Praise for *Beneath His Silence*

"Fast-paced danger and suspense from an exciting newcomer to Regency fiction."
—Julie Klassen, award-winning author of *A Castaway at Cornwall*

"A strong story of loss and forgiveness, resentment surrendered to faith, and the mercy of God. Readers will enjoy this turbulent mystery with a smile-worthy ending."
—Kristen Heitzmann, Christy Award-winning author
of *Secrets* and *The Breath of Dawn*

"This book has everything I love…a dark and broody hero, a spunky heroine on a mission, and a deeply delicious creepy manor home. *Beneath His Silence* is a rather gothic tale set in Regency England, filled with plenty of intrigue, danger, and romance to make for a very satisfying read."
—Michelle Griep, Christy Award-winning author of *Lost in Darkness*

"Grab your blanket and your chocolates and settle in for several hours because once you start reading, you won't want to stop. What a great story of second chances, romance, intrigue, and danger. Hannah Linder takes you back into the past where you just want to stay and be best friends with all of her characters. Eagerly awaiting the next installment!"
—Lynette Eason, bestselling and award-winning romantic suspense author

"With mysterious threats lurking, shadowy motives propelling characters forward, and the purest of love underpinning it all, *Beneath His Silence* is a story that delivers everything Regency lovers could ask for. A hearty *bravissimo* to Hannah Linder for her captivating debut!"
—Roseanna M. White, Christy Award winning author of *A Portrait of Loyalty*

"A classic for modern audiences! Hannah Linder dazzles with a timeless voice. I predict she'll become a staple in the Regency fiction genre."
—Caroline George, award-winning author of *Dearest Josephine*
(Thomas Nelson, HarperCollins)

"Gothic overtones abound in this atmospheric tale of secrets, lies, and betrayal. Hannah Linder has penned a twisty tale peopled with sympathetic and relatable characters that will have Regency fans cheering."
—Erica Vetsch, author of the Thorndike & Swann Regency Mysteries

"Mystery, revenge, and the challenge of forgive[...] [...] through [...]
novel filled with period appropriate details. [...]
Beneath His Silence may well prove to be your cu[...]
—Carolyn Miller, award-winning au[...]

"A heroine pursuing answers. A hero with long-buried secrets. Hannah Linder's *Beneath His Silence* is brimming in mystery, heart, and complex characters. I was captivated from page one and didn't want to put the book down until I discovered how the story ended. You won't want to miss this wholly satisfying Regency-set read."

—Susanne Dietze, award-winning, RWA RITA-nominated author of *The Reluctant Guardian, A Mother for His Family* and the Widow's Peak Creek series

"Charming, absorbing debut from Hannah Linder! *Beneath His Silence* has all the right ingredients for gothic regency—a mysterious death, family secrets, guilt-ridden hero, courageous-though-naïve heroine. Linder mixes it all with a careful hand, lending a fresh voice to the genre. I look forward to seeing more of her work!"

—Shannon McNear, 2014 RITA® finalist, 2021 SELAH winner, and author of *Elinor* and *Mary (Daughters of the Lost Colony)*

"Set in one of my favorite eras—Regency!—Hannah Linder's debut brims with mystery and intrigue! *Beneath His Silence* features a plot which keeps the reader guessing and a faith thread that lifts the heart. Fans of Abigail Wilson and Anna Lee Huber should check this novel out."

—Rachel McDaniel, award-winning author of *The Mobster's Daughter*

"Hannah Linder is one of Christian fiction's newest young writers that can easily stand alongside bestselling authors of Regency romances. Her debut release with Barbour Publishing, *Beneath His Silence,* is a riveting period romance, possessing an atmosphere of mystery and suspense. Ms. Linder has a firm grasp on the historical nuances of the era, with quick and witty dialogue reminiscent of Austen's novels."

—Rita Gerlach, celebrated author of historical fiction

"*Beneath His Silence* takes the reader on an emotional journey fraught with fears, distrust, and unknown dangers. Author Hannah Linder does a great job with this gothic-style historical romance. The setting is perfect and frames the story. Readers will pull for the heroine, wonder about the hero, and fall in love with the little boy. Fans of Michelle Griep's *Lost in Darkness* will love this book."

—Pegg Thomas, Selah Award-Winning Author of *Sarah's Choice*

Beneath His Silence

Beneath His *Silence*

HANNAH LINDER

BARBOUR
PUBLISHING

Beneath His Silence ©2022 by Hannah Linder

Print ISBN 978-1-63609-436-6
Adobe Digital Edition (.epub) 978-1-63609-437-3

All scripture quotations, unless otherwise noted, are taken from the King James Version of the Bible.

This book is a work of fiction. Names, characters, places, and incidents are either products of the author's imagination or used fictitiously. Any similarity to actual people, organizations, and/or events is purely coincidental.

Cover Design: Hannah Linder Designs
Cover Image: ©Magdalena Russocka/Trevillion Images

Published by Barbour Publishing, Inc., 1810 Barbour Drive, Uhrichsville, Ohio 44683, www.barbourbooks.com

Our mission is to inspire the world with the life-changing message of the Bible.

Member of the
Evangelical Christian
Publishers Association

Printed in the United States of America

DEDICATION

To Mother, for believing in me.

CHAPTER 1

Northston, Devonshire
April 1814

Insanity. Over and over, the word catapulted through Ella Pemberton's mind, as loud and jolting as the hard-seated stagecoach. *This is insanity.*

More than that, it was a mistake. She ought to know. After all, hadn't she told her father countless times there was no purpose, that he was only torturing a soul already battered, that they needed him home more than anything else in the world?

But he'd never listened. He'd gone to Northston again, and again, and again—until they'd stopped expecting him to stay with them.

"The truth," he'd say. He'd stumble back through the doors of Abbingston Hall, their manor house in Gloucestershire, with his eyes demented and empty. "In the name of everything holy, Ella, I must find the truth."

Mayhap if he had uncovered the answers he sought in Northston, the pain would have been less. When he had died on his bed three days past, perhaps it would have made a difference.

But he never found the truth. That strange, crazed look was never eased from his eyes. And heaven have mercy, but he died without vengeance on his eldest daughter's murderer.

The coach door swung open. "Where ye want to be goin', miss?" A calloused hand reached out. "Watch yer step, then. It be a might slippery with this dashed weather an' all."

Clutching her reticule, Ella accepted the driver's help and emerged from the coach. Her back ached, but the greater agony fluttered in her stomach. "Pray, this is Northston?"

The cobblestoned streets were clean, glistening with rain. On each side of the road, neatly trimmed bushes grew in front of wooden fences or stone walls.

The buildings were timber framed, many with thatched roofs and brick chimneys. Small townhouses, a millinery shop, a bakery, and a bookstore crowded the left side of the street, while a large bell-tower church stood on the other.

Quaint, it seemed. Pretty, almost. Didn't look at all like so many of her nightmares.

"Feedin' yer eyes on it, miss?" The driver unloaded her valise and trunk, then wiped his brow. "Where shall I take these for ye, miss?"

Ella fished a coin from her reticule and handed it over. "I am looking for a Miss Fitzherbert, a resident of Northston for longer than five years, I am certain."

"'Tis a mite far to walk. I'll send a boy to be takin' ye in a pony cart."

Ella thanked him and waited beneath a wild cherry tree, whose sheltering boughs kept away the slight drizzle. She tucked a damp curl back beneath her bonnet. What a sight she must be. But then again, it had not been easy to persuade her mother and sister she was heading for London. Even harder to pay off her young lady's maid and send the abigail away with references to another parish entirely. Mother would never find out that Ella had done the unthinkable.

In the end, this would all be worth it. She would not fail, as her father had done. She would search every crevice and badger every person and unbury every forgotten trace.

And she would destroy the man who had killed her sister.

There was no leaving until she did.

∽

Henry Sedgewick crested the ridge with speed, then drew the leather reins to his chest.

The mare slowed, swung her head, and let out a defiant snort.

"Just a moment, Miss Staverley." He rubbed the horse's neck. "We cannot very well return home without first enjoying the view, now can we?"

The bay horse pawed the ground.

The dark-stoned structure of Wyckhorn Manor stood tall along the edges of a rocky cliffside, overlooking a gray-blue sea sixty feet below. The waves glimmered and shone in the afternoon sunlight, as dazzling as diamonds against an ivory neck.

Henry urged Miss Staverley forward. How little the place had changed in the weeks he had been absent. Indeed, it was much the same as the day he had left—the manor casting long, disorienting shadows, the bushes sparse and without bloom, the windows shuttered and lifeless.

All but one.

A small hand waved at him from behind the glass, and the figure disappeared. No doubt, the child was running downstairs to meet him upon entrance.

Henry's chest swelled with anticipation. If only his happiness were not mingled with dread.

⚭

"You cannot be." Dorthea Fitzherbert wore a simple patterned gown with green ribbon tied under her bosom. Her eyes were rapt with wonder. "You simply cannot be."

Ella stood on the threshold of the Fitzherbert home, luggage stacked behind her. "Yes, Miss Fitzherbert." She cleared her throat. "I most certainly am."

"Lucy's sister!" Dorthea clapped her hands. "My heavens, I could cry. I really have no words. Come in, come in, won't you?"

Moments later, Ella had been dragged into the sitting room, seated on the red damask settee, and offered a cup of tea.

Dorthea took the armchair opposite her guest. "You might have written and told me you were coming. Mother and Father shall be ever so glad to meet you when they return from tea with the squire." Her tight black curls, alabaster skin, and expressive green eyes bore all the attractions of youthful beauty. Her smile was eager. "Lucy spoke of you so often that I feel as if I know you already. You were always such a delight to hear of, you know. Lucy told the funniest stories of you. What impish inventions she credited you for."

Heat prickled Ella's skin. How many times had she chided Lucy for giving accounts of her scrapes? Lucy had never listened, for she was as talkative as their youngest sister was good—and Ella was errant.

"Tell me." Dorthea sipped from her silver-rimmed cup. "Are you the bluestocking your sister was?"

"Certainly not. I do read some, but in most cases, only when I am ill at ease."

"I do not read at all. I detest the sight of books. I really do."

A moment's pause ensued.

Ella lifted her eyes, lowered her cup. "Miss Fitzherbert, there is a matter I must discuss with you. I have come a very long way, and I must first beg discretion."

"Miss Pemberton, upon my honor and pride, I shall not breathe a word."

A cowardly lump lodged itself at the base of Ella's throat. "I have come for the very reason my father always came. To expose him. . .to expose Lucy's husband." She hesitated. Willed the air to rush back into her lungs. Why was it so difficult to speak the cursed name? "I must know what happened. I must know why she is dead. And pray, do not ask me how I shall discover all this, for I hardly know myself."

"I shan't ask how." She wagged a finger. "But first, I imagine you should wish to see him. There is a ball at Sir Charles Rutledge's manor at the end of the week in celebration of his eldest son returning from his grand tour. I am certain Lord Sedgewick will be in attendance and I shall introduce you—"

"No, please. I do not desire him to know who I am. I should rather observe him from a distance. That is all."

"I daresay, Miss Pemberton, the name does raise suspicion."

"I shall not be Miss Pemberton during my stay at Northston." Ella returned her teacup to its tray. "I shall be Miss...Miss..."

"Miss Woodhart." Dorthea's face beamed with pleasure, as she grasped Ella's hand. "It becomes you most perfectly, and no one shall be the wiser."

∽

From within the large hearth, orange flames licked the air, crackling and sputtering. They cast warm light throughout the drawing room.

"Papa?" A small figure appeared beside Henry's armchair.

Henry pulled the five-year-old onto his lap. He never realized how desperately he needed the boy's nearness, these small touches, until the months they were kept apart. "Yes, Peter?"

"I am ever so glad you are back, Papa." Peter's dimpled fingers touched his father's buttons. "Miss Morton and I did not go out of doors very much."

"Did you not visit the seashore?"

"No." Peter's eyes were bright, his hair as smooth and flaxen as his mother's had always been. "Miss Morton does not like the water. She doesn't want the sun to touch her face."

Why would it matter to the old governess anyway? Freckles were hardly consequential at such an age. Aches and pains, doubtless, were the more credible reasons. Or was it more than that? "But you must have played other things, did you not?"

Peter shrugged, sighed, and continued to play with the buttons. "Papa?"

"Yes?"

"Why did you go away?"

"An old friend was in need of my company for a bit." Or so he had thought. He had received a letter from Major Sir Frederick Tilbury in Essex—an acquaintance of Henry's deceased father—requesting Henry's presence at his home. The old officer had been released from his duties in the Peninsular War due to a crippling leg wound he had acquired during the Battle of Nivelle. Finding the comforts of home rather less sensational than the battlefronts of France, Major Sir

Frederick's intent had been to find a suitable match for his daughter—a realization Henry reached only in hindsight. Why couldn't he be left alone, for mercy's sakes?

"Was there a seashore there too?"

"Yes, but I fear it was not half as lovely as here." Nor was the company. "And there was one small misfortune that kept me from visiting it often."

"What?"

"There was no little boy to play with. It was insufferably dull indeed."

Peter's mouth widened with a grin, and he laughed. "We can play tomorrow, Papa, and build a castle in the sand and swim in the water and—"

"So we shall, Peter, so we shall." Henry stood with the boy in his arms. "But at present, we must both find our beds and get some rest."

Peter nodded, keeping his arms tight about his father's neck until Henry tucked him beneath his bedclothes. When Henry returned to the drawing room, he froze at the threshold.

Miss Morton stood beside his armchair, the firelight illuminating her severe features. "Lord Sedgewick." She bobbed a curtsy.

He approached but did not sit. "Is anything the matter?" Only he already knew there was. Of course there was.

"May I be permitted to speak freely with you, my lord?"

"Certainly."

"I have had my belongings packed for a fortnight. I wish to depart in the morning, and I have already made arrangements for travel."

He stifled a groan. "Miss Morton, I have only just returned—"

"Precisely. I have waited most anxiously for you to do so. Conscience would not permit me to leave the child alone in this house, to the care of servants and. . ." Her sentence faltered, and she looked away.

"Has it become so very bad?"

Miss Morton's thin lips pursed together. "Yes, my lord." Tears glistened. "God have mercy on you all." She ducked her head and brushed past him—as eager to leave the room, it seemed, as she was to flee the house.

∽

Peter tackled the waves with arms wide, greeting the spray of saltwater that splashed his face.

Henry dove after him. He grabbed the boy's waist, tossed him upward, and caught him against his own chest.

Peter's squeals rose above the crashing water. "Papa." He squirmed from his father's hands. "Watch me." He disappeared beneath the foam, remained under for several seconds, then popped back up. He rubbed the sea water from his eyes, grinning. "Did you see me?"

A chuckle rumbled from deep inside Henry. "I did indeed."

"And I can do this." Peter ducked under again, managing to extend his feet into the air. He toppled over and resurfaced.

Henry clapped. "Jolly good, fellow. Where do you learn such tricks?"

The boy's cheeks brightened. "I taught myself. Do you want to make a castle now?"

Henry followed the child back to the beach, where they sat by the lapping waves and dug their hands into damp sand. When the castle was built and the morning sun had heightened, they took a stroll along the water's edge.

Every so often, Peter flung a seashell into the waves, but other than that, he remained contentedly quiet.

It was not a falsehood when I told the boy it was far lovelier here. Henry had spent many evenings ambling down Essex's coast, accompanied by the tall and elegant Selina Tilbury. She was all grace and sophistication, a woman who could not be criticized in any matter of accomplishment. In painting, she far excelled anyone he had ever seen. He supposed it was Tilbury blood in her veins, for her father had never done anything halfway.

It was certainly a match worth some consideration.

But every time she had looked at him, or laid her gloved hand upon his arm, the bitter poison rushed through his veins. The memories came back. The warnings.

God, have mercy on me.

Because he would never marry Miss Tilbury nor any other woman. All he wanted was to be left alone, to forget everything—to keep Peter from ever finding out the truth.

If only he could keep it from himself.

∞

The knock came lightly at her door, first once, then a second time.

Ella sat upright in bed. "Yes?"

"It is me—Dorthea. Might I come in?"

"Certainly."

Dorthea rushed inside, clad in a wrapper. "I could not sleep. I always used to visit Lucy at such times, and she never minded a bit." She slipped into the bed. "I had every hope you would be the same."

"I cannot promise the stories Lucy might have told you." Ella smiled. "But I can listen, if nothing else."

Dorthea leaned back against the pillows, taking a quick glance around the candlelit room. "I have not been in here since. . ." The words trailed off. "Well, since Lucy's stay with me, and that was many years ago."

It seemed strange to hear her sister's name spoken without the dreaded tone of her father. Why could they not have kept Lucy's memory sweet and happy, as Dorthea had done?

"Pray, tell me about her," Ella whispered. "Those last years."

"Well, we were never naughty, so there is really not much to boast of." Dorthea giggled. "Oh but we were shameless flirts, to be certain. I always supposed I taught her that sin, though she did seem a natural at it, nonetheless."

"Our Lucy was always rather shy and bookish."

"Oh, she was. And that is how she carefully—and most beguiling—caught the interest of so many suitors. I often envied her endearing meekness and those batting blue eyes. La, you should have seen her. It was most entrancing the way she would quietly and perfectly relate her latest novel to whoever sat by her side."

Ella chuckled. "What fun she must have had."

"Of course back then, I was rather prone to jealousy. Especially when the grave Lord Sedgewick began to court her. I had doted on him for years, you know, but he never once even smiled at me. He was quite immune to female charms, or so we all supposed, until Lucy came along."

"Did she care for him so very much?"

"I always thought she was flattered more than anything else. It was quite a feat to receive a proposal from such a man—and of his standing too. Anyone would have said yes."

Heat burned across Ella's chest. "Did you see her much after the wedding?"

"Hardly at all. He swept her away to his manor on that terrible cliffside, and since she soon became with child, she was never present at any balls or such. I did not even see her at church."

"And her death?"

"Sudden illness, they say. Yet that is a matter of controversy—at least among the gossips. I think it was your father who first aroused suspicion. Did you know how often he used to come here?"

"Quite often."

"He was never forthright about anything, yet his line of questioning always led one to believe he thought Lucy's death was not of sickness at all. But the constable has never taken action against Lord Sedgewick or anyone else for that matter, so who can know?" Her brows rose dramatically. "Although Father has never liked Constable Keats. He seems a might richer than he should be—and certain, shall we say, upstanding gentlemen have not reaped consequences for their suspected crimes." She paused, then added in a thicker tone, "If you get my meaning."

"Yes." Ella drew the covers to her neck with an involuntary shiver. "I do indeed."

The modish brick building was set apart from the rest of the village, with a white fence along the perimeter of the yard. Ella unlatched the gate and entered. She had taken only a few steps when a shuttlecock landed at her feet.

"Dear me." A fleshy man drew to a quick halt, breathing hard, his navy waistcoat dark with sweat. "What a shock, indeed. I did not expect to find a lady around the corner."

Ella retrieved the shuttlecock and tossed it to him. "A fair day for sporting, is it not?"

"Quite so. Kept it up in the air six and twenty times."

She smiled, giving a tiny clap of her hands. "How marvelous. You far exceed my meager abilities, I admit."

A flush-faced woman appeared with a battledore in hand. "You play?"

"Only when nothing else allures me." Ella faced the gentleman again. "Constable Keats, I presume?"

He outstretched his hand. "And my wife, Mrs. Keats."

The woman curtsied.

"Well." He surrendered his racket to his wife. "I am always aware of the nature of one's visit by the title with which they choose to address me. Shall we go inside?"

"Certainly."

He proceeded her to the house and into a small, disorderly study. He motioned toward a chair. "Won't you sit?"

She removed a stack of papers from the seat.

"Here, give me those." He grabbed them, stuffed them inside a drawer, and forced it shut. "Pray, don't judge the man by the room. Tidiness was never among my greater virtues."

She smiled.

"Now, miss." He sank into his chair. "In what matter might I assist you?"

How many times had her father been in this same room, perhaps this very chair? "I wish to make an inquiry. You see, a dear acquaintance of mine resided here around seven years ago. I have long since stopped receiving letters, and because I would be traveling in the near vicinity, I decided on a sudden visit."

He nodded.

"Upon my arrival, I was informed by a local that she had died."

"My condolences."

"Thank you." Ella twisted her finger around the drawstring of her reticule. "I should like to know how she. . .what circumstances led to her death." She lifted her eyes. "Her name was formerly Lucy Pemberton."

A deep shade of red colored the constable's cheeks. "Lucy." He cleared his throat. "Yes, yes. Lucy Pemberton."

A clock on the wall groaned a low, mechanical sound. *Tick-tock. Tick-tock.*

"I wish to know of her death."

Tick-tock.

"Sir?"

He leaned back in his chair until it creaked under his weight. "Five years ago, she became rapidly ill, I'm afraid. It was all rather sudden and"—he looked down as if perusing the scattered papers on his desk—"is that all you wished to know? I'm afraid I've quite a lot of paperwork."

"Her health was always impeccable. I cannot imagine her to succumb to—"

"Yes, well, we are all subject to malady." He came to his feet. "Surely you cannot gainsay that. Now if you'll excuse me—"

"Constable?"

He frowned but answered genially nonetheless. "Miss?"

"Where might I find her grave?"

"She is buried at Wyckhorn Manor." The constable strode to the door and opened it for her. "But you'll be wise to leave the place alone."

CHAPTER 2

*H*e was inside.

Ella drew to a stop before the open wooden doors. Her heart quickened painfully. He was so close, so unbearably close. She quenched the desire to flee, yet even so, her feet would not propel her forward.

"My heavens, whatever is the matter?" Dorthea waited until her parents had entered the ballroom, then touched Ella's elbow. "If you are half as graceful as Lucy," she whispered, "you have no need for qualms. I am certain you shall dance well enough."

Ella barely heard the words, nor could she summon her voice. She stepped inside the ballroom. The colors, lights, and rising music fell around her as if a stifling shroud.

"Sir Charles Rutledge," said Dorthea, nodding across the room. "He is most ravishing for his age, do you not think? I daresay white hair is rather becoming in a man—although I have heard it said that he uses wax due to his lack of volume. Myself, I would detest the solution. How would one run fingers through waxy hair?"

Ella's gaze swept across the gentlemen present. She searched each face. She had never seen Lord Sedgewick before, not even a portrait of him, yet she felt as if she would know him. Would she not sense it somehow in her heart of hearts?

She *would* because at his hand she had suffered. Lucy had suffered. Her father, her mother, even her younger sister had suffered. They had been ripped away from the gracious palm of happiness and forced into an iron grasp of hate.

For that, she'd see him pay.

∽

"How goes it, good fellow?"

Lowering a glass of lemonade, Henry straightened from leaning against the wall. He nodded at Sir Rutledge, whose fine-cut features bore a good-natured grin.

"I am rather pacified to be home, I admit," said Henry. "Yourself?"

The baronet waved his hand. "Fie. If I wished to talk of myself, I would have gone to Lady Rutledge, for she does enjoy telling me all the points in which I am lacking." He chuckled and sipped at a glass of ratafia. "How goes Essex?"

"Fair. Major Sir Frederick Tilbury was in good spirits despite the leg."

"Glad to hear it. Did you hear of Wellington's latest battle?"

"At Toulouse?"

"Indeed. A British division and two Spanish divisions. Bloody, I hear—more for us than for the French. Would not stand in Wellington's boots for the world." A slight pause lingered, in which he chuckled. "Though I doubt he has a wife who takes pleasure in cutting him to shreds, eh?"

Before Henry could respond, the subject of the baronet's jest approached them, two younger women in tow.

"Delighted to see you, Lord Sedgewick." Lady Rutledge offered a civil nod of her head. With a hardening expression, she turned her eyes to her husband. "Do come, my dear. Have you no ear at all? The orchestra is playing 'La Boulanger,' and you know it to be my favorite."

Sir Charles slid Henry a look, but schooled his features before he took his wife's hand. "Might I have this dance, my beautiful?"

She scoffed. "Do not be nonsensical, dear." She resisted when he tugged her toward the dance, saying hurriedly, "Lord Sedgewick, I neglected to introduce you to my two cousins. Miss Augusta Creassey and Miss Ann Creassey, both without partners." Lady Rutledge flicked her hand toward the women. "You may have your pick, Lord Sedgewick, but do hurry or you shall miss the dance." And thus, she hurried off with her husband into the forming line of couples.

Henry's temples throbbed.

Both women stared at him—the shorter lightly fanning her face, the taller raising her unnaturally thin eyebrows in expectation.

He recovered his voice, though the quality of his tone was deep, husky, "Forgive me, Miss Creassey...Miss Creassey." His fingers tightened on the glass. "I must excuse myself. Good day." He turned his back to them, but not quickly enough to miss the rounding of their eyes and the dropping of their dainty jaws.

How long before they spread harsh whispers of his incivility?

It didn't matter. An uncivil reputation was better than repeating mistakes he'd already made.

⌒

Ella's hands perspired beneath her elbow-length gloves, but she dared not remove them. If only the hostess would open more windows. A swim in the punch bowl was starting to sound appealing.

Dorthea did not seem to mind the heat—nor did she even seem to notice. She appeared solely conscious of the fact that Sir Charles Rutledge's eldest son was asking her to dance.

"Oh my." She tilted her head, blushed to a proper degree, then allowed him to escort her into the set.

Ella hid her grin with her fan. Perhaps Miss Fitzherbert found the younger Rutledge even more riveting than his father.

"Miss, do tell me promptly that you are without partner." A gentleman appeared before her, dumpy and short but with rather pleasing features.

"It is a bit warm, sir. I do not think I feel much like dancing."

"I say, you're in quite the wrong place then, are you not?" He chuckled. "We have all come to dance and make merry. I can't think what else there could be to do." And with a shake of his head, he bowed and walked away.

Make merry. His words echoed. Any other day, she would have taken the gentleman's hand and eagerly danced into the night. With great pleasure, she would have strolled throughout the room, laughing

22

and sipping lemonade to her heart's content.

But it was not any other night, and she had no more desire for laughter than she did for lemonade or dancing.

As another song began to fill the room with a lively tune, Dorthea appeared at Ella's side. "I came as soon as I could," she whispered. "There he is. I have only just spotted him." Her eyes darted to the westerly wall.

Ella could not look. Her throat constricted.

"There is one more thing I must tell you of him—news I heard only tonight. I think you shall find it most interesting." Dorthea patted her curls as if to assure their placement. "But there is not time to relate it now. I have already promised this dance." She turned on her heels and dashed away.

Ella was left to herself. The blood ran hot in her veins, yet still, she could not look at him. She hadn't the strength. He had so long been a faceless monster, a shadowy demon that loomed in every nightmare, every dark corner of her soul.

Oh, Father. She clenched her hands, lifted her eyes.

There was nothing to obstruct her view, nor was there any question as to which gentleman.

Lord Sedgewick stood along the wall with the last shafts of light streaming from the window behind him. He was flesh and bone indeed.

Dressed in tan pantaloons and waistcoat, with a black tailcoat and white cravat, his appearance was pompous and seemed to boast of his superior position. He stood in much the same manner, straight and rigid, coldly casting his gaze about the room.

His lips were firm and tight, and he appeared ready to escape the inconvenience of his present circumstance. Hair—the deepest brown—was tousled on the top and shorter on the sides. Sideburns invaded either side of his face. His brows were dark and concentrated. If he had looked upon her, she might have frozen.

Yet he never did.

A knot ascended Ella's throat. She whirled and fled the room, escaping into the quiet, empty corridor. She covered her mouth with her hands, squeezing her eyes shut. *Oh, Lucy.* She shook with cold, unbearable passion.

He shall not get away with what he has done to you, Lucy. Her pulse hammered. *Upon your grave, I promise.*

∞

Henry listened to the soft, disturbing sound of his own footfalls in Wyckhorn's corridor. They echoed in his mind until he was empty, bereft.

But it was better than the silence.

In those first few days, perhaps even weeks, he had not noticed the silence. There had been other things to distract his attention. Ridding the manor of her body had taken preeminence. Anything so he did not have to look at her.

A nanny had been assigned, as if any woman could restore what was lost, as if any woman could replace the touch of a mother.

The blood had been scrubbed away. There were no more stains. The constable had come and gone, the body buried at last.

That was when, to the most penetrating degree, the curse had settled upon the house.

In dim and haunting fog, this silence had woven its cold fingers through every window and down every corridor. It had inhabited every room, every stairwell. It had managed its way to the garden, touching every bursting bloom, until the petals dried and withered. After a time, the curse had reached as far as the cliffside, where the breeze suddenly lacked warmth and the horizon lost beauty.

Perhaps he might have borne it well if it had stayed within the confines of his own house and land. After all, such a fate was merited. It was his duty, his punishment, to bear whatever God laid to his charge.

But the cursed silence had not merely hovered over Wyckhorn Manor. It had crept through the very portals of his soul and lodged therein. He was forced to carry it day upon day, night upon night—until the silence festered into hate, and the hate into fear, and the fear into torture.

Tugging at his cravat, Henry opened the whining door to his bedchamber.

"M'lord." His valet jumped from a chair across the room, a book in one hand, a candlestick in the other. "You are home earlier than expected."

"There was very little to detain me."

His valet nodded, and his lips pinched in a frown of empathy.

"How was the house?" Henry asked.

"Quiet and sound."

Relief eased through him. "And Peter?"

"In bed asleep, to my knowledge."

Henry remained quiet as his valet undressed him and helped him into his banyan. Moving to a chair by the unlit hearth, Henry said over his shoulder, "Thank you, Collin. You may go now."

"Yes, m'lord." He reached for his book and started across the room.

"And Collin?"

"M'lord?"

"Do try to sleep." A grin played at Henry's lips. "Reading in the dark can be most detrimental to one's eyesight. I should not like to acquire another valet in my search for a governess."

Collin's eyes brightened with fondness. "Yes, m'lord." He shut the door soundlessly behind him.

Henry settled into the chair more comfortably, crossing his arms across his chest. Again, he was left alone with his curse.

Forgive me, God.

Tonight, he had blundered again. He had refused a simple act. A chivalrous duty, doubtless. Why had he not chosen between the sisters and honorably taken them into the dance?

Only he knew why. He'd had no wish to take their hand, to catch the familiar maidenly scents, to feel the warmth of their touch upon him. He knew what they wanted, what they all wanted. How easy it was for them to feign love for the advantage of a profitable marriage.

But he was no fool. There was danger in doting smiles—a lesson his mother had taught without mercy.

∽

Ella appeared in the doorway of the breakfast room, dismayed to find Mr. and Mrs. Fitzherbert, as well as their daughter, already partaking of their meal.

Dorthea spotted her first. With eyes still soft with sleep, she motioned Ella toward the table. "Miss Pemberton, do hurry and join us. Father shall eat everything if you do not make haste."

Ella glanced at the older gentleman, whose lips curved slightly at his daughter's jesting. He did nothing to defend himself, however, and resumed forking a sausage from his plate.

"I trust you slept well, my dear?" Mrs. Fitzherbert said.

"Perhaps too well. I simply could not awaken this morning."

A footman supplied another plate, which Ella filled with one slice of honey cake and a sausage. She was also given a cup of tea.

Mr. Fitzherbert engaged his wife in conversation of politics, a matter which he spoke of in deep and serious tones. Periodically, he read aloud from the newspaper.

His wife—whether absorbed or indifferent, Ella could not tell—nodded dutifully and made relevant remarks to all of his points.

Dorthea, however, feigned no such interest in her parents' colloquy. Her gaze slid eagerly to Ella's face every so often. Once she mouthed in silence, "We must talk after breakfast."

Ella nodded lightly, though she had no desire to finish the food. Nightmares of last night resurfaced until her flesh raised in goosebumps. She had been plagued with them for five years, ever since the letter arrived of her sister's death. Shouldn't she be accustomed to the terrors by now? Could anyone grow accustomed to terror?

Last night had been far worse. Perhaps seeing him had made the difference and given the nightmares a new level of reality and form.

Whatever the case, she had awakened in cold sweat, with her legs tangled in her bedclothes. Many hours passed before sleep claimed her again.

Dorthea nudged her knee beneath the table. "Do hurry. I simply cannot bear another minute in silence."

Ella dabbed her napkin at her mouth. "I am finished."

Dorthea excused them both from the table, took Ella's arm, and hurried her up the flight of stairs. "Into your bedchamber." She flung open the door and slammed it behind her before facing Ella with animation. "I wanted to tell you last night, but we arrived home at such a late hour that I did not wish to burden you before bed."

"Do not keep me in suspense. What have you discovered?"

"I cannot tell until you vow you shall not repeat this to a soul. If you ever say a word to Father and Mother, I shall deny the whole thing and call you a liar."

Ella's hand crossed her heart. "I vow it."

"And mind you, I am not suggesting you do such a thing…such an immensely ludicrous thing. I daresay, I would probably not have mentioned it at all had Lucy not spoken so very often of your mischief."

"Tell me."

"Well, it was mentioned last night that Miss Morton—though I don't suppose you know who that is—has returned to the village with all of her luggage. She had been at Wyckhorn for no longer than a year, I am certain. No one stays longer than that."

"Who is she?"

"The governess, Miss Pemberton. And there is more." Dorthea leaned in closer, taking Ella's hands in her own. "Lord Sedgewick is seeking a *new* governess…to bring to his home."

"Whatever are you so clumsily trying to say?"

"It means that if you wish to observe Lord Sedgewick more closely, you may do so at your leisure." She paused. "Without the faintest worry of being discovered, Miss *Woodhart*."

"I am not a governess. Surely you cannot mean that I should—"

"I do not mean anything." Dorthea shuffled backward with a daring grin. She flung open the door with one hand. "And remember, you did not hear it from me." With nothing more, she hurled herself from the room.

His home. Ella tried to breathe. *A governess.* Curled her fists. *No, no, no.*

Because she wasn't ready to face such a monstrous murderer.

And she had no intentions of caring for his child. True, the little one belonged to Lucy. Her own flesh and blood. At the least, the child surely needed protection.

But he was also just another reminder that Lucy was dead. Would Ella be able to bear even the sight of him?

CHAPTER 3

*E*lla left the Fitzherbert household without imparting her decision to anyone. Her mother would have chided her that such an act was impulsive, careless.

Perhaps it was. She did not know, nor could she help it now—for she was already approaching Northston's main street without carriage or escort.

At least she had made time to gather her gloves and bonnet. Certainly that was something to her credit.

The lulling noise and hum of village life surrounded her as she continued down the cobblestone street. She drew to a stop before a red-bricked building, squinting to see the sign. The paint, however, was so worn she could not distinguish the words.

It did not matter. She passed on with gaining speed, her chest taut. *Lord Sedgewick's governess.* Her mind stung at such a thought. Perhaps Lucy had not been errant to establish her as a trifle impish in the mind of Dorthea Fitzherbert.

But partaking in a jot of folly was not at all the same as besmirching oneself. Or endangering one's life. What would Father have said?

He would have doubtless been horrified. As would her mother.

No, Ella would simply have to find another way. One that did not mortify her pride. One that did not summon every ounce of courage she might possess. One that would not put her so close, so vulnerably close, to a man she loathed and feared.

"Top of the mornin' to you, dearie."

Ella startled. At the sight of a bent old man, however, her fears settled.

He sat on the ground, leaned back against the stone wall, with a shabby topper low on his forehead.

She offered a smile. "Good day to you, sir. I trust you are enjoying the rather splendid sunshine."

He dragged a stained hand down his chin, delighted—it seemed—to have the attention of one so far above his station. "Just a-baskin' in it, dearie. And yourself?"

She ignored his question as a sudden thought struck her, a thought the constable would have no doubt repressed. "Might I bother you with an inquiry, sir?"

"What it be?"

"I have heard most impressive accounts of Wyckhorn Manor, and because I am fond of painting, I should like to see the view for myself."

"Paintin', eh?" As if he sensed her mistruth.

"Yes." Then she added with force, "*Painting*."

"Well, 'tis a taxin' walk for such a young little chit, but if you were of a mind to go—"

"Yes, yes! Of a certain, I wish to go. Where is it?"

He explained that she need only follow the south road one-and-a-half miles, where she would turn onto a smaller road and gain sight of the ocean. Beyond that, she would find her destination on a great ledge overlooking the sea. "Which is rather a glum venue to paint, if you be askin' me. Don't you be knowin' that Lady Sedgewick's ghost lives in those rocks, moanin' and groanin' all night long?"

Her stomach plunged. "No, I had not heard." Grabbing a fistful of her dress, she departed for the south road.

∽

The portrait should have been removed a long time ago. His father should have disposed of it the day she left, should have burnt the remains so they would have nothing to taunt them.

But years had come and gone, and no one had touched the painting.

Henry stared at it, the tendrils of brown hair, the eyes so like his own, the cool and vacant gaze. His mother seemed to stare at him, whether with regret or indifference, he could not tell.

He had never been able to tell. Not even in the beginning, when she would enter the nursery and dismiss the governess for a few short hours. The touches were achingly brief. Even her smiles were elusive and never often enough. If only he had—

"My lord?"

Henry tore his eyes away. "Yes, Dunn?"

The steward's attention shifted to the portrait, but his features lacked response. He cleared his throat. "A weighty pile of letters just arrived. I took the liberty of placing them on your desk."

He nodded approval.

"A man also arrived, my lord. A Mr. Arnold."

"The tenant?"

"Yes, my lord. It seems the fellow is most desirous to speak with you about a certain quandary."

Henry departed the room with Mr. Dunn at his heels. "Must be grave, indeed, for Mr. Arnold to feel it necessary to come here."

"I rather thought so myself, my lord."

"Well." Henry reached his study and perused the sealed letters on his desk. He tucked the one from Essex to the bottom of the pile. He would deal with letters from matrimonially minded fathers at a more convenient time. "Tell me of Mr. Arnold's plight."

"I could not extract any details from him, my lord, but he was a bit sooty—and very much in a hurry."

"Why didn't you send him in?"

"I did not wish to disturb you, and he refused to wait. I assume, my lord, that he has returned to his home."

Henry retrieved a letter that had fallen to the floor. He planted it atop the pile. "I shall ride there now. If Peter inquires, tell him I shall be home shortly."

"Yes, my lord. Shall I send a servant to prepare your horse?"

A small grin tugged at Henry's lips. "No, Dunn. That is one thing I rather enjoy doing myself."

∞

She shouldn't have come.

Ella tugged the ribbons loose until the bonnet shifted to her back. She wasn't certain what she had hoped to find, or what measure of comfort she might have gained from the mere sight of Wyckhorn Manor.

But whatever she had longed for, she was rewarded with nothing. The sight only emptied her.

Far in the distance, high upon the cliffside, the manor faced the open sea. It was tall and lofty, a likeness of Lord Sedgewick himself. A strange and rugged beauty, a pinnacle of power—yet dark and forlorn, as if death had made a home in both the house and the man.

Perhaps Dorthea was right. If only she could get inside, perhaps the answers would unfold around her. Perhaps she could reach the truth her father never could. Wouldn't it then be worth it?

She didn't know. She didn't know anything, only that she had come to Northston for one reason. She had no intention of leaving without it.

Ella turned on the road, the sun warming her back. The old codger in town had been right. The walk was a trifle long. She would have done well to bring a parasol, at least.

She paused, sniffed.

Smoke?

Her eyes fell out across the sea, then to the other side of the road, where rolling terrain filled her view.

Black clouds of smoke rose in the air, appearing from behind a distant hill. No small chimney fire would render smoke to that degree.

Despite a faint warning to which she paid little heed, Ella turned to the rutted path and hastened her speed. By the time she crested the hill, her breathing came in short, raspy pants. One would have thought, with all the times she had scampered to the village back home, she would have enough wind to see her up a small rise.

Her heart caught. "Oh no."

The small cottage below was charred and black, the last of flames licking up the timbers. Smoke hung in the air. A child's whimper filled the silence.

Ella approached the scene.

A man stood nearer than the others, his face beet-red from the fire's heat. Black soot smudged his clothing, his hands.

Behind him, two small children huddled in their mother's arms. A pig lay at her side, not alarmed—it seemed—by the surrounding turmoil.

The man turned and stared at Ella.

She frowned. "I saw the smoke."

He said nothing, only drew his gaze back to the cottage—or what remained of it.

Ella's hands clasped. "Is there something I might do?"

"Nothin' to do," he said. "Nothin' anyone can be doin'."

"Silas." The woman's voice rose. "Silas, she be shakin' again."

He whipped off his hat and darted toward them, hastening the tiny child into his arms. "Water," he choked. "She be needin' water."

"I shall get it." Ella spotted a well and threw down the bucket. Her muscles strained as she yanked it out and bustled it toward them. "Here."

He dipped a cloth, wrung out the water, then mopped the child's brow. She appeared no older than three.

"What is the matter with her?"

"We don't be knowin'," the woman sniveled. "Only a few wee burns, but she won't stop shakin'."

"Perhaps the shock of it."

The sound of hooves drew their attention.

Ella's pulse throbbed as she watched the gentleman dismount, watched him throw his reins across the saddle.

His gaze brushed hers in confusion before he rushed forward. "What's happened?" He took one look at the child and touched her brow. "Is she ill?"

The girl's head fell into the father's chest. "I didn't want to be comin', my lord," he said, "but I didn't know what else to do."

Lord Sedgewick glanced at the cottage. "How did it start?"

"We don't be knowin', my lord. I was out in the field when I saw the smoke, an' then it was..." The man's chin ducked. "Then it was too late, my lord."

"She's burnt." His eyes were on the child, but his voice lacked warmth. "Load your family into the wagon and take them to Wyckhorn. Dunn shall see to her."

A sob of relief overtook the woman, and the farmer made a quick dash for the barn.

Ella's legs weakened.

Lord Sedgewick turned to her, just as she'd known, and his eyes moved down the length of her dress. His brows came together. "Who are you?"

"I was walking." Her throat dried. "I mean—I saw the smoke."

"I did not inquire as to what you were doing or what you saw." He came closer. "Who are you?"

"M-Miss Ella Woodhart." The name fumbled forth. "I only just arrived in Northston."

"You should have stayed there. This is a private road."

Fury clapped like lightning through her blood. "I meant no harm, I assure you. I only cared to see the ocean."

"There are plenty of places you might have done so." The wagon drew his attention away, and he helped both woman and children into the creaking wagon bed. He removed his greatcoat and tucked it under the little girl's head.

"My lord." The father stood before him, small and slight under the shadow of such a larger man. "My lord, I'll build it back with me own hands, but we haven't anywhere else to go—"

"We'll talk of it later." Lord Sedgewick made a motion toward the family. "You had better make haste."

With his hat back on his head, the farmer climbed onto the wagon seat and drove away.

Lord Sedgewick turned to her again. "As you are fond of walking, miss, I assume you shall find your way to Northston safely."

Her teeth clenched. "You needn't feign concern."

"I am on horseback, else I would have escorted you to town."

"Which I would have refused," she said, "as I do not wish to defame my character."

"I doubt I would inflict such consequences, miss."

She glared at him.

A faint light of amusement touched his expression, but it vanished quickly. He was mounted and riding away before Ella could say another word.

Miss Staverley needed very little instigation to break into a gallop. She rode against the wind with ease and speed, unwinding his tension.

They could've been killed. Not only that, but he'd have to find suitable arrangements for the Arnold brood. Another duty demanding his attention, as if there weren't enough already.

He rounded the curve, digging his heels deeper into Miss Staverley's side. Guilt nipped at his conscience. He'd done it again. Didn't even know who she was, or why she was there—but his temper had flared.

He just hadn't expected hers to flare back.

It was obvious from her apparel that she was of a wealthy breed, though her hair had been askew and her bonnet had dangled behind her back.

What she was doing at the Arnolds' cottage remained a mystery, to be certain. What sort of imprudent girl took strolls in the countryside—without escort, no less? And she had certainly put no effort into curbing her tongue.

Henry scowled into the wind. Her stab at his reputation had been most deliberate, as if perhaps she'd heard. He had dared to hope the village talk had ceased.

He should have known better.

With a tug of the reins, he slowed Miss Staverley's gallop into a comfortable trot. He rode to the apothecary's, strode inside, and asked for herbs that might alleviate a little girl's burns.

∞

"My heavens, whatever happened to your hem?" Dorthea had been stitching in a lavish red chair, but she jolted to her feet at the sight of her guest.

Ella peeled off her gloves. "I have taken a walk."

"A march across Egypt, it would seem." Dorthea frowned. "A muddy Egypt, I dare to say."

Mrs. Fitzherbert was seated across the room with an issue of *Ackermann's Repository*, which she lowered with a disapproving squint at her guest. "I presume you will not be too fatigued to dine with us tonight?"

Dorthea clapped her hands. "Father has invited Sir Charles and Lady Rutledge to visit." She paused to whisper, half giggling, "And their son."

Ella forced a smile. "How delightful."

"Isn't it, though? You must come with me at once to select a gown. I've been quite beside myself all day, deciding betwixt the primrose satin or the Saxon blue." Dorthea proceeded Ella up the steps and into her bedchamber. "Sit on the bed and I shall show you the gowns. You may decide which best sets off my hair."

"Dorthea—"

"And how shall I arrange my hair? I once heard his mother expounding on the art of hairstyles, and I should not like to disappoint when—"

"Dorthea, please."

The girl paused, the dress sliding from her hands. "Why, Ella, you are most pale."

"I wish to speak with you."

Dorthea sat beside her, taking her hands. "You are trembling. Whatever is the matter?"

"I went. . ." She paused, looked away. "I went to Wyckhorn, and I had a most unfavorable encounter with Lord Sedgewick."

"Does he know who you are? Has he disclosed your identity?"

"No, nothing of the sort. Yet he is as cold and wretched as I ever could have imagined. His mere presence worked to undo me."

"How horrifying."

"Yes." Ella scooted off the bed, hugging her arms. "I have made a rash decision, one I despise to such a degree that it weakens my heart."

"Ella. . ."

"I have decided to apply for the position at Wyckhorn." She turned, hot tears springing to her eyes. "I fear it is the only way I shall ever attain the truth."

∞

The quiet laughter and conversation below stairs drifted to her room. Ella had declined the offer to join them on behalf of a vexing head-ache—or rather, heartache.

She glanced at herself in the mirror. The vicar back home—who spent half of his time attempting to convert her, the other half attempting to win her heart—would have said she appeared peaked and unrested. "Our bodies, Miss Pemberton, are the temples of the Holy Ghost. Thus we must do our best to remain always restored and in good health."

As if she cared what God would want of her.

If there was a God.

Ella moved to the window. She stared out across a well-groomed lawn, watching birds flutter in and out of boughs. *A governess, a governess, a governess.* The degradable, sing-song words played over and over. Yet another insanity. How could she ever deign herself? She, a baron's daughter with rich Pemberton blood flowing through her veins and heart?

It had been wise to inform Dorthea of her decision. At least now she was accountable. It would be less easy to dismiss her plan.

He didn't care. Another thought, one that made her fingers press against the glass. *Their home was gone, and all he could consider was resuming his trip to the village.*

He had expressed a small measure of concern for the child, but even that was fleeting. What would he do with them now?

Ella had heard the soft pleas of the tenant. Worry and desperation had settled on the man's face, yet Lord Sedgewick had done nothing but dismiss him. Would he throw them out?

She pulled her valise onto the bed and began to pack. For the second time, she was prepared to leave surroundings of familiarity and safety.

But that was a small price to pay for truth and justice.

Major Sir Frederick Tilbury was persistent if nothing else.

Henry crumpled the letter and tossed it across the room. Didn't the man realize Henry had responsibilities to attend to? He couldn't simply take off at the notice of a letter to drink tea and play *bouts-rimés* with the major's unmarried daughter.

He browsed through other correspondences, wrote various responses, then moved on to his ledger. He had just dipped his quill into the inkwell when a tap came at the door.

"Come in."

A footman entered and bowed. "A visitor, my lord."

"Who is it?"

"She does not say, my lord. I believe she mentioned the position of governess."

He closed his ledger. "Send her in."

The door shut and opened again in a matter of seconds.

Henry stared.

The young lady stood on the threshold, wearing a white dress and yellow pelisse, blond curls escaping from under her bonnet. Her arms hung limply at her sides, and the shade of her cheeks was especially colorless, as if she were experiencing discomfort.

A reaction he had inflicted, no doubt. "Well." Henry rose. "Did you walk?"

"I arrived in a hackney, my lord."

"What may I do for you?"

"I understand you are in search of a governess."

"Are you?"

"Pardon?"

"A governess?"

"Oh." A flush swept across her face. "Well, I have never been before, but I am certain I could do well at it."

"You are very fond of children, I presume?"

Again, she hesitated.

He moved on. "What is your name?"

"Miss Woodhart." Her chin lifted a notch. "I am two and twenty, and quite capable of managing a child."

"Any education?"

"The best, my lord, and I am moderately accomplished in both Greek and Latin."

"Greek and Latin?" He sank back into his chair, motioning for her to do the same. "I am quite impressed, Miss Woodhart. I wonder that you are so well versed in two languages, yet seek a position so lowly."

"There is nothing lowly about a governess." Her eyes flashed. "And I was previously a lady's maid. I learned a great deal."

"And gained a wealthy wardrobe, I see."

"Her ladyship desired me to dress in vogue."

"I wonder that you ever left her."

Her mouth opened, then snapped back shut. She turned to leave—

"Miss Woodhart." Henry came around the desk and held out his hand.

She stared at it for a long time until finally her eyes lifted to his face. She placed her gloved hand in his. "Yes, my lord?"

"Forgive my ill temper. I shall send a servant with you back to the village, and you may retrieve your things."

"Thank you, my lord." A pause, a strange flicker of emotion he could not place. Then she tugged her hand free and was gone, shutting the door quietly behind her.

Henry returned to his desk, yet even when he opened the ledger, the figures were a blur. *Miss Woodhart.* He dipped his quill for the second time. Why did it seem he knew her already? Why did something in her eyes spark recognition, as if he'd held such a gaze before?

He couldn't place it. If he had spoken with her in the past, it must have been a brief interaction indeed, for the name meant nothing to him.

He leaned back and tugged the bellpull on the wall.

Minutes later, Dunn swept through the doorway and approached the desk. "I presume all went well, my lord?"

"As well as we might have hoped for. Though I daresay our new governess will be new in more ways than one."

"Then perhaps she would not be suitable—"

"No, no. She will manage quite well, and I imagine Peter shall find her charming."

"Splendid, my lord."

"Although she never said as much, I would not be surprised to learn she at one point possessed a small fortune herself, which gives me great confidence in her ability to educate Peter." Henry leaned back in his chair. "It does not much matter to me how she came to lose such a fortune or why she desires to work here. It only matters to me that she stays."

"I believe that is all our hopes, my lord."

"Let us do more than hope, hmm? See that Miss Woodhart is afforded special privileges. Put her in one of the guest rooms, the one with the view, and see that she is allowed to partake of all her meals with myself and Peter. I want her to feel as comfortable as possible. Understood?"

"Yes, but—"

"And see that she is given her own freedoms, as well. Mrs. Lundie will continue to watch over our Peter when Miss Woodhart requires her own time."

"Yes, my lord." Dunn's forehead tightened. "But do you think such arrangements. . .well, do you think them wise, my lord?"

"Maybe not." A familiar pang started low in his stomach. "But I am desperate."

And no matter what happened, he didn't want his young son to lose another woman again.

∽

Mrs. Lundie's wiry arms hooked on her hips. "Git doon from there, ye wee rascal, afore I be telling yer faither."

"Tell me what, Mrs. Lundie?"

The woman whirled, her jaw slacking. "M'lord." She pushed the frizzy gray hair away from her face. "I was just telling the wee one to be getting doon afore he hurts himself."

A rustling of leaves from midway up the oak tree confirmed her worries.

Henry grinned. "Well, if he does not care to come down, I fear he shall never know what a great secret I have for him."

A small branch parted. "Secret, Papa?"

"Come down and I shall tell it to you." He turned to Mrs. Lundie, whose lined face bore signs of exhaustion.

She wiped a continual sheen of perspiration from her skin. "I dinnae be meaning to complain, m'lord, but I'm no nanny at heart. The wee little lad has been running all morning, and with I a-chasing him like I used to chase a goat in the hielands when I was a lassie myself."

"Then I believe my surprise will be most pleasant for you as well, Mrs. Lundie."

Peter leaped from a low limb, landed on all fours, then bounded back to his feet. "Look, Papa." He held out a leaf that was crinkled from his tight grasp. "It is a special leaf. Do you know why?"

"Why?"

"It's the very highest." He raised on tiptoes. "The very, very highest leaf on the tree—"

"Lord Sedgewick!"

Henry spun around, dread slamming his stomach.

Dunn kept one hand on the door, the other clenched into a fist. "You are needed indoors, my lord."

Henry sprinted for the manor. He hardly heard when Peter's voice cried out to him.

∽

Dorthea's farewells were quiet and dejected, her smiles not given in earnest.

"Why so glum?" The door clicked shut behind the servant, who was toting Ella's trunk with sighs of exertion.

Dorthea frowned. "Quite the reality, is it not?"

"At your prompting."

"Oh, do not tell me such things." Tears glittered in Dorthea's eyes. "What shall I do if you are killed too? How can I bear such guilt?"

"You need not worry. I promise I shall not be murdered."

"One usually cannot prevent such a thing."

"Lucy was unaware of his true nature. I am not."

Dorthea dabbed at her eyes, smiled for a second, then embraced her friend. "Well, you may rest assured I shall conceal your secret to my death, Miss *Woodhart*. Not even my parents have been told."

"I did not doubt you once."

The servant returned, and Ella climbed into the chaise next to him. She waved goodbye as the Fitzherbert household grew small and obscure in the distance. She derived some comfort in the colorful streets of Northston, but even that passed them quickly.

The road loomed ahead. Empty countryside surrounded them, sublime and melancholy, murmuring sounds of evening time.

The servant did not broach any topic of conversation, for which she was most grateful. She had no heart for tedious comments on the weather, the scandal of a downstairs maid, nor any other topic a servant might possibly care to discuss.

But then again, now *she* was only the slightest bit above a servant. Wasn't she?

Yet only in pretense. There was a great difference.

As the road turned, the ocean view spread out to their left. Her eyes followed the coast until Wyckhorn Manor became visible on the top of the cliffside.

What am I doing? A thousand times with no answer. She was numb, but only because she repressed any feelings. She was too afraid of them. *In heaven's name, what am I doing?*

When the chaise halted, the servant swung her to the ground. He said nothing, only hefted down her trunk with a grunt.

Ella ascended the stone steps. She brushed back her curls, smoothed her dress, straightened her bonnet—silly things to do, of course, because she'd already made an appearance once today. Not a very good one, to be sure. More than once she had been ready to flee Lord Sedgewick's study, certain he had discovered her identity. What a fool she'd been to tell him of her Greek and Latin. What had she been thinking?

She knocked until the door opened, then followed the butler up two flights of stairs. Crossed swords and framed paintings decorated the halls, ancient faces with eyes that seemed to follow her.

She shivered.

"This shall be your chamber, miss." The butler swung the door open for her. "His lordship requested you be given this room. He felt you might appreciate the solitude."

"Indeed."

"Master Peter's chamber is at the end of the hall, adjacent to the nursery." He took a step back as if in a hurry, his eyes never alighting on her face. "I believe you are to arrive for dinner presently."

"Thank you."

"Yes, Miss Woodhart." The butler bowed and hastened away.

She entered and surveyed her room. A four-poster bed with green curtains, a Persian rug, a writing desk, washstand, and wardrobe. Very quaint and sensible. Sedgewick had suggested it?

She approached the only window and drew back the drapes. *The sea.* Her fear dissipated, her courage rose. *What a perfect, lovely sight.*

In her moments of greatest despair, she would return to this view. She would open her heart to the beauty, tranquility, and brightness of the endless waves.

It was a comfort not anticipated, but very welcome indeed.

∞

Whatever does one do with a child?

Ella's pulse was frenzied. She took one step at a time—one dreadful, daunting step at a time, until she regrettably reached the bottom. How old had she been when she'd last been around a person Peter's age? Her younger sister, Matilda, was fifteen now, herself two and twenty ...which would have made Ella twelve? A mere slip of a child herself.

Besides that, the governess and her mother had seen to all of Matilda's needs. Ella had not once satisfied her younger sister's childish whims.

I hardly consider myself one who adores children. Ella entered a dark hall, lit only with dim chandeliers overhead. *They are rather strange and devilish creatures if the village urchins are any indication.*

Of course, the son of a lord would be considerably better mannered. But mannered or not, a child was a child.

"Excuse me." Ella halted a young maid, who was dusting a flowerless vase on a stand. "Might you show me to the dining room?"

The girl directed her to impressive double doors, which were open wide as if waiting for her.

Only a weak soul would have trembled, but she did so nonetheless. "Thank you." She spoke to the maid, more to test her voice than to execute civility. Forcing her fingers to uncurl, she entered.

A long table stretched across the room, empty chairs on either side, the tablecloth sporting several colorful dishes.

Only one pair of eyes stared back at her—small, rounded, a familiar shade of blue.

Ella stared at him. Never had she expected such a likeness of Lucy.

"You may sit down if you want to." The voice was small and kind, the expression bashfully sweet.

Emotion clogged her throat. She took a seat two chairs away from him, then unfolded her napkin for the sole purpose of busying her hands. Did the child always dine at such a large table by himself? Or was his father usually present?

"You are the surprise."

Ella lifted her gaze to him. "I beg pardon?"

"The surprise for me." His blond hair was damp and brushed, his cheeks gleaming as if recently scrubbed. "Papa was going to tell me, but Mrs. Lundie told me instead. She said I should wear my best skeleton suit for you. See?"

She observed the outfit with an involuntary smile. "I see."

"Do you like mackerel?"

"Yes—"

"I don't. I have to eat it anyway if I want any tarts."

She glanced at the untouched fish on his plate. "Well, since we are the only ones present, I do not think one tart would hurt."

A beam transformed his expression, but he didn't reach for a tart. Instead, he scrunched his nose and took a bite of mackerel. "I had better do as Papa says," he said between bites.

Surprise poked at her insides. When had she ever dismissed a chance at mischief? She had never thought twice about breaking a rule.

The remainder of the meal was spent in pleasant, intelligent conversation—a reality which both intrigued and delighted Ella.

When the course was finished and his tart consumed, young Peter Sedgewick was the first to stand. "Tomorrow I will show you my favorite tree. I can climb all the way to the top."

"Oh?"

He sidled closer and stood beside her chair with eyes aglow. "And Miss Woodhart?"

"Yes?"

"You are a good surprise."

∞

Henry locked his bedchamber door behind him, listening to the silence, loathing it. His muscles ached. *God?*

He ripped off his tailcoat and tossed it to the floor, wiped the blood from his lip with the back of his hand. Would the cut be notice-able? What would he tell his son?

More lies. Always lies. He was sick of deceit.

Exhaustion drew him to his bed, but he lacked the will to rest. He reached for his Bible. The pages fell open and the words stared back at him—bold, black, never changing: "Purge me with hyssop, and I shall be clean: wash me, and I shall be whiter than snow. Make me to hear joy and gladness; that the bones which thou hast broken may rejoice. Hide thy face from my sins, and blot out all mine iniquities."

His insides opened up and wept, but no tears touched his eyes. He closed the book, drew it against his chest. His pain mingled with the silence, his heart with the agony of the words. When would it end?

Maybe never. Maybe it would always be like this. And had he any right to pray it would change?

No. He didn't. His fault. . .everything was his fault. The blood on his lip. His wife dead. His son without a mother.

God, have mercy on me. Because he couldn't change anything now. He couldn't reverse that night. All he could do was make it up to Peter and keep the truth from ever leaving this house.

If that was even possible.

CHAPTER 4

$\mathcal{T}$he house was no more alive in the morning than it had been at night.

Ella had risen early, donned a yellow dress, and escaped to the out of doors long before the child was awake. She strolled around the perimeter of the manor, took a detour through the garden, then returned to the servants' entrance. She was just reaching for the door when it came open from the other side.

"My!" A wiry little woman stared at her. "What do ye think ye're doing 'ere?"

"Why, entering I suppose." A smile threatened Ella's lips. "I live here, you know."

"Live here?" Understanding transformed the woman's features. "Och, but ye cannae be the governess, can ye noo?"

"Indeed, one and the same." Ella curtsied. "You may call me Miss Woodhart."

"And ye may be calling me Mrs. Lundie." The woman motioned her inside. "I dinnae mind telling ye how glad I am ye've come."

Ella followed her through the house. "Why so?"

"I am a housekeeper—not a nanny. At least I was." She harrumphed. "Once the child was born, all that changed. His lordship wouldn't hear of bringing a true nanny into the house, not even one with references."

"Why not?"

"I fear he was not himself those five years ago. He dinnae want strangers aboot. 'Twas not so bad for me at first when the child was a wee thing—but och, he's so spry now. Ye understand, dinnae ye?"

47

"Yes. Certainly."

"Not that Master Peter is an unruly bairn. Dinnae think that of him." She opened the door to a breakfast room. "It's just that I am a wee bit auld and such."

Ella's pulse hastened as she entered.

Lord Sedgewick sat at the small round table, his back facing her. He shook a napkin free of crumbs. "Mrs. Lundie." He turned in his seat. "Have you seen..."

The blood chilled in Ella's veins.

"Miss Woodhart." The corners of his mouth drew downward. Was that a cut on his lip?

His gaze shifted back to the older woman. "Peter is still abed, I presume?"

"Likely overslept, poor thing. I'll go and wake him."

"No." Ella brushed the woman's arm. "I shall tend to him—"

"I dinnae mind. Besides, ye have nae had yer breakfast." Mrs. Lundie motioned her toward a chair. "Sit doon and I'll be bringing the wee lad in no time."

Lord Sedgewick rose, not returning to his chair until the door was shut and Ella seated. His large hand reached for a glass. "Your chamber was suitable?"

"Most."

"And how did you find the view?" He took a bite of his brioche.

"Unmatchable." Her gaze latched onto a painting across the room, anything so she might not look at his face.

He caught the direction of her stare. "The late Duke of Cornwall."

She cast her eyes away from the painting. "He is rather solemn, I daresay."

"Not all can afford the pleasures of a happy life." Lord Sedgewick stood again. "Excuse me, Miss Woodhart." He departed the room without another glance her way.

∽

Peter's tree was not half as large as she would have imagined. Indeed, the tree she had climbed as a child was far its superior, in both height and width. She kept such thoughts to herself, however.

"I should like to show you something else." Peter made the final leap back to the ground, full of vigor after a morning spent in lessons. "Do you want to come?"

"I am quite at your disposal."

"That means yes?"

"Certainly."

He laughed and grabbed her hand.

Something stirred inside of her, a sense of surprise and uprooting. She allowed herself to be tugged across the lawn. "Where are we going?"

"My second-most favorite place."

"The tree being your first?"

"No, not the tree." He released her hand and darted toward the stable doors. He went on tip-toes as he lifted the latch. "The seashore is my favorite—and Papa's. We play in the water."

"Men do not play."

"How come?"

She entered the stables behind him, drawing in the sweet scents of hay and leather. "Because." No further explanation came to her. Lord Sedgewick played in the water?

How absurd. Such an unhappy man—at his own admission only this morning—would certainly not be capable of frolic. Not even for the sake of his son.

"Over here, Miss Woodhart." Grabbing her hand again, Peter drew her to a stall along the left wall.

A familiar bay stared back at her.

"This is Miss Staverley. Do you like her?"

"Well, I do not confess to knowing her very well." Ella stroked the animal's nose with her glove. "But she seems rather good-natured."

"Don't you like horses?"

"Only because I shouldn't."

"What?"

Ella pinched his cheek with a smile. "Never mind. We had better

49

go inside now, for Mrs. Lundie gave imperative instructions for you to take an afternoon nap."

"I am not tired at all."

"Well, then sit in your room and pretend to sleep."

His chin puckered, but he never cried or brought on pitiful pleas. He became subdued and downcast, but by the time Ella had seen him into bed, he was already beginning to yawn.

She shut the door of his bedchamber quietly. *I am fitting into the role quite nicely.* Who would have known that overseeing a child could be so easy?

She would never have guessed. Why, just yesterday she was a clumsy fool—and today she was holding his hand and tucking him into bed.

Ella returned downstairs and inquired about the location of the library. Like all other rooms of the house, the library bore signs of despondency and emptiness. Everything she touched was dead, everything she saw was dark and alone.

Lucy would have spent many hours here. Crossing the threshold took a force of will, as if stepping into the past. As if she might actually find Lucy inside.

Ella approached an upholstered chair, ran her fingers down the gilded wood. How easily came a vision of her sister curled in the chair, book in her lap, face enraptured with the story behind the cover.

A spec of silver from the stand beside the chair caught her attention.

She pushed away a stack of books and drew a silver comb into her hands. Tears stung until her vision of the hairpiece was little more than a blur. *Oh, Lucy.*

Ella pressed the cold silver to her chest. She was no longer a stranger in a house of strangers. Be it lifeless and hollow, she now had something she could touch, something tangible.

She held a part of Lucy. And she had every intention of roaming the entire house—until she uncovered each little thing her sister had left behind.

Including the truth.

Oh, Lucy, what happened to you? Why couldn't Father rest? Why does this house feel as if it's hiding you from me?

Lord Sedgewick had not been at dinner. Indeed, she had neither seen nor heard from him in two days, except once when she had glanced out the nursery window earlier this morning. He had been riding Miss Staverley toward the gates. Even from a distance, his stance was erect, his arrogant head held high.

She detested that arrogance. How had Lucy been so blind? A handsome face was certainly not everything.

"Miss Woodhart?"

Ella scooted across the settee to allow room for the little boy. "Yes?"

"Will you read to me?" He laid *The Tour of Dr. Syntax In Search of the Picturesque* upon her lap, though she suspected it was the illustrations—not the story—that most captured his interest.

Whatever the case, he lasted no more than ten minutes before several yawns proved it was nap time.

Ella walked him back to the nursery, where Mrs. Lundie rose from her chair and readied Peter for bed, despite his tired protests.

Ella stifled a yawn of her own. Why was her sleep so elusive in this house? All night long, even in slumber, there was a restlessness. An uneasy twinge. The need to search out all the secrets, even if they did frighten her.

When Peter had fallen asleep and Mrs. Lundie began to doze in her chair, Ella slipped from the room and back down the stairs. Perhaps she shouldn't have. What right did she have to wander the house this way?

But the butler had made it very clear she was permitted certain privileges—and if Lord Sedgewick and his house were so much alike, perhaps an exploration of the halls would teach her much.

Her footsteps thudded away the silence. So much silence. Why was every corridor, every chamber so quiet? And for a manor this impressive, why were there not more servants scurrying about?

She had half expected to find Mr. Arnold and his family in residence, but had yet to lay eyes on any of them. Certainly, they were being cared for in the servants' quarters, weren't they? There was hardly time for them to have been situated in another cottage. Or had Lord Sedgewick...

No, he would not have thrown them out. Even the most miserable of creatures would not have sent a family so destitute into the streets. After all, they were *his* responsibility.

"Miss Woodhart." A square-faced, compact man filled a doorway to her left. "Have you lost your way?"

"No, indeed. I have just been acquainting myself with the premises."

"Large and impending, are they not?"

She chuckled. "Well stated, sir. I fear I shall be eternally lost in these endless halls."

He closed the door behind him, seemingly a study, and offered her a slight bow. "I am Mr. Dunn, Miss Woodhart. I am the steward here at Wyckhorn."

"What a strain you must be under. Such a large estate."

"Not at all. I rather like it here, miss."

She could not imagine why.

"But I am afraid I do have duties to attend to. If there is anything I might do for you first—"

"There is something."

His brow quirked. "Yes?"

"I wished to inquire after a Mr. Arnold and his family."

"Oh?" His voice lilted in surprise. "I had not realized word reached the village so quickly."

"I believe they were brought here after the fire. Is that so?"

"Why, yes, miss." His hands crossed behind his back. "But you need not concern yourself. They have already been removed from the household."

Shock lowered her jaw. "They—"

"Dunn!"

Both heads snapped around as Lord Sedgewick rounded the hall corner.

Ella's fists clenched.

"Dunn," he said again, calmer. "I require your assistance a moment." He stood in riding clothes, hat in hand, sweat curling the tips of his dark hair.

"Yes, my lord." Dunn spared her a small nod and hurried to his lordship. They disappeared from view, the sound of their quick footfalls echoing back into the silence.

Removed from the house? Was such a man even human?

Ella's hands clasped together, shaking, much as she'd seen her father's do a hundred times. *"I hate him, Ella. Not just for what he has done to Lucy—but for what he has done to hide it. Am I the only one not blinded by his lies?"*

Her soul wept in answer to the memory. *No, Father. You are not the only one.*

And before she left this house, she would reveal the depths of his cruelties to the whole world.

To all of them.

⌒

"What was she discussing with you?"

Dunn opened the third drawer, rummaged through it, then shut it again. "I am quite sorry, my lord, but the letter seems to be gone."

"Did you hear me, Dunn?"

The steward glanced up. "Nothing beyond the ordinary, my lord. Why do you ask?"

"I thought she might have experienced a difficulty with Peter. Why else would she seek you out?"

"I was under the impression, my lord, that she merely wandered by my study. I do not think it was intentional."

"Taking tours of the house, then?"

"It would seem to be thus, my lord."

Henry crossed the study and brushed through the papers again. "That letter needs to be found."

"Is it very important?"

"Yes. Do you think I would have bothered you were it not?"

Dunn blinked, paled, then took a step away from the desk. "I am certain it is just misplaced. I shall locate it."

Henry sank into his chair. He dragged his hand across his chin. "No, you may resume whatever it was you were doing. I am no doubt the one who lost it."

"Whatever you say, my lord."

"And Dunn?"

"Yes, my lord?"

Henry held the man's eyes. "Is she doing well with Peter?"

"I cannot say, my lord. I have not had ample chance to observe." A hint of a smile touched his lips. "Although I do recall a bit of laughter penetrating the walls, now and again. It was a pleasant sound, indeed, my lord."

"Yes." Henry turned his eyes to the windows. "I imagine it was." How long since this house had known anything but misery? How many years since the air hadn't smelled of death, since the curse hadn't made a home in the walls?

There'd been no laughter for a long time. Longer than he could remember. What an agony that his son must remain in such a place.

But maybe now things would be better. If Miss Woodhart could offer the boy love, if her presence could bring him laughter, if the truth of his own mother could forever be kept from his ears...

Maybe Peter could escape the punishment.

The punishment Henry had brought on them both.

Evening provided the first chance for Ella to return to the stables. The building and stock were far more impressive than Abbingston's, as her mother had always discouraged her father from wasting time improving such a small aspect of their estate. Her father had loved horses, but he must have loved her mother more. Beyond travel, he spent very little time riding or lingering at the stables.

Her mother had always wished Ella to do the same. That alone, perhaps, was why Ella had instead ridden so often. Besides, it was most in fashion to ride—and to ride well. It was considered the elevation of loveliness and grace.

A different motive, however, drew her here. She entered, closed the door behind her, and shuffled across the straw-littered floor. "Anyone about?"

A young boy peered around a stall. At the sight of one obviously unexpected, he scrambled to his feet. "Miss." He whipped off his cap. "I mean—I am." A pause. "I am about."

She laughed at his jumbled response. "Very good. Mr. Dunn said you might assist me with a mount. May I have one saddled, please?"

"A horse? You be wantin' to ride, miss?"

"Yes."

"Oh." He flew into motion. "Yes, miss—right away." He expressed uncertainty about locating a sidesaddle, but soon produced one from the back, notwithstanding the dust. "I'll shine it for you real good, miss, just as soon as you be gettin' back."

Ella smiled her thanks, mounted, and rode beyond the black gates of Wyckhorn Manor. Freedom surged within her, like wellsprings gurgling over and saturating her. What would have happened if no one had ever built the first house? If mankind had learned to survive and adapt without the horrid, enclosing walls of shelter?

A frown pulled at her lips. What nonsensical thoughts—yet what reality they might be to the Arnold family. Could her suspicions be true?

Well, she would know soon enough.

Ella dug her heels into the animal's side, spurring the animal faster up the familiar road. She reached the top and stared down into the valley. Her stomach knotted.

She'd been right.

∞

"Well, that is quite the tower." Henry stooped over his son. "How much higher do you plan to go?"

"Not very much higher." Peter sat on his knees, reaching for another block on the Turkish rug. "I don't have many blocks left."

"Well, it is a good thing because I am ready to place one young man in bed."

"I'm not a man." His tongue poked between his teeth in concentration. He fixed another block on the tower. "Men do not play. That is what Miss Woodhart says."

"Miss Woodhart." He tried her name again, disconcerted by the way it sounded on his lips. What was it about her that bemused him so? She was familiar yet strange to him, in likeness to a dream that comes and goes, leaving only faint impressions of remembrance.

"Tell me." Henry fingered a strand of his son's hair. "What do you think of Miss Woodhart?"

"She isn't old like Miss Morton and Mrs. Lundie."

He coughed to hide a desire to laugh at the boy's bluntness. "No, she is not old."

"And she is pretty." The tower crumbled. Peter groaned and covered his face. "My tower!"

Henry scooped the child into his arms and swung him into bed. "You may build it again in the morning."

Peter burst into a laugh. "Can you swing me again?"

"Swing you?"

"Into bed, Papa. Please?"

Henry obliged, then tucked the bedclothes around his son's neck. They whispered prayers quietly before Henry shut himself out of the room. He was just turning when—

"Lord Sedgewick." Miss Woodhart halted in the hall, a candlestick illuminating her features. The light danced in and out of windblown curls. "I was just retiring to my room."

"I see." He took a step forward. "Allow me to escort you."

"I would not think of robbing your time."

Her refusal irked him, although he couldn't exactly say why. "I am in the habit of distributing my time at my own discretion."

"Do you govern all choices at your own discretion?"

"Don't we all?"

"Some have scruples, my lord."

He leaned forward into the darkness. "Which you suggest I lack?"

Hard, luminous eyes glared back at him without flinching. "I admit I am no crusader of the poor, but the thought of rendering a small family houseless unsettles even me."

"I am quite confounded as to which family you believe I have bestowed such cruelty."

"I wonder that you have forgotten it so quickly. It was only mere days ago that their house was devoured in flames."

"The Arnolds?"

Her lips pursed. "Your steward gave me permission for a ride this evening, in which time I rode by their house. There remains nothing there but ashes and misery—"

"You are very candid, Miss Woodhart, and I am afraid it is not to your furtherance." He took a step into the light beaming from her candlestick. "I suggest you learn to quell that vicious tongue." He brushed past her and descended the stairs in the darkness, feeling a bit betrayed of himself when a smile upturned his lips. What was the matter with him anyway? Must be some kind of fool to let his own governess speak to him so, to let her accuse him of such things.

But then again, he was used to being accused. He just wasn't used to having a woman do it. And he was not about to assuage her intrusive concern.

Strange little thing, she was. Unlike any woman he'd ever known. He was used to the smiles, the purring voice, the feigned innocence, and delicate flattery. All things he'd grown to hate because he understood them as a knife wound understands a blade.

But this?

This was different. She was different. No danger or pretense hid in the way she approached him, in the way she met and held his eyes.

She seemed, almost, as if she had no ulterior motives at all.

CHAPTER 5

From behind Ella, Peter sighed. "I cannot climb my tree."

"Nor can we take our venture to the seashore." Ella turned away from the rain-washed window. "I suppose there shall be other days."

He plopped into a large chair by the hearth. "Will you read to me?"

She was getting rather tired of dear Dr. Syntax, but at least his travels entertained her young charge. "Very well. You remain here, and I shall fetch a book."

She hurried toward the library, but she must have taken a wrong turn because the ornaments were unfamiliar to her. Why could she not remember where she was going? Abbingston Hall was exceedingly more logical—and not half as large.

The hall ended at a doorway.

She would have turned away, only the large wooden door was opened to a crack. Soft, indistinguishable noises drifted into the hall.

She drew closer. She shouldn't have, of course, but she always did what she shouldn't do. With a small nudge of her finger, she pried open the crack without sound.

An empty room stared back at her.

How odd. Hadn't she distinctly heard someone?

She slipped inside and closed the door behind her. Her gaze swept across the green-and-gold draperies, the flowerless vases, the unused hearth.

Then she saw the painting. The life-sized woman hung on the wall, framed in polished silver. Her eyes were narrow and tight, painted in the lightest shades of blue and green. She was beautiful despite her rigidity. Was there coldness on her face, or was it only the strokes of the painter that made her appear so detached and unhappy?

"What are you doing?"

Ella's breath caught, but she couldn't turn. What a fool she'd been, what a fool she always was. If only she were sensible like Matilda—

"His lordship would not like you here, Miss Woodhart."

Slowly, she turned. Her tension lightened. "Oh." She swallowed hard. "Mr. Dunn, I thought you were—"

"Forgive me if I spoke harshly." The tips of his ears reddened. "I was simply taken aback. This is a"—his gaze swept to the painting—"very private room, miss."

"Which I did not intend to intrude upon." She did a hasty bow. "Forgive me, but I must continue my search for the library."

"Shall I direct you?"

She avoided his gaze as she swept to the door. "No, sir. I shall locate it myself." She all but ran from the room.

She could only hope he would not inform Lord Sedgewick what she had done. She was in enough peril already after last night. But pray, what was so private about this room?

And who was the woman in the painting?

Henry was ill-prepared for the sight and unaccustomed to the odd sensations. He couldn't have said if the sensations were warm or cold, if they comforted or inflicted—only that he was transfixed. He could not move.

She sat in the chair he usually occupied, with her elbows on the upholstered armrests, Peter in her lap, his fingers twirling one of her stray curls.

She did not fuss at him for it, nor did she even seem to notice. She read in tones soft, animated, as if the story had come alive to her. "'For Dolly's charms poor Damon burn'd. Disdain the cruel maid return'd: but, as she danc'd in May-day pride, Dolly fell down, and Dolly died—'"

"Died?" Peter leaned up.

"Died indeed," echoed Miss Woodhart, brows raised theatrically. With eyes wide and solemn, Peter settled back and listened.

Henry should have made himself known. He knew that. It was a breach of etiquette to linger in the doorway as a common eavesdropper.

But if there was comfort for him here, he could not disrupt it. He had always wanted his son to have the one thing he himself had never possessed—a mother's love.

Yet that was the very thing he had ripped from Peter's life. The very thing he could never give back.

"'And now she lays by Damon's side. Be not hard-hearted then, ye fair! Of Dolly's hapless fate beware! For sure, you'd better go to bed, to one alive, than one who's dead.'" A smile dimpled her cheek as if to soften the extremity of such a mature theme as death. Then her eyes lifted, roamed the room—paused and rounded.

Henry emerged from the doorway. "You have an impressive voice, Miss Woodhart."

Peter climbed off her lap, and she snapped the book shut. "I was not aware I had an audience."

Was *she* scolding *him*? He rather thought so. Didn't the woman know her place? And for heaven's sake, why was he not rankled by her unseemly candor? How odd that he should be amused by such a chit of a girl.

"Papa, it has stopped raining." Peter tugged at his coat. "May I go out of doors?"

"I believe it would be in order to ask your governess."

His eager grin turned toward Miss Woodhart. "May I?"

"Yes, and I shall go with you."

He clapped his hands and squealed, but his spirits dampened some when Henry instructed him to return the book to the library first. He pelted from the room.

"And do not run in the house," Henry shouted after him.

"I need not be in suspense as to why you are here." Miss Woodhart remained seated, but her back arched and stiffened. "Though I do not know what I might do now, with the exception of apologizing."

Henry stared at her. What was she talking about?

"Which I am very good at," she added.

"Good at what, Miss Woodhart?"

"Apologizing." Her head cocked. "But should you not first care to hear my opinion of the painting? I assure you, my lord, I shall not dare say she is solemn."

Unease tightened around his throat. "It seldom matters to me what others think."

"With my opinion falling among the least, I presume." She glanced away for a moment, sighed, then returned her gaze to him with no small amount of prejudice. "My apologies nonetheless, my lord. It shall not happen again."

Peter bounded into the room again panting for breath. She rose to greet him.

"Won't you come too, Papa?"

He shook his head. "Another time."

Hands clasped, Miss Woodhart and his son quit the room. The sounds of his happy chatter, the feathery trail of her laugh. . . They melted into a silence he knew all too well.

If only she would love his son. If only she would offer him what no woman ever had, a mother's faithful heart.

Every little boy needed that.

Henry knew.

∽

Ella shuddered and drew her wrapper tight around her. Thunder shook the sash window of her bedchamber. Lightning brightened the darkness, illuminating the raging sea—then the world plunged back into blackness.

How odd that she should desire to sit here, with her fingertips pressed against the cold glass, and her position so close to the turmoil outside. It was late enough that the house was doubtless asleep. She had no wish to prowl in the night, to venture out into passageways that were black and endless.

Yet it was something she must do. This was, after all, the reason she had come.

Taking her pewter candlestick, she slipped quietly into the hall. At various times when she knew herself to be alone, she had investigated all the rooms on this floor. She had discovered nothing. She had also searched below stairs, but since there were no bedchambers, she had found very little to interest her.

Thus, she approached the stairway and started up. The steps creaked beneath her, as if from lack of perpetual use, and the feeble candlelight invaded deep shadows.

She reached the landing.

Dark, empty space spread out before her, but she was not so afraid as to turn back. No. She most certainly would not do that. Courage was her virtue—wasn't it?

She had great difficulty swallowing, but such could easily be explained, for the hallway was dusty and stifling. She padded to the first door and tested the knob. It turned with a small creak, but she hesitated. What if she stumbled into Lord Sedgewick's chamber?

No, it was not possible. Lord Sedgewick was located in another wing of the house—Peter had informed her so. There was no chance she would be discovered. She had never seen anyone approach this floor, least of all the lord himself.

She pushed inside the room and swept around with her candle. Nothing. It appeared to be little more than an old guest room, long since abandoned if the dust was any indication.

She continued down the hall, opening doors, peering in alcoves, slipping in and out of shadowy places.

She entered another bedchamber and leaned inside.

Candlelight spread a glow across a canopy bed, a dressing commode, a Sheraton fire screen, a bookshelf. . .

Ella's heart leaped to her throat. The bookshelf. Of course there would be one, of course it would be here. Lucy would dare not go anywhere without her volumes.

Ella's hands shook as she approached. She brushed her fingers against the dusty spines, recognizing many of them, wondering why no one had missed them from her father's library.

How Mother would have scolded her sister for taking them from the house. It was the only defiant thing Lucy had ever done in her life.

A roar split the air.

Ella jumped, whirled. Her heart settled when she realized it was only thunder. She was being as fearful and timid as Matilda. A smile upturned her lips at the thought, and she turned—

Movement caught her eye. Something small, then a rustling noise.

Her stomach lurched. Her flesh raised in goosebumps. With a throbbing chest, she lifted her candlestick.

Light cast itself into darkness. The bed was illuminated.

I have the greatest of imaginations. Sweat formed on her skin. *It is only the storm—*

The bed creaked, as if under a weight. The curtains rippled.

A scream lodged in her throat, but she flew away so quickly the light flickered into darkness. She darted into the hallway. She ran blindly, cupping her mouth. *It wasn't the storm.*

She found her bedchamber and locked the door with her key. *Dear heavens, it wasn't the storm.*

∞

Henry glanced at her plate for the second time.

Miss Woodhart sat alone with him in the breakfast room, one finger idly circling her cup of cocoa. As if sensing his scrutiny, her head lifted.

He perused her face—the light, delicate features, the sharp blue eyes flecked with gold, the tight blond curls that framed her cheeks. Upon most encounters, he found her challenging and accusative, as if the need to defend herself was ever present.

But now she was pensive and pale, and her cool gaze made him lower his fork.

"Are you well, Miss Woodhart?"

She took a small sip of her cocoa as if an answer to his question required contemplation. She finally nodded. "Quite, thank you."

"I trust the storm did not make sleep elusive."

"I am not afraid of storms." Was he in error, or had her chin trembled on the last word?

He scooted from his chair. Hesitated. Why was he getting ready to do this? "I shall talk to Mrs. Lundie and inform her that Peter will be entirely in her care for the day. You may take advantage of the time and rest."

"I do not need rest."

"Then you may enjoy the day to do as you please. Perhaps an outing?"

A protest shaped her lips, one second before she sighed and nodded. "I do have a letter I should like to send. Perhaps I shall go into the village."

"I shall talk to Dunn about an escort."

"Do not bother."

Why did she gainsay everything he said?

"I have no need of one, and I should rather enjoy the time alone."

His mouth twitched with irritation. "Go and write your letter, Miss Woodhart."

She narrowed her eyes, pursed her lips, and departed from the breakfast room.

Henry dragged a hand across his chin. Frustration battled against something else, something undefined that he could not place. Why had he extended privileges to her? Of what consequence could it possibly be to him if she had not slept last night, or if she was growing ill, or if she traveled to the village without escort?

No difference at all—except for the sake of his son.

"My lord, I have the greatest of news." Dunn swept into the room and produced a small letter. "It is no small wonder you misplaced it, my lord, for it had slipped under the desk by mistake. The housekeeper spotted it only this morning."

Henry eased the letter open. He read over the messy scrawl until his fingers tightened into fists. "One thousand pounds." He surrendered the letter to his steward. "Go and get it."

Dunn's eyes shifted to the handwriting, then rose again with dejection. "Again, my lord?"

Henry's gaze roamed to the window, where a green branch scratched at the glass.

"Perhaps there will not be any more—"

"There is always more, Dunn." Henry raked his fingers through his hair. "Father was a fool to cumber me with this."

"With due respect, my lord, your father cannot be to blame."

"No." Henry grabbed his hat from the corner of the desk. "But I know who can."

This was all lies, of course, but at least Mother and Matilda would be pacified that she was having a good time. Ella even added a section— on her mother's behalf—of the lessons society had administered to her. *I have become of the dullest nature since arriving in London and have not partaken of any mischief at all.*

She sealed the letter and tucked it inside her reticule. She donned a Pompeian-colored dress, a fichu, and a bonnet with matching red ribbons.

Peter was waiting for her in the hallway, with Mrs. Lundie fussing at him about the vices of running throughout the house. "Dinnae ye ken ye cannae do that when ye're auld, lad?"

He answered her quietly, but his gaze stayed on Ella. "Why are you leaving, Miss Woodhart?"

"To post a letter. One cannot remain detached from the rest of the world, you know."

He took her hand as they headed for the stairway. "Who did you write it to?"

"My mother."

"Oh."

His silence wrapped cords around her heart—cords that tightened until she hurt for him. "Peter—"

"You aren't coming back, are you?" His fingers squeezed and his gaze besought her.

She knelt before him, kissed his cheek. "You cannot think me so horrid as to break our engagement."

"Engagement?"

"You do not remember? Did we not plan to visit the seashore?"

"Oh." A soft smile crept to his lips. "We did."

"Then do not ask silly questions." She kissed him again, then charged him to return to Mrs. Lundie, who waited at the head of the stairs.

Ella found a footman waiting for her below. "Miss Woodhart, are you prepared to leave?"

"Oh—yes."

With one hand pulling open the door, he motioned her outside. "The phaeton is awaiting you, miss."

Had Lord Sedgewick told them? She was not quite certain what to think of that. She was still in puzzlement as to why he bothered giving her such liberties in the first place. Had he treated all of Peter's governesses so attentively? Then why had he destroyed his own wife?

Her steps halted, every nerve frayed. "Lord Sedgewick."

He stood beside the phaeton, his topper shading half of his face. His hand outstretched. "Do close your mouth, Miss Woodhart. It is most unbecoming."

Resentment shuffled her backward. "I cannot know why you are offering me your hand. I have no intention of—"

"*I* have no intention of sending you to the village alone. As for myself accompanying you, I am only doing so because other business is required of me. I did not see the justification in sending a servant when my company will do. Now give me your hand."

She surrendered, not due to a lack of confidence, but due to a mind too stunned to retaliate.

He climbed next to her. He was close enough that she caught the first faint scent of cologne, the lavender and citrus mingling with the late morning air. He gathered the reins and clicked to the horses.

The phaeton eased into motion. She clasped her hands as the iron gates disappeared behind them. Perhaps she should have been frightened. Maybe she was, she didn't know. . .only she kept stealing glances at his face.

His profile was smooth, his chin tight and erect. He glared at the road with pale eyes—or *was* he glaring?

She could not tell. In fact, she had been able to determine very little about him at all. He was as distant and discourteous as Dorthea had led her to believe. Yet at other times, he seemed almost kind. How could one possess the ardent affection of an innocent child, yet bear such iniquity upon his soul?

It hardly mattered. Her estimations of character had never been precise. Not even in paintings.

Her father had been different. He had known the truth. He had recognized the lies and had died still trying to unveil them. How could she do any less?

"Peter holds you in the highest regard."

She bit the inside of her cheek. Hesitated. "Well, his affections are returned."

"My son does not love in part."

"Nor I."

"He is a sensitive child."

"I fear you misjudge him. I would tribute him with intelligence and strength before I would wound his character with sensitivity."

His jaw clenched. He slapped the reins on the horses' rumps, remaining wordless for the space of a few heartbeats. Then, glancing at her again, he said, "My son never knew his mother."

As if he hadn't ended her himself, as if the blood weren't on his hands. Her throat worked up and down, but she hadn't the will to look at him. "How did she. . .die?"

"Illness." Sharp, emotionless. The reins slapped again. "But then again, I suppose you are already more than aware, Miss Woodhart."

Panic ascended. Still, she could not speak. Did he know? Had he discovered her, had he—?

"The village gossip is audacious and conceived by persons of the lowest nature. Very little truth can be found among their prattles."

"You deny their allegations?" A question, not a statement.

His pause lingered. Guilt clipped his tone. "Their misconceptions are hardly my concern. I told you before, opinions mean very little to me."

The countryside stretched out before them, rolling greenery and stone fences. But however picturesque it might have been, not even the sunshine could warm the scene. Coldness shrouded her until it entered her veins and pumped her heart.

And she knew her father had been right.

CHAPTER 6

The tavern door snapped shut behind Henry with a loud click.

From their seats around crudely built tables or from leaning positions upon the wooden kegs, a few local fishermen stared in silence. A woman strummed a lyre in the corner—though it seemed to lack some of its strings—and the discordant sound struck the air with strain.

Their eyes shifted to the counter, where another gentleman reached for a tankard. He flicked a coin to the proprietor. "You might invest in new floorboards, fellow." His mustache twitched. "And a new instrumentalist, in the doing." As if he'd already known Henry was present, his eyes lifted with a smile. "Lord Sedgewick, won't you join me?"

Henry approached the counter, laid his palms flat. "Mr. Swinton."

"In flesh and blood, my lord." He bowed with exaggeration. "Won't you join me for a tankard of ale? I am afraid this establishment can boast of very little else."

"I recall the place to be your choice."

"Ah, so it was." The gentleman leaned forward, grinning. "But that was for your sake, my lord. I wished to spare you any embarrassment possible."

"There is no embarrassment, I assure you." Henry produced the note from his pocket. "Good day—"

"Wait a minute." The man's fist snatched the fabric of Henry's coat. "I have waited a great many years for this, as described in my letter. Indeed, I had no inkling as to where he'd gone after he departed Cheltenham in the middle of the night—"

"Consequences of gambling." Henry shrugged him off. "Your debt is paid, Mr. Swinton."

"I tend to see it differently." The man's mustache twitched for the second time. "Dash it all, why didn't he deliver himself? Does he always send another fellow to pay for his own folly? I do wonder, my lord, what the good residents of Northston would think if they knew the behavior of a certain gentleman—"

Henry's hand groped for the man's cravat. "I wonder what they would say if I were to crush your throat, Mr. Swinton? If we are so eager to give them gossip, I shall be more than inclined to oblige you."

Mr. Swinton's eyes bugged. "No." His breath was raspy, panicked. He struggled out of Henry's grip and shuffled backward, knocking his tankard with his elbow. The liquid dripped from the counter, even as he rescued the note from ruin. "No, my lord, you see—"

Henry glared at him.

He shifted, colored, then looked away. "As you said before, my lord," he said. "The debt is paid." Stuffing the note inside his coat, he stormed from the tavern.

The door clicked shut behind him.

And Henry's shoulders caved the same time his heart sank lower in his chest. For mercy's sake, how long would he have to endure all this? His father should have never written such a will. Should never have made such stipulations, such unbearable stipulations.

But then again, his father hadn't known what would happen years after his death. He hadn't known what Henry would do on some quiet night, or how the blood on his hands would change everything.

If only he had.

If only they all had.

"Mr. Arnold." Having just posted her letter, Ella spotted the brown-coated man on the street, his face scarcely visible under the large hat.

He must not have heard her, because he continued on his way in hurried steps.

Ella darted after him. "Mr. Arnold!"

The large hat turned. Underneath, a shadowed pair of eyes met hers and widened. His lips hesitated as if he had forgotten her name.

Perhaps she had never introduced herself. "Mr. Arnold, I am ever so pleased to see you." She reached for his hand and gave a slight squeeze. "You do remember me, don't you?"

"Why, yes, miss." He withdrew his hand diffidently and ducked his chin. "'Twas a day I won't be forgettin' none too easy."

"How fares the littlest?"

"Well, miss. The Almighty be watchin' o'er her—o'er us all, I reckon."

Lord Sedgewick certainly was not.

"An' e'erything is startin' to look bright again." He shook his head. "I sure couldn't be seein' how after the fire an' all, but with the new house—"

"New house?"

"Yes, miss—"

"However did you manage to find a place so quickly? After you were forced to leave—"

"Leave, miss?" He pushed his hat back. "We wouldn't e'er want to leave."

"But Lord Sedgewick—"

"Settled us on a different patch o' land, not far from where we was before. 'Twas a bigger house an' all. Ground richer too. But Lord Sedgewick said it was fittin' on account of my missus being with child again."

"Oh."

How had he arranged all that so quickly? And why had he never told her, even when she accused him of her false suspicions?

"I—I didn't realize."

"Fine man, his lordship. Came to the new place e'ery day for a week after the fire, helpin' an' all, cheerin' up the children, bringin' things for the missus." A smile stretched across his weathered face. "Even helped me start on the barn with his own hands, he did."

His own hands? Couldn't he have sent a servant?

"Well, I best be goin', miss." Mr. Arnold tipped the brim of the large hat. "Good day to you, now."

Good day, indeed. How was she supposed to face his lordship now?

☙

She was already waiting for him in the phaeton when he returned. He settled next to her in silence, took the reins, and brought the horses to a slow trot out of town.

"My letter is sent." Her voice took on a quality of cheerfulness. "Has your business been attended to?"

A smile curved at the remembrance of Mr. Swinton's frightened dash from the tavern. "Yes, I daresay it is."

Silence.

Then, "Only one letter?"

"Pardon?"

"You sent only one letter?"

"I had but two people to write, and since they both reside in the same dwelling and will no doubt read aloud, one letter was sufficient."

"Two people," he said. "Mother and father?"

"Mother and sister."

"I see."

Silence again, in which a deep sigh escaped her. With a sudden jerk of her head and a clasping of her hands, she said, "My lord?"

"Yes?"

"I do not take pleasure humbling myself, but as I mentioned before, I am more than familiar with apologies." Rosiness settled over her cheeks. "And I fear, most ashamedly, that I owe you one."

Amusement attempted to produce a grin, but he did not wish to offend when her words were given in such earnest. "I shall be more prone to accept your apology after I am made aware of your wrongs against me."

"I should think you would already know."

"There are so many"—the grin finally unearthed—"that I cannot guess which one you wish to make amends for."

To this, she only sighed again and crossed her arms. "Why did you not tell me where you had placed the Arnold family?"

"I do not recall your asking."

"Would you have left me in error indefinitely? I had a most ill opinion of you." She held out her hand. "And pray, do not say it again."

"Say what?"

"How apathetic you are to the estimation of others. We have been over that quite enough."

He shook his head, half startled, half intrigued by her wit and effrontery. The rest of the ride was taken in silence, but it was silence of ease and pleasure. He did not even mind when her sleeve once brushed his, or when the smell of her hair wafted his way—all things he would have detested before.

Why should she be any different from the others?

CHAPTER 7

*D*aytime cast the room under a different spell entirely. Ella faced the bed which had so frightened her before. Now it stood dusty and still, with the curtains peeled back. Dust motes floated in the air, faint and almost invisible until they passed under the light from the window.

Ella approached the bookshelf. She touched the titles again, as she had done only nights ago, before moving to a small secretary in the corner. A stack of letters drew her attention. Hmm, hmm, only cheerful accounts of balls, it seemed. All were signed affectionately by Dorthea, but there was no mention of Lord Sedgewick.

Sliding open the many drawers, Ella discovered her sister's pendant watch, her peacock quill, and a few other treasured possessions.

Had her sister still kept a diary? Of course she would have.

She always had in younger years. Ella had invaded her sister's room on more than one account, stolen the diary, and read every last page before giving it back. She had even memorized a few quotes from it, and delighted in Lucy's blushing cheeks as Ella recited them aloud.

What a naughty sister she'd been.

Finding very little else at the secretary, Ella searched beneath the bed, on top of the nightstand, and inside of the white wardrobe. Cobwebs weaved across the dresses and the scent of mold was pungent.

Ella closed the wardrobe and retrieved her gloves. Peter would be finished with his nap by now, and with the good weather upon them, she had promised their visit to the seashore.

She paused, however, before she departed Lucy's room. She glanced back at the bed, the straightened pillows, the wrinkleless spread. Had she only imagined the movement and noises? Or had Lord Sedgewick been sleeping in his dead wife's bed?

∽

Ella dipped her first toe into the water and shivered. "Oh my."

"What is it?" Peter took a giant step and caught a wave to his midriff. "It's not even cold—"

"Peter!" Ella groped for his collar and tugged him back. "You are not to get wet, young man. There will be no time to bathe before dinner, and I cannot have you seated at the table smelling of sea salt." She caught herself. Was that her mother's voice coming out in her?

Surely not.

Even so, a laugh escaped at the thought. "Then again," she said, "sea salt does not smell so very bad."

Peter must not have heard her, for a crawling sort of creature had distracted him back to the beach.

Ella watched him play, watched him drop to all fours as he inspected the little crab. With hesitant fingers, he patted the crab's back—but drew back quickly and cackled.

What a pleasant sound, his laugh. So harmless, guileless, and genuine. There was never pretense in his kindness, nor trickery in his sweetness. He lived happily and feared nothing.

And he was good. His heart bore the tenderness of Matilda—and then some. Every once in a while, when she tucked him under his bedclothes, he would close his eyes with a prayer.

She pretended not to listen. Even tried not to. What foolishness the child had been taught—but even so, the words penetrated. They haunted her.

Ella gasped as a wave hit the back of her legs. "Oh dear." She took a step, but something sharp jabbed her bare foot and she yelped. She might have kept her footing, only another wave impacted her. She splashed backward.

"Miss Woodhart!" Peter stood over top of her within a second. "You fell!"

"What an astute observation." She groaned as another wave smacked her back, wetting her hair. "Well, there is nothing to be done about it now." She pulled herself to her feet and was just turning when—

"Oh no." She murmured the words before she could stop them.

Lord Sedgewick stood, his Hessian boots in the sand, his arms crossed over his chest, and stared into her. She could not read his expression, but she was certain a rebuke was on his lips.

Her gaze dropped to her shoeless feet, then back to his face. For all her experience in conjuring excuses, she had not the faintest with which to call on now. She was quite helpless.

"Papa, I found a crab." Peter broke the silence and hurried to his father's side. He relocated the crab, who had taken a hiding place under a pile of sand, and both father and son stooped to examine the animal.

She wished there was a pile of sand large enough for her to hide under. She wrung out her dress the best she could, took great care in sneaking to her shoes without drawing attention, and made at least one part of her appearance presentable—her feet.

Peter laughed at something his father said. Then, lifting the crab with caution, he took the creature toward the water.

No, Peter, please. But her silent plea did not reach the little boy, and just as she had feared the father rose.

He brushed the sand from his breeches and approached her. "How do you find the ocean, Miss Woodhart?"

She would have expected anything, any measure of scolding or condescending. But she had not been prepared for him to laugh.

She moved backward, gaping at him. "My lord—"

"Do not tell me Miss Woodhart is out of sorts." He glanced away, then back to her face. His smile broadened. "I have yet to see such a thing."

"I am not out of sorts at all. I am merely wet." Her brow quirked. "And I suppose you have never fallen?"

"Many times. Are you hurt?"

"Do not be nonsensical." Her chin jutted forward. "As if one could be hurt with a cushion of sand to catch one's fall."

"I am sure it has been done."

She huffed and crossed her arms. "Are you quite finished patronizing me? I should rather bear your wrath than your dashed humor."

He laughed again, a sound that put her faintly in mind of Peter's. Then he outstretched his hand. "I shall walk you back."

"I am not finished."

"Oh?"

"Yes, I am still enjoying the ocean, if you do not mind."

He nodded and dragged his hand along his jawline, as if trying to prevent another grin. Then, with a sigh, "Very well, Miss Woodhart. If you do not object, I shall take Peter back with me. I believe a new suit shall be in order before dinner." He did not wait for her answer, only gathered his son's hand and trekked back up the path toward Wyckhorn Manor.

She did not wish to eat dinner at his table. To be subject to more humiliation in one evening would be more than she had the strength to bear.

Besides, she did rather like the sea. If she had been awed by the view at her window, she was much more so now, as she sat staring at the endless rolling waves. They foamed and lapped and crawled further onto the sand, drawing ever nearer to where she sat in her wet clothes.

She wondered if anything in London could have possibly been so wondrous. She was always apt for a good time. She had entertained many a suitor, danced many a dance, and laughed at any ridiculousness presented by her opulent friends.

But what could be greater than this?

Yet still, she was empty. Her life back at Abbingston had never been enough. Her mother, father, sisters, acquaintances. . .they had never been enough. Even now, with a view transfixing and lovely, she had not enough.

She little knew what she needed, only that she needed something. She wondered if she would ever find such a thing. When she finished this quest, when the truth was brought forth, could she be happy? Would that be enough to end her hungers and satisfy her inner soul?

The vicar said she'd be helped if she prayed, but she didn't believe him. She was repulsed that her father had turned to such weakness, that in the end such a rash conversion should erase the lifetime theory of independence and unbelief. Yet another way in which his death had been in vain.

Ella scooted back as the water drew too close again. The sun dipped lower into the red-streaked sky, until finally it burned into the water and cast the world into twilight.

She would probably escape anyone's notice if she returned now. Dinner would certainly be past, and she would not be required another meeting with the dreaded Lord Sedgcwick today.

She shook her dress free of wet, clumpy sand. How gritty and—

"Lucy?"

Ella froze. Her lips opened, but she could not speak, could not turn.

"Lucy?" The voice was behind her, muffled and low.

Slowly, she turned.

A figure emerged from the thickening darkness. Lord Sedgewick? He stood before the path, rocks on either side of him, with the night shadows hiding his face. "Lucy." Again, but not a question this time.

"I-I'm not." Her heart squeezed. "I'm not Lucy."

Thicker and thicker fell the darkness until she could scarcely make him out at all. But the whispered word carried across the air with a moan, "Lucy."

No.

"Lucy." Closer.

No, please—

"Lucy." A cold hand curled at her wrist.

Ella screamed. She wrenched free and darted away, but the sand prevented speed. She fell, drew herself back to her feet. Couldn't tell if he followed. Couldn't even hear his whispers, only the constant ebb and flow of the sea.

She stumbled into a rock at the base of the cliff. Her legs nearly buckled as she sank behind it, pressing herself against the hard stone. Her breathing was loud, raspy, but she muffled the sound with her hands. *Please go away. Please leave me alone.*

For the first time, she wished she could pray.

☙

Henry jerked awake, his Bible sliding between his legs. He lifted it from the floor and smoothed the pages that had wrinkled.

"I rather think reading would be more profitable in the morning time, my lord." Dunn placed another log into the hearth.

Henry rubbed his eyes with his thumb. "I tend to agree." He stretched his legs, stifled a yawn, and loosened the cravat from his neck. "What were you telling me a moment ago?"

"Only that Mr. Arnold was most appreciative of the new pig you had delivered."

"Good."

"Another tenant has a difficulty with his well, but he was most determined to resolve the issue himself."

"Who is it?"

"Mr. Cluett, sir."

"He is rather advanced in years. Send a servant out to help him in the morning."

"Consider it done, sir."

Henry yawned for the second time. "Anything else?"

A line formed between Dunn's light brows, but he hesitated and turned back to the hearth.

"What is it?"

"Probably little more than a daft man's worries."

Henry approached him. "Tell me."

Dunn finally lifted his eyes. "Miss Woodhart. She has not yet returned and it has been dark for over an hour—"

"Why didn't you tell me?"

"I know how you. . ." His sentence faltered. "I did not think you

80

wished to be bothered."

Henry growled and hurried for the front door. The butler was nowhere in sight when he pulled on his greatcoat and ran into the night. In hindsight, he realized he should have taken the time to light a lamp, but he knew the path so well he had no difficulty reaching the bottom.

"Miss Woodhart!" His shoes kicked against the thick sand. "Miss Woodhart!" The water made crashing murmurs, deafening his voice. He hollered louder. "Miss Woodhart!"

How insane that she had insisted on remaining behind. He should have come after her when she did not attend dinner. Why had he not realized?

"Miss Woodhart!" He stormed along the beach, then turned back around and drew closer to the cliffside. He cupped his hands around his mouth. "Miss Woodhart!"

A slight movement caught his eye, a flash of white against something dark.

He bolted into a run. "Miss Woodhart!"

The white moved again until he recognized the shape of her dress against a rock. She shrunk tighter and turned her face away.

"Miss Woodhart." He bent next to her in the sand, touched her shoulder.

"Please!" A sob choked the word as she pushed him away from her. "Please, leave me alone—"

"Miss Woodhart, I only intend to help." His hands sought her arms, drawing her away from the rock.

Her face finally lifted to his, but fear only twisted her features, as if the sight of him alarmed her.

"There is nothing to fear, I assure you." Tenderness leaked into his voice, something new and unfamiliar to him. "May I carry you?"

"No."

He lifted her anyway, and she did not struggle against him. She was wet and trembling in his arms—and weightless. His heart burned with something unexplored, but he accounted it only for pity.

In silence, he carried her back to the manor, up the two flights of stairs, and into the bedchamber he had instructed Dunn to assign her. He laid her on top of the bed, easing his arm from behind her head.

"I shall send someone to attend to you."

Wet lashes blinked up at him as more tears pooled her eyes. She turned her face away and didn't make a sound.

He departed from her chamber. What had she been doing out there? What had inflicted such fear?

Maybe she was afraid of him. He only knew that something inside of him surged with new emotion, a startling need to protect.

And more than anything, he wanted to ease the fear from her eyes.

"How is she?"

Mrs. Lundie finished unrolling her sleeves down to her wrists. "Weel enough, I suppose, m'lord. A wee bit frightened."

"Yes." His chest rose with a sigh. Frightened of him, no doubt. Had she taken all the village gossip to heart?

"Weel." Mrs. Lundie patted down her apron. "If ye dinnae need me, I will be aff to bed."

"Thank you. Do rest as late as needed in the morning."

A smile upturned her wrinkled lips. "Ye worry about the world and all that's in it, dinnae ye noo?" She turned to leave.

"Mrs. Lundie?"

"Yes?"

"Did Miss Woodhart say anything at all?"

Something passed across her expression, a hesitation that drew her face into a frown. "She asked a wee bit about Lady Sedgewick."

Henry rubbed damp palms down the sides of this thighs. "And what did you tell her?"

"Nothing." The candlelight deepened the lines on Mrs. Lundie's worn face. "I dinnae tell her nothing, m'lord."

Ella curled beneath the bedclothes, her skin still tingling with cold and dread. She had slipped from her bed only once, the moment Mrs. Lundie had left her, and twisted her key to lock the bedchamber door.

Even still, she could not be safe. Lord Sedgewick no doubt had another key. After all, he'd killed Lucy, hadn't he? With all the halls and rooms and stairs, Lucy had not been able to escape him. If he designed to kill Ella now, what could she possibly do to stop him?

Notwithstanding, she couldn't be certain. If only there had been a moon, a sliver of light, she might have seen the man's face. She might have known for sure who it had been.

She was left with the tangled horrors her mind had formed. Sometimes, she knew it had been Lord Sedgewick. His eyes, his tone, his physique outlined in the blackness. Other times, she recalled a sense of relief when he bent next to her. When he had lifted her into his arms, hadn't her terror subsided?

What could it all mean?

She was numbed with her fear, hollowed from her unvoiced and unanswered questions. Sometime through the night, she drifted into sleep, but even then, she was plagued with nightmares.

Strangely enough, it was not Lord Sedgewick who oppressed her in the dreams. Instead, he was the rescuer who carried her back to a haven of warmth.

"If ye're feeling a' right, Miss Woodhart, there's a wee laddie who wants to see ye."

Ella shifted position in her bed, brushing back her unkempt curls. "A wee laddie, ye say?"

Mrs. Lundie chuckled at Ella's attempt at a Scottish lilt, then opened the door. "A' right, ye can come in noo. She's back to her auld self, indeed."

Peter entered as Mrs. Lundie made her departure. He approached her bed quietly at first, eyes wide and waiting. "How come you are sick?"

"I am not sick at all." Ella patted the bed. "You may sit, if you like."

He climbed onto the bed, but instead of sitting next to her, he made a comfortable seat on her lap. His arms wound around her neck. "I cried."

Ella's hand stroked his back. How fascinating that such a little thing should conform so naturally to her as if he belonged, as if Lucy had known she would need him. "What a silly thing to say. Why ever should you cry?"

"Because." A pause. "I was really sad."

"But why, Peter?"

"My mamma died." He sniffled. "And Dolly in the book."

"The book was not real."

"But my mamma was real." His eyes lifted to hers, lashes spiky with tears. "Are you going to die too?"

"I shouldn't think so." At least she hoped not. After all, Lucy had been unprepared to face a killer. Ella wasn't. "In any event, you should not worry about such things—or I shall never read Dr. Syntax again."

"Never again?"

"Never." She tickled his tummy until he rolled off her with hysterics. She tossed a pillow to him, and within the moment, a happy war had begun—a diversion they were both in desperate need of.

For the next several days, Henry made himself as scarce as possible. His only regret was that he could not see more of his son, but he did not wish to frighten Miss Woodhart further. On the eve of last night, he had returned a book to the library, only to find her seated in the chair his wife so often occupied, a book open in her lap. Why had she looked so much like Lucy always had?

Miss Woodhart did not seem to be reading, though, and at his entrance, she paled. With a quiet murmur, she had excused herself and fled.

Now, Henry unfolded the letter on his desk and read his latest correspondence:

Lord Sedgewick,

I shall not waste any time on niceties, for I am too set on gaining your consent to do me the largest of favors. I have no means with which to bribe you—though I daresay, I wish I had—but if you do not comply, I shall be left to the mercy of feminine company for an entire day. Therefore, I call upon your sympathies when I beg you to attend a rather dull picnic my wife and son have arranged. Miss Fitzherbert, Miss Creassey, and another Miss Creassey shall be in attendance, along with the sisters' two young siblings. They are nigh to Peter's age, and I do believe an outing to be healthy for him, if you would permit such a thing.

If you should decide to come, we shall take three carriages. My wife insists we venture to a point she has often painted—though not very well, and do not mention my opinions or I shall be hanged—so do be prepared for a bit of a climb.

Respectfully in wait of your response,
Sir Charles Rutledge

On any other day, Henry would have felt few qualms about casting the letter aside. He had no wish to fulfill social obligations, especially when female company was involved.

But perhaps the outing would serve a noble purpose. Miss Woodhart was doubtless in need of fresh air, air that was not tainted with the endless scent of death.

Besides, he did not wish for her to be afraid of him. Perhaps it was a subtle way to return to her presence without placing her in any imagined danger.

He caught his thoughts. Balled his fists. What was he doing? As if it truly mattered what she thought of him or if she shivered in ungrounded fears. If she was susceptible enough to believe the village talk, why should he care?

He landed his fist on the desk. He would attend the picnic for Peter's sake. Miss Woodhart would come along as it was jolly well her responsibility to look after the boy. And that was that.

Ella's fingers glided down the keys, but she did not press them. Among her other failures, she had never taken the time to learn the pianoforte. Nor any other instrument, for that matter. She wondered if there was anything, beyond her father's title, to accredit her an accomplished lady.

A tap came at the open door.

Ella turned, sighted her intruder, and tucked her lip between her teeth.

"Am I disturbing you, Miss Woodhart?"

She little knew herself. She suspected Lord Sedgewick was angry with her—rightly so, of course—but she could not untangle her own feelings. "No." She scooted from the piano bench.

He strode into the room, dark hair tousled across his forehead in waves. Intense eyes held hers. "I wish to make my apologies for the other night."

"No fault can be laid to your account, I'm sure." Unless he had been the man in the dark.

Lord Sedgewick's hands tightened at his sides. "If you were in any mortal danger, I should like to be made aware—"

"No danger, my lord." Her gaze perched on the harp across the room, an escape from his piercing eyes. "What a lovely instrument."

"You play?"

"Not even a little."

"The pianoforte?"

A remorseful smile formed. "No, I cannot play anything. And even if I could, I have not a voice to accompany it."

He said nothing to this, and the silence stretched long and thin.

She made a step for the door. "You must excuse me, my lord, but Peter is undoubtedly awake from his nap—"

"I must have a word with you."

Her heartbeat thumped. Was it from fear? Or something else? "Yes?"

"I have been invited to an outing tomorrow, and I desire Peter to be in attendance."

"I shall prepare him."

"Yes." Silence again. "Your attendance is required, of course."

"Me?" Her hands dropped to her sides. "Oh, my lord, I really do not think I am—I mean, that I would—"

"The boy will need his governess."

What could she say to that?

"The carriages shall arrive at ten." He made a slight nod and departed the room.

Ella hurried behind him. "I do not wish to go."

He continued to walk away, his footsteps heavy in the wooden hall. "A lady's maid should have the greatest advantage over any other governess. I am certain you have been exposed to society's circles. You shall do fine."

"I am ungraceful and shall only prove to mortify you."

"You are not ungraceful." His steps paused and he faced her. "And the only way I should be mortified is if you were to unleash your untamed tongue."

A burning sensation crawled across her cheeks. Not because his words had been spoken unkindly, or harshly, or with any condemnation at all.

But because they had been spoken almost endearingly.

She whirled away from him and fled back into the music room alone.

☙

Whatever had transpired at the beach had not affected her greatly. She was of the same poise, manner, and forthrightness—unscathed, it seemed, from the trauma of that night.

She had not appeared daunted by him, either.

Henry stifled an inward chuckle at the thought of her excuses. Ungraceful? She was a great many things, but ungraceful and incapable were hardly among them.

No, every move she made was with ease and confidence. Not something taught or learned, but something to which she was born, as if elegance itself took dwelling inside of her. Yet for all her grace and assurance, she had beheld him most oddly only moments ago, as if disconcerted. Clear, blue, glassy eyes had blinked up at him—one second before she flew from his sight. Never known someone so puzzling, so impetuous, so beautiful.

Beautiful?

His stomach twisted with old pains, pains he hadn't the courage to live without.

He would not be a fool again.

⚭

The carriages arrived not a moment later than Lord Sedgewick had warned.

"Come along, Peter." Ella grasped his hand, her fingers squeezing his in panic she dared not express on her face. *This will be insufferably disastrous. I'm convinced of it.*

Lord Sedgewick moved ahead, spoke to Sir Charles Rutledge—whose topper barely fit out the carriage window—then strode back to her and Peter. "You shall ride with the other children and their governess." He glanced at another carriage with a hint of a grin. "Expect a lot of noise, Miss Woodhart."

"Is there any way I might escape this wretched destiny?"

He did not warrant her an answer, merely turned and climbed into Sir Charles Rutledge's carriage.

Ella sighed. The carriage assigned to her was smaller than she expected, and she was placed between Peter and another little chap, whose red hair was topped by a military-style hat.

On the other side, a middle-aged woman sat with tight knuckles clasped in her lap. She was rather pretty, though plainly adorned, and the constant shifting of her eyes led Ella to believe she was of an anxious disposition. With a careful smoothing of her pinafore, she leaned over to the little girl beside her. "Jane, do stop fidgeting."

The little girl had scarcely moved, but at the reprimand, her little back arched straighter.

"What is *his* name?" The hat came off and a pudgy finger pointed across her lap. "I think I am older."

"Josiah." His governess' scold was immediate. "Do sit back and be silent."

Ella had never taken pleasure in the nonsense of children, but neither could she sit by and allow the little tots to be prisoners of silence. She spoke on their behalf, "It is a rather sensible question, don't you agree, miss?"

"You may call me Miss Trowbridge."

"And I am Miss Woodhart."

The woman's eyes darted again. "Go ahead and speak then, Josiah, but do so in quiet tones."

Josiah's grin peered at Peter. "Well?"

"I'm Peter, and I'm five." Peter demonstrated with his fingers.

"I'm six." Great pride was derived in protruding one extra finger. "But Jane is only five."

"It is not kind to boast," came another stern rebuke.

The little boy did no more than mumble an apology before he presented ten other questions to Peter.

Ella let her eyes roam to the window, frustration and unease unwinding inside of her. The carriage ride was intolerable enough— but when the carriage stopped, her true tragedy would unfold.

If she knew even one person in attendance, if they had seen her at a dance, if she had spoken to them. . .

Everything could be ruined.

∽

Miss Trowbridge exited first, tugging Jane down with her. Josiah leaped to the ground next. Then Peter.

Go on. Her heart whirled. *You cannot hide from the inevitable—*

"Miss Woodhart?" With raising brows, Miss Trowbridge glanced back at her. "Pray, aren't you coming?"

"Why, of course." Ella fidgeted with her bonnet, as if that had been her reason for delay, then climbed from the carriage.

The others were busy alighting—Sir Charles Rutledge, Lady Rutledge, then Lord Sedgewick from one carriage. From yet another came two fair-faced girls, followed by the younger Rutledge, who extended his hand to. . .

Dorthea?

Ella's stomach flopped.

With a laugh that floated and a smile most beguiling to the man before her, it took nearly a minute before Dorthea's gaze roamed the others. Her expression shifted, her complexion paled, and the widening of her eyes was nearly unearthly.

Oh, please. Ella's teeth sank into her lip. *Behave well, dear Dorthea, or you shall spoil everything.*

As if the plea had reached her, Dorthea's chin tipped in a quick nod. With a smile so faint no one else could have possibly detected it, Dorthea turned back to young Rutledge and engaged him in a topic.

Picnic preparations began immediately. Blankets were spread, wicker baskets unpacked, and various foods distributed on plates provided by Lady Rutledge.

The children had a space of their own, which Miss Trowbridge was in charge of superintending. They were placed far enough away that their noise could not disturb, which was most unnecessary, due to the governess' incessant discipline.

Ella was bid by Sir Charles to remain with the others, but other than his brief instruction, she received little more acknowledgment from anyone else.

Indignation burned away her appetite. The pigeon pie, on most occasions her favorite, had very little taste. Was this how all inferiors felt? How demeaning to be treated as if one's presence was not noticed. Had she ever treated anyone thus at Abbingston?

Ah, yes. She most certainly had. Not out of meanness, of course, but rather from a lack of thought or consciousness. She resolved to do better in the future.

Dorthea's laughter drew her attention. "Oh no, Hugh. You cannot be serious." Her hand stroked young Rutledge's lapel. "Almack's Club? I do wonder if you are telling the truth. Did you really attend?"

He lowered his tumbler of claret. "Have I ever provided reason for you to doubt me, Miss Fitzherbert?"

"None to speak of." Her lashes batted. "But I am certain there were many ladies of suitable *ton*, and I wonder that you were not hastened into matrimony."

"How could I?" he said. "With one so lovely waiting for me in Devonshire?"

Pink suffused her cheeks, and the playful exchange quieted into sweet glances back and forth.

Sir Charles made a general statement on the excellence of the roast fowl, and Lady Rutledge quickly refuted his praise with remarks on how dry she found the meat.

Ella glanced at Lord Sedgewick, not for the first time.

The fair-faced girls—which had both been addressed as Miss Creassey—sat on either side of him. Their infrequent attempts at conversation were returned with brief mumbles, and finally, they begrudgingly left him in silence. He tore open a fruit turnover without engaging matters with anyone.

"I say, what was it again? Miss Woodham? Woodhox?"

Ella's focus shifted to Sir Charles. She lowered her fork. "Woodhart, sir."

"There we go. I was not so very far off, now was I?" He chuckled and bit into a cucumber. "How do you care for your position at Wyckhorn, then?"

"I am tolerably contented, sir."

"Tolerably." He chuckled again, his joviality seeming a bit keener after three glasses of sherry. "Well, if one can say they are tolerably contented, they have reached a higher summit than most of us." He lifted a toast. "I commend you."

"I as well," said a Miss Creassey. She made a definite scoot away from Lord Sedgewick and twirled her finger around a ribbon. "To live in a manor with those of unsocial attitudes would be most insufferable."

"Agreed," echoed her sister, with a glower at Lord Sedgewick. "Insufferable, indeed."

Ella looked at him, watched his lips flatten without response.

Her measure of forbearance drained. How dare they talk of him so? Not that she bore any good thoughts for him herself, but to hear anyone attempt to humiliate was not something she could bear. She pointed her gaze to both sisters. "About whom do you insinuate, pray?"

Almost in unison, the pair flushed. "Why—I—"

"Oh—er—"

"Surely not Lord Sedgewick?"

The blushes faded into pallor. The sisters exchanged looks. The rest of the party fell into silence.

Lady Rutledge was the first to speak. "Young girl, you are quite out of your place." Sharp, cold voice, accompanied by vicious eyes. "How dare you speak so brashly to those above you?"

Ella's chest caved, but she didn't speak.

"I have never in my life witnessed such insolence. This is truly shocking." Lady Rutledge removed her plate from her lap, flung her napkin to the ground. "You are a very uncouth little devil and should be held accountable for your appalling actions."

Silence.

Ella sought Dorthea's eyes, but the girl turned her face away before any comfort could be derived.

Ella swallowed. Her pulse bumped up and down, up and down.

"Well?" Lady Rutledge again. "What have you to say for yourself?"

She felt the heat of Lord Sedgewick's gaze, but she could not look at him. She had not the courage. Instead, she said only, "If I said what I really wished to say, I fear you would be even more outraged, my lady."

A gasp, but Ella did not wait to hear what would follow. She hurried from the blanket and walked away—her legs not breaking into a run until she was well out of sight.

∽

"You took very little heed to my warnings."

Ella stiffened at the sound of his voice, though she had heard his footsteps behind her. Why had he followed her? Only why shouldn't he? She had humiliated him, marred his reputation in the eyes of all present.

She did not turn. "Scold me harshly if you must. I am certain nothing can inflict more punishment than what has already been said."

"Nothing has been said against you, Miss Woodhart."

She smeared the tears from her cheeks and stared beyond the trees, beyond the field, until the vastness overwhelmed her. "Do not laugh at me now."

"You cannot think I would laugh at your tears." There was something about his voice, the husky quality, the deep tone.

She faced him, faced eyes that were probing and soft.

"Lady Rutledge's good opinion can only be found in superficial nonsense," he said. "Her taste lacks wisdom, and her favor can only be gained by those who are equally mercenary and unhappy." Tenderness etched along his mouth, leaked into his voice. "To gain such favor would have been a dishonor to you, Miss Woodhart. And to meet with her disapproval can only be accounted as an honor."

Moisture pricked her eyes again until the tiny rivers escaped down her cheeks. "I should have held my tongue."

"And I should have used mine." With his gloved thumb, he reached out and eased his finger across her cheek. Her tears were dried quickly, gently, then the touch was gone. "Shall we go?"

"I shall remain here until you are ready to depart." A pause. "Please do not make me face them."

"I am ready to depart now." His gaze never wavered. "And if anyone faces them again, it shall be me."

∽

Insanity had slinked itself around his good sense and choked it out. Touched her? Wiped her tears? What had he been thinking?

The carriage was uncomfortably quiet. She sat on the other side with Peter already asleep against her shoulder.

Shouldn't have followed her away from the others. Should never have caved in a moment of softness. Should never have left the picnic early, confining himself to a carriage where they were forced to be alone.

The wheels dipped in a hole and Peter's head lolled forward.

She readjusted him against her, smoothed the hair from his forehead, and glanced up. "He is most fatigued." A smile widened her lips. "Young Josiah is a more vigorous playmate than myself, I fear."

He nodded, his lips curving in response, but he hadn't the will to speak. He dragged his eyes away from her. *Smiled at me.* Rage returned in waves that were suffocating, drowning. *Smiled at me just like the rest of them.*

Only why had he smiled back?

CHAPTER 8

*T*he diary had to be here. Somewhere, lodged under a piece of furniture, hidden beneath a stack of books. There was no question of *if* there was a diary, only where it was located.

Ella sat in the quiet room, rubbing sticky cobwebs from her fingers. She shoved the last of the books back into the bookshelf. Nonsensical idea that had been. As if Lucy would be daft enough to hide her secret thoughts in the most obvious of places.

But where else could it be?

She went to the bed again, but qualms hindered her from unfolding the coverlets. As if touching them would unveil the fear, make her closer to the man who had hidden here nights ago.

She yanked back the coverlets anyway, eased her fingers across the bed in search of a lump, and turned over the pillows. Nothing.

I shall never discover the dashed thing. With hurried movements, Ella restored the bed to tidiness. Her eyes swept back to the corner, the secretary. Had she overlooked something?

She opened and closed all the drawers for a second time. The last drawer had considerable difficulty closing. She gave it a hard push. *Oh dear, it's broken.* What would Lord Sedgewick say if he knew she had blemished his property?

She slid out the drawer. Good heavens, it appeared as if some inept carpenter had sawed away half the drawer, making it much shorter than the others. But what was preventing it from closing?

She fished her hand inside. More cobwebs, then…something cold?

Her heart spun a whirl. She latched onto the object and tugged it out.

A small wooden box sat in her lap, with gilded claw-feet and ornate paintings across the lid. Must have fallen over when she'd hurried to open the drawer.

Lucy's. She'd never seen it before, but the very touch of it raised her flesh in bumps. She tried the lid. Locked. Within must be the greatest of secrets for Lucy to take such deliberate precautions. . .

A noise drew Ella to her feet. She clutched the box against her chest, listening, eyes pinned to the closed doorway.

But the knob never moved, and when she was certain the noises had faded, she slipped the drawer back into place. With the box under her arm, she stole from the room and hurried back downstairs.

She tried to assure herself no one had seen, no one had been watching her, no one knew she'd taken the box.

But all her senses warred against her, and she was just ridiculous enough to believe they were right.

∽

"Let me do that for you, m'lord."

"No." Henry dragged the saddle off his horse, sparing a glance at the stable boy. "Miss Staverley and I have a rather undeclared agreement, you know."

"M'lord?"

Henry reached for a brush. "She has promised to ride well for me only if I attend to her myself—and with the utmost care." With a slight grin, he pulled a lump of sugar from his coat. "I am bound, therefore, and cannot leave the task of grooming to any other."

The stable boy made a sound in slight resemblance to a chuckle, then moseyed away to another part of the stable.

Henry glided the brush down the horse's back. His thoughts lingered, drifting again and again to a scene he had no reason to recall. She had defended him. The acknowledgment lodged in his throat and pushed down a portion of his hatred.

He had never known anyone in his life to stand up against Lady Rutledge. What had propelled Miss Woodhart to do so on *his* account?

What could she possibly hope to gain?

Surely she was not so conceited as to think she might gain his affections if she impressed him well enough. She was a governess, an inferiority. There could be no reward in securing his good opinion.

But then again, Miss Woodhart had never strived to impress. On the contrary, many times she had been quick to fault him and even quicker to speak her mind—heedless, it seemed, of what *he* might think of *her*.

Then why had she defended his honor at the cost of her own humiliation?

Questions, so many questions. They didn't matter, and he couldn't attain the answers even if they did.

He hung the brush on a peg, led Miss Staverley into her stall, and went for the house. The butler took his greatcoat and hat.

"I do believe Dunn is looking for you, my lord." The butler smoothed the greatcoat as he looped it across his arm. "Shall I take your gloves?"

Henry stripped them off. "What did he want?"

"I do not know, my lord."

"Where is he now?"

"I believe he determined to wait in your study, my lord."

Henry headed straight for his study, but before he even touched the knob, the steward swung open the door.

"My lord." Panted, raspy. "My lord, you are needed upstairs."

His gut tightened. Dunn's footsteps fell in place beside him as they navigated through the hallways, up the stairs, up the stairs, up the stairs. They creaked and groaned, sounds he loathed but couldn't escape. Could never escape.

He paused at the rise of the steps. "Go back, Dunn. I am no longer in need of you."

"But, my lord, today it is most—"

"I said I do not need you!"

Dunn's lips pinched, yet not with anger. His eyes offered comfort, but it was scant relief to Henry's dread.

"Yes, my lord." The steward fled back down the stairs and out of sight.

Henry entered the hall alone. He did not look when he passed his wife's bedroom. He never did, as if ignoring the room would make it go away—just as he did his mother's portrait.

But they never went away. Neither of them. Even dead, they still haunted him, tortured him, plunged him deeper into grief.

Then he came to another doorway. One he couldn't ignore if he wanted to.

CO

Ella did her best to devote attention and enthusiasm to her young charge, but her mind's sole thought was on the box she'd left in her chamber. She glanced out the window, seeking any indication of night's approach.

"Miss Woodhart?"

"Yes?" Ella leaned over to inspect his work.

"Can I be done?" He pushed away the quill. "I want to play. I want to climb my tree, please."

"Please." She mimicked his entreaty with a smile. How very often she had pleaded to be dismissed from studies that only bored her. "How shall you ever write letters if you cannot pen your name, Peter?"

"But my name," he said with a pout, "is very long."

"How should you like to have the name Jehoshaphat?"

His nose scrunched. "I wouldn't like it. Miss Woodhart?"

"Yes?"

"Is Josiah's name bigger?"

Ella helped him count the letters, and he seemed a bit encouraged to learn his name was a smaller feat than his friend's. They continued studies for a little over an hour, at which time they prepared for dinner.

Lord Sedgewick was not in attendance. Peter did not ask of his father's whereabouts, but he seemed markedly quiet and solemn throughout the meal.

The evening stretched long and quiet. When the time came to tuck Peter into bed, Ella did so quickly and bade him to say his prayers to himself.

"How come?"

She drew the bed linens around his small neck. "One cannot always say prayers aloud."

"Do you?"

"Do I what?"

"Say your prayers out loud." He blinked, waiting. "I never heard you before. I hear Papa, though."

A burn crawled up her chest. "Oh?"

"He prays with me."

The thought of Lord Sedgewick's eyes shut in veneration, lips mouthing psalms and praise—why was the image so contradicting to everything she knew of him?

Doubtless, he prayed for the child's sake. He would not otherwise deign to pray himself, would he?

"Miss Woodhart?"

She scooted from his bed. "No more chatter, Peter. You must go to sleep now." After an exchange of goodnights, she departed his chamber and found her own.

Eagerness rooted out the niggling thoughts the child had planted, even as she grabbed the wooden box from where she'd placed it under her bed.

She utilized a hairpin to insert into the lock. She twisted. *Pray? Why should a man of Lord Sedgewick's iniquities care to pray?* Twisted the other way. *Or did the guilt drive him to such nonsense, just as the grief drove my father?*

The lock clicked. A spasm of anticipation unrolled inside of her, and her fingers hesitated for the space of a heartbeat.

Sucking in a breath, she lifted the lid. *Lucy's diary.*

∞

The man's form was hunched, his shoulders caving as if broken under a heavy weight. He faced the window, but it offered no light, no view below. Not this time of night. Only faint, silvery shafts of moonbeam.

Henry stood braced in the center of the room. Sweat formed on his skin, rolled down his temples, but he didn't bother mopping it away. How many hours had it been already?

He didn't know. Too many to count, too many to comprehend. Shouldn't have stayed, but what choice did he have? He would not have a servant deal with what he had wrought himself.

The man at the window touched the pane. Too quickly the silence was gone, the terror returning. "How long must I bear chains?" Both palms pressed against the glass, fingers splayed. "I suffocate in this prison. . .I suffocate."

Fury churned in his stomach. "There are no locks on your door, Ewan."

"No locks." A deep chortle that held no mirth, only scorn. "No locks, yet I can never leave."

"You may leave when you wish."

"Destitution would not serve me well. If you would only but give me a small sum, I could afford the greatest of pleasure." There it was, faint and intangible, but still distinct enough to recognize. As if the years hadn't passed, as if the former person had emerged from somewhere inside of him.

But the lucidity was fleeting. "Where is your wife?"

Silence.

"Where is she?" Fingers scratching the glass. Curling back into balls. "I saw her today. . .touching things. . .moving things and. . ." Silence again.

Henry stared at his back.

"No, I didn't. I didn't see her. . .didn't see her because she's. . .dead." His fists plunged through the glass.

Henry dove, caught his arms. "Ewan—"

"Lucy!" His scream rent the air. Blood on his hands, arms, seeping into his shirtsleeves, but he lunged for the window again.

Henry yanked him back.

"Let me go!" Ewan flailed, then he thrust a fist into Henry's throat and tore away.

Henry doubled over. Air dragged itself into his lungs, every breath painful and stinging. When he lifted his eyes, he saw Ewan propelling his body out the window.

Henry didn't try to stop him. Not this time. Couldn't grab him in time anyway.

But Ewan never jumped. "Lucy." No longer screaming, only moaning, sobbing. "Lucy...I only want to be free...only want to see you..."

Henry drew him away from the window.

As if in fear, Ewan scampered to a corner and hunched, dragging his knees to his chest. His shoulders caved again. Empty, luminous eyes gazed into the darkness. "Lucy?" He rocked back and forth. "Mamma is coming back...she's coming back..."

Henry towered over top of him. Emotions coiled around his heart, and he little understood how so much hate could bequeath such pity.

He turned and walked away.

∞

On any other night, Ella would have been asleep. She wouldn't have heard the stairs creaking, wouldn't have noticed the heavy footfalls passing by her bedchamber door.

She lowered her sister's diary. There could be no mistake where the person had come from—there was only one set of stairs from that direction.

Go to sleep. She blew out the light and curled deeper into bed. Her heart couldn't settle. Did she dare slip from her room?

If she could only catch a glimpse of him. If she could just know who had hidden in Lucy's bed. Could it be the same man who had accosted her at the beach? Or was it truly Henry as she'd imagined?

She lit a candle and hurried into her wrapper. She left her chamber soundlessly, afraid if she hesitated any longer, she wouldn't go at all.

She slipped toward the stairs and caught the last flicker of light as the figure disappeared down another flight.

Oh, Lucy. Emotion reared inside her, brought alive by the words she'd read in the diary. There had been nothing informative in anything she'd read, only poems of nonsense or frivolous accounts of days spent at balls or outings.

But they had drawn Lucy's heart nearer to her own. The way she penned the words, the things she said, the endearing and happy way she said them. . .

Ella blinked hard. Curse the man who had destroyed such a life.

The figure reached the landing and dove into another dark hall.

Pinching away her candle's flame, Ella hid along the shadows of the walls and followed in silence.

A door opened but never closed. Gone was the figure and his light. Had he entered the room?

Ella eased toward the doorway. Only a quick glance, then she'd leave. She leaned her head past the opening—

From behind, a hand caught her mouth and yanked her backward.

A scream rose, but couldn't escape. Her panic had no outlet. *No, no.* But even as she thought the words, the hands were already spinning her around.

Lord Sedgewick. Fear fell apart inside of her, replaced with something she didn't know, didn't understand.

His glare pierced her. "What are you doing?"

Doing? Her lips parted, but nothing emerged.

His bare hand grabbed her elbow. "Come."

She told herself to run, to fight against the strength tugging her into the room she'd sought, but all she could do was obey him.

The door clicked shut. Then, deeper, "What are you doing?"

"N—nothing." She despised the tremor. Straightened her shoulders. "I was not doing anything amiss, your lordship, and I demand to be released from your grasp."

His hand jerked away as if the touch of her suddenly burned him. "You seemed very interested in the contents of this room." Dark brows jutted. "Which I do wonder at, as you have visited it many times since arriving at Wyckhorn."

Ella's eyes swept across the drawing room. There was a fire in the hearth, blazing warmly and glowingly, as if daring to strike against the oppression in its space.

"Is your curiosity satisfied, Miss Woodhart? Or shall I further assist you?"

"Do not demean me." Rage hinted in her voice, but she could not be stopped for anything. "You can hardly condemn others for menial sins when such superior iniquities mar your own conscience. Provided, of course, you have one at all. I do wonder that your child has such wholesome qualities when you, my lord. . ." Her sentence fell apart.

Something seized his expression, some measure of pain that could scarcely be seen in the dark. He turned away from her, strode to the chair, and sank into it with nothing to say in return.

Ella could not move. *He'd been in Lucy's bed.* The thought hardly seemed to matter. *He was the man in the dark, the man who frightened me.* Why did she struggle to believe that?

He was the one who killed your sister. Pain sliced through a heart already in shreds. She should have turned and fled. There was no doubt danger. She needed to leave.

Yet her feet drew her forward until she sat in the chair next to him. For the first time, she could see him clearly in the light from the fire.

He wore no coat, only shirtsleeves that were rumpled and damp as if he'd been sweating. The neck gaped open, revealing the broad collarbone, a small patch of hair. . .his neck. A bruise purpled and swelled where his Adam's apple worked up and down.

He must have known she was staring because he turned to face her. Shadows hung under his eyes and haunted his expression. "Have you more to say, Miss Woodhart?"

No, she could never have said more. Not when her words were so hurtful, not when his voice was so quiet, deep. . .vulnerable.

She had beaten him, and she hadn't even meant to.

Sympathy threatened her judgment. How could she ignore what he'd done? If he bore misery, she should be grateful. If she could whip him with pain, she should rejoice. Wouldn't her father have? Wouldn't Lucy?

Ella Pemberton certainly would have. How many times had she lain in bed, weeping because of a father who was never home anymore, longing for a sister she could never touch again? How many times had she yearned to destroy the man who had done this to them?

Ella Pemberton wasn't sitting beside him now. Miss Woodhart was. "You are injured."

He did not move. The flames cast moving light across his face. "My lord?"

Finally, he looked at her. "Do not pretend to be affected, Miss Woodhart. One who views me so despicably could not possibly empathize with my pain."

My pain. The words echoed back and dove into her. They dug deeper and deeper until they formed a pit inside her soul. "I do not view you despicably."

"Village talk must have pronounced me a most offensive person. I wonder you came at all." His lips twitched in a smile without humor. "Did they not tell you of my wife's ghost? Or perhaps they did. Perhaps that is what you were in search of tonight."

"Did you love her?" The question arose without warning.

His muscles tensed. He faced the fire again. "No." Flat, hollow. "I've never loved a woman in my life."

Ella did not know what to say to him. She knew, just as she'd known before, just as her father had known. He had lied about Lucy's death.

And he had just lied again.

∽

Long after she had gone, Henry remained. He should have prayed. Most nights like this, when he stumbled away from Ewan's room in the night, he did pray. Such was his only solace, his only peace.

But he could not pray now. Too much guilt hung between himself and heaven. Sometimes he thought he broke through. Maybe he did. Certainly God had forgiven him, hadn't He?

Other times there was no breaking through. There was no comfort to be found, no balm thick enough to cover his open wounds.

God, why did she say such things? He had grabbed her, frightened her in a moment of surprise and anger.

And she had lashed back. Maybe she shouldn't be faulted. Everything she said was true. He had accused her of believing the village talk—as if it were all lies, as if he were innocent of the charge.

But he wasn't innocent. He had killed his wife.

Enervation pulled his head into his hands. *God, what do I do?*

No answer.

His heart bled, always bleeding. He was tired of bearing the guilt, tired of hurrying upstairs. He was tired of what awaited him inside. He was tired of accepting the cruelty, flinching under the blows—when all he was trying to do was save Ewan's life.

Sometimes he almost walked away. Sometimes he was tempted to lock the door and never return. But then he remembered why Ewan desired to end his own life.

And Henry knew that was his fault too.

CHAPTER 9

$\mathcal{I}$f Ella knew how to pray—if she had any wish to do so—she would beg for a sudden trip to send Lord Sedgewick away from the manor. Facing him so soon after last night's events was unbearable.

But as it was, when she arose early and entered the breakfast room, there he sat.

The coward inside of her wanted to turn and wait for Peter.

"Miss Woodhart." The greeting was everything she'd imagined, cold, gravelly, and accompanied with an obvious scowl.

She sat across from him. A cravat concealed the bruise she'd witnessed last night. "Lord Sedgewick." She lifted her cup. "I half hoped you would not be present."

"I am sorry to disappoint you."

"Not disappoint, my lord." She lowered the cup with a clang. "I am only uncomfortable—a condition I rendered upon myself."

"Another apology?" Ire slipped into his tone. "Or are they spared for more worthy subjects?"

"I am sorry."

He jerked to his feet. "And I am sorry," he said, "that I cannot accept apologies as readily as you distribute them. A word spoken is a word finished, Miss Woodhart."

"A finished word may be erased."

"But never forgotten." Was that sadness she sensed?

Regret throbbed at her chest. "If I can do anything to make amends, my lord, lay it upon me."

"You speak in haste. Be thankful I shall not hold you to your offer."

"Anything I say is in earnest, Lord Sedgewick." Heat climbed the back of her neck, nestled around her cheeks. "Though it is of the greatest misfortune that my tongue whips so readily, you may never be at a loss as to what I am thinking, nor must you dissect my prattles for truth. Thus, I shall say it again. I shall do anything to make amends, my lord."

For all his display of anger, there was no evidence of any now. His lips parted as if he wished to speak, but he never did. He clamped his mouth shut and quit the room.

∞

"My lord, there is a visitor arrived."

Henry turned from the window. "Who?"

"Sir Charles Rutledge, my lord."

Henry sighed and followed his butler through the house. He parted the sitting room doors and entered. "Sir."

The older gentleman rose, hat in his hands. "Ah, Sedgewick. Forgive my unexpected visit, but I did desire a word with you."

"Certainly." Henry motioned him back into the chair. "Tea?"

"No, no. I am forced to drink enough of the confounded stuff in the presence of Lady Rutledge." At the mention of his wife's name, Sir Charles frowned. "She is, in essence, why I am here."

"Oh?"

"I wish to offer my sympathies for the events of the other day. Everything turned out rather badly and—"

"Regrets should not be offered to me, sir."

Sir Charles appeared at a loss. "Eh?"

"My governess." Henry crossed his arms. "If you are prepared to offer an apology on behalf of your wife, I believe Miss Woodhart should be present. She was, after all, the one offended."

Sir Charles leaned back in his seat and chuckled under a strain. "Well, she was not entirely guileless, was she now?"

"I found no fault in her actions."

Sir Charles shifted. "Oh." Cleared his throat. "Yes, well, do send her in then."

Henry left the room quickly. He had to admit, he admired the man for stepping away from his wife's skirts enough to do something of his own—even if his efforts were ill directed.

Why was he bothering to fetch Miss Woodhart? He snorted at his own folly. Shouldn't last night have sealed his heart in stone?

She had scorned him, rebuked him, shamed him. Try as he might, he couldn't cling to the anger. He wanted to, needed to. If he thought long and hard enough, he could unravel her morning apology and deem it unfit for acceptance. Her actions *were* unacceptable.

Then why had his dreams been invaded by her? Last night, as he lay still in his lonely bed, why had her face swum in and out of the darkness?

Yes, he'd forgiven her. He'd forgiven her before she even asked him—a bafflement he couldn't understand.

Opening the door to Peter's nursery, he found her lying on the floor, hands behind her head.

"Papa!" Peter rushed forward and grabbed his legs. "You come to play with us?"

He caught Miss Woodhart's glance as she scooted to her feet, batting flyaway hair from her face.

"No, Peter." Henry pinched his son's nose with two fingers. "I've come to steal Miss Woodhart away from you for a small time."

"Can I go too?"

"I am afraid not."

By this time, she had approached them, wariness replacing the usual defiance. She didn't speak until they walked beside each other, the nursery behind them. "My imagination plagues me with all sorts of fates, Lord Sedgewick."

"What?"

"Fates," she said again, "which you have chosen in return for my apology."

A wry grin started at his lips. "They are grave, indeed."

"Pray, is there a dungeon?"

His eyes slid to hers, catching the faint smile. He had anticipated strain and tension after the events of last night and this morning, but camaraderie seemed more to describe the mood between them. And somehow...well, somehow he was glad. Even if it did make him a fool.

"No. Something far worse, I am afraid."

"Pray, do not withhold any longer. I am thrown to your mercy."

At last they reached the sitting room, and he swung open the doors before her. He swept his hand inside. "After you, Miss Woodhart."

Her eyebrows lifted, but she entered with her shoulders straight.

"Ah, Miss Woodhart." Sir Charles clapped his hands on his knees. "What a pleasure to see you again."

"Likewise, sir." She bobbed a curtsy, unruffled—it seemed—by his presence. "I trust you are doing well?"

Henry walked to the mantel and remained standing.

"Quite, Miss Woodhart," returned the other. "May I inquire how the young charge is getting along?"

"Splendidly, I assure you. I have never known a more brilliant child."

Henry's heart swelled at the praise. He recalled her words earlier and knew she did not say them in civility, but in truth.

Rutledge came to his feet. He slid a half-frightened, half-defiant look to Henry, then sighed loudly enough to be noted. "Miss Woodhart, do forgive my mention of an unpleasant event, but you see, I've been feeling rather remorseful about the whole ordeal and thought perhaps if I spoke to you myself. . .well, spoke on behalf of Lady Rutledge, I might. . ." The sentence dissolved in another sigh.

Miss Woodhart's eyes brimmed with kindness, gentleness, and—amusement? She took a few steps closer with the authority and poise of a queen. "You are a dear man, Sir Charles. And though I cannot attest to bearing good thoughts of your wife, I could never hold ill feelings toward you."

"Well spoken." Rutledge practically glimmered. He took both of her hands and kissed them. "You are a dear girl yourself, Miss Woodhart. And if confidentiality may be kept for a moment, I might dare to say that I hardly bear good thoughts of my wife, either. She is a rather galling creature, is she not?"

Neither Henry nor Miss Woodhart answered, but he noticed her lips pull together as if avoiding the catastrophe of a laugh.

Sir Charles took his departure moments later, and the spacious sitting room became much smaller than it had been before. Almost stifling.

He had imagined she would make her exit, but she only sighed and wiped her brow. "How very strenuous."

"I would not have guessed you to be under strain, Miss Woodhart."

She smiled. "I can only be grateful Lady Rutledge did not make a visit."

"I imagine you would have handled yourself no less, even if she had."

The smile faltered as if his words had given her pause, and startled her in their compliment. Had he ever seen her blush? He could not recall, but she did so now, and it crept along her cheeks and livened her face.

"Well." Her movements were abrupt as she smoothed her dress and started across the room. He barely heard the words, "I must attend to Peter," before the door shut in her wake.

Tonight, dearest diary, I danced a trifle too many dances and am now suffering from the sorest of feet.

Ella fell into the words, so alive they nearly raised her sister back from the dead. So rich with detail, so lively with the mention of music and color. How easy it was, while reading these pages, to feel as if one were there at the ball too.

Then the pace changed, the music seemed to silence. Even the ballroom disappeared as her imagination followed her sister's tiny script...

I only slightly noticed his careful glances, his slow approach toward myself and my company. But when he asked me to dance? No. That was nothing I had anticipated. Not from Lord Sedgewick himself.

Ella shut the diary. Perhaps she should have read more, but she didn't want to. *Lord Sedgewick himself.* As if he were above mere mortals, as if he were in a realm all of his own, as if he were superior to any other man.

And maybe he was.

Ella tossed the diary away from her. She slid into her bed and blew out the candle, but the darkness only formed shadows that haunted her. *What is the matter with me?*

Nothing. There was nothing wrong. Today he said something kind to her—which he had done before, only never in a tone so soft—and now she was ready to excuse his offenses?

No, she most certainly wasn't. She was not like her sister. She would not be wooed and charmed by arrogance and pride, no matter how handsome the gentleman, how rich his purse. Lord Sedgewick was a killer.

Father had said so.

Ella could see through Lord Sedgewick's lies. And what had he been doing upstairs so near Lucy's bedchamber? Where had he acquired the bruise?

If Ella were braver, she would have gone upstairs to find out. Courage such as that, however, would take a great deal more coaxing.

How much time did she have left? How soon before her guise as the governess was discovered?

∽

"M'lord." Collin halted in the doorway. "You should have summoned me."

Henry brushed at his sleeve. "Why the deuce for? One would think I was not capable."

"It is not that, m'lord, only. . ." The valet rushed forward. "Here. Allow me to assist with that cravat. You are doing a most reckless job of it."

"You are as fastidious as a woman, you know that?"

"So you often say, m'lord."

111

Henry harrumphed and allowed Collin ample time to tidy his cravat and hook on his watch fob. "Now go and find a dashed book to occupy your mind," said Henry. "Heaven knows you need something."

Collin coughed. "Yes, m'lord."

Henry went below stairs and decided against breakfast. The stables drew him instead, and he threw open their doors with gusto.

"Oh my." The hushed words dipped into the silence like the drop of coins on cobblestone.

Henry stepped forward. "Miss Woodhart."

She backed away from a horse, the familiar uplift of her chin returning. "You are rather rambunctious, my lord. You have succeeded in startling the livestock."

"And not the woman?"

"Pardon?"

"Did I startle the woman?"

She resumed her petting of the horse. "I was only momentarily cautious, as I was not quite certain where the interruption was coming from."

He took a few strides toward her. "Fond of riding?"

"Yes."

"Are you prepared to do so now?"

Her gaze flew to his. "Are you?"

"You are either unfortunately senseless, Miss Woodhart, or amusingly clever."

"If you cannot tell which," she said, "then I can do nothing to help you."

A laugh escaped before he could control it. The way she reacted— the blush again, the softening of her eyes, the smile that came and went.

"Well." She stroked the horse's nose once more. "I had better return indoors."

Part of him wished to stop her, to ask her to ride with him as he had subtly suggested.

But he didn't have the time. She gathered her dress in a gloved fist and departed as if she didn't care to ride with him at all.

And it only made him want her more.

⟡

Want her? He could not possibly want her. She was well beneath him in every sense. She was also impertinent, outlandish and. . .beautiful. She was beautiful.

No. He kicked his heels into Miss Staverley until the wind stung his face. He would not think such thoughts. They were impermissible. Reckless. Dangerous.

She was just like the others. She would cut him and take no pity when he suffered. She would abandon him, and if she couldn't hurt him in that way, she would betray him.

She would. She would. Over and over again, until he half believed the words. He almost built the hatred high again. Almost.

But would she?

He told himself she was just like the others, only she wasn't. There was no pretense in her spirit and no artificial sweetness in her temperament. If she smiled, it was because she was happy. If she laughed, it was because she was amused. If she spoke, it was because she had something of worth to say. Or some cutting remark aimed at him.

She was real. She was enchanting. She was the first woman he had ever known who seemed worthy of his admiration. He half wished he could give it to her. What would it be like to—?

No. He cut his thoughts short. There were too many years of hating, too many hard lessons he'd learned too well. The risk was too great.

Besides, a heart as battered as his didn't know how to love.

Even if it wanted to.

⟡

Ella lingered at the stairs. Daylight offered her more liberty to investigate, and Peter was down to the seashore with his father.

There could be no better time. For Father's sake, for Lucy's sake, she must not be spineless.

She took the first step, gripping the banister—

"Where ye be going?"

Ella turned as if unstartled. "Up the stairs, Mrs. Lundie." She managed a smile. "If I am permitted."

"Weel, there's nothing up there for ye."

"Then why shouldn't I go?"

Mrs. Lundie scowled. "Ye be wanting me to tell Lord Sedgewick? Dinnae ye think I won't."

"Why should that displease him? I know him to have visited the upstairs just the other night, so he cannot be so very set against it."

"Set against it, he is." Mrs. Lundie threw a disgusted look toward the stairs. "An' if ye've any brains, ye'll be set against it too."

"I have been before." The confession slipped before Ella could prevent the mistake. "Up these stairs, I mean."

Eyes widened in shock. "Ye should'nae—"

"It is quite the curiosity that Lord Sedgewick should place his wife's chamber in such a remote section."

Defense sharpened her tone. "'Twas nae always there."

"What?"

"She used to be in the west wing, she did. With her husband, until. . ."

"Until what?"

"Till the sickness. After she was gone, they carried all her things up these auld stairs."

"And he returns for what purpose?"

"Ye been seeing things, ye hae." Mrs. Lundie reached out and grasped Ella's arm. "No one's been up there in a long, long time."

"But—"

"There's a wee child who'll be returning to us soon. We had better go and wait for him." With a hard tug and frown, Mrs. Lundie hurried Ella away.

CHAPTER 10

*O*h no. Henry sank his forehead into his palm. Dashed old coot, what was he doing?

"Something the matter, my lord?"

"Yes." Henry threw the letter at his steward. "Major Sir Frederick Tilbury is the matter. The man ought to be shot."

"Shot, my lord?" Dunn asked as he retrieved the letter from the floor. He scanned the contents, then looked up. "The punishment seems to exceed the crime, I fear."

Henry stepped around the desk and spun a globe with his finger. "Of all the dandies on the earth, why should he choose me?"

"It is not as if he has requested you to *marry* Miss Tilbury, my lord."

"His intentions, no doubt." Henry overturned the globe. "He is out of his league. He should bloody-well leave the matchmaking to his finicky wife."

"My lord—"

"Write a letter and tell him I cannot receive visitors."

"But my lord—"

"But nothing. I do not have time to squander on a woman so high in the instep, nor do I wish to prepare the manor to meet expectation." He went to the door. "Besides, Wyckhorn is no place anyone should wish to visit."

Dunn did not answer.

"Tell her father I send regrets." Henry slammed the door behind him. The last thing he wanted was another woman in this house, someone who would remind him of everything, of all the hurt he couldn't untangle from and the distrust that felt like habit.

Unlike Miss Woodhart.

She was the only woman he knew who didn't make him hate.

Certainly there was *something* lining these shelves that a child would find pleasure in. Ella strolled along the bookshelves, paused to inspect the thinner volumes, then frowned. No, Peter would not find pleasure in senseless poems.

The door whined behind her. Snapped shut.

Ella glanced over her shoulder—and froze. "Oh."

A man stood across from her, sweat glistening along his brows. Dark, sunken eyes blinked. Once, twice, a third hurried time.

Unease fingered around her nerves, but she kept her expression fixed. "How do you do, sir?" A rigid curtsy. "I do not believe we've met."

His skin was bloodless as if daylight seldom warmed his cheeks. His lips twitched. No sound left. Why would he not speak to her?

"Yes, well. . ." She glanced around the room, then back to him. "I was just prepared to depart, so you are at liberty to enjoy the silence." She started forward, but he didn't move.

He stayed planted before the door, his shoulders bunching, his fists forming.

Ella's calm evaporated. "Sir, please excuse me—"

"I hate the silence." He flattened against the closed door. "I hate the silence. . .my prison."

Prison?

His fingers turned the lock. "You hate it too. . .I know you do." Away from the door. Stepping closer. "Do you not hate it, Lucy?"

Lucy. Her blood rushed faster, colder. She shuffled backward until she hit a bookshelf and could go no farther.

"Lucy." Whispered again, but he didn't follow her. "I have wanted to die a thousand times. . .but the prison will not let me free." A broken sound left his lips. He turned, fumbled with the lock before he fled.

Ella sank to her knees in a heap. *I do not understand.* Her hands pressed into her eyes. *I only know I am afraid.*

⌒

"Peter?"

"Yes, Papa?"

"Did Miss Woodhart not wish to eat dinner with us?"

"She is not hungry."

"She said so?"

"No." Peter inserted a chunk of potato into his mouth, then spoke around it, "But I don't eat when I'm not hungry."

Henry leaned back in his chair. "How were your lessons?"

"We didn't do any."

"Why not?"

His shoulders lifted in a shrug.

Henry scooted his plate away and rose. "Excuse me, Son."

"Papa?"

"Yes?"

"Must I finish my mackerel?"

Henry spared a glance at his plate. He grinned. "This once you may go without." He didn't wait for his son's delight, only hurried out into the hallway and located Mrs. Lundie. "Have you seen Miss Woodhart?"

"No, m'lord." The old woman straightened. "Is something wrong?"

"When did you last see her?"

"Only earlier when she mentioned the garden."

He went outside, following the path to the garden. Lucy had come here often, but he had never gone with her. Sometimes he had watched her from the upstairs windows. How lonely she must have been. Why had he never appeased that loneliness? Yet even if he had, would it have made any difference?

He drew to a stop when he caught sight of Miss Woodhart's shadowy figure. She plucked at a bush, drew a flower closer to her face, then sank to the stone bench.

He didn't wish to disturb her. He shouldn't be out here at all. What was he doing?

He turned to leave.

"Who is there?"

The panic made him still. Was that fear in her tone?

"Pray, who is there?"

He stepped away from the shadows, close enough that the moonlight would subside her fears. Unless her fears were him.

She should not have ventured out here. Not alone in the dark. When she left the library, she should have stayed in her chamber. Something had been wrong in her room, something she couldn't place, as if certain objects had been moved and touched—

Lord Sedgewick's figure loomed in the moonlight. "I did not wish to induce alarm, Miss Woodhart."

Her tension uncoiled. She didn't know why. She wished she were afraid of him. At least then she could understand herself.

"You did not arrive for dinner."

"Am I required?"

"No."

She brushed the flower off her lap. She should have said something by way of an excuse. No doubt he was troubled as to why she had not fulfilled Peter's lessons.

What could she say? That a man had accosted her in the library, whose eyes seemed strangely mad? Or that the contents of her room had been disturbed, even though nothing was missing?

He must have heard her sigh because he stepped closer. He hovered over her bench with serious eyes that probed her.

She looked away. "I did not realize you granted visits to the garden."

"It is not my pleasure."

The silence made her skin raise in bumps. Why did he stand so close? She caught his scent again, something wild and citrus, and she wondered why it was starting to seem familiar. "Forgive me, but I must go—"

He caught her elbow as she stood. No gloves. "I did not realize you visited the garden either, Miss Woodhart."

"I have very little appreciation for assortments that will only die tomorrow. I should rather devote time and attention to things that never change."

"Flowers are not meant to last forever." His fingers loosened. "Yet for every one that dies, God supplies a new one."

"You have no need to feign pretense with me, my lord. I am not a little child who must be taught religious anthems."

"I did not think you were."

"Pardon?"

"A child." He released her but didn't step backward. "Do you not believe in God, Miss Woodhart?"

"I have yet to see proof of Him."

"I see." Disappointment tightened his lips, took away a portion of the tenderness in his voice—but he didn't try to persuade her. "You need not return indoors on my account. I shall leave you to your thoughts."

He strode away with shoulders straight and proud. Then he paused. Foliage had cast him back into the shadows, but his eyes still reflected moonlight. "If you have not seen proof of Him, Miss Woodhart, I daresay you have never really looked." He was gone before she could speak.

Not that she could have spoken, anyway. She lowered herself back onto the bench, hugging her arms, unprepared for the emotions wringing her heart. *He was so very disappointed.* Tears burned. *In me.*

Nothing he said should have mattered. It should not have punctured her so. The vicar had written her more sermons than she cared to remember, all of which she had thrust aside and forgotten without injury. *But Lord Sedgewick. . .*

She closed her eyes. *What if he is right?*

∽

The bed offered her no comfort. The only solace she took was at the window, where she had drawn up a chair and huddled close, thankful for the moonbeams to brighten the view. *"If you have not seen proof of*

Him, Miss Woodhart, I daresay you have never really looked. . .never really looked. . ."

She hardly knew what proof was or where it might be found. Had Father found such a thing? Is that why he had made the deathbed conversion the vicar had later told her of?

She didn't know. Her mind raced with questions to which she had no answers—questions she had always chosen to leave buried.

When the clouds obscured the moon, she retreated back to her bed. She lit a candle and opened her sister's diary. She read with little interest until inconsequential ramblings turned into a subject of more gravity. The proposal.

A strange throb irritated her chest. Her sister depicted everything so clearly—Lord Henry Sedgewick arriving in his curricle, requesting Lucy to take a stroll, then taking her hand as he offered her a marriage:

He is so impeccably handsome that I can find fault in him only in the murmurs of others. His lips seldom—if ever—smile, yet even that has stirred my interest. I do not know exactly why I want to marry him, only that to reject such a man would be an injury to my character I could never dismiss.

Ella pressed the diary to her chest. She should have scoffed at her sister's foolishness, at her inability to resist a man such as Lord Sedgewick.

But Ella couldn't scoff. Not when she was beginning to understand her sister's heart.

A trip to Northston had kept Henry away from Wyckhorn for the length of the day. The returning ride was longer than usual, and the sunset across the horizon, although striking, only intensified his restlessness.

Why should he be so bloody eager to reach home? No reason, of course—beyond that of his son.

He heaved a sigh. The tension built, vanished, then built again.

Never should have followed her into the garden, where the night air carried her whispers, and the moonlight illuminated her eyes.

Her eyes. His soul smoldered. *How empty and sad they were.* The disbelief and faithlessness had cast her face under hesitancy, vulnerability, as if there were a part of her he'd never witnessed.

He wanted to uncover that part. He wanted to, longed to, needed to.

Only he couldn't. He was a fool to even partake of such aspirations.

Wyckhorn Manor appeared before him, haunted in the evening's deepening dusk. He stabled his horse. By the time he reached the house, the interior was dark and quiet.

Where was his butler? No matter. He didn't need a servant for something as menial as removing one's hat.

A flicker of light drew his eye.

Henry pulled off his coat before it could be done for him. "You needn't assist me. . ." His words fell as the figure drew closer.

Miss Woodhart halted only when she was close enough that he could have reached out and touched her. Which he wouldn't.

"I believe the butler was feeling rather poorly." Her smile was limp. "I overheard Dunn suggest he retire early."

"Wise choice."

The candle seemed to tremble in her grasp, but she said no more.

He hung his coat. "Peter behaved well for you today?"

"Quite. He always does."

"Good." A lengthy pause. "Good," he said again, for lack of any other sensible way to break the silence.

Still, she stared at him. Then, in a whisper of thread, "You must know you have plagued me, and to such a degree that I can no longer sleep."

"Plagued you?"

"How easily you cast shame and guilt upon another's shoulders when I should think—" Her chin puckered.

"You should think what, Miss Woodhart?" His legs stiffened, waiting for her answer, but it never came.

Tears glistened instead. "I cannot believe in God when such terrible events have befallen me."

"I did not believe in God until they did." Blood soaking his shirt, the hallways echoing with his footfalls, his child's wailing scream as he threw open the chamber door. . .

"Your wife." She must have known by his expression. He couldn't read hers.

"Yes," he said.

"Yet by your own admission you did not love her—"

"Do not accuse me, Miss Woodhart." Fury burrowed within him but left just as quickly. Hurt filled its place. "You should not accuse so fervidly about things you know nothing of."

A small sound left her lips, whether a gasp or a moan he could not tell. Her features twisted, one second before she turned and left.

Henry slumped back against the door. He wanted to follow her, to tell her the truth of himself and of God.

But the truth of himself would only appall her.

And the truth of God she'd have to find on her own.

Ella wished she had the strength not to cry. There was no reason for tears, no reason to question elements that had never fit into her life.

Father. Her pillow absorbed the sorrow. *Father, why did you let the grief turn you into a believer?* He had been weak, but she wouldn't be. She did not need a hand she could not see, could not touch, could not comprehend.

Where had God been when her sister was murdered? Where had He been when her father lay on his deathbed, a weak and broken old man who'd never see justice, never know the truth?

Footsteps.

Ella constrained a sob, fear overpowering the tears. *Someone is out there.* The man who had followed her to the beach, cornered her in the library. . .

The sound stopped outside her door. A small, soft thud, as if an object had been laid to the ground. Then the footsteps walked away.

Her breath came in short gasps. What should she do? Remain in bed, of course. The door was locked. No one could harm her if she stayed inside.

But for all her warnings, she could not stop herself from slipping to the door and hurrying it open. She snatched something black from the ground, locked the door behind her, and scuttled back to her coverlets.

A book. She turned the leather over in her hands and read the imprint. *A Bible.* She'd never read one of her own accord and only half listened when someone else read it to her. Like the vicar.

A note slipped from the pages: *Perhaps this shall offer you proof, Miss Woodhart.*

CHAPTER 11

*T*he days passed until they stumbled into a week. Henry's break-fast meal was eaten without her company, followed by his noon meal and his afternoons. Dinner was the only time Miss Woodhart allowed herself into his presence, but most of her conversation was bestowed upon his son.

The Bible. He ached at the thought of how she must despise him. Perhaps she was right. Perhaps he had overstepped himself and meddled with topics that were none of his affair.

But even if he had known she would treat him so coldly, he would have delivered the book. What she thought of him mattered little. If there was any chance she could see, any chance she could know the truth about the Savior who died for her...

It would be worth it. Henry retired to his room early and fell into an empty bed. *It would be worth it if she could meet God.*

No. Ella's eyes darted across the pages of her sister's diary. *No, no, no.* This couldn't be true. Lucy wouldn't have, couldn't possibly have. There was some mistake.

She was good. The weak thought penetrated her panic. *Mother and Father doted on her.* Not because of her beauty or her intellects, but because of her wondrous good nature.

She wouldn't have done this thing.

Yet the more Ella read, the more her defenses melted into doubts. *Ewan.* Who was he? Someone in the house, someone who had groped for Lucy's lonely heart and taken advantage.

Ella had read dutifully for the last week until she understood the marriage her sister had endured. Lord Sedgewick had been aloof, his intimacy scarce, his smiles nonexistent. He had given her rule of the house, but not rule of his heart.

How devastated Lucy must have been. She had committed her life to a man of a stony soul.

But the devastation should never have driven Lucy to such a sin, such a dark affair. If only it had been once, her sister's wrongdoing might have been pardonable.

But every page of the diary deepened the truth.

Lady Sedgewick had been unfaithful to her husband.

Ella took extra care in preparation for dinner that night. Guilt turned her stomach in knots she couldn't undo, didn't deserve to undo. Why was she always hasty?

In hindsight, her injudicious actions were always a shame to her. Her life was filled with apologies and regret!

Lord Sedgewick had given her the Bible. She kept the note beneath her pillow, where she drew it out every night and read it over again. She didn't know why, only that a part of her was warmed that a man such as him would care.

For his kindness she had returned coldness. She had been so overwhelmed with her sister's accounts of a forlorn marriage that she had avoided him to every degree possible. Even Peter had questioned her.

"Why do you not like Papa anymore?"

She had pinched his cheek with a laugh that was forced. "Your papa is only busy, Peter, and I have no wish for either of us to disturb him."

Pulling one last curl around her face, Ella descended the stairs in a muslin gown and coquelicot-colored spencer jacket.

Peter sat alone when she entered, with Mrs. Lundie tucking a napkin down his suit. "Well, dinnae ye look nice tonight, Miss Woodhart."

Ella took her seat. She glanced at the lord's empty chair with a twinge of discomfort. "This all smells quite delightful." Which was hardly true. She could not smell the dishes at all.

"That it does, indeed," said Mrs. Lundie. "'Tis a shame Lord Sedgewick could nae be here."

"Where is he?"

"Out to warn the tenants, he is. Ne'er seen a man so occupied with the likes of others."

Then why did he neglect to love his wife? She stopped herself. She would not come to Lucy's defense any longer—not now. Was it possible Lord Sedgewick had not been in error?

"'Tis a tairible storm a-coming, ye ken."

"Storm?"

"Och, 'tis why Lord Sedgewick rode out to be warning them. Hae ye nae seen the clouds gathering?"

Lord Sedgewick returned before dark and, upon entering the drawing room, asked if Peter was already in bed.

"Yes." Ella rose. "But only just so."

He nodded and left. She could not blame him, of course. Did she imagine he would always be amiable and ready to forgive her misconducts?

She settled back into the chair. Perhaps he would return to the drawing room. She would know no rest until she made amends.

But the minutes stretched into hours until the windows became dark and sprinkled with rain. She gazed into the hearth with a yawn. *If he comes back, I can make my apology.* Her eyes drifted shut. *If only he comes back.*

Henry's arm flung free of the hand gripping him. He drew back with a fist. *Ewan—*

"M'lord." Collin's voice invaded the silent bedchamber. "M'lord, it is me."

Henry's head fell back into his pillow. "What the devil are you doing?"

"I am sorry, m'lord, but I thought you would want to know."

"Know what?"

"There's a ship, m'lord. Caught in the storm, we think—and heading for the rocks."

Henry ripped out of his bedclothes. "Fetch my clothes." He dressed in shirtsleeves and breeches, tugged on his boots, then ran downstairs.

Dunn stood waiting for him. "My lord, if the vessel hits the rocks, there may not be survivors. There is very little we can do."

"How close is the ship?"

"We cannot tell, my lord."

Henry threw open the door. "Get every able-bodied man down at the beach, and bring the rowboats—"

"Your coat, my lord!"

Henry was already out in the rain, with the door slamming shut behind him.

Ella awoke disoriented. "Dunn."

The steward and a maid stood side by side, their frames blocking the warmth of the hearth from reaching her. "Get blankets and plenty of bandages prepared. We do not know how many, if any, we shall need to attend to." The maid hurried away.

Blankets? Bandages?

She moved from her chair. "Dunn?" she said again.

Weariness etched around his eyes. "Miss Woodhart, I am quite puzzled as to what you are doing down here."

"I must have fallen asleep." She smoothed unkempt curls away from her face. "What is happening?"

"Quite a lot, Miss Woodhart." Dunn's gaze roamed to the window. "May God be with us all tonight." He left the drawing room, and Ella followed behind until they reached the front door.

Servants were already rushing out, the roar of the rain drowning out their pounding footfalls.

Dunn was the last to leave. He jerked on a coat, then mumbled as he grabbed another, "Fool man has not the sense to think of himself."

She caught him before he swung the door shut. "Lord Sedgewick?"

"He is likely to get himself killed. You better stay inside, Miss Woodhart, and say your prayers."

The moment he was gone, she hurried upstairs, made certain Mrs. Lundie was with Peter in case the storm should awaken him, then found her cloak and flung herself into the downpour. Water soaked the velvet as she stumbled down the path to the beach, her mind frenzied by bellows of men and claps of lightning.

When she reached the beach, movement in the water caught her attention. *A ship.* The vessel plunged and rose in each angry wave, close enough she could hear screams from the deck.

"They're sinking!" Someone's shout cut through the chaos, then the ship splintered and disappeared.

No, please.

"M'lord!" Another scream. Lord Sedgewick was dragging a rowboat toward the water.

Her heart slammed. *No.*

∞

The waves smacked against his body, threatening his balance.

Collin's hand snatched his arm. "M'lord, if you go out there—"

"Enough!" Henry jerked out of his hold and climbed into the vessel. Water lapped over the edges, one second before his valet lunged in after him.

Collin groped for an oar. "I am coming too, m'lord."

"Collin, no—"

A wave struck the boat, careening them to the left as the ocean gulped them farther from the shore. Darkness everywhere. Couldn't even see in front of him.

God, please. The oar was ripped from Henry's hands. Gone. His chest seized. "Collin, keep hold on your—"

Lightning split, illuminating the waters, casting light upon bobbing figures in the ocean.

"There, m'lord! I see them!"

Another wave. It crashed over top the rowboat and plummeted them to the bottom of the craft. *God, help.* Salt stung his eyes. Couldn't breathe. Wiped the water away, but the darkness prevented sight. *Collin.*

The boat overturned. Cold water devoured him. *No.* Sinking, flailing. He pushed himself upward until his head broke the surface.

Something latched onto his shirt. A hand?

He grasped the fingers, drawing the person to him.

"Help."

I've got you. Another wave dove them under, but the arms encircled his neck and clung to him. He stroked until they surfaced. *God, please.* He rasped in air. *Please get us to shore.*

Because he didn't want to die. Didn't want to leave his son.

Please.

The boat had disappeared, swallowed by the angry sea. They were not going to return. Ella and the others stood helplessly on the shore, buffeted by the winds and rain.

Lord Sedgewick and Collin didn't stand a chance.

Dunn stood beside her, blinking against the rain. Were those tears on his face?

"They are gone." Ella's hands cupped her arms. "Are they not?"

"God, be with him," said Dunn. Not in answer to anything she had said, but in prayer. "God, be with them all, I beg of Thee."

She wished she could pray. She wished she'd read the Bible Lord Sedgewick had brought to her room. She wished she'd been given a chance to spill through another apology.

"A body," said Dunn. From down the shore, three men tackled the waves and drew a form from the water.

Her insides shriveled, but she hadn't time to cry.

Another body washed to shore.

Lightning flashed. One of the men she didn't recognize, the other familiar and young. A sob escaped. "His valet?"

Dunn watched the other servants turn him on his back and pound his chest, but the steward must have known there was no use.

After a few moments, the servants rose. They cast long, silent glances among them before one finally said, "Collin is dead."

CHAPTER 12

*T*hey carried the bodies away. How long before the rest of them washed to shore? How many would there be? Or maybe they wouldn't wash ashore at all. Maybe they had crashed into the rocks, broken and mangled, then dragged back into the sea.

Ella shivered and accepted the hat Dunn offered her.

"To keep off the rain, Miss Woodhart," he shouted over the wind. "Though I wish you would return indoors."

She couldn't. Not where Peter slept upstairs, oblivious to what had happened. Who would tell him?

Your father is dead, Peter. The words whispered across her consciousness, but she forced them away. *No, he is not dead—*

"Dunn." A servant trotted toward them, panting. "Dunn, sir, a few of the men have spotted movement."

"Of what kind?"

"Could just be the mast of the ship, sir, not yet sunk."

Ella scanned the waves. So much turmoil, so much churning, so much crashing white. . .

Lightning again. "There." Dunn stepped forward. "That thing. . . that is no mast."

"Sir?"

"The rowboat." Dunn broke into a run. "Let's get the men out there. There's people hanging onto the edge!"

⟜

"Hold on." The arms clamped tighter around his neck. "Hold on." Over and over again, until the water filled his mouth and he couldn't speak.

He knew she was a woman. Sometimes her dress tangled around

131

his legs. Other times, he heard the choking of her sobs.

For a long time, he heard nothing. He wondered if she was dead. Another life on his conscience. Didn't matter, though. Not now.

The upturned rowboat dipped again. His fingers lost hold of the edge. *No.* Under again. Couldn't keep on like this. Couldn't carry the weight. Couldn't rise to the top.

God, I beg. Air again, but the relief lasted only a moment before the boat thrust itself into his face. He took the blow without sound and groped for the edge. *Stay afloat.* All he had to do.

"Help. . ." Her voice again.

Then another voice carried over the waters. "Lord Sedgewick!"

Help.

"Lord Sedgewick!"

Here. . .help. . .

"Lord Sedgewick!" Drifting farther away, until he couldn't hear anymore. Or maybe he had gone under again. Yes, he was underwater. That was why he couldn't hear, why his name was no longer called, why he could no longer breathe.

Rough hands hauled him up. *God?* He was lifted, dragged, then laid back against hard wood.

". . .still breathing. . ."

Beating his back until his mouth sputtered with water.

". . .saving the girl. . .not responding. . ."

She's already dead. Another death on my hands. His last coherent thoughts before another sea of blackness devoured his mind.

The water foamed across Ella's half boots.

Servants tugged the rope until the boat slid onto the sand. Two men piled out of the craft, but Dunn remained. "Take the woman."

Woman?

A limp form was lifted from the vessel. Her white arm dangled in the air, but no one spoke if she was dead or not. She was carried away.

Ella crept to the boat.

Servants crowded around, hoisted another body, then laid him across the sand.

He is dead. She went forward when she had no right, and she knelt next to him where it wasn't her place. "Is he. . ."

"No." Dunn knelt too. "No, he is alive."

Lord Sedgewick's eyes were shut, his lashes dark and wet. A gash cut across his forehead, and a tiny trickle of blood slid down an ashen face.

Ella brushed his cheek. Just a faint whisper of a touch, but his eyes opened.

He stared at her—confused, no doubt, why one who had treated him so coldly would caress him now.

She hardly understood herself.

"We had better get him inside." Dunn rose and pulled her back.

The servants lifted Lord Sedgewick into their arms and hurried him away.

∞

Henry sat close enough to the hearth that his skin reddened and tingled.

Across the room, Mrs. Lundie's slow, rhythmic snores filled the silence. She'd watched over him, no doubt, until sleep claimed her. She would be angry if she knew he had slipped out of bed.

Impulse had driven him into the rowboat. He shouldn't have. He should have known they didn't stand a chance, that he was risking more than his own life.

Collin had paid the price.

God, forgive me. His eyes burned. *I wish to heaven there was no more guilt.* He was weary of failing. He was weary of awakening sick and lying down with a thousand regrets.

He should be accustomed to it by now. Even as a child, he had been less than what he should have been. He didn't know how. He never knew for sure—only that there must have been something because she left anyway.

"Mother, please." His father had held him back with one arm, Ewan

with the other. *"Please do not go."*

But nothing they had said stopped her. They had never known why.

Henry jumped when a knock sounded at the door. Too soft to be Dunn's, too high on the door to be Peter's. "Who is it?"

"Miss Woodhart."

He did not wish to see her. He half wondered if he had imagined her down at the beach. Certainly he had imagined her hand on his cheek, hadn't he?

"May I come in?"

He was dressed in no more than his nightclothes and banyan. What did she think she was doing here?

"Lord Sedgewick?"

"The door is unlocked." His hands fisted. "Come in."

She entered fully dressed, though the curls around her face were limp. She glanced to Mrs. Lundie opposite the room. "Dunn said I might come for a moment." Color rose to her cheeks. "We thought you would be asleep."

"What did you wish to derive from a sleeping man?"

"Nothing but a measure of comfort."

"Comfort?"

"Yes." Her eyes fell. "I wished to see for myself if you were well."

If he possessed any strength at all, he would have ordered her away. He would have rid the room of another threat, another person who might deepen his wounds.

But as it was, when she sat down next to him, he did nothing to stop her. Undoubtedly, she must have known the impropriety of such a situation. Where was her sense?

Her eyes lifted to his with warmth and empathy as no other woman's ever had. "You must have known the danger," she said.

He hadn't stopped to think.

"Your life might have been taken so easily."

But it wasn't. Another, more innocent than he, had been taken instead.

"My lord." Now there were tears. How beautifully they glistened. "The fate of your valet cannot be blamed on your courage."

"My courage, Miss Woodhart, or my recklessness?"

"You are too severe on yourself."

"With reason." Collin's life was not the only blood on his hands.

Silence dropped a curtain between them, but it lasted only for the space of a heartbeat.

"You were at the beach," he whispered.

The rose color touched her cheeks again. She nodded.

"Why?"

Her gaze melted into his, as probing and deep as anything he had ever known. She removed herself from the chair and left without saying anything.

His heart sank. How foolish to wish she would have told him she cared.

Ella had remained downstairs helping attend to a young sailor who had washed ashore. He died in the early hours of the morning, however, and his body had been carried away.

Dunn shared a small breakfast with her in the kitchen. "I am most grateful, Miss Woodhart, for your diligence in all of this." He set down his teacup. "You have a good heart."

A good heart. Ella had never endeavored to do anything good. On the contrary, she was most usually troublesome and ridiculous. Never once had anyone spoken such words to her.

"Is something the matter?"

"No, no." Ella smiled. "I was eager to be of service. I am only sorry the poor fellow died."

"I was not only speaking of him." Dunn returned the smile. "Your endurance of the storm and rain was most commendable. You must care for his lordship a great deal."

She did not answer. How preposterous to think she could care for a man who had destroyed her sister's life, as well as her father's. Yet

Lucy had not been innocent. What could that possibly mean?

"I would ask one more small favor of you, Miss Woodhart." Dunn removed his napkin. "If you are not too fatigued."

"What would you have me do?"

"The woman who was rescued last night. I thought perhaps you could relieve the maid I sent to watch her. Mrs. Lundie will be with Peter until you are ready."

"Certainly." Ella departed the kitchen and made her way to the bedchamber. She eased open the door as quietly as possible, dismissed the maid, then took her place in the chair.

Exhaustion nudged at her, but she chose to study the woman rather than sleep.

Pale and of lovely features, the stranger's face was surrounded by auburn ringlets. Her lips were bow-shaped, her cheeks smooth, and her lashes of the darkest shade.

How beautiful. A green thread of envy tightened about Ella. *No wonder Lord Sedgewick went to such strains to save her—*

"I quite abhor being stared at." The woman rolled her head to face her. "Pray, who are you?"

Ella blinked. Twice. "Uh, Miss Woodhart."

"Charming." She scratched the end of her nose with her finger. "You may call me Miss Tilbury. Now will you kindly adjust this pillow? My head is in a most vicious state of pounding."

"I would imagine." Ella held the woman's head long enough to modify the pillow. "Is that better?"

"Quite, thank you. Are you the same maid who tended to me before?"

"No, I am not a ma—"

"Good, because I detested that creature. She had very cold fingers, and after nearly drowning in that formidable sea, I should not be forced to endure frigid hands. One would have thought she could have warmed them before prodding at me so."

"No doubt, she did not think of it."

Miss Tilbury frowned. "Well, I daresay she should have." She directed emerald eyes to the door. "Has Sedgewick been to see me?"

"You are acquainted with his lordship?"

"Acquainted?" A droll smile curved her lips. "Why, I would venture to say we are much closer than that. I would not have traveled all the way from Essex to visit a stranger, now would I?"

A stab of hurt. "Then he knew you were coming."

"Why, you are an enigma! You cannot suggest I would arrive without first sending a letter?"

Ella rose. "Excuse me, Miss Tilbury, but I have other duties—"

"Wait." She leaned forward. "Deliver a message to Sedgewick for me."

"He is not well himself."

"He cannot be so injured that he would not wish to see me."

Ella's fingers dug into her palms. "Very well. I shall tell him."

"And girl?"

Fire seared up the back of her neck and leaked into her answer, "Yes?"

"Do fetch me smelling salts. I am afraid I do not feel well at all." With that said, Miss Tilbury collapsed back into her pillow, and Ella made a quick escape.

Prolonging the inevitable was a most craven attribute. She should have entered with her ward and at least spoken to Lord Sedgewick.

She certainly shouldn't have lingered in the doorway, unseen by the man as he bestowed hugs and kisses upon his child.

"What happened to your head, Papa?" Peter curled beside his father in the huge bed. "Did you fall off Miss Staverley?"

His chuckle was warm, easy, a sound very contrast to what she knew of him. "What an honor that would have been," he said, "but I am afraid I was beaten by something far less noble."

"What, Papa?"

"A rowboat, but you mustn't tell a soul. I cannot have the coxcombs of England thinking I can be knocked about by a mere slip of wood, now can I?"

Peter grinned. "You can't be knocked by anything, Papa."

Another laugh, just as his eyes lifted to the doorway. His expression changed. "Miss Woodhart."

She despised the way her own heart betrayed her—how it throbbed faster and squeezed, even knowing it shouldn't.

"Did you wish to speak with me?"

"No." She took one step backward, then remembered Miss Tilbury's demand. She eased back into the doorway. "There is a request for your presence, my lord. Miss Tilbury greatly desires to see you."

She watched for any sign of eagerness, but his features remained unaffected.

"Come along, Peter." Ella motioned to her ward. "Allow your father his rest, for we must begin your lessons." She ignored the child's sigh and the father's disconcerting eyes.

Long after she had left his bedchamber, however, Lord Sedgewick's laugh remained in her mind. Had Lucy cherished that laugh?

Or had her sister even noticed it?

The diary. Ella did not wish to read anymore. Every page she conquered was more difficult, leaving her with more wounds than before. *Ewan, Ewan.* Who was this stranger who had bewitched her sister's judgment?

"Lucy." Her skin crawled. The strange man. . .the one who had frightened Ella so many times. *Of course. How could I not have realized?* The resemblance was so clear. The same hair, same eyes, same build as Henry.

She turned to the next page and read on—words of secret nights, of love that was wild and forbidden, of passion nearly too great to conceal.

Then she read of the will.

The stipulation.

My beloved Ewan is ever entreating me to run away with him, to marry him—but Henry has told me of their father's will.

Deceased Sedgewick, God be with his soul, must have known his youngest's vices, his sins of gambling, thus the stipulation that Ewan inherits nothing Henry does not bestow on him. As for Henry, he has no choice. For the rest of his life, he is to provide for his brother.

Ella stared at the pages with ripples of disgust. Henry's brother? The man at the beach, the library, behind the bed-curtains. The one who had wooed Lucy from her husband. . .how could this be? What kind of man would steal his brother's wife?

And Lucy. Had she not cared for Henry at all? The threat of poverty must have been the sole tie keeping her in this house. How long did she imagine she could go on like that?

Slipping away in the night, writing of another love in her journal, deceiving the husband who knew nothing of her scandalous heart.

How much kinder if she had run away with the man called Ewan.

How much more merciful if she had told Lord Sedgewick the truth.

Though Henry's strength was returning swiftly, he half wished he were still weak in bed. At least then he would not be forced to make such an insufferable visit. *One I would not make at all were she not the major's daughter.*

He entered behind the maid. Selina Tilbury was seated, dressed, and decorated. Almost as if she'd prepared for him. Which she undoubtedly had. "Miss Tilbury."

She held out her hand. "Lord Sedgewick."

Out of courtesy, he brushed his lips against her bare knuckles. He dropped her hand just as quickly. "I am thankful you are safe, Miss Tilbury. Your father will doubtless suffer at the thought of what could have occurred."

"But did not occur," she purred, "thanks to you."

"I wish I could have done more."

"Indeed. When I ponder any time at all on the dresses and turbans that now litter the ocean floor, I quite despair."

"I was referring to lives, Miss Tilbury."

"Oh." Her dimples deepened with a frown. "Of course."

He waited a moment, then two—long enough that he might excuse himself without causing offense. "Well, Miss Tilbury, I had better leave you to your rest—"

"How considerate of you to worry over me." She rose, offered her hand a second time. "I hope, now that I am here, we shall see quite a lot of each other. Truly, your brief visit to Essex was not half long enough."

"Months is hardly brief, Miss Tilbury."

"To one so ardent as myself, I am afraid, it is very brief indeed."

Emotion unwound inside him, hatred he knew all too well. "Excuse me—"

"Wait." She took one step closer. Alarmingly close. "I cannot think so lowly of you as to assume you do not know why I am here. I regard you as a most insightful man, Lord Sedgewick, thus my reason for being so candid."

He refused to meet her eyes. "Proceed, Miss Tilbury."

"My father has great expectations for his only daughter, and it seems his search for a proper match has long since ended." A smile. "For me, as well."

"Oh? Then I must offer felicitations. Who is the dandy?"

She gaped. "My lord?"

"You did say, Miss Tilbury, that your search had met an end?"

"Why—yes." Bewilderment silenced anything further she might have said. She sank into her chair and mumbled something about a maid who had never returned with her smelling salts.

CHAPTER 13

*H*enry turned from the window. "Dunn?"

"Yes, my lord?"

"Who is moving along the beach?"

Dunn approached behind him. "I believe Miss Woodhart mentioned something about viewing the wreckage. I am certain she will make her way back before dark, my lord."

"I am not so certain." Henry started from the room. "She did not possess such foresight last time."

His steward followed. "You are going after her, my lord?"

"Yes."

"I could just as easily send a servant. I fear you have not regained all of your strength, and to make such a walk could prove to be strenuous."

Henry hesitated. Why shouldn't he send a servant? If Selina Tilbury were down there, he doubtless would.

But she's not Selina Tilbury, and she's not Lucy, and she's not my mother. He grabbed his hat on the way out. "No, Dunn, I shall go after her myself."

☙

Ella's foot nudged something in the sand, a fragment of wood. *Can this be proof?* She lifted it, hesitated, then hurled it into the water. Supposedly the water a Creator had breathed into existence. *Oh God.* How senseless to pray to Someone she didn't even believe in.

If you have not seen proof of Him, I daresay you have never really looked. His words again. If only she could forget them. They lingered in her dreams, accompanied by the haunting image of Peter whispering his prayers.

Ella kicked at the sand. She shouldn't have come. Once, the beach had been beautiful. There had been something special about the view, the sand, the water.

But the storm had tainted the beauty, and the scent of death still choked the air. *How could God let that happen?*

A movement diverted her attention. She squinted. *Lord Sedgewick?*

He approached along the beach, the evening sun playing in the dark waves of his hair. He stopped close enough that she breathed in his scent. "Taking a stroll, Miss Woodhart?"

Warmth pulsated her heart. She hardly knew why. He was the cause of her torment, her plagued dreams, her new questions. Why had he done this to her? Couldn't he more easily have left her alone?

"You do not appear well."

"Nor you." She raised her eyes to him. "Is there not anyone who can confine you to bed?"

"Not when other duties need attending."

"Such as calling upon your most recent guest?"

"Yes, I am afraid that is a duty, indeed." Did she imagine the disgust in his tone?

"And is chasing the governess out of doors also among your duties, my lord?"

"No." Softness crept into his gaze. "No, such a task as that could only be accounted as a pleasure."

Pleasure? Her warmth dissipated into unhappiness. He should not say such things, not to her. He should not try to make her care for him. He should not try to persuade her of his faith. He should not be here now, alone with his son's governess.

"Miss Woodhart—"

"I found something." She stepped away and reached for a small comb she had found in the sand earlier. She thrust it at him. "Miss Tilbury's, no doubt."

He grasped the item, but his fingers slid across hers.

"It is quite a lovely piece. I used to wear one most similar in my hair, but it was of a different color and—"

"Miss Woodhart." Stepping closer, he dropped the comb. "Whatever is troubling you?"

"Nothing."

"Perhaps you should not have returned so soon. The storm was most horrific and with the wreckage still here, there is little doubt why you should be disturbed—"

"It is not the storm, Lord Sedgewick." She drew in air. "It is you."

Dark brows lowered, but he didn't glower, only stared. "The Bible offended you."

"Not offended, my lord."

"You read passages?"

"Only some." Tears edged up her throat. "Only enough to plague me further than your words already have."

"I fear I can offer you no comfort."

"Then offer me proof."

He scanned the sea, the cliffside, then returned to her gaze. "You are standing upon it, Miss Woodhart."

"I can believe that God created the world," she whispered, "but how can I believe He is the author of such dreadful circumstances?"

"I cannot convince you, Miss Woodhart, nor can I make you believe." The evening shadows deepened around them. "I can only testify of Him. I am afraid the rest is something you must discover yourself."

Henry sat at the head of the breakfast table and cut a morsel of roasted fowl in half. The meaty scent intensified. His favorite course—and the major's daughter was ruining it for him. Did she never stop chattering?

"And the sugar sculptures were magnificent and most delicious," said Miss Tilbury. "They replicated the Regent's most impressive garden, if you can even imagine such a thing."

"No. I cannot."

"Of course, I inquired as to who had created such masterpieces.

Her Grace introduced me to the confectioner himself. A quite charming Frenchman by the name of Benoit Lachapelle. He even expounded on his impressive carving tools and molds."

Miss Woodhart, who had remained silent throughout the course of the meal, glanced up with a wry smile. "Charming, I'm sure."

Miss Tilbury must not have caught the sardonic tone because she rambled on with great detail of her most recent painting. "Which has won the admiration of nearly everyone to which I've presented it." She straightened her citrine pendant. "Even Lord Worthington remarked on how exquisitely I captured the contrast between the setting sun and the evening twilight."

Henry lowered his fork at her brief pause. "I occupy no doubts but that your painting is remarkable, Miss Tilbury. I am certain you shall have ample chance to paint a new masterpiece to present to the earl."

"Painting requires a good deal of time," she said. "Time I should rather spend on matters of greater importance."

"Of course. You may do whatever you wish." Henry leaned forward in his chair. "You must excuse my absence, however, for business takes me away today."

Miss Woodhart's face snapped up at the words.

Even Peter paused and frowned.

"Business? What sort of business could call you away when you have a visitor?" Miss Tilbury reached across the table and pressed her hand atop his before he was prepared to withdraw.

He slipped from her touch. "Nothing of great importance, but something I must see to nonetheless." He stood. "My deep regrets, Miss Tilbury."

"Regrets cannot balm my disappointment." A demure smile formed. "But rest assured, I shall not return home until you are first back at Wyckhorn."

Henry paused at his son's chair and laid his hand upon the little boy's shoulder. "Do finish your breakfast, Peter, and try to be diligent in Miss Woodhart's lessons."

"Will you be gone a long time?"

"No, Son." Henry rubbed his soft hair. "I shall be home within the week." His son smiled and offered a goodbye, and Henry was forced to pass the chair that stirred great mayhem within his chest. "Goodbye, Miss Woodhart."

Her neck craned to look up at him. "Do take great care in your travels," she murmured.

"And do try to make haste." This came from Miss Tilbury, who exited a sigh soft enough to be within the bounds of polite behavior, yet loud enough to be noticed. "I shall be quite bored and dejected without you here to entertain me, my lord."

Henry made a slight bow in response and hurriedly quit the room. At least for a few days, he would be without Miss Tilbury and her incessant prattles.

He would be without Miss Woodhart too. Away from her accusations, her untamed tongue, her negligence in keeping with society's rules. Why did those things mean nothing to him?

Indeed, he would almost miss them in his few days away.

He would almost miss her.

∽

"I am leaving."

"You cannot be blamed. I would leave too were I not in a prison."

Henry took another step into the room. Dust motes cascaded from the ceiling. "I shall not be gone long, but I felt you should know."

"Why?" Ewan rose from the bed. He came to his feet in wrinkled clothes that hung on his frame. "So I shall prevent the murder of myself until you return?"

"God forgive you for such words."

"No, Brother." Ewan stumbled forward. "God forgive you for killing her."

"I would have died that day to prevent such a thing."

"But you didn't."

Guilt thronged him. He turned to leave—

"Henry!" Ewan leaped forward and grasped his arm.

"Yes?"

"Why do you not let me die?"

"If you really wanted to, you would have found a way to do so by now. Nothing I can do would have stopped you."

"Yes." Panting, shaking again. "Yes, yes, I can if I want to. I can escape the prison and be with her. . .and there's nothing you can do to stop us, not this time. . ."

"Let me go, Ewan."

"But I cannot be with her yet." The clutch on his arm finally loosened. "Not until I have watched you suffer for what you've done. . .for what you've done to both of us."

Henry bolted from the room. He went for the stables and swung his saddle across Miss Staverley's back. *As if I haven't suffered.* From deep inside surged the pain, each stab accompanied with an image, a sound, something that drew him back to that night.

The bed was large. He shouldn't have noticed she was gone, and it shouldn't have mattered. It wasn't as if he loved her. He had married out of social obligation. Lucy Pemberton was a sensible escape from the desperate mammas who plotted and connived to see their daughters well espoused.

And she had given him an heir. Perhaps that, more than anything, had softened the coldness of his heart. He had almost believed he cared for her. In some small, insignificant way, he had felt as if they were finally becoming one.

If only I had stayed in bed. Henry leaned his forehead against the saddle. *Why didn't I stay in bed?*

He'd been foolish enough to think something had happened to her. He awoke Dunn first and sent him out of doors to check the grounds. Then he went to his brother's chamber with the inane hope that Ewan would help him search for his missing wife.

"My lord?"

Miss Woodhart. He turned. "I am just leaving."

"I will not detain you."

"Is something wrong?"

She drew closer in her pretty blue dress, with a blooming color of roses on her cheeks. How lovely she was. If he could spend the rest of his life only looking upon her, he would be satisfied. He could not think of touching her, though. Not with his bloody hands.

"Dunn told me why you are departing." A faint smile. "I find it most commendable."

"There is nothing commendable about it."

"A letter would have sufficed."

"I met Collin in Wiltshire nearly seven years ago. He was fourteen when he left his parents to serve as my valet."

"You must have been very close."

"He was equally close to his parents. I cannot bear to deliver such news in a mere slip of paper. It would be a disgrace to them all." He reached for Miss Staverley's reins and pulled the animal toward the stable door. Fresh air swarmed his hot face. He mounted without looking at the woman in the doorway.

"I only wished to thank you for the Bible, my lord—and to make a small plea."

"Ask what you will."

"If there should be any room in your prayers, I thought you might say one for me." A pause in which her eyes filled again. "That I might have the strength to believe."

His breath caught. "You need not make such a request, Miss Woodhart, for you have had my prayers all along."

Ella brushed her hand down the velvety cheek, then removed the bangs from his eyes. "You are very tired tonight, aren't you?"

Peter shook his head, but his eyes drooped nonetheless. "When is Papa coming home?"

"Most any day now."

"I miss him."

"I know."

"I wish someone would say prayers with me."

Ella's fingers stilled. "You say them quite nicely by yourself."

"Can't you say them with me? Just one time?"

"Peter, I—"

"Pray that Papa will come home soon? And pray I will be a good boy. Papa always prays that, and I try really hard."

"And you do very well." She dropped a kiss on his forehead. "I have never known a better little boy."

A grin split his face, but a yawn was quick to replace it. "Please, Miss Woodhart?"

She couldn't do such a thing. Not when the prayer would be forced from lies, and the praise ushered from a heart of unbelief.

Even so, she folded her hands. Hesitated. "God, return Lord Sedgewick home safely and quickly, for Peter misses him greatly." She paused long enough to peek.

Peter's eyes remained shut.

"And help Peter to be a good little boy." *And help me. . .*

"Amen." Peter nudged her. "Now you say amen."

Her chest burned. "Amen." *Only it isn't amen, because it wasn't a prayer at all.*

Something was wrong. Ella could tell by the way the pen marks were unsteady, the way Lucy's words were scratched more deeply and with less effort. Should have known. Disaster. Terrible secret. What in the world was Lucy talking of?

Then the words struck with force: *Henry shall never know the child is not his—and neither shall his brother.*

Ella clapped her hand over her mouth. She slipped from the bed, approached the window, and pressed the diary against her chest. *Peter is Ewan's son?*

Compassion writhed within her soul, a soul more empty than she'd ever realized. How could this be? Did Lord Sedgewick know?

Had Lucy told him before she. . .before she was killed?

Didn't make sense. Nothing did. There was so much hidden and so much she didn't know and so much pain right here in her hands.

She slung the diary away from her and covered her face. Tears climbed her throat. What would it do to Peter if he ever found out the truth?

What would it do to Lord Sedgewick?

CHAPTER 14

*Y*ou have done what?"

"Not I, my lord." Dunn's lips pinched tighter. "Miss Tilbury."

Henry yanked off his topper and threw it to the side. "Dash it, fellow, I only left for six days. Can you not keep Wyckhorn safe from such a caper-witted woman in that short time?"

"I am sorry, my lord, it is just that she—"

"I care very little what she said. There will be no ball." Henry stopped short.

Miss Tilbury swept from the drawing-room doorway, a book in one hand, a quizzing glass in the other. "Oh, my lord. You are returned."

"You had no right."

Her lips parted. "My lord?"

"You had no right to plan such an occasion without first consulting me."

"That is just it, my lord. The ball was to be a surprise." Her gaze slid to Dunn. "You told him?"

"Miss Tilbury, I—"

"You did well in doing so, Dunn. Now go and see what can be done about reversing the invitations."

"Just a minute." Miss Tilbury's knuckles whitened around the book. "My lord, may I first speak with you before any action is taken?"

"Action *will* be taken."

"Very well, but will you deny me a few short moments? That cannot be so very much to entreat, now can it?"

Henry sent a glare toward his steward, clenched his fists, then followed Miss Tilbury into the drawing room.

She deposited her book and quizzing glass on a stand. Then she sighed, facing him, pulling her lips into an exaggerated frown. "I daresay, there is more of my father in you than I care to note. Are all men so intractable?"

"That depends on your selection of men, I would think. Some are more than willing to become docile and manipulated creatures, ruled by a feminine goddess." He jabbed a thumb into his chest. "I am not one of them."

"I might have taken offense to your speech, my lord, if you had not so delicately called me a goddess." Her eyes glimmered. "Is that how you think of me?"

"I hardly think of you at all unless forced."

Her mouth dropped, but she composed herself quickly. "Your temperament is most ill today. Was your journey very taxing—?"

"Let us stay to the matter at hand. How am I to retract this disaster you have brought upon Wyckhorn?"

"A ball is hardly a disaster."

"To me, it is."

"Why? Are you not fond of dancing?"

"It is bad enough that society's expectations force me to attend events where I am talked of and speculated by all the gossips. Why should I want them here, whispering about me in my own house?"

"It cannot be all that bad." She cocked her head. "Besides, Dunn must have forgotten to inform you."

"Inform me of what?"

"The ball is being held tomorrow." A smile curled her lips. "Which is much too soon to be put to a stop."

⌘

Oh no. What a tragedy that Ella should chance upon him like this— alone in the confines of a tiny hallway. She drew to a stop. At least he had yet to see her. How disheveled she must appear after chasing Peter in and out of the garden. If she could only slip into a room without being seen. . .

"Miss Woodhart." His voice carried. Strong, deep.

She shivered. How could she wish for an escape, when at the same time she longed for his nearness? His eyes were unbearable to her. Unbearable because of what she knew, what his wife had done.

"You have returned," she said as he strode closer. "I did not expect you."

"You didn't?"

"Not here." A pause. "In the hallway."

"Oh." A smile lightened his face, scaring away the shadows. "Have you been out of doors?"

"Yes."

"In the tree?"

"Only for a small time, but I confess I am afraid of heights, so we reverted to a game of running instead."

"What sport." He reached out, touched her hair.

My lord. . .

"Here." His fingers returned with a small twig. "It seems you have brought a bit of the tree down with you."

"Yes." Breathy. "It seems I have."

"If you'll excuse me, Miss Woodhart." With another small smile, he bowed and continued on his way.

Ella hurried toward her own chamber. What was wrong with her? Tripping heart, dampening palms. . .

She had not come here to care for him. Quite the opposite. He had harmed her sister—or at least that's what Father told her. But who was to say Father was right? He hadn't known the true story any more than Ella had.

If Lucy had been killed, Lord Sedgewick was not to blame. He couldn't be. He was different from anyone she'd ever known, kind in ways she'd never imagined. What sort of man worked alongside his own tenants when a servant could have done as much? What sort of man prayed on his knees with his son every night? What sort of man cared if Miss Woodhart, a mere governess, believed in God?

He was worthy of something she'd never even considered giving him before. Her respect.

∽

Ella bit the inside of her cheek for the third time. Meals were becoming quite insufferable. Why could the woman not hold her relentless tongue? And if she could not be prevailed upon to do that small task, why could she not broach subjects that were not of herself?

Why Lord Sedgewick would have her here at all is beyond me. Ella stabbed an egg ball with her fork. *Beyond her wealth, beauty, accomplishments, and...*

Ella dropped her fork back to her plate. *Well, beyond that she is quite uninteresting.*

"...At which point I had already promised away all of my dances," Miss Tilbury continued. "But he was a man from university, so I could not very well turn him down, now could I?"

Lord Sedgewick made a slight nod of his head.

"Oxford, I believe. Is that where you attended, my lord?"

"Cambridge."

"Oh, that is right. I always forget such things." She chuckled with a flip of her wrist. "But anyway, I was in such a predicament about the dance—"

"Miss Tilbury." Ella glanced at the woman's untouched plate. "You have hardly eaten. Does the goose not appeal to you?"

The woman's smile hardened. "Yes, well." Her chin lifted as her voice became huskier. "As you see, I have not yet finished my soup."

"Then perhaps you should. It is quite excellent, you know, but may fail to be so if eaten cold."

"Well, I never—"

"On the matter of dancing." Lord Sedgewick cleared his throat. "I fear I am quite out of practice."

"Oh, my lord, you must allow me to refresh your memory," said Miss Tilbury. "I had the most excellent dancing master in Essex, and I am—"

"But we shall need music."

"Oh, yes, of a certain." Her eyes narrowed to Ella. "I don't suppose you play?"

"No, not at all."

"Dance?"

Ella's heart beamed. "Yes." *Quite well, actually.*

"Then I suppose you shall have to do for now." Miss Tilbury lifted her chin with resolve. "I shall observe from the pianoforte and assist you best I can, my lord."

A faint sparkle appeared in Lord Sedgewick's eyes. "Very well."

The music room had been silent for so long. Sometimes, when his wife assumed no one was listening, he had heard the sounds coming from within. She had played just like his mother. Just like Miss Tilbury.

"Ah, there you are at last." Miss Tilbury's fingers stilled on the keys. "What shall I play? I can produce most any melody, my lord."

"Play what you wish." His gaze slid across the room. "Unless Miss Woodhart has a preference."

"No." She turned from the window, her finger releasing the drapery. "I do not."

"Very well. Let us begin with this." And thus, Miss Tilbury flew into a melody that filled the room.

A pounding started at Henry's temples, moved to his chest, and settled at his heart. "Miss Woodhart, may I have this dance?"

"There is very little need to be formal." She accepted his hand, but she wore no gloves.

Thank heaven he wore his. He could not fathom a touch so intimate. These slender fingers against his own. "I did not imagine a lady's maid would know how to dance."

She guided him into the first few steps. "I did not imagine a lord would not."

As if to deny her words, his memory urged him into the next move of the dance. They moved with ease, gliding back and forth, falling in step with the music.

Her mouth widened with a smile. "Your memory is not so impaired, my lord."

"I suppose it compares to riding a horse. One never quite forgets."

"Am I to think this was a scheme?"

"To gain what, Miss Woodhart?"

"A dance, perhaps, with Miss Tilbury?"

"No." He swept them farther from the pianoforte. "But if I had foreseen this, perhaps I would have been guilty of such plotting."

Her expression faltered. Confusion lowered her brow, flattened her lips, took away the sweet gleam in her eyes.

He wanted to scold himself. He half wanted the guilt to return, one more time, and scare away the feelings he knew he should forbid. Why couldn't he be afraid? Where was the hatred?

"You forget yourself, my lord."

His stomach clenched, but he didn't answer.

"I am only a governess."

I know.

"And your dancing skills are not lacking." She stepped out of his arms so quickly his mind reeled. "Excuse me." She rushed from the room as if he'd wronged her.

Perhaps he had. What right did he have to taunt her heart? What right did he have to taunt his own? Especially when such a match could never be.

The music stopped. "My lord?" From the pianoforte, Miss Tilbury stared at him, brows raised, cheeks flushing. "My lord, I. . ." Her lips half twitched as if she wished to say more. Instead, she managed a smile. "Come stand next to me and I shall play another tune. It seems your dancing lesson is finished."

∞

Ella slammed her door behind her. Her empty room swallowed her alive. She could still hear the music drifting in the distance and wondered if Lord Sedgewick stood at Miss Perfect's side, listening to the angelic notes.

As if it mattered. To him, Ella was nothing more than a governess. To her, he was nothing more than the killer of her sister.

But he looked at her differently. In a new way. With eyes that were soft and raw and tender, almost as if he—

No, she could not think such a thing. Not ever. How could this happen? How could he feel this way? How could she?

If only she felt for him as she'd always felt for the vicar. Annoyance. Disgust. Indifference.

But no, it wasn't the same. Henry's presence stirred her. His voice undid her. And all her doubt of him was morphing into strange, warm reverence she couldn't escape.

This was never supposed to happen.

And it couldn't go on.

Ella came to her knees beside the bed. She reached under for her sister's diary. Maybe reading Lucy's words, her own thoughts of him, would help make sense of all this confusion. . .

Her hand met empty space. She stretched her fingers. Felt nothing.

Oh no. She dropped low enough to peer into the dim shadows. *No.* The diary was gone.

Ewan slipped back into the darkness. He loved the darkness. That was where they used to meet. Sometimes in the shadows of the staircase, where her kisses delighted him. Other times in the black space of his bedchamber, where he'd listen to her whispers of love.

He held the diary in his hands. *Need a light.* Despised the light, but he needed it. With trembling hands, he lit a candle and set it close to him.

Then he opened the book. *Lucy, Lucy.* How precious to see her words, to have them at last. If only he had known before of this diary, perhaps he would not have been so lonely. Perhaps his prison would have known some comfort.

With sweating fingers, he flipped through the pages. The same pages Lucy had touched. The same pages upon which her breath had fallen. The same pages, perhaps, that had caught a tear or two from her eyes.

Ewan thumbed all the way to the end. The last page. He read again, then again, then again. *The child.* The core of his soul shook. He cradled his head with both hands. *Lucy, why didn't you tell me?* He hurled the diary away from him. *Why, why, why?*

He wanted to weep, but he couldn't. Sad, very sad because Lucy had never told him the truth. Yet happy. So very, very happy—because once more he had something Henry didn't. There was a thrill in that. Same thrill as wooing Lucy, as stealing her away, as gaining her love without his brother ever realizing.

But in the end, Henry had realized.

And he had anguished.

Just like he would do again.

CHAPTER 15

I really cannot be certain about this."

Mrs. Lundie drew out a voile dress, the color closely matching an early budding red rose. "Ye dinnae need to be certain of anything, Miss Woodhart. His lordship said ye were to come, so ye are."

"But I do not think Miss Tilbury—"

"Miss Tilbury is nae lady here yet, noo is she?"

Yet. The word thudded against Ella's chest. "I dare to venture she never will be. Now"—she tugged the dress from Mrs. Lundie's hands—"this will not do at all. If I am to go, I shall not attend looking like an ape-leader in this old thing."

"But Miss Woodhart—"

"Never mind your fuss." Ella flew to her selection of gowns and reached for a handful of golden silk. She drew it out. "I have something more fitting for the occasion. What do you think?"

With eyes widening and a tentative smile, Mrs. Lundie finally nodded. "I think ye'll be the loveliest thing I hae e'er seen."

∞

The guests entered through the ballroom doors, some in pairs, others in small, clustered groups. Their eyes skidded to Henry. Careful, curious, amused. Then, one by one, they filed toward him.

The gentlemen tipped their hats and made general complaints on matters of war. The ladies took turns curtsying and smiling, but the moment they strolled away, whispers flew behind ivory fans.

Repulsion needled through him. Could they not delay their murmurs until they were out of his sight? He half wondered what they said of him. And if they thought so ill of him, why did they compete for his attentions with their coy glances and practiced smiles?

"Well, you look pink of the ton." Sir Charles Rutledge appeared, having already helped himself to a glass of lemonade. "I rather thought Lady Rutledge had lost her senses when she told me of your invitation."

"It was not my invitation."

"Oh?"

Henry grimaced as a large ostrich feather rose above the others. "The culprit approaches," he murmured. Then, with a slight bow, "Miss Tilbury."

"Lord Sedgewick." Auburn curls wound tightly against her powdered face. "Forgive me for not arriving sooner. The maid provided me is less than nimble, I fear, and sorely lacking in the ability of arranging hair." A dimple appeared. "Do you think my hair tolerable?"

Henry frowned, silent.

"Er—I find it quite stunning, miss," Sir Charles supplied. "Do you care for a glass of lemonade?"

She bestowed a faltering smile upon him. "How kind, sir, but I must decline."

"Then perhaps I can persuade you to join the set with me? I am certain my wife can have no objection."

Miss Tilbury's lips pursed, but if she had planned another excuse, it must not have come to her fast enough. She allowed Sir Charles to escort her toward the others already beginning to form in lines.

Henry made his way to the other side of the room, where he lingered by a large plant whose leaves offered him a bit of seclusion.

Only then did he see her.

Miss Woodhart stood across the room, the silk of her golden gown catching the light of the chandeliers. In her hair, she wore a chaplet. Sweet little ringlets dangled along her cheeks, ending at her jawline where a smile was already forming. Was she looking at him?

He couldn't be sure in the distance, but it hardly mattered. Two young Corinthians from the village approached—one handing her a glass of lemonade, the other kissing her gloved knuckles. Moments later, she was swept into the dance.

The music made a vicious pound at Henry's temples. He hadn't desired to dance in so many years. Perhaps never. There had never been a reason to tempt him.

He swallowed hard and kept his eyes away from Miss Woodhart. For half an hour he managed to avoid the supposed pleasantries of conversation, though at one point he'd been forced to change locations, for the two Creassey sisters had been approaching.

He diverted himself with wafers and a piece of cake.

"I must say, Lord Sedgewick," said Lady Rutledge, with her own plate of cake in hand, "I am rather mortified to see a certain individual in attendance."

Henry's eyes roamed back to the dance, where he caught a flash of gold. "I can think of no one present who might offend you, my lady."

"Oh, do not be daft with me, my lord! You know very well of whom I speak."

"Granted, but I am afraid there is nothing I can do to alleviate your discomfort."

"Well." Lady Rutledge leaned closer. "I have never seen a governess in my life dress like *that*."

"Like what, my lady?"

"So. . .modish, you know."

"If her dress is envied, my lady, perhaps I can direct you to her seamstress."

"Envied?" She scoffed. "Hardly so. I am merely at sixes and sevens as to why she would be here in the first place."

"Ponder the matter no further, my lady. I required it."

A gasp. "Well, that is rather shocking."

Henry froze.

Movement across the room, a dull shock of brown hair. . .

"One would think, after the disaster of her last social outing, you would keep the little chit under lock and key until company has departed."

Henry's stomach roiled. "Excuse me, Lady Rutledge."

"Well!"

Leaving behind his plate, he weaved through a group of ladies. "Pardon me."

"Oh, Lord Sedgewick," said a woman, "you must allow me to introduce you to—"

"Another time, I'm afraid." Henry slipped away farther. Panic made a slow rise through his chest. *Please, God. . .*

Half hidden in a dark corner, the figure turned. Luminous eyes caught his and held.

Henry halted close enough to be heard. "Ewan, what are you doing here?"

"If you do not let me dance with her, we shall only slip away later," came the whisper. "You cannot prevent us."

"Dance with who?"

"Lucy."

"She is not here."

"But I see her."

"Ewan, she—"

"There." Ewan's thin, pale hand lifted to the dancers. "See how beautiful she looks? Her dress. . .her dress is golden like her hair. . ."

Blood rushed cold through Henry's veins and he seized his brother's arm before he had time to think.

Glances stole their way. More tongues to waggle.

"Ewan, this is not the place. We shall discuss the matter upstairs."

"My prison. . .you cannot hide me forever."

"Ewan—"

"Go to the devil, Henry!" Ripping away from him, Ewan cursed and flew from the room.

More eyes drifted toward Henry. Even Miss Woodhart stared his way until the dance forced her attention back to her partner.

He exited with all their dashed gazes following him. There was nothing left of his reputation anyway. He was a blackguard to all of them, to himself, to the wife he had killed.

He ran up the stairs and found the door to Miss Woodhart's room swung open. "Ewan."

His brother stood by the window, tears wetting his cheeks, fists at his sides. "She is dead."

"I know."

"Yes." Sobbing. "Of course, you know. You killed her!"

"Ewan—"

He flung forward and sprang a fist into Henry's mouth. Then another.

Henry caught his arm. "Not here," he rasped. "I'll take you to your chamber—"

"No, no, no!" Ewan collapsed, pressing his hands over his ears. "No, no, no. . .I won't go back into my prison. . ."

"You have no choice." Henry dragged him to his feet. Blood stung his lip. "Do you hear me, Ewan? You have no choice."

"One day." Ewan staggered. Fury spun in his eyes, slipping out into his voice, "One day I shall be free, and the one in chains shall be you, Brother."

Henry yanked him from Miss Woodhart's chamber.

"I shall see you suffer."

Up the stairs.

"I shall watch you ache, as I have ached."

Henry kicked open Ewan's door and shoved him inside.

"Lucy had it planned all along." Ewan stumbled back to his bed with more tears. "And now we'll watch you die together."

"No one is going to die." Henry started from the room but paused. "And Ewan?"

His brother lifted miserable eyes.

"If you ever invade Miss Woodhart's chamber again, God forgive me for what I shall do."

His brother only turned his face into a pillow and spoke not a word.

"My." Miss Tilbury fluttered her face with a fan, her smile not quite reaching her brooding eyes. "You look most exquisite, Miss Woodhart."

"Thank you."

"And your dress is quite the masterpiece. Silk?"

"Yes." Ella turned to an approaching gentleman.

With a bow, he offered a quick smile to Miss Tilbury before his eyes turned to Ella. "You are quite the dancing creature, if I may be so bold, miss. Whoever was your caper merchant?"

"A—"

"Oh, I am certain she cannot answer, sir, for she is only but a governess. Certainly she could not afford the pleasures of a dancing master," said Miss Tilbury.

The gentleman glanced to Ella in question.

"Yes," she said. "Miss Tilbury is correct." Excusing herself, Ella made a quick departure toward the other side of the room. She approached the plant, the place she had spotted Lord Sedgewick hiding only an hour before.

It was empty. Where had he gone? And why had his brother appeared in dusty clothes, evidence that he had been kept away for so long?

As soon as Lord Sedgewick left, murmurs had filled the room, dulled only by the sounds of the orchestra. How unfair of them to speculate, to judge him—

"One usually does not linger here unless intending to avoid."

Strange, that she should know his voice so well, that it should evoke such a fluster inside. She turned to greet him. "You sound as if you have made use of the place often."

"Quite."

She studied his face, the handsome curve of his jaw, the pale shades of his eyes. Then his lips. She lingered there without meaning to, her stomach twisting. "You are hurt."

He glanced away.

"Your brother?"

"You have learned a great deal in the time I was absent. What more have they told you of me?"

"I did not share in their whispers."

"Why not?"

"Because nothing they have to say could be of interest to me." She paused. "Only your words matter."

He met her eyes then, his gaze warm and sad, until finally a smile broke through. "Let us speak of my brother no further, Miss Woodhart." He opened his hand. "I believe I would rather dance, if it's all the same to you."

∞

Stay in his prison, they screamed at him. He was tired of listening. He was tired of hearing them scream. He couldn't stay in his demon chambers any more than he could have stayed away from Lucy's love.

He was iniquitous. He always had been. Perhaps that's why she left. . .his mother. Couldn't have been Henry. No, Henry had never been unruly, never raised his voice too loud or run about the house.

Even in later years, when she'd already gone, Henry had never gambled and imbibed brandy. That was the reason, no doubt, why their father had turned his back on Ewan too. They all despised him.

Henry only provided for him because of the will. As long as Wyckhorn belonged to Henry, he was to care for his wicked younger brother, the one they'd all rather do without.

Ewan had tried to oblige them.

If only he could die.

But Lucy had loved him. She had kissed him, held him, whispered warm words to him. The first balm his bleeding soul had ever known . . .and now she was gone.

Ewan's steps were silent as he slipped back down the stairs for the second time. Music rose from below. Was his brother dancing, laughing? Didn't matter. He wouldn't be laughing forever.

The nursery door had been unnoticed for so long. Only wicked memories lived inside. Another prison.

He pushed the knob without sound and slipped inside.

Under the window stood the little bed, where a sleeping figure lay without movement. Small, slow breathing filled the room.

Ewan crept closer. He dared not touch the child, not yet. He only stared into a face he had never really looked at before.

Lucy's face.

His own face.

CHAPTER 16

*E*arly morning sunshine cut through the draperies, casting a shadow beyond Miss Tilbury's rigid stance. "I trust I am not inconveniencing you greatly, my lord, by requesting this moment alone."

"Hardly. How can I be of service?"

"In that, you can no longer assist me. There is nothing you might do for me at all."

"Oh?"

"You saved my life, Lord Sedgewick, and I shall not soon forget the sacrifice involved in such a feat. Indeed, I was foolish enough to imagine your heroism and my father's wishes would all result in a very pleasant ending." She turned. "This past evening rather dashed the last of my hopes."

He stiffened at her tone but did not speak.

"I heard some rather—shall we say?—scandalous tales concerning your past. As you know, I cannot jeopardize my own reputation by remaining in this home a moment longer, nor would I have come in the first place had I known."

Anger stirred. "Very well. I shall have a servant escort you to Northston."

"How soon?"

"As soon as you wish."

She nodded curtly. "I hope to spare all of this from my father. He has a rather odd respect for you, and I am hesitant to dash his good opinion."

Henry frowned.

"Good day." Miss Tilbury went for the door, but she paused before she left. "Oh, and my lord?"

"Yes?"

"I shall also try to discourage my father's anticipations for a betrothal. Even if your character hadn't been tainted, his wishes would have been in vain."

"How so?"

Her voice hardened, though accompanied by a thin smile, "You are quite in love with another woman."

∽

What could the alphabet—or even the Latin alphabet—have in comparison to grass and sunshine?

Ella could only endure studies and books for so long.

"A walk?" Peter echoed her, accepting the cap she offered.

"Yes, indeed. Unless you should rather complete your studies first."

"Oh no, Miss Woodhart. I shouldn't like to do that." Peter took her hand as they made their way out of doors, where a late morning gust rushed through the grasses and stirred the trees. They followed the road until the heights of Wyckhorn grew smaller in the distance.

"Miss Woodhart?"

"Yes?"

"I can run very fast."

"Oh?"

"Yes." He swung her hand. "Do you want to see?"

"Then I shall have to walk all alone."

"But I will come back for you. Please?"

Ella tugged loose her hand. "To save you a bit of steps, I might just run alongside you."

His eyes widened. "You?"

"You do not think me capable?"

"But your dress—"

"Oh, Peter! All ladies are not made of porcelain." Before he could respond—and grabbing a fistful of fabric—Ella darted ahead of him.

She heard a thrilling shout, a laugh, then the pounding of little feet chasing after her.

Her speed increased. One by one, the curls of her hair unraveled, falling free. . .disgraceful. It didn't matter. Who would possibly know? She could amend the mess before her return to Wyckhorn, and no one would be the wiser.

What would Lord Sedgewick think of such a thing? Would he glance upon her as disapprovingly as her mother always did? Would he—

"Miss Woodhart!"

She slowed at the crest of the hill, chest heaving. "Can you not catch up, then, Peter?"

"Your hair!" Glee filled his laughter and brightened his eyes. "It's all falling down!"

"So it is." She glanced at a group of rocks alongside the road. "Let's sit a moment and I shall remedy my disarray."

They plopped down on warm stone seats, where a view of the sea stretched out below.

Ella wound her hair back in place as Peter reached out and stroked a curl.

"It's so pretty," he said. "And long."

"Which can be a vexation at times." Ella smiled. "Be grateful you are of the male persuasion."

"Male persuasion?"

"A boy," she supplied. She glanced back to the road—

Ewan.

"What is it, Miss Woodhart?"

She came to her feet, perspiration trickling down her temples. She groped for Peter's hand. "We had better hurry home."

"But our walk—"

"Will be resumed later."

He was close enough now to hear them. Close enough that a few short steps would cover the distance. Dark hair was messed across a pale forehead, but he made no move to brush it from his eyes. "Miss Woodhart."

He knew her name?

Her fingers clamped tighter on Peter's hand. She forced a nod. "Sir."

"Taking a stroll?"

"Yes," Peter answered. "And Miss Woodhart ran with me because she is not made of porcelain. And her hair even fell down."

He blinked. Liquid, hazy eyes drifted to her hair, lingering, lingering, lingering...

"Come, Peter. We must return." She pulled him forward and tromped through the grass. Couldn't walk on the road. Couldn't get that close to him.

"Lucy?"

She froze. Tears surfaced.

"That is not my name, sir."

"If only it were." He said nothing else, and Ella rushed Peter away. She glanced back only once, but the road was already empty.

Ewan was gone.

✿

Henry knew the moment they returned. Their voices drifted through the walls, followed by his son's laughter and the closing of the large door.

"You had better go upstairs," she said, "and change into a clean suit."

"I will." Peter's strapped slippers echoed as they darted across the marble floors and up the stairs.

Henry emerged and met her at the base of the steps. One glance at her and he couldn't control his smile. "If Peter looks half as unkempt as you, no wonder he was instructed to change."

Her lips remained flat. "You may laugh all you wish."

"I am not laughing."

"Not everyone is content to live their lives in a cage, my lord. You and my mother and all the peerage in England may forever argue your cause, but I shall not be persuaded—"

"Persuaded of what, pray?"

A curl fell across her forehead. "Oh, never mind." She started past him.

He caught her elbow before she could ascend the steps. "You may be a bit presumptuous, Miss Woodhart, and may lack certain habits of good etiquette." His voice lowered. "But in dancing, you exceed many—and in loveliness, I have known no equal."

Color flooded her cheeks. Her eyes dropped to his hand, then back to his eyes, but she didn't pull away. "Was that Miss Tilbury in the carriage?"

"Yes."

"A hasty departure, is it not?"

"Seems she feared for her reputation."

"By staying?"

He shrugged.

With eyes a strange delight of compassion and amusement, she nodded. "I admit to surprise," she whispered, "as I did not think Miss Tilbury to yield when something so desired was at stake."

"I believe she has the battle proficiencies of her father in knowing when to retreat."

"Were her efforts so very futile, my lord?"

His heart hitched with the strange wish that she could care. "Entirely." His fingers released her, but even when she'd ascended the stairs and left him alone, his soul still rejoiced from the touch.

Miss Tilbury's words had been in truth.

The tap on her door came softly.

She didn't move. Dinner had already come and passed. No one would disturb her now, not at this time of evening unless Ewan—

"Miss Woodhart?"

A pause, a breath. "Lord Sedgewick?"

"Yes, may I speak with you a moment?"

She snapped shut the Bible and slid it under her bed, unwilling for him to see she'd been reading. It would only give him hope that could prove to be false.

She opened the door.

He stood in a green frock coat and tan pantaloons, with his beaver hat twisting in his hands. "I hope I am not disturbing you."

"No." She had not seen him since the day before when he'd spoken to her at the stairs. Peculiar, how such a short time could seem so lengthy. "No," she said again. "You are not disturbing me."

He didn't speak, only looked at her. She sensed something, a vulnerability in his expression, as if the words he hunted for did not come without pain. "You were right in one point yesterday," he said finally, "and most wrong in another."

She waited.

"Not everyone cares to live in a cage."

"And the point to which I was wrong?"

"I cannot be categorized with your mother, nor all the peerage in England." A smile broke through his hesitancy. "Would you join me in a ride?"

A thrill passed through her. "Now?"

"It is late, I know, but I shall not keep you long."

"Give me but a moment and I shall change."

"Splendid." He offered a bow. "I shall prepare our mounts."

Until now, he had been faultless. He had asked for nothing, sought for nothing—and if his soul was tempted, it was only because temptation lingered so close. The same breakfast table, the same ballroom, the same house. He could not have escaped her if he'd wanted to.

Which he didn't.

And that is my downfall. Henry swung her saddle atop a gentle roan, tightened the cinch with hands that shook. *What am I doing?*

He was falling of his own choice. He had gone to her chamber and asked her, just as any other gentleman might have asked a woman to court. Any consequences now were self-inflicted.

"She is lovely."

His nerves swirled at the sound of her. "He, actually."

"Pardon?"

"The horse." He turned. "His name is Alphonse."

"A French name." She followed him from the stables, then allowed him to swing her atop the animal. "Much more inventive than Miss Staverley."

"Yes, well"—he swung atop his own horse—"Miss Staverley has never said much in way of complaint." Instead of following the road, he took the lead down a steeper, grassy path.

The farther they trotted away, the quieter the earth became, as if all of nature conspired to give them a moment of peace.

I want to love her.

Could he? Did he know how? He'd never loved a woman in his life. His governess had administered discipline in place of kindness. His mother had only visited him sparingly, and then she had left. Even his own wife had been little more than a stranger to him.

But he wanted to love.

Hardly mattered that she was a governess. Rumormongers had already hung his neck with a rope and left him to dangle. What did it matter now what they said?

Doesn't matter. Softness crept into all the places so long empty, so long cold. *Doesn't matter at all.*

Because if there was a chance for happiness, for the first time in his life, he was willing to pursue it.

Warm evening air bathed her face and rippled through her muslin skirt. Countryside spread out before them, green and rolling, as lovely as the wall murals back at Abbingston Hall. An orange, hazy sun dipped lower on the horizon. Was that a faint scent of salt she could still catch in the breeze?

She took great care with her reins. Not too close, yet near enough that she could study the frame of his shoulders, the way his hair curled at his neck. A knot bobbed in her throat.

He had been silent for the entirety of the ride. If he had no desire to speak to her, why had he brought her along?

She couldn't speak either. How had it come to this? Strange, unsettling emotions she wanted no part of—yet they chased her so hard she began to need them. Need him.

Alphonse threw his head with a snort. His ears flicked.

"Whoa, boy."

Lord Sedgewick turned in his saddle. "Hold him—"

The animal reared.

No. Ella jerked the reins, but her body was already losing contact.

Arms grabbed her from behind, pulling her into another saddle, against a hard chest. "Whoa, there." His voice in her ear, even as he reached over and grasped Alphonse's reins. "It's all right."

She wasn't certain if his comforts were meant for the horse or her, but her fear melted. *In his arms.* She tried not to think of it, to bask in such a thought.

Just as quickly, he lowered her to the ground. "An adder." He pointed to the bushes, where a brown snake slithered safely from the threat of pounding hooves. "I should have noticed."

"Even now, he is hardly distinguishable in the grass." Ella smoothed back her flyaway curls. "You cannot be faulted."

He dismounted and tied both horses to the branch of a sea buckthorn. Then he stood before her, as close as he'd been when they danced. "We shall wait for Alphonse to regain his wits."

"He is quite out of sorts, isn't he?"

"Yes." Deep, careful eyes stared into her. She saw Peter in their depths—the same real, unfeigned love.

Love? No, that couldn't be. To gain the love of one so noble, one so brave, would be unthinkable.

"You were not frightened, were you, Miss Woodhart?"

Yes, she'd been frightened—but it had lasted only as long as it took him to rush to her rescue. Miss Tilbury could not be faulted in her endeavors. To be saved by such a man was no small honor.

His hands framed her cheeks.

My lord. Warm, beautiful emotions danced within.

"Were you?" Whispered this time. His thumbs stroked her cheeks.

"No." How tender was his touch, as if he'd never cherished any-thing more in his life. Maybe he hadn't. "If one ventures to live life outside of a cage, one must expect a bit of peril." Her heart sped. "But in all peril, there can always be found a bit of comfort."

A vein bulged in his forehead, then tears shimmered in his eyes. She wasn't certain what she'd said, but in the end, it only made him smile. "More than a bit, I daresay." He leaned forward, pressed warm lips against her cheek. Even when he withdrew and helped her back atop her horse, he did not say another word.

They returned to Wyckhorn Manor, where the evening had turned to twilight, and the sea made low roars in the distance.

Lord Sedgewick escorted her to the door. He smiled, tipped his hat, then took the horses back to the stables in a silence she was begin-ning to love.

∾

The thought was surreal, intangible, even when he held the diary in his hands. He read the words again. Would to heaven the truth could become real to him.

Henry's son. Ewan pressed his fingers into his eyelids, massaging, comforting. *Henry's son is mine. . .my son.* He ripped the paper from the diary. Hated to destroy something Lucy had treasured, but if he could slip such a paper under his brother's chamber door. . .

Oh, his face. The anguish, the grief of knowing. Would Henry weep at the knowledge? Would it alter his love for the child?

No, not Henry. He would do anything he could to conceal such a secret. He would destroy the paper and keep the truth from ever reaching Peter's ears. No one would ever know.

Cannot happen. Ewan returned the paper to the diary. *Peter is mine and I shall have him.*

How?

The child was seldom alone. There would be little chance of steal-ing him away from Wyckhorn's walls without the nanny or governess

174

interfering—unless, perhaps, at night.

Lucy, Lucy. Ewan sprang to his feet and hugged his arms. He paced about the room, following the walls, pausing at every corner. *Lucy, what do I do?*

Perhaps this was his chance. He had wanted to kill Henry for what he'd done, for how he'd harmed her. But would leaving his brother alive be a greater affliction? Henry would have no one left without a son.

Yes, yes, no one left. Just as Henry had done to Ewan. Now he'd feel the pain himself. He'd know what it was like to want to die, to try to die, to live to die.

Almost here, Lucy. Ewan's lips curved in a trembling smile. *Just a little while longer before the man who killed you suffers.*

CHAPTER 17

$\mathcal{M}$orning came long before Henry was prepared to see her again. He deprived himself of breakfast to avoid speaking with her. He enclosed himself within the stifling four walls of his study to avoid even a glance of her.

How clumsy he must have been last night. Touching her face as he had, whispering in tones he'd hardly realized himself capable of—yet never once speaking his heart.

Declaring his love had never been a difficulty he'd had to face. He had never feigned affection for Lucy, only offered her marriage. It was expected. It was the duty of all sons and daughters of the nobility to carry on honorable bloodlines, to espouse riches to riches despite matters of the heart.

Could he offer Miss Woodhart something more? Could he summon words of love to her?

Old doubts dampened the ecstasy of such a thought. He imagined his feelings were returned, but what did he know of such things? Was it possible she would accept a proposal for the wealth he offered? Or worse yet, not accept at all?

He pushed away the books on his desk, all his dashed letters, his correspondences—along with his doubts. If he had to dismiss fear for the place of happiness every day, he would do so. He would not allow his mother or Lucy to ruin his chances.

He roamed through the house until he caught their faint voices within the nursery. He burst inside.

Positioned in the window seat with one foot dangling off the edge and the other tucked under her dress, Miss Woodhart lowered her map.

Peter lifted his head from the scroll end of the bench. "Papa!"

Unfamiliar emotions scratched at his throat. "What do we have here?" he asked, glancing to the map.

"Oh, nothing of great importance." Miss Woodhart folded the paper.

"She showed me where the lions live. They eat people. Have you ever been to Africa?"

"No." Henry approached and tugged the map from her hands. "No, I have not."

"I'll show you." A tiny finger pointed at the brown sketch of a continent. "Can we go there?"

"I am afraid it is a mite distance from us, Son."

"Oh." Peter slipped off the bench. "May I play with my blocks now, Miss Woodhart?"

Her eyes lifted to Henry's before she answered. "Yes," she said after a pause. "For a minute or two."

As the child scrambled to the other side of the room, Henry sat next to her. He realized too late how tiny the bench was.

A warm flush bathed her cheeks. "Peter seems greatly interested in geography."

"An interesting topic, I'm sure."

Silence. The only sound was the wooden blocks as they were stacked carefully on top of one another.

"You must forgive me for last night, Miss Woodhart."

"Forgive you?" Wide, eager eyes captured his. "For what, my lord?"

"I never intended to..." The words drifted as his hands still tingled with the memory of holding her cheeks. "I never intended to bestow such affection, nor compromise you."

"Then your apology springs from regret?"

"Only for your sake." An unsteady pulse thrummed his heart. "For myself, I can only be grateful."

Tenderness transformed her features, and when she reached out and grasped his hand, a new burst of joy unfurled within him. "Then you had better keep your apology, my lord, for I want nothing of it."

◌

Throughout the day, he remained close to her. When Peter's tower had crumbled, as it always did, Lord Sedgewick had gotten on the floor and helped build it back. When she'd returned to Peter's studies, Lord Sedgewick had stayed and offered small rhymes to help his son remember the alphabet.

Many times, she had reminded Lord Sedgewick of the responsibilities he must be neglecting. She was torn betwixt the fascination of having him close, and the stifling need to put distance between them. Why was breathing so inanely difficult?

Was he so affected? Could that explain his strangeness? His apology? His desire to be close to her?

The thought filled her with wild sensations long after the day had ended. She snuggled deep into her bed, and with her candle lit, opened the Bible once more. *"Consider and hear me, O LORD my God: lighten mine eyes, lest I sleep the sleep of death."*

Her soul echoed the words as her heavy lids drifted shut. *Lighten my eyes, God. I long to believe.*

◌

She was just like Lucy. Over and over came the thought. Into the night, through the day—until it almost seemed she was alive again. But in the end, he knew she wasn't. Lucy had loved him—and the governess didn't. She shrank away from him just like everyone else, as if he were some sort of mad, devilish creature.

Only he wasn't mad, and if the devil was in him, it was only because Henry had placed him there.

No qualms, no qualms. He reached her chamber door long before he was ready. Weight settled in his stomach until the candle in his grasp began to shake. She didn't deserve to die. He shouldn't kill her. Even if it could look like an accident, he shouldn't destroy something so beautiful just because she wasn't Lucy. Just because she despised him.

Cowardice drew him away from her door. The quaking light made disoriented shadows in the hall as he started away. *Now I shall never escape with Peter.* He stole a glance back. *Never destroy my brother. . . never see him hurt. . .*

Ewan whirled back around before his conscience could interfere. He eased open her door and crept without sound into the black room.

Her bedchamber key and unlit candle sat by her bedside. He couldn't see her face. He was glad. He could almost imagine it wasn't Miss Woodhart at all. Perhaps it was his mother. Yes, that's who it was. He would be glad to see the flames devour the woman he hated. He would savor the sound of her scream.

Ewan dipped his candle to hers until her wick caught with flame. Then he scooted it closer to her bed as the flame groped for her bed-curtains.

She never stirred.

Ewan grabbed the key, locked the door, slipped outside. *No qualms at all.* He didn't return to his room. Instead, he lingered on the stair-well, knees drawn to his chest, and listened for the first painful cry to stab the air.

⚭

Sleep of death. . .sleep of death. . .

Over and over again, until the words grew hands to seize her. They dragged her through inky blackness, casting her into flames the vicar had warned her of. Devouring her, eating her, burning her in hellish torture. . .

Ella jerked upward. Sleep disoriented her, made her half believe the fire had escaped her nightmare and leaked into her bed.

Then a flame licked her arm.

"No." She thrust herself backward, swatting away the fire on her sleeve. *It is real.* Panic sent her sprawling across the floor, groping for the knob of her door.

It wouldn't open. Locked.

My key. On her nightstand, but the flames had already devoured it. "No." The murmur turned into a scream. "Help me!" She forced her fists into the door, pounding. "Help! Fire!"

No one answered, as if her voice had been overpowered by the crackling sound of fire spreading across her bed. Orange flames crawled up the curtains, the bedlinens, the pillows.

She hammered again. "Help!" Why would no one come? She screamed again, again, again, until smoke constricted her lungs. "Please, someone! Help me..."

She whirled around as the fire spread to the rug, bursting it into bright color. She grabbed the edge and whacked it against the wooden floor, but the flames only nipped at her fingers.

"Miss Woodhart?" The small voice penetrated her chaos.

Ella stumbled back to the door, coughing. "Peter, is that you?"

"Why are you screaming?" he whimpered.

"Get your father. Hurry!"

"Why won't it open?" He must have tried the knob. His voice rose an octave. "Why is there smoke?"

"Peter, please. Get your father!"

He never answered, but his footsteps faded down the hallway. Could he run faster than the flames?

❦

"Papa! Papa!"

Henry rolled out of bed with blurry eyes. "Peter?"

The door swung open and a small, dark figure ran and leaped into his arms. "Papa, she is burning."

Henry pressed the boy's head into his chest. "Did you have a bad dream?"

"No, Papa!" Peter flung himself back. Tears cascaded down white cheeks. "Her door won't open...and I saw smoke...and it woke me up because she was screaming..."

"Who, Son?"

"M—Miss Woodhart."

Henry swung Peter into his own bed. "Stay here."

"But Papa." Peter's hand snatched Henry's sleeve. "I—I don't want her to die."

Fear like he'd never known stabbed at his gut. "She won't."

CHAPTER 18

A thousand steps. The hallway was endless. An eternity had come and gone before he reached her bedchamber.

God, don't let this happen. Smoke already lingered in the air, hot and stifling, as he jerked the scorching knob on her door. "Ella!"

No answer.

He slammed his body into the door. Then again. Pain bruised his shoulder with the third impact, but the hinges began to give. *God, please.* He ripped the door free and it crashed behind him.

Hot smoke blasted him. "Ella!" He shielded his face with one arm and stepped inside. His eyes stung. Flames reached for the side of his nightgown, but he smothered them. "Ella!"

The sound of breaking glass drew his attention to the other side of the room. So much smoke. He caught the faint sight of her figure by the window.

God, have mercy. Henry pushed his way toward her.

She was on her knees in front of the window, her mouth to the broken glass as if gasping for fresh air.

"Ella." He latched onto her shoulder, pried her back, hoisted her into his arms. He dove back through the smoke and flames, into the hall.

Other faces were already appearing—Dunn in his nightcap and slippers, other servants with disheveled hair and rounded eyes, all with copper-handled buckets already in hand.

"My lord. . ." Dunn's whisper carried.

"Get the fire out." Henry squeezed past them, started down the stairs.

The echo of Dunn's orders and frantic footsteps made the house come alive.

She's bleeding. Henry raced down the steps with her arm dangling, the red trails dripping to her palm, through her fingers. *God, she's bleeding.*

He was too familiar with blood, the coppery scent, the red stains. Nausea churned his stomach as he lowered her to a chaise lounge in the drawing room. "You are all right, Miss Woodhart." *Make her all right, my Savior.*

Stricken eyes stared back at him. She didn't blink, didn't speak.

He laid her sticky hand in his. "Are there burns?"

Her tongue rolled over her lips. "N—not many."

A measure of relief coursed through him. He lifted her arm. "You broke the window?"

"F—for air." Moisture welled in her eyes. "I—I could not breathe... the smoke..."

"Do not try to speak." Henry rose, warring between the thought of leaving her or staying close. But she needed bandages, a maid to search for burns, a servant to ride for flaxseed oil.

"Papa?"

Henry jerked toward the doorway. "I told you to stay in my chamber."

His son, appearing very small and slight in a doorway so large, held his hands clasped in front of him. His eyes lingered past Henry to the chaise lounge. "Did she die?"

"No, Peter."

Features scrunched, he smeared away tears from his cheeks. "I was f—frightened." He hiccupped. "I didn't want her to be in the ground like Mamma."

Henry approached his son and scooped him into his arms. He breathed in the scent of little child. Swallowed down tears. "I prayed she would be safe, and God has shown mercy."

"I prayed too," said Peter. "Can I stay?"

"Miss Woodhart does not feel well."

"I know, but maybe I can say my prayers to her. That will make her feel better."

"Very well." Henry carried him to Ella's side and planted him on the floor next to her.

Without seeming to notice the blood, the little boy lifted his arm over top of her chest and pressed his face close to hers. "I love you," came his thread-like whisper. "God will make you better."

Her only response was a slight murmur, but her lips turned with a smile.

Henry hurried from the room, wishing he could speak his love as easily as his son.

☙

Ewan didn't return to his chamber. If he had, he would have found some way to end his agony—and he couldn't do that. Not now. He had to stay alive for Lucy, if not for himself.

The fire is out. He slipped into the old bedroom, as forsaken and forgotten as his own. Lucy's presence came alive again, as if the mere furniture and keepsakes she had touched still carried her spirit.

His skin prickled with the thought. "Lucy?" He tried her name in the silence, strode to her bed and grabbed up her pillows. "In the name of heaven, answer me!"

But she didn't. Never did. Only listened to him from some obscure place in the room.

"I am sorry. . .sorry I failed again." Sobs shuddered his voice, but he muffled the sounds in her pillow. "I cannot get our son. . .nothing worked. . . yet I will. . ."

With a moan, he curled on top of her coverlets. He ripped the bed-curtains shut and welcomed a darkness he loved. His mother should have burned. He wished she hadn't escaped. He wished the flames could have hurt her as she'd wounded him.

Forgive me, Lucy. He sank his teeth into the pillow, shaking, weeping. *I promise we'll be free.*

❧

The probing hands and gentle ministrations should have comforted her. The shadow of Mrs. Lundie against the paper hangings, moving this way and that as she sang an old Gaelic tune should have eased Ella into the arms of sleep.

But her nerves were still sharp, frenzied. She lay motionless as a young maid wound a bandage around her arm.

"Too tight?" the girl asked.

"Och, what are ye doing?" Mrs. Lundie came around the bed. "Get out of the way, if ye cannae do it right. Here"—she slid into the girl's place and began to unravel—"this is how ye do it."

Ella's pulse throbbed beneath the fabric. "Mrs. Lundie—"

"Now dinnae ye be whining, lass. All ye need is a bit of rest."

"And Peter?"

"What of him?"

"He seemed. . ." Ella licked dry lips. "Very out of sorts. I do not wish to inflict him with worries."

"Ye've inflicted more than him, I'd wager."

"What?"

"Never mind." Mrs. Lundie drew the bedlinens to Ella's chin. "Now, close yer eyes and I shall sing to ye a wee bit longer."

"No, please do not stay." Ella's throat tightened. "You must get some rest. I shall sleep more soundly in silence."

"Verra well." With a kiss that was almost motherly planted upon her forehead, Mrs. Lundie doused the candle. "And dinnae be fretting about yer dresses and trunk and sich things. Ye'll be happy to know they were pulled out before much damage could be done." She smiled then and left the room with a soft tune carrying after her.

My fault. The burn of the words ran deeper than her wounds. *The candle. I must have forgotten to blow out the candle.* How could she have been so thoughtless? How much of the room had been damaged?

Then another thought pierced her. *The Bible.* The only thing Lord Sedgewick had ever given her and she had destroyed it. She was reckless, careless, incapable. Her mother had been right in all of her endless scolding.

The words of the verse came back to haunt her, as cold as they'd been in her dream. *Sleep of death. . .sleep of death. . .*

Her soul writhed. *Oh, God, was the fire my punishment? My penalty for unbelief?* She trembled in the lonely darkness, half wondering if God had wished her to burn in those flames—or if He had rescued her from them.

∽

"My lord?"

Henry looked up. "Dunn?"

"Yes, my lord." The steward stepped forward, the tassel on his nightcap singed. His gaze shifted to Henry's chair, then the door beside him. "I had a most difficult time locating you, my lord."

"The ordeal has deterred me from sleep."

"Understandably." Still, Dunn's eyes lingered to the closed door. "Miss Woodhart?"

Henry rose without answering. "Do say what you have come for."

"I only wished to return your mind to ease, my lord. Forgive me if I am disturbing."

"The fire is out?"

"Just so, my lord."

"Any other rooms affected?"

"None but a bit of the hallway, but we managed to stop it there."

Henry clasped his hands behind his back. "Very well. You have eased me. Go and do the same for yourself, for morning will come quickly."

"Yes, my lord." Dunn bowed, but his gaze latched onto the door once more. "Is she quite all right, my lord? I must know."

"She could have been killed."

"Yet she was not."

"There was blood."

"Which washes away, my lord."

Not from everything. He had a shirtsleeve hidden in his chamber

185

to prove it. There were still stains, stains that would never come out.

⚸

Pounding at the glass, thrusting her hands through, breaking her skin with the jagged edge. She plunged, only the fire was there too. Couldn't be happening. She fell so hard the air left her, yet still she screamed. Flames circled her, crackling with demon tunes, laughing with cold derision. Then they leaped at her, even as she thrashed them away—

"Miss Woodhart."

She jerked, but couldn't pry open her eyes. *Lord Sedgewick.* Sweat descended down her temples. *Please, help me.*

"There is no need for fear," came his voice again. "I have had you placed in the west wing where no harm shall come to you."

No harm. Her mind clung to the words, half believing, half dreading.

"Come now. Open your eyes, Miss Woodhart." Fingertips slid down her cheek. "Ella."

She could resist no longer. With tears, she opened to him bent over, eyes close to hers. Did he realize how close he hovered over her, or that his breath fell upon her face? Indeed, she could count every burst of color in his eyes.

The knot in his neck bobbed as if his thoughts aligned with hers, but he didn't pull away. "Your cries awoke me."

"From your chamber?"

He glanced away, quiet for the space of a few heartbeats. He faced her again. "The fire is out."

A defense sprang to her mind, a story that would likely have escaped her from trouble—only she didn't want to lie to him. "I—I do not think I blew out the candle."

"It matters not."

"Matters not?"

"There will be no more graves to dig. That's what is important."

She should have known his character enough by now. She should have foreseen his kindness. His regard for human life far exceeded anyone she had ever known. Such a man could not have killed anyone, least of all her sister.

"Ella?" Strange, how his voice rang differently. Deep, husky, soft, like something from a dream. "Ella, I wish permission to speak my heart to you."

His heart. She could not fathom that his could match her own. She only managed a nod.

"You see, I. . ." His forehead tightened as if the words were hard in coming. "I. . ."

"I know."

His eyes sought hers.

"I know," she said again. "Because I too have no words to describe such a thing. Yet I've heard it called *love* by more than one poor fool."

A smile chased away all the shadows, all the fears that lingered about him. "Fools, indeed." He drew away and backed to the door without once tearing his eyes away from her. "Do rest soundly, Miss Woodhart, and I shall be near if you need me."

Her nightmares diminished in the warmth of his happiness. *That may be a very long time, my lord. A very long time, indeed.*

CHAPTER 19

The room was charred and sweltering. Even the late summer breeze, invading through the broken window, could not steal away the stench of smoke.

Henry's boots crunched over shards of glass. He gazed out the window—the dewy grass along the cliff, the faded rocks, and the sea that met a brilliant sky. He didn't know why he'd requested this chamber for her, only that a part of him had known she'd appreciate the view.

She shall need new accommodations now. She could not remain in the west wing. He hardly knew why he'd placed her there, only that keeping her close had seemed imperative after the fire.

Perhaps he could suggest the room opposite Peter's. There were lovely draperies on the windows, a sizable bed, and plenty of space for any furniture she might have need of. Yes, she would be most comfortable there. A logical solution.

As the thought formed, another was pushing through. One he scarcely had the courage to comprehend.

No. He crossed the room and tugged the remains of her bedcurtain to the ground. The heavy fabric fell in a heap at his feet. *God, I cannot.*

He wasn't ready for another wife. He wasn't ready to move Miss Woodhart into his bedchamber. He wasn't ready to cast his bloody shirtsleeve into the fire for fear she'd discover it in his things.

She must have questions. All the speculating murmurs had doubtless reached her ears, arousing doubts she had failed to voice. He had no right to keep the secrets from her any longer.

If she was to be his wife, she must know the truth.

Every step she took in the blackness took her farther from the west wing. She half expected her mother, at any moment, to appear from behind and order her back to bed.

What a silly thought. In all the times Ella had gotten out of bed, her mother had never once caught her—and if she had, her father would have come to the rescue. Or had her mother known all along?

She didn't know and it hardly mattered. What she wouldn't give to see the both of them again, seated before the hearth with each in their own place. Mother had always settled on the settee, cross-stitching with Matilda cuddled next to her. On the other end, Lucy had held a book or a letter—either of which she would read out loud in soft tones. Father had occupied a chair closest to the hearth, and he often drifted asleep until Ella invaded his lap. She still recalled the rhythm of his heartbeat.

But that is gone. Ella's hands reached into the darkness and pulled open the bedchamber door. She slipped into a room that banished old memories with the gentle touch of new ones.

Sweet boy. He didn't stir when she settled onto the edge of his bed and swept her hand down his cheek. She kissed his brow. *My dear little Peter, if only I could rescue you from hurt.*

Heaven forbid that Peter should ever know the truth. He'd already lost a mother. To lose a father too—

"Peter?"

Ella sprang from the bed. She couldn't see, couldn't recognize the figure in the darkness. "Lord Sedgewick?"

No answer.

"My lord?"

The figure remained still, erect, silent.

Ella's legs buckled as she took one step forward. "Ewan?"

Something dropped at his feet. Without ever saying anything, he fled from the room, leaving the door open behind him.

Ella rushed to retrieve the object. Her blood ran cold.

The diary.

If he'd read it. . .then he knew.

⚭

She should have stayed in her chamber as she was told. Mrs. Lundie had advised her to rest, had insisted she stay in bed. She could have seen Peter in the morning. Why had she done such a thing?

But Ewan would have come anyway. What would he have done if Ella had not been there? Awaken his child? Read him the diary?

Ella leaned against the mantel, exhaustion making the tears run faster. *Lord Sedgewick—I've got to tell him.*

Something needed to be done. Ewan could not be permitted to see Peter whenever he wished as if Peter were his son.

Because he wasn't. Not anymore. Lord Sedgewick had raised him, loved him, nurtured him. That meant more than any bloodline.

I can't tell him. Ella gripped the diary in her hands. She glanced down into the small flames and lowered the book, hesitating. *Perhaps Ewan only wished to see the child. That would be natural. Maybe he'll never speak a word of what he knows.*

She was right not to tell Lord Sedgewick what she had seen tonight. It would only hurt him—and Peter.

With her vision a blur of tears and firelight, she tossed the diary into the flames. Was she doing the right thing?

⚭

She opened her bedchamber door after Henry's second knock. She stood before him in a white linen dress and bandaged arm. In two short days, her cheeks had regained their rosiness, her lips their smile. He shouldn't have stared, but he couldn't stop himself.

"My lord."

He cleared his throat. "How do you feel?"

"Well, thank you." She stepped into the hall and closed the door behind her. "Though I would greatly appreciate it if you would inform Mrs. Lundie that I am not an invalid. She has the most exasperating notion that I should remain in bed."

"Should you?"

"No." Her smile widened. "One more moment in there and I shall shrivel away and die."

"Then it seems I have rescued you, does it not?"

"For the second time."

His heart raced at the warmth in her tone, but he did not look away. Instead, he grasped her hands. "Would a ride out of doors alleviate your distress?"

"I feel a bit too tender for a saddle, I fear."

"Would a gig suit you?"

"Oh yes." She hurried back into her room and returned wearing a stovepipe bonnet and lace gloves. He tucked her hand in the crook of his elbow.

Never had the journey to the stable taken so long. Never had the stable boy moved so slowly as he prepared the horse and gig. *God, help me tell her.*

"All ready for you, m'lord." The stable boy led the horse and gig to them. "But there 'pears to be rain a-comin'."

"We shall return before that." Henry lifted her, hands spanning her waist, and planted her upon the seat. His chest worked faster as he went to the other side and joined her. "Ready?"

Her eyes were curious, wide, as if she sensed his tension. "Yes."

He gave the whip a small crack, and the wheels lurched into motion. The gray morning sky stared back at them—sad, gloomy, as if prepared to unleash a torrent of tears. Shadows loomed across the road, cast by stone fences or age-old trees. Familiar rolling hills stretched endlessly ahead. From not far away, the ocean waters made low, roaring warnings of a pending storm.

What would she think when she knew the truth? How would she look at him? Would she keep the secret he'd hidden for so long? He told himself she'd understand, that compassion would override any shame. Hadn't she nearly said she loved him?

He'd nearly said it too, only he hadn't. Maybe it was just as well.

"Did you speak with Peter this morning?"

His mind shifted to her question. "Yes."

"At breakfast?"

"Afterward. He slept late, so I went to wake him myself."

"I see." Silence again, silence he hated.

Tell her. The road turned in a small curve until the ocean noises became fainter. *Dear Savior, help me tell her.*

But he didn't, and the horse kept plodding farther away until the sky began to rumble. Moist, tropical scents filled the breeze.

"Perhaps we should start back," she said at last. "I believe there shall be rain, after all."

He didn't answer. Without looking at her, he turned the horse toward home. Light sprinkles of moisture blew into his face as if tears from heaven. *God, please.*

Then her fingers reached for his and tugged the reins away from him. She pulled back and the horse stopped. "My lord, you cannot think me blind enough to not perceive your pain."

His eyes raised to hers.

"And if I am the source of that pain, let me offer remedy. If you regret the feelings you implied before—"

"I regret nothing." His chest throbbed. "And if you wish to offer me remedy, become my wife."

First it was in her eyes—that soft, sweet glow that so quickly sparkled with tears. Then it was on her cheeks, a spreading shade of pink. And her lips. He tried so desperately not to search, not to look—but it was there too. He wondered if this was the sight of love.

"You forget," she whispered. "You forget that I am a governess."

"I have forgotten nothing."

"But people shall—"

"Let them talk."

Silence.

Then, as if in amazement, "Your wife? You wish me to become Lady Sedgewick?"

"Yes." He hesitated, swallowed hard. "But only after you know what has happened to the last lady of Wyckhorn."

∞

Ella stared at him while cold fear clawed away her ecstasy. For the first time, she didn't want the truth. She didn't wish to know things that would disappoint her heart, that would devastate her love for him.

He is innocent. The words came again, the ones she'd come to believe. He wasn't capable of hurting anyone, of taking a human life. No matter what her sister had done, he wouldn't have murdered her. He was innocent. He had to be.

But even as her mind cried the words, his face told her differently. "Ella." He got no farther than her name before a noise disrupted the quiet.

Both of them turned, just as two matching bays pulled a hackney beside their gig. The door swung open, and a black hat poked out into the rain.

Ella gasped. *No.*

The vicar climbed out, shoes sinking into the mud as his pale face lifted to hers. "I prayed to God I would find you, Miss Pemberton."

Lord Sedgewick's eyes snapped to hers.

"What are you doing here?" Instant rage lent a tremor to her voice. "You had no right to come."

"Matilda said there had been no letters—"

"I have been busy."

"I was afraid for you." The vicar's forehead tightened as his gaze slid to Henry. "And I have come to do what I should have done a long time ago, but lacked the courage for."

"Mr. Beaumont—"

"Please get down, Miss Pemberton, and do not suffer me with complaints." He caught her waist before she could squirm away.

Lord Sedgewick did nothing to stop him.

"Return her to Wyckhorn long enough to retrieve her things, then see that she is brought back to the village," the vicar told the driver, as he opened the hackney door wider. "And do not be persuaded by her pleadings, for I am only performing the will of the Lord."

She struggled against him. "I won't go."

"Forgive me, but I am afraid you do not have a choice." With strength she had never imagined him to have, the vicar hoisted her into the hackney. He slammed the door hard.

No. Ella pushed at the door, but the wheels were already turning. She fought for a glance of Lord Sedgewick's face.

He never looked up.

"I am not a man of great strengths, my lord, nor do I possess any abilities with weapons." As the vicar spoke, he drew a pistol from his coat. "But for all my deficiencies, I am still quite capable of pulling a trigger."

"Then pull it." Henry remained rigid in his seat. He didn't think, didn't ask questions—only remained as still as possible, a statue in a world that no longer made sense.

"You cannot think this will be easy for me." Wet hair stuck to the man's skin. "Especially as a man of the cloth. Do you have any idea how this could destroy my congregation?"

"My sympathies, sir."

"Do not mock me. I have undergone far too much pain, far too much agony to be mocked." His skeletal throat bobbed. "Every one of them believed she had gone to London, but I knew the truth. I am as acquainted with Ella's hatred as I was her father's."

Hatred. The word slapped him.

"If I were any kind of man, I would have gone after her myself. I would have spared Ella from danger. I would have avenged the life you took."

"You know nothing of my wife's death." Henry almost didn't recognize his own voice, the menacing growl in this tone. The sudden need to defend himself after all this time.

"On the contrary. Lucy's father knew you were lying all along. It was only a matter of proving it." Spittle flew from his lips. "Which is what I intend to do right now—once and for all. Now get down."

Henry climbed out of the gig and stood before him.

The vicar took a step back. "All you have to do is tell me what happened. After that, the law and God may punish you."

"My wife was sick."

"You must not understand. I am going to kill you, Lord Sedgewick, if you do not expose yourself."

"Then you had better do it." Henry took a step forward.

The vicar retreated one more step. The pistol began to tremble. "There is no going back now, you see. I cannot let you live to murder Ella as you did her sister."

With another step, then another, Henry approached. He stood close enough to grasp the gun, but he did not. A part of him wanted the absurd little man to pull the trigger. Wanted to die where he stood. Anything would be easier than facing Ella. . .Pemberton.

The vicar's tight shoulders collapsed. His pistol dropped to the mud. "God have mercy on me," he muttered. "I am not a man at all."

Henry never answered. He climbed back into his gig, leaving the vicar and his pistol motionless in the rain.

Lucy's sister. He flicked the whip for the fifth time. *Her sister, come to destroy me.* He should have known. His mother had taught him well— but not well enough. By the time his wife had betrayed him, the lesson should have sealed his heart in stone.

But he'd let another woman penetrate his bulwarks. What a stupid, wretched fool!

When he reached the stables, he leaped down without bothering to take the horse inside. He ran to the manor, burst inside.

She was waiting for him. He knew she would be. She should have hidden in fear, escaped while he was away so he wouldn't kill her too.

Isn't that what she believed of him?

But no. She stood there with tears big enough that he might have thought they were real. She was more deceiving than Lucy had ever been.

"You are unharmed." Her words were strangely calm.

He ripped off his wet coat, slung his hat to the floor.

Dunn appeared in a doorway.

"Henry." Odd, that she should speak his name now, of all times. "Henry, please, I—"

"Do not give me another apology." His chest hurt. "If you would like to shoot me too, I shall provide a weapon."

She blanched. "I love you."

He hated the sound of those words. They cut him. Deep. "Get out of here."

"I love you." Again, louder this time. "I cannot deny I came here in pretense, but you must know that my heart—"

"Your heart!" His fists balled. "Your heart, Ella *Pemberton*, is as wicked as your sister's." He started past her, but she latched onto his arm.

He flung himself out of her touch. Then he leaned forward, towering over her. "You came here for the truth, Miss Pemberton, and now I shall give it to you. I killed your sister."

A wretched sound escaped her. "I do not believe you."

"I have a shirtsleeve upstairs to prove it. If you don't believe that, speak to the man who buried her."

She shook her head.

"Dunn." Henry whirled to the doorway. "Tell her, Dunn."

His steward shook his head. "My lord, I—"

"Tell her!"

Dunn's voice cracked, "She was shot when we buried her."

Ella's hand flew to her mouth. Still, she shook her head. "I cannot believe this of you. I cannot."

"Then that makes us even, Miss Pemberton, because I cannot believe you." Henry drew away from her and brushed past Dunn on his way through the doorway. He paused only feet away, however, and said without turning, "See that she is removed from Wyckhorn immediately, Dunn. She is never welcome within these walls again."

CHAPTER 20

Three servants entered her bedchamber in the west wing. Without a glance, two lifted her trunk and the other carried away her valise. The only man remaining was Dunn. "There is a carriage awaiting you outside, Miss Pemberton."

"I cannot leave."

"There is no choice."

"I won't." She lifted eyes that were blurry, stinging. Regret choked her. "Dunn, please. . .I must speak with him again."

"There could be no good in that."

"I beg of you—"

"I am sorry, Miss Pemberton." His features remained impassive, but accusations arose in his eyes. "I fear anything you could say would only hurt him more."

"I never meant to hurt him." Shaking hands clasped in front of her. "I only came for the truth."

"Which you have attained. There can be nothing else for you now."

"There is." Her heart ached. "Dunn, I love him."

Pain twisted the steward's face. "The tragedy, Miss Pemberton, is that *he* loves you." He took a step to the side and motioned her through the door, never saying a word until he had escorted her to the carriage. "You had better not return, Miss Pemberton."

She flinched against the words, as the carriage door slammed shut. "I intend to."

∽

Henry entered the room. He shut the door carefully without sound, so as not to disturb the silence. There was no sense fighting his curse.

He'd already defied it once. Even believed, in some unbroken place in his soul, that the grace of God had permitted him happiness.

Fool. He took slow steps deeper into the room until he stood face to face with the life-size portrait.

Lifeless eyes stared back at him.

He had been eight when the artist had arrived at Wyckhorn. Often times, Henry would slip into the room while she posed, as fascinated with the bright colors of paint as he was with the man's strange accent.

His mother must have been fascinated too. The earnest smiles Henry had always longed for were bestowed so freely upon the stranger, and the laughter she never gave Henry's father became frequent in those hours of painting.

Not three months after the portrait was finished, his mother had left. He'd never seen her again.

God, why? Henry's fingernails sank into his palms. *Was it the painter?*

He'd always wondered, always kept a hold of the man's face in his mind. Was that what had drawn his mother away from him?

No.

He couldn't hate the artist with the strange, alluring accent—because he knew the truth. His mother hadn't loved him. Not ever. She had betrayed him for things more brilliant, just as Lucy had done.

And now Ella had betrayed him.

Stabs punctured his gut, then twisted. *Fool, fool.* Over and over again, until he felt sick with the words. *God, why did You let me be deceived again?*

He should have seen the resemblance, the same shape of her eyes, the same voice of sweetness and honey.

God. His hands gripped the framed portrait. Tears pushed at his closed eyelids. *God, why?*

Silence.

Why?

More silence, as if to taunt him, as if to deepen his hurt.

A sob pushed through. His teeth clenched as he ripped the portrait from the wall. He slung it to the ground and kicked it away from him.

His mother's cool, strange eyes stared upward.

God, I loved her. He sank to his knees and tried to muffle his miserable sounds. *I loved them all.*

꩜

The crack in the door wasn't very big, only large enough that Ewan might see the painting on the ground. And Henry. On the floor, accompanied by noises of grief.

Yes. Ewan retreated backward. *Yes, yes, let him cry.* Pain was the only thing Henry deserved. Justice was being fulfilled as if God Himself had ordained it.

From a quiet place in the stairwell, two maids whispered to each other. Most of it, Ewan didn't understand, talk of deceit and lies and Lucy's sister—but one thing he knew for sure. Miss Woodhart was gone.

The manor was returned to quietness. Death loomed again, as tangible as Lucy's hair had ever been, or as soft as her skin had ever felt.

He will pay, he will pay. Ewan slipped back through the house unseen, like the shadow of a ghost. *It is time, and Lucy is ready, and there is no one to stand against us.* He nearly wept with the joy of that thought. *Tonight.*

꩜

The carriage stopped in the middle of the road. Voices outside, then the door swung open and a drenched Mr. Beaumont climbed in.

Ella glared at him.

He took off his hat, pushed back his auburn curls, then wiped the rain from his face.

"Thank God you are safe," he said, as the carriage began to move. "I was left to innumerable thoughts of what he could have done to you."

"Why did you come?" She squeezed her hands into fists to stop the trembling. When he didn't answer, her voice rose, "Why?"

"I—I only wished to avenge your sister."

"You are lying. You did it for me."

"No, no, Miss Pemberton, not only you. My thoughts were of your father too."

"Have you forgotten your religion, vicar?"

"No, I—"

"You what, Mr. Beaumont? Are you so madly in love with me that you would stain your holy coats with blood and pollute your saintly heart with revenge?"

"Yes." Splotches of color brightened his wet face. "I would have slaughtered him for you and committed far worse sins than that. . .but I have failed. Now I can do no more than help you escape with your life before he—"

"My life is in no danger, Mr. Beaumont. And even if it were, I would not call upon a man so despicable as you to rescue me."

His lips slackened. "You have wounded me greatly."

"Then I have only repaid what you have done to me."

"Ella, please." He seized her wrist—

She swung her other hand into his cheek. Once, twice, until finally he released her. With a quick sob, she swung open the carriage door. "Driver! Driver, stop the carriage!"

The wheels came to a slow halt.

She tumbled outside. "I shall walk from here. Continue on without me."

"Ella, please," came the vicar's pleading. "Do not harm yourself on my account. It is not safe to walk unaccompanied, and you shall catch your death in this rain. . ."

But the driver frowned and shrugged. With a crack of the reins, the horses started away.

The food had no taste, the room no warmth, the air no familiar sound or scent of her.

Peter sat in his usual chair, with his head hung low over an untouched plate. A few times, he glanced up. What a pity his young eyes already knew the marks of pain. They were red, puffy, so full of questions.

Henry had no answers. "Eat, Son."

His child nodded. He pushed the pickled vegetables to the other side of his plate with his fork. Tears dropped into his food.

"Peter?"

His son's face turned away.

Sorry. The word rent through Henry as he rose from his chair and went to him. *I'm sorry, Peter.* He lifted the boy from his chair until the little arms squeezed his neck. "You're all right."

"W–why, Papa?" The tiny voice cried in his ear. "Why did she want to leave us?"

"I'm sorry, Son."

"We have to do our lessons."

"I know."

"And Mrs. Lundie has to take care of her until she gets all better." Peter's frame wracked. "Doesn't she, Papa? Doesn't Mrs. Lundie have to take care of her?"

"Peter, she is gone." Henry's voice gave out on the words. "And I would move heaven and earth to bring her back to you, but I can't."

His son never answered, only shuddered in his father's arms until Henry carried him to bed.

He tucked the bedclothes under Peter's chin. "None of this was your fault, Son." He smeared tears off the little cheeks. "You must know that. For you, she would have stayed forever."

"Then why did she leave?" Peter's chin quivered. "They all go away. Mamma and Miss Morton and Miss Woodhart. . .they all go away."

I know. Henry leaned in and pressed his lips against Peter's wet cheek. *I know, my son. I know.*

∽

Darkness came faster than Ella had expected. The rain no longer pelted. It fell softly enough to make her dress heavier.

She stumbled to a stop.

Farther ahead, the village lights of Northston beckoned to her like rays of hope.

But there was no hope. Ella did not believe in God, nor in salvation, nor in anything else she'd ever been taught by pompous fools like the vicar. She had no need for such things. She had always managed her own life quite suitably without the help of any immortal Creator.

Only she hadn't. She had managed nothing well. She had failed at everything she had ever endeavored to do—and hurt others in the doing. She had hurt Lord Sedgewick, who had never been anything but kind to her, who had given her the Bible, who had been willing to love her.

I don't know what to do. The cry awoke. *God, I just don't know what to do.*

She doubted He heard the prayer. If she were His child, perhaps He would listen. If she believed, perhaps He would care.

But she wasn't and she didn't.

God.

Her legs shook. She blinked hard against the rain.

Are You listening?

No answer. She wondered what Lord Sedgewick would tell her to do. If only the Bible hadn't been destroyed, maybe she would know. Maybe the truth she sought *was* in those pages.

Or maybe she knew the truth already. Wasn't it God who had rescued her from the flames in her chamber? Wasn't it God who had kept her awake at nights, haunting her with Lord Sedgewick's words and the verses in the Bible?

I am weary of unbelief. She covered her face with her hands. "God, do You hear me? I said I am weary with unbelief. I want to believe in You." She hesitated, swallowed. *I do believe in You.*

Her skin prickled with a presence she'd never known, a presence that crept into a place of her soul yet undiscovered. *And I want to be saved, Christ. If there's any mercy left, I want to be saved.*

∞

The damp night air wafted in from his open window, filled with scents of the sea. Long hours ago, he should have been in bed, seeking refuge in the oblivion of sleep.

But Henry desired rest as little as he desired food. *She is gone.* How sorrowful and empty rang the echo of those words. How they slipped into all of his tender places and bruised. How they destroyed a part of him he had imagined was restored.

He knew the hatred would return. Perhaps it already had, only not enough to numb him.

Should have never let her come here. How close he'd come to making her his wife. He'd been prepared to entrust her with his home, his son, his heart—all the things that meant the most to him.

But they meant nothing to her. He knew that now.

Something creaked.

Henry turned from the window. Frowned. "What are you doing?"

"Heartache keeping you from sleep, Brother?" Ewan's lips twitched, as if in a smile. "At least the one you love is not murdered."

Henry moved to latch the window. "You had better go back to bed."

"I hate my prison. I am never going back."

"Ewan—"

"No!" From the folds of his black coat, he drew a gun. "This time, I am the one to speak."

"Where did you get that?"

"Familiar?"

"I said where did you get it?"

Ewan's eyes were a strange blend of rage and amusement, his lips still swaying between a frown and a smile. "I would think you would remember. It is the gun you killed her with."

Henry took a step forward. "Give it to me."

"No."

"Ewan, I shall not say it ag—"

Gunfire blasted through the room.

Henry was flung backward, upsetting a chair, toppling to the ground. His fingers fumbled for his thigh and pressed into the wound.

Ewan edged closer. "You have been spared, Brother. You still have your life—more than you gave Lucy."

Henry lurched to his feet. Pain disoriented his vision and made his brother's eyes seem like fire. "W–what are you doing?"

"Destroying you."

"With that?" Henry's gaze dropped to the gun. "If you had desired to kill me, you could have done it then."

"I wish I had, but then I might have never known the truth. . . might never have found her words. She is dead, yet she speaks to me still. Did you know she speaks to me?"

"Give me the gun, Ewan."

"She says things in her death that she never spoke in life. . .things about you. . .about the child."

"Ewan." Henry outstretched a bloody hand. "The gun—"

"He is mine." At first they were faint, whispered words. Hardly distinguishable. Then they came again with force, "Your son is mine . . .my son."

"You don't know what you're saying."

"Don't I?"

"You're out of your head. You're mad—"

"The diary." Ewan's voice lowered. "Or did you not know your wife kept one? Did you not know she wrote of her love in those pages. . .as if she wanted me to find it. . .to know I have a son."

Henry dove forward. His fist flew into his brother's face, then he grabbed his coat, slammed him against the wall. *Lying.* Hands groping for Ewan's neck, fingers digging into his pulse. "Lying," he rasped. "You're lying!"

"No." Ewan's eyes were bright, fervent, as if he enjoyed the torture. Then his knee swung upward, catching Henry's thigh.

Pain exploded. A groan slipped from Henry's throat as he collapsed.

Ewan's foot struck his face. Once. Twice. Then another kick that made blood sputter from Henry's lips.

No. Henry lifted on his elbow. Rough hands pinned him to the floor. *Ewan—*

"No more prison," came the panted words. "I am escaping with my son. . .and there will be no more prison."

Henry ripped free, but knuckles bore down and slammed him back. "I. . .won't let you." Struggling.

Another blow. "You cannot stop me."

"I will find. . .you."

"No." Ewan's lips twisted as he bashed once more into Henry's face.

Blackness caved in, cold and vague. "No." The words gritted through clenched teeth. He tried to rise. "No. . .not Peter."

"You can keep us no longer."

No, God.

"I shall take him from you, just as you took Lucy from me." Ewan rose. "She wants it that way. The child is ours."

Henry dragged himself upward, groped for Ewan's boot.

But his brother scampered away. The door slammed shut.

And locked.

CHAPTER 21

*W*ait here, miss, and I shall fetch Miss Fitzherbert."

"Thank you." Ella dripped upon the Axminster carpet as the maid left her alone in the dark sitting room. A clock on the wall ticked away the minutes.

At last, a candle swept through the doorway, and Dorthea appeared with paper curlers tied in her hair. "My dear, dear Ella! The maid just aroused me."

Ella prevented her from a hug. "You mustn't touch me, for I am frightfully drenched and dirty."

"Oh my, but you are bandaged. Lord Sedgewick has tried to kill you—"

"No, he did not harm me." Exhaustion shook her knees. "He only asked me to leave."

"And sent you walking into the storm? My heavens, did you walk all the way from Wyckhorn?"

"I walked of my own choice."

"Oh my, but—"

"Please, Dorthea." Ella rubbed at her eyes. "I can bear no more questions."

"No, of course not. I shall have the maid heat some water while I find something for you to wear. Wherever is your luggage?"

Had she left it in the carriage? It hardly mattered. "I—I don't know."

"Never mind. Follow me upstairs." Dorthea took her arm, chatting quietly on the way up the stairs about how difficult it had been for her to conceal the secret. "Do you know how often the topic of Sedgewick arises? Talk of his new governess too—and I burdened with the knowledge I could not tell." She swung open a door. "And the social events. Dear Miss Pemberton, I could hardly look at you without giving it away. I hope you do not mind that I stayed at such a distance. I thought it may give way to suspicion if we appeared too familiar."

"Yes." Ella entered the warm room. "You did right, Dorthea."

"I thought so." She lit a candle. "My, how pale and cold you appear!"

"Just a bit weary."

"Well, do lie down, and I shall have the water sent up. You shall be comfortable in no time at all."

Ella sank to the edge of the bed. "Thank you."

Dorthea's face was empathetic and soft in the candlelight. "You are most welcome, Miss Pemberton. I am only glad to see you have not been murdered by that wretched man."

He is not a wretched man. Ella shivered and curled onto the bed. *No matter what he might say of himself, I cannot believe he murdered anyone.*

∞

Someone would have heard the gunshot. Someone was coming, had to be coming.

God. Colors made circles in front of his eyes as he grasped the doorknob. Didn't budge. *Please do not let this happen.*

He thrust his shoulder into the door, then again. He backed up and lunged for it, but the pain sent him sprawling to the floor.

Blood leaked beyond his hand, seeping down his trousers, even as he heaved himself back to his feet. A sob shuddered through him.

Ewan was taking his son. He was stealing him from his little bed.

Peter wouldn't understand. Probably wouldn't even fight, only do as he was told. He was good. He had always been good, always such a good boy. . .

Dear God, please. With another plunge, Henry threw himself against the door. Over and over and over again, until the pain made him senseless and the blood oozed onto his boots. *Please don't take my son.*

Ewan wiped the sheen of moisture from his forehead. How long did he have before the house was no longer asleep? Before the servants came running up the stairs, opening and closing doors, murmuring about the strange sound that had awakened them—just as they'd done before?

But there had been nothing any of them could do. It'd been too late. She'd been dead before she ever hit the floor.

The horrors of that night pounded at his chest as if crying to be released. They made him run faster in the darkness. They made him hope that Henry bled to death in his chamber. They made him forget any notions of killing himself, because for the first time, there was something to live for.

When he reached Peter's door, he wiped more sweat from his face. Then he threw it open and watched as the child in the bed raised his head.

"Papa?"

Ewan dashed toward him. "We have to go."

The groggy face inched backward. "Is it morning?"

"Yes, yes. . .morning." Ewan grabbed the child into his arms, startled at the way Peter's body stiffened.

"Where we going?"

"Away."

"With Papa?"

"Yes." *But not the Papa you think.*

As if comforted by the words, Peter's head leaned into Ewan's neck. He yawned, rubbed his eyes.

"Go back to sleep." Ewan's whisper echoed in the corridors. He hurried, slipped downstairs, and found the room he had not entered in so long.

Henry's study had the same smells their father's always had. Leather, books, ink—a strange mixture that drew him back into a childhood he'd hated. He approached the desk and opened just the right drawer.

The money was there, as he'd known it would be. He stuffed it into his pocket, smiled, and eased the drawer shut.

He was almost free.

"M'lord?"

"Slide the lock!"

"Oh yes, m'lord, but is everyth—"

"The lock, woman! Hurry!"

There was a mumble, a rattling sound, then the door swung open. "I heard the shouts an' bangin', m'lord, and wondered wot—"

"Get Dunn." Henry stumbled past the maid. "Get all the men. Hurry!"

"Right away, m'lord, but you be bleedin'. . ."

Henry broke into a hobbling run, his breaths coming out quick, choppy. Halfway down the stairs, he slipped and rolled. Pain exploded in waves so great they were deafening.

No. Gripped the banister. Dragged himself back to his feet. *My gun. . .got to get my gun.*

Something stirred below. The whining of a door.

"Ewan!"

No answer.

Henry lunged down the steps. The night air fanned his face as the door moved back and forth with the wind. "Ewan!" He bellowed the words as he flung himself into the darkness.

There was no answer, only the fading echo of a horse galloping away.

"Miss Pemberton?" A pause, a nudge. "Dear Ella, can you not hear me?"

Layers of sleep began to erode.

"You have a visitor awaiting."

Ella's eyes flew open. *Henry.* He had come to talk with her, to offer her a chance to explain—

"A Mr. Beaumont arrived more than an hour ago," said Dorthea, "and I could not let the poor man wait a moment longer."

Her hopes deflated. "Send him away."

"Oh, I cannot! Father is speaking with him now, and the two are getting along splendidly. How embarrassing it would be for all of us to send him away now—and him being a vicar."

A groan filled Ella's throat. She ripped back the covers and stepped barefoot onto the floor.

Dorthea crossed the room and lifted something. A dress. "Recognize this?"

"That is mine." Ella's gaze dropped to her friend's feet. "My luggage—however did you retrieve them?"

"Not I, Ella, but the vicar." Dorthea tossed her the gown. "And if you ask me, he seems a bit tender-eyed when he speaks your name."

Without looking at her, Ella took the dress. She held it close to her chest. *So had Henry.*

<hr />

Dunn's face was a blur, his voice a drone. "Lie down, my lord, I beg of you."

"I only came for a fresh horse."

"Yes, my lord, but—"

"Enough!" Henry sagged against the doorframe of the front entrance. "Now go and pack me provisions. Quickly."

"No."

Henry's gaze snapped up. "What did you say?"

"I said no, my lord, with all due respect. You and the men have been gone the length of the night. God knows how much you have bled, but I shall allow you to bleed no more. Now please, my lord, come lie down."

Never in his life had Dunn ever gainsaid him. Henry's mind hurled with a reprimand, but maybe the man was right. After all, how much could he do for Peter if he was dead?

"Fine. Hurry."

Dunn took his arm and led him into the quiet drawing room, where he positioned him on a sofa. "You stay here and I shall fetch bandages."

"And provisions."

"Yes. That too, my lord." He hurried away.

Henry slid his eyes closed, exhaustion cramping his body, his mind, his soul. He and the servants had been gone all night, following empty roads, roaming soundless woods. He would have never come back without Peter, except the horses could plod on no farther.

"I know very little of this sort of thing," said Dunn upon his return, as he ripped at Henry's trousers, "but I shall do the best I know."

"Do it quickly."

"The bullet is still there."

"Then dig it out!"

Dunn's face paled. He nodded and began to wipe the blood away with his rag. "You have seen the constable?"

"No."

Dunn reached for the knife. "Then you must allow the servants to accompany you again—"

"There's no need!" Pounding filled Henry's temples. He drew in air. "There's no need," he said again, "because I shall find him alone."

"Do you think that wise, my lord?"

"I know my brother better than anyone." Henry eyed the blade in Dunn's hesitating hand. "Now use that."

"I am no doctor—"

"I do not care if you slice off my leg. Now use it."

Dunn nodded, murmured, "Yes, my lord. You were saying?"

"Anyone else would hinder my speed. Every minute lost, they gain distance." The knife sank into his flesh and every muscle strained against the pain. "I. . .I need every moment if I am to catch up with them."

"But he will not. . ." Dunn's words caught. He dug deeper before speaking again, "He will not harm Master Peter, will he, my lord?"

"I. . .do not. . .know." Henry gripped the sofa and gritted his teeth.

The knife twisted farther into his wound. "But if he does…I'll kill him."

The knife twisted farther into his wound. "But if he does…I'll kill him."

Mr. Fitzherbert's comment on the weather could be heard from the hallway, followed by the vicar's monotonous praise of the view from his church bell tower, from which point he could detect an upcoming storm.

"Yes, yes, storms are much better borne when one is made aware," answered Mr. Fitzherbert. "Do you not think so, Mrs. Fitzherbert?"

Ella entered in time to see his wife smile and nod—until her gaze swung to the doorway. "Miss Pemberton, you are here at last."

Ella curtsied.

The vicar came to his feet. "I hope you were not disturbed on my account."

"Yes, I was."

Mrs. Fitzherbert gave a small gasp.

"Though Dorthea has informed me that you returned my things, for which I should be grateful."

"Yes," said Mrs. Fitzherbert. "That was a most *kind* gesture, Mr. Beaumont."

The vicar clasped his hands, then unclasped them. "Won't you sit, Miss Pemberton?"

Ella sat without looking at him.

He had no more than returned to his own seat before he sprang back up. "Perhaps you would enjoy a walk? I am certain Mr. and Mrs. Fitzherbert would relish the return of their privacy."

Both offered denials, but the vicar still approached her. He held out his hand. "Shall we?"

With her back stiff, Ella grimaced as he walked her outside, where he directed them to a small garden path that wound around the house. When they were out of view of the windows, Ella jerked away her hand. "I must speak with you."

"And I with you." His steps slowed. "In hindsight, I realized the error of my injudicious actions. But please know that if I have hurt you

213

in any way, I have done far worse to my own dignity."

"And what of Lord Sedgewick?" She tried to curb the anger, but a bite still sharpened her voice. "Have you any inkling of what you have done to him?"

"He does not concern me. Nor should he concern you, if I may be so bold."

"You may not be so bold," she snapped. "And he does concern me."

"What are you saying?"

"I am saying you may forever put away any notions of gaining my heart, sir. It has already been taken."

He blanched. "Him? You have fallen prey to that…that blackguard?"

"You know nothing about him."

"Only that he killed your sister—"

"I know him incapable."

"And your father?"

Fury stirred. "What about him?"

"What would he say to such a thing? If you recall, he wanted only for you to marry a man who would not harm—"

"My father wanted me to marry you, Mr. Beaumont. Let us not talk in circles, shall we?"

His shoulders caved as his eyes turned to pleading. "Is there nothing I might do to win you, Miss Pemberton?"

"No." She hugged her arms, looked away. "No, I am afraid not, sir. I think you had better leave."

"What shall I tell your mother and sister?"

"Tell them nothing."

His chin dipped in a nod, but he seemed to lack a voice. Taking his hat into his hands, he offered a bow. "Perhaps you will return to Abbingston soon. I know you are dearly missed by all."

"Thank you."

He nodded again, perspiration dotted above his frowning lips. "Then this is goodbye, Miss Pemberton." He started away, returning the hat to his head.

"And Mr. Beaumont?"

He turned quickly. "Yes?"

"There is something I must thank you for." She hesitated, unable to meet his eyes. "All those years there was not one of us who could reach our father, who could offer him comfort. None, that is, save you."

A flush crossed the vicar's face. "I did not do much."

"Yes, sir, you did. You led him to Christ."

"I did not think such a religious decision would mean anything to you, Miss Pemberton."

"It didn't." Joy unfurled inside her. "Until I became a believer too."

Mr. Beaumont's face said all the things his lips never spoke, and with a teary smile, he turned and walked away.

The house was quiet when Ella returned to the sitting room. Mr. Fitzherbert stayed buried behind a newspaper, and his wife gave none-too-subtle grunts about the poor vicar.

Dorthea came to her rescue quickly enough. "Oh Ella, has your visitor left so quickly?"

"I wonder that he did not depart sooner," said Mrs. Fitzherbert, "with the sort of unamiable company he received."

Dorthea reached for Ella's hand. "Come, you have not had breakfast. We must find you something to eat."

When they had escaped the room, Ella drew to a halt. "I must ask a favor of you."

"Breakfast first, then we shall talk—"

"No, immediately. Please."

"Oh." Dorthea faced her. "Of course. Ask me anything, and I shall give it to you."

"A carriage?"

"Certainly, if you wish. Do you desire a ride? Why yes, that is just what you need. I shall go too, and you will feel much better—"

"I must go alone."

"Alone?" Dorthea's eyes widened. "You are not going back to

Wyckhorn? Surely you would not go back there."

Ella squeezed her friend's hand. "I must."

"I cannot let you."

"Dorthea, please—"

"I cannot be a part of your death, my dear Ella, for I am entirely too fond of you."

"Then I shall have to walk." Ella pulled away. "And there is nothing you or anyone else can do to stop me."

"Wait." Dorthea snatched her elbow and tugged her back. "You are ever the impish creature Lucy told me of."

"Then I may have the carriage?"

"Yes." Dorthea sighed. "You may have the carriage. I only hope it will return you."

And I can only hope it does not.

There it sat, gilded by the afternoon sun, as unchanged as it had been yesterday. Wyckhorn Manor was lovely. Sad, somber, quiet—yet ever lovely, as if God had bestowed more grace upon that rocky cliffside than anywhere else.

The carriage wheels disturbed the air, announcing to the world her entrance into a place she no longer belonged.

But her heart belonged. Would belong always, no matter what Henry said.

God. The small whisper of a prayer rent through her. The carriage stopped. The door swung open. *God, make him listen to me. Make him understand.*

With shaking limbs, she managed each step toward the entrance. The shadow of Wyckhorn fell over top of her like a shroud.

Please. At her first knock, the door ripped open—almost as if in panic.

A pale butler stared back at her. "Miss Woodhart." A pause. "I mean, Miss Pemberton."

"I must speak with his lordship."

"I—I am afraid that is impossible."

"I know he does not wish to see me, but if I may be permitted one word with him—"

"His lordship is not at home."

"Oh." Had he gone to the village? "Well, I shall wait for him."

"Another time."

"There is no other time." Her mother would have been proud as she drew on her years of training, drawing herself to her full height and using her firmest lady's voice. "Now let me in this instant."

His face growing whiter, he stepped aside and allowed her entrance. "I am sure Dunn shall want to know you are here."

"Certainly. May I see him?"

"He is in his study."

"Thank you." Ella brushed past him and navigated through the corridors that were finally—achingly—familiar. When she reached the steward's study, she tapped on the unlatched door.

"Who is it?"

She hesitated. "Miss Pemberton."

Silence, then a small sigh. "Come in."

She entered the small, leather-scented study. Sharp stabs of light escaped around the sides of the drawn curtains.

Dunn sat at his desk, fingers woven into his hair, shoulders sagging as if he'd known no rest. When he glanced up, his eyes were bleary, reddened. "You can be of no help. You might as well return to the village."

"Is that where Lord Sedgewick has gone?"

"What?"

"To the village. The butler said he was not home."

Dunn rose as if he'd aged ten years overnight. "Then you have not been told."

"Told what?"

"That Ewan has taken Master Peter." Dunn sank back into his chair with a moan. "And heaven knows if Lord Sedgewick can ever bring him back."

CHAPTER 22

He cannot be gone.

Ella darted from the study, down the halls, panic driving nails through her chest. When she reached the doorway, the butler still stood in his place, eyes snagging hers with apology.

"Miss Pemberton—"

She groped for the door, ripped it open.

"I wanted to tell you, Miss Pemberton, but I did not know if Dunn would want you to know. . ."

Warm air smacked her face as she flung herself outside. Ewan would not return him. He would escape as far away as he could and hide as long as he needed.

I should have told. She pumped her feet faster and made her way toward the stables. *I should have told Henry everything.*

Instead, she had thrown the diary into flames. She had kept her lips sealed about Ewan's appearance on their walk, about his late-night visit to Peter's room. How could she have known he would abduct the child?

I couldn't have known. The words came over and over again without balm. *I couldn't have known—could I?*

Didn't matter now. Peter was gone, and Henry was searching for him. If he never found them, he would doubtless be wild enough to kill himself. If he did find them, Ewan was likely to do it for him.

She had ruined his life in more ways than one.

"Miss?"

The shabby head of the stable boy stepped around a stall, wiping his hands on his trousers. "Can I be helpin' you?"

No. There was nothing he could do. Nothing she could do, no way she could possibly make amends for what she had done.

"Miss?"

If only she could. . .

"Miss, do you be needin' something?"

"Yes." The word was out before she had time to think. Her pulse raced. "I need you to saddle a horse."

☙

Darkness fell again. Another night. How he loved the blackness, the open air, the chill that rose his flesh.

Peter's hands wrapped around his little arms. Every once in a while, they loosened long enough to wipe the tears from his face.

"Do not cry." Ewan had breathed the words again and again but to no avail. Why could his son not listen?

A small wind rustled around them. Peter shivered in his nightgown.

"I should have brought your clothes." Ewan pressed the boy closer. "Never mind, though. It little matters. We shall be arriving soon."

"Where are we going?"

"To a village."

"Why?"

"To see your mamma. . .you will like that."

"But she went to heaven. Papa said she did."

"He lies." Ewan's hands were clammy against the leather. He should have worn gloves. "He lies about everything—and he is not your papa!" How many times did he have to tell the boy? Why could he not understand?

He will. As soon as they saw Lucy, as soon as she told him everything, Peter would believe. He would know the truth. *Yes, yes, he will.*

Ewan told himself not to worry when Peter's sobs lifted again, nor when his small frame doubled over.

He is only crying for his mamma, came the reassurance. *And they shall be together soon.*

The horse tracks had led her into the forest. Beneath a canopy of greenery and upon a floor of leaves, she had discovered a world most surreal and beautiful.

But the beauty was marred with dread, the sweet smells tainted with fear, the brilliant colors dimmed with guilt.

Then came the darkness.

She could no longer follow his tracks. There was no comfort in knowing Lord Sedgewick was just ahead, because all sense of direction had fled from her as quickly as blackness fell.

I am lost. Coldness tingled in her blood. *No, I am not lost.* What would her mother say? Rash, impetuous girl. How could she do such a thing? What did she hope to gain?

She didn't know. Henry's forgiveness was something she would never obtain. Peter's return was likely a feat too impossible for her to even assist. So why was she here?

Questions, questions, always questions. She had answers for none of them.

Something snapped.

Ella froze in her saddle, squeezed the reins. She glanced around her, skimming through the blackness, searching—was that a movement?

Doubtless an animal. She sat for a while longer, but when she heard nothing more, she urged the horse forward. The saddle rocked her, lulled her. She wondered if Dorthea would send out the constable when she didn't return. Ella could almost hear the girl's wails of murder.

A yawn escaped her, then another. Was she even going the right way? She would end up across the world if she was not careful.

Better stop. Twisting the reins around her fingers, she swung herself to the ground. "Come on, Alphonse." She tugged him toward the outline of a tree and looped the reins across a hanging branch. "We shall rest until morning."

He swung his head, as if in consent.

Then the noise again. Closer.

She didn't have time to run—

"Turn around." Something small pressed into her back as if the point of a gun.

She turned and stared into a face only barely visible in the darkness.

Her heart spiraled to her feet.

CS

"What are you doing?"

She wore a dress dark enough that he couldn't outline her figure. Couldn't even tell she was a woman.

Henry took a step forward.

And she took one back.

Hurt nipped his chest as he thrust the gun back into his coat. Was she truly afraid of him?

"Peter." Her single word came out raspy, shaken. "Have you—"

"No."

"They cannot have gotten far."

"Far enough."

"But surely—"

"Surely what, Miss Pemberton? Surely Ewan shall return my son? Surely I shall find them come morn, and this nightmare shall end? Do not underestimate my brother, Miss Pemberton." Small, spiraling fragments of anguish went through him. "Do not underestimate him."

Her breath inhaled and exhaled, then she edged forward. "I want to go with you."

"No."

"I want to help."

"No—"

"I love him too!" Now she stood beneath him, staring up into his face with all the fear, all the grief, that was pent inside of his own self. "Can't you see?" she said. "I cannot return to Northston and do nothing."

"You would be doing nothing out here," he said. "Nothing but hindering me."

"I would not slow you down."

"A chance I cannot take."

"Henry." His name again, his Christian name. Had she any idea how the sound pierced him? "Henry, you may think of me what you wish, but I must come with you—for Peter's sake."

"And what of my sake?"

Silence slithered between them, as the eyes he used to love overflowed again. Even in his hatred, they were still beautiful, beguiling.

"You can do nothing for Peter. You can do nothing for me." He forced the words past a dry throat. "In the morning, you shall return to Northston."

∽

She had long since curled by the fire he had made, with his coat over top of her and his saddle beneath her head.

Henry stoked the flames. She should've never come out here. Should've never tried to follow him, tried to threaten his bulwarks again with the sweet compassion on her face.

Perhaps her love for Peter had been real enough. It was her love for him that had been feigned.

Doesn't matter. He snapped the stick and shoved it into the flames. His wound burned. Never been so tired in his life, but he couldn't sleep. He was too afraid of where his dreams might take him, what sort of horrors they would press into his mind.

He had enough nightmares when he was awake. Nightmares of where Peter was, what had been done to him. Had Ewan struck him as he had Henry so many times? Was he in pain?

Yes, he was in pain. They were all in pain, even Ewan.

My fault, my fault. Henry held his head in his hands. His chest heaved with sobs that had no sound. *Dear God, why did you let me kill her?*

If only God had punished him then, destroyed him the day it happened.

But He hadn't. He had let Henry keep on living, and He had let him raise his son, and He had let him learn to love again.

And now He was taking it all away.

Do not do this, God. Tremors wracked his shoulders. *I will suffer anything, but spare my son—*

Something touched his shoulder.

He didn't look up, didn't pull his head from his hands. *Go away.*

"Henry. . ." Softly. "Henry, do not despair."

He wanted to escape her. He wanted more than anything to rid himself of her touch, her voice, her presence. But in the end, he only sat there, too battered to force her away.

"You must know that Peter shall be found."

If only he could know.

"And no harm will come to him."

How could she say that?

"Henry. . ."

His eyes lifted and caught hers, his anger mingling with his guilt, his guilt with his heart, his heart with his love. He was confused, bereft, even as he pushed her hand away. "Spare me your pity, Ella. I cannot bear it too."

"Is compassion pity?"

"What does it matter? I deserve none of it."

"Because of Lucy?"

"Yes."

"Because you killed her?"

"Yes." He spread his hands in front of him. The memory of blood tingled his skin. "Yes, because I killed her. What else would you have me say?"

"The truth."

"You have heard it."

"Then tell me again."

He looked away, stared into the fire. The flames crackled and popped, throwing burning ashes into the air. "It is not something you shall wish to hear about your sister."

"I want to know."

"I kept the secret for all of our sakes. I did not wish to tarnish my wife's name, nor send such news home to her family—nor did I wish for scandal to ruin my son." His thigh throbbed in rhythm to his chest. "Her love was for another." A pause. "Ewan."

She didn't speak.

"I was naive enough to be alarmed when she was missing from my bed. I took my gun. I thought something had happened to her." He massaged his leg. "I found her in my brother's chamber."

She didn't so much as flinch.

"I was in a rage, half out of my mind with anger. I don't remember much, only that Ewan and I grappled. . .struggled with the gun. . .and it went off."

"And Lucy?"

"She was hit in the neck, died before I even reached her."

Everything was quiet, the only sound the faint sputtering of the fire, the light wind in the trees.

Then her voice, small with tears, "It wasn't your fault."

"I pulled the trigger."

"It was an accident."

"Was it?" His teeth clenched. "We were fighting. . .I was so angry . . .almost wanted to kill my own brother."

"Is that. . ." She exhaled. "Is that why you pulled the trigger? To kill him?"

"I've been asking myself that question for the last five years." His head fell back into his hands. "And I don't know. God forgive me, Ella, but I just don't know."

∞

Lucy wasn't here. They stood in a town that had long since fallen asleep, beneath a sky that seemed to mock him with sniggering, twinkling stars.

A tortured groan pressed within, but he couldn't release it. He had the boy to think of now. . .his son.

"Come on." With his hand seizing Peter's, he trudged them across dirty cobblestones toward the only establishment with any lights. A tavern. He hesitated at the door. Maybe she was inside, waiting for them. Maybe she knew they'd come here.

"Lucy." He kicked his way inside, dragging Peter after him.

Seven pairs of eyes met him with suspicion. None of them soft, sapphire, and lovely.

Distress whipped through his stomach. Confused, so confused. Where was she?

Dead, came the traitorous voice. *She is dead.*

But Peter needed his mamma. She had to tell him the truth, make him unafraid. They were free now, all of them. Where was she?

"Wot you doin' standin' there, gov'nor?" A woman whose paunch made her apron swell came swinging from behind the bar. "There's not an ounce of ale to be had in the bleedin' doorway, you know."

Ewan tightened his grip on Peter's hand. "A woman." His throat tingled. "Have you seen a woman. . .a woman looking for us?"

"Not no one the likes of you would be likely to 'ave," she said. "Wot's the matter with the brat, now? He's all dressed like he's ready for Bedfordshire."

"What?"

"The nightgown, fellow! Don't he 'ave no clothes?"

Ewan ignored her. "We have to wait. . .to rest. . ."

"Aye, aye, spit it out, will you?"

"A room." Ewan dug into his pocket and pulled out a few coins. He marched forward and pressed them into the woman's beefy hands. "We need a room. . .to rest."

"Follow me." With her dingy apron strings swaying, she preceded them through a narrow hallway and pounded at a stained door. "Out of there, Voisey! I 'ave a real lodger for once, now 'urry it up."

The door yanked open, and a bedraggled man came stumbling out, greasy hair strung into dazed eyes. "Wot the—"

"Out, out!" The woman reinforced the words with a hard shove.

Her voice changed as she turned back to Ewan. "Inside, gov'nor, and the room's all yours. Want me to bring some bingo for you?"

"No. . .no."

"Not a drinkin' man, eh? Well, just as well, I reckon." She started to leave but swung back only a few feet away. "And mind our little friends the rats, that they don't be climbin' in your bedclothes to snuggle. Fearsome little devils, they are."

Ewan pulled Peter into the room before the woman could say more. The door made a final, wretched click—almost like the slamming of a prison cell.

Peter stood in the center of the room and looked up at him. Tears again, brighter than ever, but he uttered nothing.

Don't. Ewan withdrew from the child, flattened himself against the wall. *Do not look at me like that.*

The boy still stared, with eyes as hurt and empty as Lucy's had been in death.

No, no. Panic drove away the bliss of freedom, replaced it with chains that were new and cold. Ewan sank to the floor. He held his son's eyes. "I see Lucy." The only thing he could think to say, the only comfort he could grope for. "I see Lucy in your face. . .your eyes. . ."

"I—I want to go home."

"No."

"Please." A shudder. "Please, I—I want my papa. I want to go home."

"No. . .cannot." Ewan thought of Wyckhorn, the bedchamber where Lucy's presence still visited him, the halls that reminded him of her embraces. *Yes, yes, go home.*

But Henry's image cut through the hope. He could not go back. They could never go back.

With tears coming loose, Ewan crawled toward his son and grabbed him.

At first Peter struggled, pushed away, wept.

But in the end, he finally became still in Ewan's rocking arms, as if freedom was as bitter to him as it was to Ewan.

She knew he was awake. Every few minutes, leaves crunched beneath his Hessians, or a twig snapped as he rounded the fire.

When the sounds approached her, her heart quaked. She was tense, paralyzed—then he prodded her shoulder through the fabric of his coat.

"Wake up." His breath washed over her.

She forced open her lids.

Early morning sun cast his face under faint light, revealing a man very unlike the Lord Sedgewick she had known days before. His jaw was shadowed with growth, his skin discolored and sunken, his eyes the palest color of ice. He appeared wretched enough to be ill.

"I shall leave you now." He rose and frowned at her.

She struggled to her feet, his coat in her hands. *No.* Emotions made a slow circle around her heart, around his, binding them together. If only he could sense it too. *Please, I want to go.*

He took one step back. "You know the way, I presume?" Hard, dry voice. When she didn't answer, he said again, "Miss Pemberton?"

"Yes." Her temples hammered. "Yes, I know the way."

"Then you require no assistance from me?"

"None at all."

He nodded. Didn't meet her eyes. "Very well." Lips pressed tightly together, he turned and limped toward his horse, one hand gripping his thigh as if he had been injured.

Such wounds will heal. Ella's vision blurred as he mounted. She gripped his coat tighter against her chest. *The ones I inflicted will not.*

Nor would the ones he'd inflicted upon himself.

He had told her everything. Did she despise him, fault him? All through the night, she'd lain on the other side of the fire and wept. The sounds were muffled as if she hoped he didn't hear.

But he did.

And every tear cut through him.

Don't care. Henry hurried his horse past the trees, farther away from her. *Doesn't matter.* She'd shown him nothing this morning, no sign of how she felt. He longed for the days her tongue had lashed him, jabbed him without hesitation. Her silence was foreign. How much easier it would have been to bear her insults rather than her voiceless tears. But what did it matter?

If she didn't blame him, he blamed himself. If she didn't hold him responsible, Ewan did. If she didn't hate him, she should.

My God. Henry shut his eyes. *For once, let me know the truth. I need to know if I tried to kill. I need to know why the gun went off.*

There was no answer.

Please, God.

Nothing still.

And the woods were as lifeless as his soul.

CHAPTER 23

A shot shattered the silence.

Ella froze in front of her horse.

Then it happened again.

Leather reins slipped from her fingers so fast she couldn't grope for them. "Alphonse!"

The horse reared, stomped, and then reared again.

"Alphonse, easy—"

Another gunshot exploded. Eyes wild with terror, the animal bolted.

Ella broke into a run. *No.* Adrenaline increased her speed. Where were they coming from? Gunshots—

Something latched onto her dress. A branch. The dress ripping sounded as loud as the distant shots. She slid onto the prickly forest floor, needles driving into her arms, her neck, her cheek. She lay still, barely breathing. *What is happening?*

She waited. One minute. Two minutes. Three. Was it safe?

With a grunt, she pushed herself up and swatted needles from her hair. *Alphonse.* After hours of riding, she'd dismounted and led him onward on foot, hoping the road was somewhere ahead.

The shots had frightened them both.

Now what?

Did she follow her horse back into the denser woods? Or was the road just ahead, as she'd imagined?

Frustration filled her. She was beginning to share her mother's bad opinion of horseflesh. When had she ever needed the assistance of one so much and been failed so miserably?

"My."

A whoosh of air left Ella's lungs, as a man stepped out in front of her. Her blood turned cold. She hurled herself backward until a tree stopped her.

The man approached. Beneath a battered continental hat, a round face peered at her with flaming cheeks. Long, stringy hair curled to the tops of his shoulders. "My," came the word again, as if in surprise. He lowered his gun. "What's a biddy like yourself doing alone?"

Alone. The echo of his tone chimed in fast pace with her heart.

"Hmm?"

"I..." She forced herself to stand straight, tall, as if his presence did not affect her. "I am not alone, thank you, sir."

"Not alone, eh?" A smile distorted his smudged face. His eyes did a quick scan. "Others hiding in the treetops, are they?"

"Do not be daft, sir."

"Me? What a nasty charge, indeed."

"I fear I can supply a far nastier one."

Patchy brows arched.

Ella nodded toward the gun. "You are undoubtedly the bird-witted fool who so recklessly frightened away my horse and disturbed nature's quiet."

"Blameworthy, I am."

"Have you no sense at all?" Anger stampeded away her fear. "Had I been riding my horse instead of leading him, I might have been killed!"

"Ah, but you are right. A fool thing it was to be shooting at a poor ol' fox, for the greedy hope of filling my groaning stomach. I stand chagrined." The man did a slight bow and doffed his hat. "What can a poor fellow do to make amends?"

"Save finding my horse, there is very little."

"We must think of something."

"I am sure there is nothing. Alphonse is doubtless long gone."

"And your companions?" His eyes glittered with unsettling amusement. "Will they not share a mount with you?"

Ella's fingers curved into tight balls. She looked away without answering.

"If only all liars were as unpracticed as you, my biddy." He stretched out dirty, red-tinted fingers. "Clement Solomon Becker, miss, and you have not a reason to fret."

She stared at his hand without moving. "Sir?"

"Waiting beyond those trees, my maiden, is a wagon." The smile again, slithering slowly without ever reaching his eyes. "Allow me to amend my wrongdoings by offering you a ride."

She should have resisted him. She should have declined his offer and retreated into the woods in search of Alphonse—and let God handle matters if she never found the animal.

But after three small shakes of her head, the man had merely shrugged and started off.

Fear had clamped around her throat. To be left alone in strange and foreboding woods *with* a horse was hazardous enough. To be left alone *without* a horse was terrifying.

Besides, the man could not be all that bad, could he? A little dirty, a little uncouth, but certainly not the sort of man she need fear—right?

So in the end, she had sped after him and climbed aboard the wagon, which was waiting alongside the road just as he'd promised.

He settled next to her with a smirk. "Care to handle the ribbons, biddy?"

"My name is Miss Woodh—err—Miss Pemberton." How long would it take for the lie to dismiss itself? She took the leather reins he offered.

"Thank you, my maiden." He leaned back and situated his flintlock musket between his legs. "If the lady thinks she can bear up to the task, I'll be cleaning my gun."

"I must reach Northston. I presume you are willing to take me there?"

"I offered you a ride, now didn't I?"

"Yes." She gave the reins a small ripple and turned the wagon back onto the road. No more had she done so when he reached over and snatched the reins from her grasp. "What are you doing?"

"Pardon me, lady, but you're going the wrong way."

"I most certainly am not—"

"Northston, you say?"

"Yes."

"Well, then, 'tis a jolly good thing I came along when I did, else you would've landed yourself in Linby."

"Linby?"

"Eh, my biddy. 'Tis a small village, one I'll be passing through myself." He bullied the horses into a sharp turn until their wagon faced the flat, northward horizon. "After I take you to Northston," he added, with slanting lips. "Of course."

"No." The small word, forced out by empty gums, caused Henry's chest to tense. "No, me good sir, I hain't seen no such people."

"The boy is five, fair-faced, light hair."

"No," the cobbler persisted. "You been to the blacksmith?"

"Yes."

"An' Darby's tavern?"

"Where can I find it?"

The cobbler turned back to the door of his shoe shop, answering as he locked the door, "Down the street an' past the church house. Dreadful, I say, that the two should be so bloomin' close together. . ."

Henry didn't remain long enough to hear the rest. He plowed through a puddle in the road, sidestepped a fishwife with her tots, and jogged toward the church. As soon as he'd passed the stone building, a smaller structure caught his eye—rustic, faded, and unsightly in the shadow of the church.

He pushed his way inside and approached the counter.

A woman rose from behind the counter with a rag and wet hands. "Wot 'ave we here?" A grunted laugh. "Two 'andsome faces—an' all in the space of two days. I'm a-feelin' rightly honored, gov'nor."

Two. Henry's hopes bludgeoned the walls of his chest. "Who was the other?"

"Wot?"

"The other gentleman. Did he have a boy—"

"Strange sort of cuffin, he was. But aye, he had a boy—an' a sad one, to be sure."

Henry's palms pressed into the counter, and his breath caught with the words, "Are they still here?"

∞

Ella rubbed her arms, her back screaming against the jostling seat. Gathering clouds hurried the shadows of evening and intensified her discomfort. "Must you drive so carelessly?"

"A thousand pardons, lady." He lowered his continental hat on his forehead. "My other passengers have not complained the length of the journey, you see, and myself"—his huge shoulders shrugged—"well, I don't be minding the bumps."

Ella glanced at the back of the wagon. Woolen blankets hid the oblong outline of what lay beneath them. "Passengers?"

"Aye, two of them."

"I cannot imagine what you mean." Her eyes shifted to his slowly. "I am the only one here."

"Only living one."

A knot jumped in her throat. She forced her gaze ahead. "You mean..."

"Dead they are, to be sure. On the left is Mr. Ashbrook, fine fellow of rather quiet manners—and on to the right is his son, young Ashbrook, of equal silence." A small pause. Then, in a dragging voice, "God rest their souls."

Ella folded her fingers together in her lap. She forced her eyes down. "Relatives of yours?"

"No, but dear Mrs. Ashbrook—mother and wife, I presume—is paying a fat price for their deliverance to Quinbury." And with the words, the sky began to let loose tiny droplets of water. "What do you think of that, my biddy?"

"Nothing, I'm sure." Ella breathed in the moist air. "How long until we arrive in Northston?"

He didn't answer.

"Mr. Becker?"

With one hand dabbing away the moisture on his brow, his gaze slid to hers. Then went lower. Lower. Lower again, until his eyes rested on the tear of her dress. "What a shame such a lovely piece of finery should be wasted." His cheeks dotted with color. "And all to my blame too."

Unease rushed heat up the back of her neck. "Are you deliberately avoiding my question, sir, or are you uncommonly deaf?"

A smile, a chuckle, then another snap of the reins. "Perhaps we should lay the blame to that fox, eh? Weren't for him—"

"Mr. Becker." Ella sat straight in her seat, teeth grinding. "If you do not answer me, I shall—"

"Shall what?" The question drawled with an air of humor, but the laugh that followed seemed brittle, threatening.

Ella whirled, threw a foot out of the wagon.

A giant hand yanked her back. Seams ripped. "Not so fast, my biddy."

She writhed out of his touch. "What—what do you think you're doing?"

"Trying to keep you from tumbling over."

"Then stop and let me down."

"A fool I'd be if I did that." In an instant, his pudgy red fingers pulled a pistol from his coat. "Besides, I've an obligation now, haven't I? A debt to you, so to speak—and do not think that Clement Solomon Becker leaves his dues unpaid."

Ella scooted away from him, squelching a panic that suffocated her. *No. . .*

"Now look. Is that a village up ahead?"

Housetops and smoking chimneys jutted into the air, their sight a mixture of terror and relief.

"Not Northston, I fear, but I didn't think you would mind a wee change of plans. Besides, Linby has the most charming. . .quarters. Very private, you know?"

The wagon's wheel dropped into a pothole and climbed back out, almost unseating her. She licked dry lips. "I shall scream," she managed, clinging to the wagon seat. "Release me this moment, or I shall scream."

"With only a bird or two to hear." The misty wind rustled his greasy waves. "And what a shame. Then you'd have to join Mr. Ashbrook and his son—a fate I'm sure both of us would rather avoid."

The steaming bowl of mutton churned Henry's insides, brought bile to his throat. When was the last time he'd eaten? He didn't know. Hardly mattered.

He hammered his fist onto the table. "I thought you said he would be here by now."

"So I did, so I did." The woman—shouted to as Darby by some in the room—came waddling toward him with a ladle. "Tasted 'er yet?"

"No."

"I know it ain't much, but it won't kill you to 'ave a bite."

"About this man." Henry lifted his eyes. "You're certain he spoke with my brother?"

"Well, if your brother is the bloke with the kid, Voisey spoke with 'im, all right. Sat right o'er there, if you don't believe me." She pointed to a small table positioned in the corner of the room, where a constant drip of rain leaked through the poor thatch and splattered the floor. "Woke early, the man did, and right off started playin' cards with my man Voisey."

"Your husband?"

"More like the louse I keep 'round to run my errands. Husband's a despicable word, you know, and ain't neither of us made use of it in years." As if sensing his desperation, she hooked her hands on broad hips. "As I was saying, he sat there—that fellow, I mean—and played a winnin' game of faro. Then he was askin' where he might buy clothes for a small lad."

"Voisey recounted this?"

"I was passin' with drinks when I 'eard him say it."

"Where did your husband send him?"

"Didn't send him nowhere, he didn't. Our own was just about his size once, so Voisey put up an outfit on account he had no more guineas. Lost again, that's the way with my man, and the stranger took his boy an' left."

Henry raked his hands through his hair, sighed.

"But like I was sayin' earlier, Voisey went after him. Probably 'oping to talk the gent into another game, so's he can win back what he lost. He'll be back soon, though. Always is."

He didn't know if the chance was worth the wait, the lost time. What if Voisey hadn't followed them? What if, every second he sat in this chair, he was losing distance?

God. Henry pushed away the bowl of nauseating mutton, covered his face with shaking hands. *Please, God, don't let me fail.*

Besides the patter of rain hitting the canvas-shrouded coffins and wagon wheels rolling through gravel, the rest of the world was still.

Linby. In the twilight hues, the buildings seemed enormous, as if they towered with the intent of imprisoning her. *Dear Savior, do not let this happen.*

If only she had been rational instead of following a man who hated her into woods she could not navigate. Why had she done such a thing? And even after she'd found Henry, why had she allowed him to abandon her?

In her heart, she knew why.

Henry had been right. She would have been in his way, muddled his thinking, carved more burdens into his bleeding heart.

He needed no such distractions. Not if Peter was to be found.

"Whoa." The wagon wheels slowed alongside a gritty brick building, stopped in the mud. "I don't think Mr. Ashbrook and his son will be minding if we leave them here for the night, eh, biddy?"

Run, run. Racing thoughts pounded as quickly as the rain in her face. Just as soon as he started off the wagon. . .

"Now Mrs. Ashbrook might not feel too kindly about her husband and son spending the night in the rain." His teeth flashed in the growing darkness. His shoulder turned, and a foot dropped over the edge. "But like I said before, the two of them are quiet fellows who—"

Ella leaped. Her feet came down in thick mud. She plunged forward.

His shout rang after her. Rising in volume. Nearing in distance.

She sprinted around a brick corner, slammed into something hard, wooden, a crate. The impact sent her sprawling backward.

And right into engulfing arms.

No. Her scream was suffocated with a wet, pudgy hand. *No—*

"What a gutsy little wench." He jerked her around, slammed her back into a brick wall. He panted hard. "My! Have to catch my breath after that."

Her fingernails dug into his hands, but instead of a yowl, he only grinned.

"Goodness, goodness." Slowly, his grip loosened from her mouth. Slipped to her throat. "Now, shall we have a little discussion about this?"

"What. . ." She had to swallow, start again. "What do you want with me?"

"I should think that would be guessable."

"What?"

"It's simple, really." The foul scent of his breath intensified as he leaned closer. "But as I am neither a fan of rainy nights nor deep scratches, I would much rather constitute an agreement."

Slivers of horror invaded her, numbed her. "What are you saying?"

"Be my friend—or rather, my traveling companion to keep me warm on the days to come."

"A–and if I refuse?"

"Then tell me now." His fingers curled into her neck. "And you shall join Mr. and Mr. Ashbrook instead."

The creaking hinges of the tavern door groaned, chipping away at his layers of sleep.

Henry lifted his head from the table. How had he let himself doze?

"'Ello there, strangers. Weather's a nasty sort o' chap today, ain't it?"

Disappointment stung as he realized Darby wasn't speaking to her husband. How much longer before the blasted fellow returned?

"Wot'll it be, then? A good ol' pint of ale?"

"More than a pint, if you please."

"An' for the lady?"

Henry scooted his chair to look behind, where two figures had just sat at a table. *Ella?*

"You have a tongue, my biddy." The man's face turned to Ella's. "Name anything outside of Grosvenor Square, and it's yours."

She must not have seen Henry yet. Her eyes remained fixed on the air in front of her, as if staring at floating dust motes would provide the answer she searched for.

The man finally shrugged. "Just the ale, then."

What is she doing? Henry's hands slipped to the worn arms of his chair and squeezed the splintery wood. Did she know the man?

No, of course she didn't. Judging by his frayed coat and overly patched breeches, the man had never known a respectable person in his life.

Then why was she not resisting him? Why was she with him at all? And in a tavern, of all places?

He started to stand.

The whining door slammed open again, louder this time, letting in a rainy gust of cool night.

Henry's eyes did a swift circle—first catching Darby's hurried scowl of recognition, then traveling further until Ella's widening eyes met his, then on to the dripping stranger who filled the doorway.

A booming female voice filled the silence. "It's 'bout time you got yourself 'ere, Voisey."

CHAPTER 24

enry. His shoulders, cut sharp and erect, held with as much pride as the day she'd first seen him at the Rutledges' ball. The curve of his jaw—jutted and clenched. His eyes, though watching the men, were bloodshot, weary, sagging, but somehow comforting as if all his weakness could not mask his strength.

Henry. His name again. If only singing it in her mind could draw him to her. She waited for the distraction to pass, the stranger at the door to go away, Henry's gaze to settle back to hers.

But he turned his back instead. "I shall have a word with you, man," drifted his words.

"Biddy?"

The wet stranger in the doorway moseyed toward Henry's table. They both sank into chairs.

"My pretty, pretty biddy."

Henry's chair scooted a bit, angled just enough that if he glanced over, he would have a clear view of her. But why wouldn't he look—

"Uh-hum." Clement tugged a tendril of wet hair from her bun. "Do pay attention, my maiden, or we shall never get acquainted."

Rage demanded she swat him away. She clenched her fists instead. One move back into his coat and the point of his pistol could be looking down her throat.

"Sure you'll have no ale?"

She turned her face away.

In response, the man's fingers jerked her hair.

She winced, cracked her lips—

"Now, now," he whispered. "Mustn't forget Mr. Ashbrook and his son, eh?"

Tears built, grew, overflowed. She swatted them away. "You are despicable."

"Among other things."

She caught the motion of Henry's head, then stilled as his eyes finally drifted to her.

Please. The pleading ushered more tears. *Please help me, Henry, please—*

"That was a quick downin', gov'nor." A hefty woman marched in front of her view. "Want some more, do you?"

"No." Clement's hand slithered around her wrist. "Not as thirsty as I thought."

"Mayhap a bite o' mutton, then?"

"No, but a room, perhaps."

"It'll cost you two pence."

"No price at all." With one hand still on her wrist, he dug into his vest and slid the money across the table. Then he rose to his feet, tugging her along with him. "We'll see the room now, if you please."

"Follow me, gov'nor."

Ella's eyes made a frantic dart for Henry, but he seemed engaged in what the other man was telling him.

"No sense dragging, my biddy."

A few more paces and they would be passing into a hallway, trapped within dingy walls, doomed—

"That's far enough." Henry's words sliced the air, low, chilling.

Clement froze first, then her.

"I'll be right with you, gent," yelled Darby, as she continued her first step into the hall. "Lemme show these folks to their—"

"I'm afraid that will not be necessary." Henry approached, scooping up the two pence still left on the table. He tossed them at Clement. "Your refund, sir."

"By George, what is this?"

"Not much of anything, unless you care to rile me." Henry neared another step. "Which I doubt you do."

The man's fingers became possessive on her wrist. "Forgive my saying so, gent, but you hardly look the brawler."

"Shall I deliver a demonstration?" Another step forward. Henry's fingers splayed, curled, then spread again, as if preparing to deliver a blow.

Just as quickly, her wrist dropped free. "No, no, my good man." Clement's voice shrilled at the same time his cheeks dappled red. "If you would rather we move on, we'll be right on our way—"

"I am certain you'd do better alone, sir."

"Alone?"

"Yes." Henry took a final step until he towered over the shorter man. "Alone."

Without so much as a glance her way, Clement Solomon Becker slinked away from Henry's shadow, beelined for the door, and banged his way outside.

Henry was torn between the traitorous need to pull her toward him, or the faint warning to step away. He did neither. "Who was he?"

Wet hair plastered to the side of pale cheeks. The cheeks with tears. The cheeks he longed to slip his hands across. "That hardly matters." Her bottom lip quivered. "Thanks to you."

Thanks to him? She wouldn't have fallen prey to such a man had he not been senseless enough to leave her alone. More guilt pumped ire into his veins. "You shouldn't have followed me in the first place."

No retort.

"You had no right to."

She looked at him, as if at any moment her composure would crumble away.

He hadn't the heart to say more, to scold one already so punished. He grabbed her hand—frigid, tiny, shaking—and pulled her into a chair.

He sat across from her. "Are you hurt?"

She shook her head.

"Cold?"

Another shake.

He leaned in closer. "Ella, I am sorry."

"It was not your fault."

"Did he accost you on the road?"

Her sigh was weary. "Please, it doesn't matter. None of it matters." More tears. "Peter?"

"They were last seen on the road to Tresum." He held her eyes. "I intend to ride through the night."

"In the rain?"

He nodded.

"I want to go with you."

"Impossible."

"Henry—"

"I shall see about an escort before I leave, and you shall have a decent room to yourself. You must get dry." He hated the softness in his voice, the way his soul reached out and embraced her, even when his hands stayed put.

"But there is no time to find an escort."

She was right. Every moment spent cost him dearly. But what could he do?

"You can take me with you." As if she'd read his thoughts. As if the answer were simple.

He shook his head. "I shall not drag you through night and rain. I could not."

"All ladies are not made of porcelain, my lord." Was that the shadow of a smile? "Besides, I cannot see you have a choice."

He didn't want to take her. He didn't wish to expose himself to one who could hurt him so easily, who could destroy him so effortlessly.

But she was right. His son's life was in his hands.

He had no choice.

Sometime through the night, the rain stopped. The storm clouds that had obscured the moon parted, allowing silvery light to cast its beam around the world.

She wished for the darkness again. How much smaller the pain when she did not have to look at him.

He rode before her, his hat crowning his head, his tailcoat much darker with the stain of water. His shoulders slumped. She knew he tried hard to keep them straight, to keep his back erect—but in the end, they only caved again. When had he last slept? When had she?

Every hoof squished and sloshed in the road. Tree branches quivered and moaned. Somewhere far away, a tawny owl lifted a low *kee-wick, kee-wick, kee-wick.*

If only she were home. If only she were nestled in the chair at Abbingston Hall, with Matilda humming sweet notes and her mother fussing at the draft in the air. . .ever fussing. . .

"Do you suppose we should position our chairs closer to the hearth, my dears?"

Kee-wick. Kee-wick. Kee-wick.

"Yes, yes, we must certainly. It is uncommonly chilly this evening, and above all, we must stay warm. . .very warm. . ."

"Ella?"

Her head snapped up, just as she straightened from a dangerous lean. Had she—?

"You were asleep." His horse retreated backward until he faced her in the moonlight. "We must stop."

"No."

"I shall not have you ill with fatigue." Even as he spoke, his own weariness seeped the life from his tone. Did he ever once consider himself?

She pulled her gaze toward the sky. "It shall be morning soon. We cannot afford the lost time."

"Nor your illness."

"I assure you, I am more than capable." She told her lips to lift, to smile. "Truly."

In answer, he only nodded. In the soft, bluish hues of moonlight, he urged his horse back ahead and plodded on.

⁂

Another town, another place. Yes, the people said. They were here, they said. No, the boy wasn't harmed, they said.

But what did they know?

Of course, he was harmed. He had been ripped away from all he knew, kidnapped into a dangerous fleet of madness. Oh, but to hold him, to comfort him!

"Well?" Ella stood in a dress that was no longer soaked, but a wrinkled mess. "Have they been here?"

"Yes." He brushed past her and grabbed the reins. Didn't mount, though. Little point. Not when he had no idea where to go. "He could have taken any of three roads from here."

"Surely someone must have seen them depart."

Hope glided past his doubt. Yes, she was right. Wasn't she?

God, make her be right.

"We shall ask everyone," she said. "God in His kindness would not abandon us now."

He glanced to the face bathed in morning sunlight, into the cheeks ripe with color, even after such a wretched night. Why should she speak of God when she couldn't believe in Him?

He pulled his mind from such a distraction. Draped the reins back over a white fence. Cupped her elbow.

"Where are we going?"

He led her across the street, where a small inn was settled between a dressmaking shop and a library. "First, I am going to secure you a room for a few hours of rest."

"And you?"

He swung open the inn door. "I am going to turn Tresum topsy-turvy until I discover which road they took."

⁂

The tap came once, twice—but before she could open her eyes, it swung open. "Miss Pemberton?"

She jolted from the bed, ripped away the coverlets.

He stood in the doorway as propriety demanded. Did he forget the sweet night he had rescued her from a nightmare? When he had hovered over her and spoken softly of his love?

"I must depart immediately."

His words struck a chord of dread. Why had he not said "we"?

"A stage will be leaving in the morn which will transport you back to Northston." He thrust a hand into his pocket. "Here are the funds—"

"You may keep them." She rose. "My plans are unaltered."

"They took the road for Quinbury. It cannot be reached in a day and there are no inns along the way." His eyes bore into hers. "I have no wish to compromise either of us."

"There is no need to be concerned for your reputation, my lord."

"Only for yours."

"Mine is my own concern."

He scowled, but not before she caught the faintest light of humor in his gaze. With a grunt, he reached out and took her arm. "You are quite the impossible creature."

Strange, how the strong hand dragging her from the inn felt so much like loving affection. If only it were.

He was bleeding again. The crimson stain on his trousers was growing. She was sure to notice and he didn't want her to, didn't wish for her pity.

With one hand gripping his thigh, he rode faster. She'd just have to keep up. The warm hours of morning had ebbed into a bleak, gray afternoon. Was it going to rain again?

Heaven forbid such an agony. He was cold enough already, chilled deeper than the congenial weather should have made him. *Must You curse us with more rain?*

But as the afternoon shifted into evening, the somber clouds never once wept their tears. As if God had answered his prayer. As if God, in this one instance, had lent a bit of mercy.

Forgive me. He shouldn't blame his Savior for problems he

deserved, torments he had wrought. *I shall bear any punishment. Send the rain to devour me, but just don't let my son be harmed.*

"My lord?"

He drew the reins and turned in his saddle. Already, the dusk made her face less distinguishable, if no less lovely. "Yes?"

"It is nearly dark."

He didn't answer.

She nudged her horse closer. "Shall we ride through the night?"

Yes, we must. If they were ever to find Peter, if they were ever to make up the distance lost. But even as the thoughts persisted, he knew they couldn't. Her body was as wilted as his, her eyes as pleading as they had been in Darby's tavern when the strange man had held her captive.

The weary horse beneath him would not make it through the night. "No." He shivered. "No, we shall find a place to rest."

She nodded and kept up with his pace until he spied a small barn in the near darkness.

"This way," he said. He led her away from the road and down the small meadow, where they dismounted and walked their horses toward the leaning structure. He pried open the door, motioned her in.

Why must she be here?

The door rattled with finality when he eased it shut. The darkness swallowed them alive. The even sound of her breathing disrupted the quiet.

She turned. "There are no animals."

"I did not think there would be." He strode past her and took her reins. Tried not to notice the way her fingers brushed his. Tried not to inhale her scent.

"How did you know?"

"We have not passed a farm in miles." He pulled both horses into separate stalls with dry hay. "This was probably abandoned years ago."

As if in testament to his statement, a wind made the boards overhead creak and groan. Somewhere in a corner, the distinct flutter of wings soared past them.

A shudder shook her, but her lips uttered no distress. How would

Miss Tilbury have coped? He must be beyond exhaustion if he was thinking of her.

"Here." Slipping his hands on her shoulders, he guided her through the blackness and into an empty stall. He kicked through moldy, damp hay to ensure no varmints were burrowed within. "Just lie down there and I shall get you something to eat."

"Thank you. I am quite starved."

He nodded, walking away from her. *Why must she be here?* The thought again, until it rooted itself into his bed of anger. Cultivating, growing, overtaking. *God, why?*

He dug into the saddlebags, retrieving bread, cheese, a tinderbox, and an unlit candle. Dunn had packed well, almost as if he'd known all along there would be two of them.

Which was impossible, of course. No one could have possibly known.

Least of all Henry.

With the provisions, he made his way back through the darkness. If only he'd had time to prepare his heart, to let the wounds heal into scars.

But the pain was too fresh, the hate too unsettled, and he didn't even know how to fight. He was defenseless.

He reentered a stall that was small, stifling—and sat down beside a woman whose eyes were already snatching his.

"Is that a candle?"

"Yes." He handed her the chunk of bread, then the linen-wrapped cheese. "Eat all you wish."

She ripped the bread in half and took a bite. "Mmm, this is good."

He didn't respond, merely focused on the tinderbox until he had nursed a flame. He touched it to the candle.

A flickering, orange glow forced back the darkness. How softly the light rested upon her face, catching her hair, illuminating her eyes.

Then her gaze lowered. The bread slipped past her fingers and landed in her lap. "My lord."

He knew without looking. Didn't answer, didn't move.

"My lord," she said again. Then her eyes lifted. "Henry, you're bleeding."

"It is nothing."

"Nothing?"

"Yes." He exhaled. "Nothing."

Her hand reached out—

He snatched her wrist before her fingers ever alighted on his thigh. "Ella, no."

Her pulse became frantic beneath his touch. "It must be attended to."

"Not by you."

"Am I so despicable?"

Despicable? Yes, she was that and a thousand other things to him. She had deceived him, betrayed him, slaughtered him in more ways than she could ever know.

And now she was burying him alive.

"Henry." Choked. "Have I no hope of ever obtaining your forgiveness?"

"Would it really be such a trophy?"

"Not a trophy." Tears slipped free like rivers, blazing with the light of the candle. "But I know I can never know happiness without it."

If his hurt were not so unbearable, he might have eased the pain in her eyes. He might have offered the forgiveness she begged for. He might have smeared away the tears that came so quickly.

But he couldn't.

The moments came and fled, with her eyes never once leaving his and the tremble of her shoulders wracking harder.

Then a sound escaped. A small sob, one she caught in the palms of her hands, even as she turned her face away from him.

He pulled himself to his feet and fled the stall. The candle shook in his grasp. *God, this is more than I can bear.*

∞

The slamming door echoed into the stillness.

He is gone. Ella sat with her hands wound around her knees, salty streams burning her dry lips. Another sob depleted her strength. *No, no, no.*

He couldn't go out there. There was no shelter against the cool wind—and what of his leg?

She dragged a hand across her eyes. Pain exploded, her heart shattering from the pressure. *Peter.* The name penetrated and buried her deeper. *Peter. What is to become of all of us?*

If only they could be returned to Wyckhorn, where they had played in the garden, smiled in the corridors, and laughed at the breakfast table. She wished they had never left.

Or that she had never come at all.

No, that couldn't be true. Lord Henry Sedgewick had shown her Christ. In the midst of all their lies, an ounce of truth had wiggled through and changed her. For that, she would be eternally grateful.

It was all she had left.

Rubbing away the tears, she came to her feet. She gathered the bread and cheese and slipped through the darkness without sound. When she reached the door, her veins surged with cold. Dare she follow him?

She gave the wood a small push.

A whine, a moan, then the door swung back in a gust of wind.

Ella took one step into the night.

Positioned along the side of the barn, Henry sat with the candle by his leg, his bloody trouser ripped open at the wound. His head snapped around. "What are you doing?" Was it her imagination, or were his words uncommonly frail?

She inched toward him with her bread and cheese. Pitiful truce offering. She laid it beside him nonetheless.

For a moment, she thought he would say nothing. Then he peeled back red-stained fabric. "Dunn lacked the foresight to include bandages in my provisions."

She hunkered beside him. "Perhaps this." Quickly, she unwrapped the cheese from its linen and thrust it toward him. "Is it large enough?"

He tossed the old aside, grabbed the new. "Yes." Husky voice. "This is fine."

The small praise wrestled back the demons of his former words. She rose, swallowed, turned to leave—

"Ella?"

Her hand paused on the door at the same time her heart ceased to drum. "Yes?"

"Thank you."

Another sob edged up her throat. "You are welcome, my lord." And she hurried back inside with the horses.

CHAPTER 25

*T*wice, he passed by it without glancing over. He only clung to his son's hand and tried to keep his feet moving. *No, no.*

Ewan stopped, exhaled. *Must walk away.* Yet even so, he pivoted back around and dragged Peter with him.

The entrance to the Quinbury gentlemen's club stared at him with luring eyes, and just when he shook his head again, the tall door swung open.

Out stumbled a gentleman whose cravat was stained with sweat, whose eyes bore the dazed look of one who had lost a great deal.

But I won't lose. Ewan tugged Peter out of the man's way. *Our funds are dwindling, and I must provide.*

After all, he had a son to think of.

He had Lucy to think of.

Straightening the lapels of his coat, Ewan entered a tall-ceilinged room with chandelier light and evening shadows making a clashing war. Top hats, a few feather plumes, worn red chairs, and giant rounded tables filled every inch of space.

Peter peered up at him. Little brows pushed together in confusion.

"Just stay beside me," Ewan said, "and remain silent." As if the child would really cause commotion. Indeed, he had not spoken in days. Or had it been weeks? Years?

Ewan hardly knew. All he understood was the running, the escaping. He'd never realized it would be so hard, or that Lucy would remain so elusive. Where was she? Didn't she know they were waiting on her?

They needed her, the both of them. Needed her more than life. Needed her more than this.

But right now, this was all he had.

"So there I was with thirty-two cards and—ahhh!" The backside of a tailcoat bumped Peter against the wall, making a sconce clatter. "Excuse me—oh my. Why the devil is there a lad in here? Of all the things." And the gentleman hiccupped and staggered away.

Ewan pulled Peter back to his feet. "This way." Body heat and cheroot smoke inundated them as they squeezed into the room designated for the game of hazard.

As soon as they crossed through the doorway, a gentleman tossed up a die.

Ewan caught it quickly. *No, no.* The detested warnings of Henry and his father returned to rake at his conscience. They had never wanted him to gamble, never trusted that he was capable of profitable luck. Perhaps there had been debts, but if they had only let him play longer, he could have paid them in full.

Yes, yes. His palms perspired around the cold die. *Yes, yes, I could have won.*

A familiar, pulsing thrill entered him. He motioned Peter toward an empty corner. There was no one to stop him now, no one to stand in his way.

And I will win.

⌣

The sun was already poking through the cracks in the old barn—and still he hadn't stirred.

Ella took one more step. Hay and boards creaked under her, so she stopped. Should she wake him?

Yes, Peter needed them. Every lost second dashed their chances into smaller fragments.

But in the end, she sank to the ground and sat there, staring four feet away at a man whose lashes were longer than she'd ever realized.

Heat, shame, emotion turned her heart upside down. She shouldn't stare like this, shouldn't devour every crevice of his face as an ogling child.

But I may never see him again. After all this was over, any remnants of Miss Woodhart would be dead. Only Miss Pemberton would remain—and Lord Sedgewick had never fallen in love with that young woman.

I cannot lose him.

An errant piece of hay tickled the side of his face, making one of his eyes twitch. Hair, dark and untamed, fell across his forehead with sweat wetting the tips.

Upon quick glance, one might have mistaken him for a street beggar—his chin darkened with growth and his skin smudged and colorless.

But even then, beneath all of that, honor shaped his expression. Strength held his lips in a line that teetered between despair and hope.

And pride, always pride. Pride she had hated, she had mocked—but pride she now loved, for it had built a man stronger than she'd ever known.

As if sensing her scrutiny, his lashes eased open. At first he stared through groggy, narrowed lids. Then realization struck. "Why did you not wake me?" He forced himself up. "How long has there been light?"

"Not long."

"How long?"

"I do not know, but your rest—"

"My rest is nothing to Peter's life." He reached for the stall and lifted himself. His knees swayed, buckled—

Ella scrambled forward. Her arms slid around a shirt that was mopped with sweat, as his arms came in around her.

"Sorry." Deep in her ear, unstable. He eased himself away. "I didn't mean to—"

"You're fevered."

"No."

"And you're weak."

"No—"

"Henry, you cannot keep on like this."

"I have no choice!" Blazing eyes swung to hers. "What would you have me do, Ella? Find a hole to sleep in while my son is being stolen from me?"

"I did not mean that."

"Then do not gainsay me. We must keep going." He started past her.

Ella grabbed his arm. Heat soared through the fabric and scorched her hand. "But you shall do Peter no good at all if you are dead."

"If I cannot do him any good," he whispered, "that is just what I'd rather be."

⁂

He shouldn't be drinking. He knew that, had always known that. He wasn't like other men, because the poison went all through him and numbed his mind.

Sometimes he welcomed such oblivion.

But not now. Not with so much at stake.

"You the caster again, are you?" Two dice clicked against each other, as the bald-headed man rolled them in his palms. "I should think you have lost enough."

Lost enough. The words hurled into his stomach. Couldn't think.

"Leave it alone, Mr. Reeves. If he's of a mind to get ruined, I'm all for letting him."

"Aye," chimed another voice. "Now give the gent his dice."

Ewan thrust out an open hand. "Once more. . .one more time."

Mr. Reeves frowned. "Have you anything left?"

"What?"

"Gingerbread, fellow. Have you any left?"

Ewan cursed the ticking in his ear. What was that ticking? He scanned the room in one swift glance until they collided with a long-case clock. *Eleven o'clock?*

"I suggest you take your son home," said Mr. Reeves. "He's been quite the sport about all this, what with sleeping in a blooming chair all night."

"I cannot."

"Cannot what?"

"I cannot take him home. . .can never take him home. . .now give me the dice, Henry!"

"Henry? What the—"

Ewan threw himself forward, tackled the man against the wall. "I mean it. I shall not be imprisoned by you any longer."

Other hands hauled him back.

"Swallow your spleen, man."

Another brushed at his coat. "You're a bit tap-hackled, that's all. Now, what say you to another game?"

Ewan dragged his sleeve across his forehead. He reached for his goblet, gulped the rest down. "Yes." He retrieved the dice from the floor where they'd landed. "Yes, one more game."

Henry squeezed the leather reins so hard that his fingers ached. Everything ached. His head, his neck, his chest, until the ache spread into his blood like an icy river. Engulfing, cold waves. Devouring him. Why was it so cold?

In the name of Jesus, give me strength. The cry shuddered him. He dug his heels into the horse and swayed, working to stay upright. Why was God doing this to him?

As if the five years of agony had not been enough.

He wanted to pray again, wanted to beg. But he possessed no more strength. He was depleted, even of faith.

No, not true. His vision plunged into darkness, then surfaced just as quickly. *I do have faith, God. I must have faith.*

The saddle slid away from him. He tried to grope, tried to regain his balance, but his face smacked gravelly dirt. Pain jarred every corner. He pushed up, up, up.

His shaking arms gave out beneath him, and he landed back in the dirt.

A gentle pull turned him over.

The sun glared into his eyes, but even that could not warm him.

Cold, so cold. Why was it so cold?

Soft, warm hands slid over his face. "I'm so very sorry, my lord."

His eyes shut against his wishes.

"I want to help you."

Hurry.

"We must find Peter."

Please.

"I don't know what to do."

No. The last words made a roar before blackness swallowed him.

All morning she'd watched him hunkering over his saddle, knowing he would eventually tumble off.

Panic stitched a pattern across her chest, as she pulled his head onto her lap. *Please, Henry.* Why wouldn't he wake up?

At least he'd fallen along the side of the road. At least there would be no chance of a fast-riding carriage coming upon him unawares, delivering another tragedy.

God, what do I do?

His leg was bleeding again.

She ripped back the fabric and tossed away the linen now stained red. The sight of butchered flesh gagged her.

I'm so sorry, Henry. Because he'd suffered so much, because he couldn't go on, because Peter was likely lost to them.

I'm so sorry we have failed.

He was glad his father was dead. He wished Henry was dead too.

Ewan took one step back, then one step forward. Nausea flipped his midsection upside down a hundred times, a hundred million times.

They shall never find out.

He was penniless again, a failure again—but his father and brother would never know. That was the only solace Ewan had left.

"No feathers to fly with already, man?"

"Well, here, then. Hand the dice over, will you?"

"If he had a house and wife to wager, I don't doubt he would." This came from Mr. Reeves, who had a voice strangely similar to Ewan's father and brother.

Ewan dropped the dice into his empty goblet. "The devil with all of you," he muttered. He staggered away from them, collided with a gentleman he shoved aside, and swiveled his gaze to the forgotten corner.

He blinked.

Peter? Rubbed his eyes. Jerked someone else out of his way. Covered the small distance in unstable strides.

He drew to a stop beside the chair.

The empty chair.

CHAPTER 26

A lord, ye say?"

"Lord Sedgewick of Wyckhorn Manor." Ella kept her voice steady with an effort.

"Ne'er heard of it."

"Near Northston."

"Oh?"

"Yes." The man's eyes strayed to Henry's limp form, then up and down her ragged dress, before finally returning to her face. Disbelief lit his eyes with a touch of humor. "That's a Banbury tale, if e'er I heard one."

"It is no tale, sir, and I shall recompense you for your time." Ella reached down and dug into Henry's pockets. She pulled out a shilling. "Here, this is yours if you oblige us."

At the sight of silver, the man hopped down from his pony cart. "Lord or ragpicker makes no ne'er mind to me. I haint' goin' no further than Quinbury, though."

"Is there a doctor there?"

"How would the likes of me know?" He came close enough to snatch the coin, which he bit. "But there won't be room for all three o' us in the cart."

"I shall ride behind. Now will you help me up with him?"

"I've a cranky sort o' back."

"Surely, sir, you do not fathom I can lift him on my own."

"Mayhap not, but I can't see failin' my back unless there were. . ." He paused, wiped his hands on his trousers, and cocked a grin. "Well, mayhap something to make it worthwhile."

Frustration licked away the last of her patience. She pulled out two pence and smacked it into his hand with force. "Now hurry up."

"As you say, lady." And the man hefted Henry's form over his shoulder, grumbled something about his back, and deposited the body into the cart.

∞

"My son. . .have you seen my son?"

Another shake of the head, a mild oath.

Ewan reached for someone else, a middle-aged man at a faro table. "My son. . .have you seen him?"

"Bad form, man. Leave me be, will you?"

"But my son—"

"I say, are you quite finished?" This came from a brawny gentleman who rose from his red chair. "No one has seen such a person, I assure you, and we are all trying to play a game, if you please."

"My son." A murmur under his breath, as Ewan stumbled away from the table. The noises, the colors, the aromas—they all clubbed him in the stomach at once. He doubled over and vomited, shaking. "My son."

Gasps came from behind him, more curses, then a rough hand grabbed his arm. "A few too many you've had," came the deep voice, as the door was thrown open. "Come back when you can keep from casting up your accounts, eh wot?"

Ewan landed on his hands and knees. "Lucy. . .Lucy, help me. . ." He came to his feet as a couple swept by him, condemning him with their glances.

The same way his mother had always looked at him, then his father, then Henry.

But not Lucy.

She never looked at him that way, only smiled at him with warmth and fondness.

"Because she loves me." He panted the words under his breath and stepped into the street. "And she loves our son."

Ewan had to find him.

ⓒ

"I want to see him." Ella stood outside the door in a hallway growing dim with eventide.

The doctor's small, veiny hands pulled the knob. "That is no fresh wound, miss."

"No."

"How many days?"

Her mind raced. "I—I do not know." *A lifetime.* "How is he?"

"Awake, but only just so."

"And his fever?"

A small shake of the head.

Ella's throat jabbed with pain. "I want to see him," she said again.

"Very well, but I have cut a vein in his arm to let him bleed. I trust the sight shall not frighten you?"

Yes, she was frightened. She was frightened that the man she loved was lying in a strange inn—bleeding and weak—and there was nothing she could do for him. She was frightened that a little boy she had welcomed into her heart was now deep in the clutches of a madman. She was frightened that the God she had finally surrendered her heart to wasn't answering any of her prayers.

As if some of her fears were translated in the silence, the doctor nodded. His voice deepened with empathy, "Do have faith, child." He patted her shoulder. "He is no frail man, you know."

"I know."

"And with some rest and food, he may very well be on the mend." The doctor started past her. "In a day or two, of course."

Ella might have wept.

A day or two was something they didn't have.

ⓒ

She was haggard and dingy, her dress torn and stained, her hair askew along her face. She padded toward his bed with reluctance, as if coming closer were a feat too difficult.

Henry glanced at the bowl beside his bed. The blasted man should have put it away, spared her the sight of so much blood.

Her eyes drew to it first. Slowly, tearfully, she lifted her gaze to his face. Her lips quivered. Never spoke, though.

"Your dress." His words exited with tremor. "On my. . .thigh."

"You were bleeding."

"Dunn should have packed bandages."

"Yes." Small, whispered. "Yes, he should have."

How he hated the way a stillness crept into the room and settled, like an icy layer of snow that would not melt. He blinked with effort, lids so heavy. He tried to think. "Will you. . .sit?"

She didn't.

He watched expressions flit across her face—the bravery subsiding into fear, the faith sinking into doubt, the hopes crashing into defeat. "You said I should believe in God," she said.

"What?"

"You said I should believe in God—and I did." A pause. "I do."

It didn't make sense but it sent his heart rate into a frenzy that hurt.

She crept closer to his bed. Faced him with questions, anguish, and a feeble light of trust. "Henry, why is He not answering me?"

"I do not know."

"Why is this happening to you? To Peter?"

"My faith is too frail, Ella, to lend any strength to yours."

"That is not true."

"Isn't it?"

"Henry. . .please pray." She closed her eyes, breathed out cries that had no sound. "Please pray this will all be over. . .please."

∞

At first he couldn't tell, so slight was the figure in the distance, so shadowed in twilight hues.

Peter. Ewan broke into a run. Air bathed his wet face, spiking his blood with adrenaline. *Peter, wait.*

Another figure hurried his son around a dark corner.

Ewan sprinted. He spun around the building and lunged into the alley, halting just shy of a man's broad back.

A whimper rose, confirming one thing—he had found his son.

"Well, well, good sir, I see you have at long last found your ward."

"My son," Ewan said. He reached for the boy—

"Ah, ah." The outline of a round face and a continental hat became visible in the increasing darkness. "I fear the child has certain qualms about accompanying you, my good man. Is that not so, Master Peter?"

No answer, only sniffling.

"Poor child ran away, you see, and had I not discovered him when I did, he might have been snatched away by gypsies or—worse yet—discovered by prowling street waifs."

"Who are you?"

"A friend of the child."

"He's my son—"

"Stolen from his papa," finished the man, "who is none other than a lord. I presume you know all of this?"

"Get out of my way—"

"A lord who would doubtless be very eager to gain him back."

Ewan swung a fist for the man's jaw, but his wrist was caught before the blow ever landed.

"Now, now, good sir, let us not be hasty about all this. Shall we talk?"

Ewan twisted his hand free. "Lucy needs him. . .needs our son."

"Lucy?"

"Yes, she needs him."

"I am certain she does. Now"—the man backstepped twice and hoisted Peter into the bed of a wagon—"allow me to amend my ill manners. Names are most important, eh?"

Ewan's eyes darted to Peter's. If only it were not dark, if only he could glimpse the eyes that so reminded him of Lucy.

"What is yours, good man?"

"Sedgewick."

"Fine, fine. I am Clement Solomon Becker." The man tipped back his continental hat. "What do you say we constitute a deal?"

CHAPTER 27

Thirty-two cards weighted the world, his whole world. He sank into the red chair and gulped in air that reeked of cheroot.

"A good man, you are." Clement Solomon Becker sat across from him. "And a wise choice you made too."

Ewan smacked the deck onto the table.

From beside him, Peter's fingers twisted. Dimples. . .his hands bore dimples. Why had Ewan never noticed before?

"Shall we go over the rules once more?"

He knew them well enough. They were grounded into his mind as deeply as Lucy's whispers, the ones he had treasured over and over again. *"Ewan, my pearl, you are divine. . .and I love you. . ."*

"A simple game of piquet."

Lucy, help.

"The victor leaves with everything."

Please, please.

"If you win, Mrs. Ashbrook's blunt is yours." He poured a stack of coins onto the table. "And if not, you shall relinquish the child to me, and I shall return him to the lordy. For a price, of course."

Ewan wiped at the deck, scattering the cards. "No, no. . .I cannot." He shook his head. Again, again, again. "No."

"I was under the impression you were a gambler, good man, from the child's accounts."

"Yes. . .yes, I am." He tightened his knuckles into fists. "My father forbids it. . . .Henry too. . .but I can win."

"Ah yes, I am certain you can."

"Lucy loves me."

"Does she?"

"Yes, yes, yes." Shaking everywhere. He grabbed Peter's arm and jerked him to his feet. "I have to take him to her. . .our son."

"Sit down, good man."

"I have to take my son to her!"

"Do you?" Becker's smile widened with ease, as one finger idly flipped a golden coin. "What a shame you shall appear before her empty-handed."

"What?"

"Without funds, man. What shall she think of you?"

"She loves me."

"But she believes you can win. Are you so willing to disappoint?"

A pocket of memories burst within—images of his mother's disappointed looks, her stiff smiles, her cold aloofness.

"And if it is the boy you are concerned for, you needn't occupy a worry." The chair squeaked as Becker leaned back. "I shall return him to the papa from whence he came."

"He's *my* son."

"So he is."

"Lucy's son."

"Yes."

"Henry will never have him."

"Perhaps not."

Ewan collapsed back into the chair. Throbbing pain pierced his temples. Perspiration stung his eyes. Fear stacked in his stomach. "Deal."

Becker gathered the cards with stubby hands. "With pleasure, my good man."

∽

Wretched, ghastly shapes licked inside the room's sooty hearth. Half the time, Henry fathomed himself in a nightmare, a dark place with no windows and no air.

But then he would hear her breathing. How faint and lulling was the cadence, like the gentle music of a breeze rustling branches.

She should not be in here. His eyes remained shut. *Why is she in here?*

He'd fallen asleep and expected her to be gone. Never could have rested if he'd known otherwise.

Ella, I love you. The hearth's light illuminated her. *I love you.*

Her head was leaned back into the chair, her arms folded across her chest, her lips gaped only slightly.

I love you so much I could die.

He'd loathed the proximity that the barn had forced upon them. Now he wished for it again. He wished there were black and empty stalls to run into, to escape in. He wished he were not in a room small enough to detect her breathing, bright enough to watch her sleep.

Ella, how shall I heal? Tears gathered, swelled, overflowed. He would have wiped them away, but he hadn't the strength. *How shall I heal this time?*

He told himself there was a way. He told himself he'd find a path that would lead him into each tomorrow. He told himself, someday, he'd know the lack of pain.

But he didn't believe himself.

Yet more lies he must live with.

◌◌

No more dimples. He couldn't see them, because they were engulfed in a massive, pudgy hand.

Becker's lips moved, sneering, talking—but it was all a roar Ewan couldn't understand. All he could focus on was Peter's eyes. He clung to them like the mast of a ship going under, as if letting go would plunge him under cold waves.

Strange, but he already felt like he was drowning. Water everywhere, flooding his cheeks, slipping into his lips, tasting like saltwater.

Becker's fingers squeezed his shoulder as he passed. "Good man," came the jibe, then something cold was pressed into Ewan's hands. "For your Lucy, wherever she is."

He stared down at it. A small stack of coins, glinting from chandelier light, but they slipped through his grasp and clinked on the floorboards.

Ding.

Ching.

Flop.

His ears screamed with the sounds—then he heard the worst of all.

The door easing shut behind him.

"No." Ewan pivoted, gasped.

They were gone. His son was gone.

"No, no, no, no." His hands slipped over his ears. Weak legs gave out beneath him and he landed on top of worthless coins.

He couldn't even weep.

"No." Henry's voice ricocheted against all four walls. "I said no, and I shall not be defied."

"You are in no condition to command."

"And you are in no condition to walk outside of this inn." Why was everything with her so difficult? "Not dressed so."

"My pride can endure the buffet."

"Your pride is not my fear."

"Then what is?"

"Are you such the fool? Or do you only play a poor argument?"

Rebuttal shaped her lips, but instead of answering, she whirled for the door.

"Ella, do not go—"

She flung it open.

Henry swung his legs out of bed so fast his head spun. "Ella, wait!" His knees hit the floor before he could reach her. "Wait." Pain scratched away any voice he might have had, and he gripped the side of the bed with a growl.

Fool woman. Did she think all the world would treat her considerately—and dressed in dirty tatters, no less? What if she should run into another blackguard like the one at Darby's tavern?

Or what if she should run into Ewan?

⁂

There was no respite. Just a blur, a bottomless tumble into madness. He didn't know where he was. Prison?

No, he'd escaped.

And this was freedom.

Ewan swayed in the alley and took one more step. His body smacked into the building. His cheek dragged along the wet, mucky brick. *Freedom, freedom.*

Cries broke from his lips, with the same dying sounds Lucy had gurgled.

But he wasn't dying. Oh, how he wished he were! How sweetly and gently the lap of death would rock him, soothe him, heal him.

"Henry! I shall kill you, Henry!" Rage came and fled, as quickly as it took him to force another step. He couldn't hold onto it, couldn't nurse the anger any longer. He had no feeling. He was empty, devoid, a shell.

My son, my son. Why had he lost again? He always lost, lost everything, everything he loved. *My son, where are you?*

More steps, closer to the street.

Where, where?

People sauntered by, horses, wagons, and carriages. None of them looked at him. None of them loved him.

Cool water splashed his legs. A puddle? He didn't care. Didn't matter—

Someone stepped into the street across from him. At first it happened slowly, a rise of emotion through his numbness, a torch of light in all his barren tombs. He stared without blinking. Breathed without exhaling.

Because she was here. Only a few feet away.

Lucy.

Ewan bolted into a run.

⁂

Perhaps she should have listened to him. For the first time in her life, she had *wanted* to listen. How could that be, when she'd spent her whole life disobeying everyone?

Ella smoothed down her dress with a gloveless hand. What she did or didn't want hardly mattered—not with Peter's future dangling in the balance.

If Ewan and Peter had been in Quinbury, she would find out. She would ask the questions Henry would have asked. She would go the places he would have gone.

There was no other choice.

"Excuse me, miss." A plain-clothed man bumped past her, a young daughter on his elbow. "Clumsy of me."

She hurried past with a small nod, then avoided a woman who came sashaying by with a broad parasol. Why must there be so many people?

If only the town were smaller. If only the world were smaller. How could they ever find Peter in—

Hands grasped her shoulders from behind. "Lucy."

An explosion rushed up her spine as he jerked her around. "Ewan—"

"Lucy, you have come." His strength hurled her out of the street, into the alley. "You are here."

"Wh-where is Peter?"

"I waited."

"Peter—"

"I waited so long, but you never came."

She tried to wriggle out of his touch, but his grip only tightened. Should she scream? But if she could find out about Peter—

"I did not want to lose the child too." He wagged his head. "My son...I did not want to lose him."

"Where is he?"

"Gone."

"Where?"

"Gone, gone, gone." His hands tightened painfully on her shoulders. "Lucy, I waited but you never came...waited in prison...waited always..."

Ella pushed against his chest, but he backed her further into the alley. Further from the street, from the people, from escape.

"I tried to die for you, but he would not let me. Did you know?" Closer. "Did you know I tried to die for you?"

"Tell me about the child."

"I love you."

"Tell me."

"More than anyone, I love you. . .and you love me." Tears slipped loose, making grimy channels down his cheeks. "Tell me you love me, Lucy. I want to hear you say you love me."

"Then you shall tell me where Peter is?"

"Gone, gone."

"But where—"

"I want to hear you say it. Say the things you used to say, Lucy. I want to hear you say them."

Silence.

Burning flames crawled along her skin.

"Why?" His question rang with fear. "Why will you not say them?"

"Ewan—"

"Why?"

"Because I am not Lucy." The words exited half whisper, half sob. "My sister is dead."

For a moment, he did not move. One of his eyes twitched, as the dark pupils widened with grief. Then senselessness. Then rage.

Ella's back slammed against a brick wall.

"You love Henry."

"Please—"

"You love him! You have forsaken me like her. . .my mother. . ." Shaking, beating her head into the wall.

Pain cracked her skull. Then again, again, again, until a scream lifted.

His hands hurried higher to her neck. "Why did you have to do it, Lucy?"

Again.

"Why did you have to betray me?"

Again.

"I loved you. . .loved you so. . ."

She kicked, but she couldn't see. Blackness hovered over her vision. Why was something crawling on her, dripping down her neck?

Now his fingers dug into her throat.

Harder to breathe, harder to fight away the blackness.

"I left my prison for you, Lucy. Why did you have to—"

A shot ripped away his words. Must have torn away his hands too, because they loosened one finger at a time until the air flowed back into her lungs.

Then he toppled in front of her.

And Ella sank into a heap.

⤬

"Someone get the constable." A scruffy boy darted off at the command. "You other men, grab his bleedin' body."

Murmurs rose from those peering into the alley, then grunts as the body was hoisted into several arms.

"Where to, fellow?"

"I don't be knowin'." The man in charge finally turned to her, his gun still dangling from one hand. Wasn't he the one she'd bumped on the street? "The dead house, ye wants?"

"No." Scratchy, whispered voice. She pulled herself to her feet. "No, take him to the Banter Inn on Dowington Street. He. . ."

"He wot?"

"He is an acquaintance."

"Not a friend though, eh?" Shoving his gun back behind a woolen coat, the man gave a glance to the alley's entrance. "Sarah, ye be comin' over and helpin' me with the maiden."

His daughter hurried forward.

Carefully, the man took Ella's arm. "Now, we'll be gettin' ye straight to the constable, so's ye can tell him I had no choice but to—"

"No."

"Pardon?"

Ella eased free. "No, I must get back to the inn."

"An' so ye will, but the constable will be wantin' to have a word with ye."

"I—I would be most grateful if you would tell him where to find me." Her legs shook as she took a few steps away. "But I must get there before..."

"Before wot?"

Before the body. Ella started away. *Before Henry sees.*

The man's strides caught up with her. "Ye will tell the constable wot happened?"

"Of course."

"If Sarah hadn't o' dropped her hankie, I'd o' never heard the scream." Should she thank him?

"Like as not, he would have killed ye."

Yes. Ella quickened her pace away from him, from the alley, from everything. *Yes, I know.*

∞

If he hadn't the strength to comb the whole of Quinbury, at least he could make inquiries downstairs.

He descended each step with a strong grip on the banister, then slipped into the crowded coffee room. He took a seat at a table with four other patrons, who gave him a brief nod before resuming their conversation.

"Just brought the corpse in, an' I don't know but what he's the man I saw the other night."

"Aye?"

"That fellow who spit his bloody accounts on the floor?"

"And dropped his coins the very next day?"

"Aye, one and the same. Souls like him oughtn't gamble."

"Excuse me." A man with a glistening brow leaned in from the door. "Any strong gents in here who wants to carry a carcass upstairs?"

A few volunteering hands went up, followed by the scratch of wood on wood as they scooted out of their chairs.

"Ain't by no chance a Lord Sedgewick in here, huh?"

Henry stood. "Here, sir."

"Good." The man wiped his brow with a ratty sleeve, then motioned to someone behind him. "All right, miss, there he be."

He was halfway to the doorway before she filled it, with something dreadful twisting her expression, with something strange emptying her eyes.

He halted inches away. "The body?"

"Ewan's."

He pushed past her for the steps. She called after him, but he didn't wait to listen. Instead, he followed the four men up steep stairs as they carried a limp form into an empty bedroom.

By the time they'd all filed out, Ella was next to him, grabbing his arm. "There was no help for it, my lord."

"Peter?"

"They were not together."

Henry started into the room.

Her hand didn't loosen. "Henry, please, there's no need to go in there—"

"I want to be alone." His arms flexed beneath her grip. "I want to be alone." Then he pushed through and sent the door hurling shut.

From across the room, a dead and scroungy face stared up at the ceiling. His eyes were still open. Why were they open?

Henry drew himself forward. A sob churned, but instead of sound, only shook his shoulders. "Where is he?"

Ewan's dry eyes didn't blink.

"Where is my son?"

Still, nothing.

Henry should have known. Even in death, his brother only wished to torture him. "Where. . .where. . ." Henry's hands seized the motion-less shoulders. He shook hard, digging his fingers into flesh without feeling, inflicting pain into one who could no longer hurt.

Then a cry finally escaped Henry's wrath.

He sank his face into his brother's chest, making fists around the fabric of his coat. He should have hated. He needed to hate. For Peter's sake, for his own sake. . .why couldn't he hate?

"I am sorry." If only the dead had ears. "I am sorry, Brother, for killing her."

∞

"Where is she?"

A man at the bottom of the steps glanced up from his broom. "Constable just took her in the coffee room, he did."

Henry headed for the doorway. When he entered, the room was less crowded, the scent of coffee more nauseating.

Ella.

At the end of a table, she sat alone with a man, her back as stiff and erect as the iron gates of Wyckhorn. Dry blood crusted at the nape of her neck. How had such a thing escaped his notice?

He didn't know, didn't really want to know. His brother was dead. Wasn't that enough to endure without bearing the details?

Even so, he approached and slid into a chair next to her.

She didn't turn to look at him. Instead, fast-blinking eyes remained fixed on the constable's face. "Yes, sir, I knew him."

"Who was he?"

No answer.

Henry supplied it for her, "Ewan Sedgewick."

The constable's red-rimmed eyes made a casual turn toward Henry. "And who are you?"

"His brother."

"Interesting." He flicked his hand to Ella. "Continue, Miss Pemberton."

"H–he forced me into an alley. He thought I was. . .I mean, he always thought I was. . ."

"Thought you were who, Miss Pemberton?"

"Someone else."

"Odd, do you not think?"

"Ewan was. . ." The last color drained from her face. "He was not well, sir."

"I see. Go on."

No, do not go on. Rage and hurt mingled, as Henry listened to whispered words that made him want to bash his fists through the walls of time. He should have been there. He should have stopped this from happening. He should have protected her, defended her—

"And then he was dead."

The constable never flinched. "Wrapped up case, it seems. The fellow got the finish he deserved."

"Maybe I could have prevented it." Ella's shaking voice rose. "Maybe if I had pretended to be Lucy, said the things he wanted. . .he would still be. . .still be. . ." Her shoulders collapsed with a whimper.

Henry reached for her. "Ella."

She scooted away from him. "Constable. . .if that is all?"

He stood with a brief nod. "Quite so. Want me to see to the burying?"

"Yes," Henry answered. He pulled coins from his pocket, aware that her chair had become empty. "See to it there's a headstone."

"Elm coffin?"

"Yes."

"What of the coffin covering? Velvet or black baize—"

"It does not matter. Just see to it." Henry hurried after Ella. He grabbed the banister, pulled himself up creaking steps, and caught her partway down the hall. "Ella, just a moment."

"Please." With his touch, she froze. Her eyes never made it farther than the lapels of his coat. "I cannot talk anymore."

"Then do not talk."

"Henry—"

"No." His hands grabbed her face, but she backed herself into a wall. "No," he said again. "Do not speak, only listen."

"You blame me."

"Never."

"I have hurt you." Her eyes lifted to his neck, then his mouth, then his eyes. "Again."

Forgiveness sprang to his heart in one pulsing moment. If only it could so easily spring to his lips.

"If there were any hope left of finding Peter, I have destroyed it," she said. "And for all your anguish at Ewan's hands, he was still your flesh and blood."

"You can no more blame yourself than I can."

"But I should have listened to you."

Guilt. He recognized the dark, plaguing demon in her eyes—the same one he had lived with for five long years. He would not have her suffer on his behalf, on Ewan's behalf, on anyone's behalf. Not as he had suffered. "No, Ella, you have done everything right."

"I should never have followed you. We shall never find Peter and you are ailing and I have—"

His lips stopped her words, dissolving them into the bittersweet taste of passion. Oh, if only he could but live here. No malice, no pretense, no threat. Just soft, throbbing lips that yielded to his own, as if the brief haven was as blissful to her as it was to him.

"You were meant to follow me." His kiss dragged to her cheek, as his thumbs caressed her warm jaw. "I shall regain my strength, and we shall find our Peter."

Our Peter? His own words half mocked him, half delighted him.

But if nothing else, the small phrase rewarded him a smile.

And a bit of life leaked back into his soul.

"He is here."

Henry reached for the covers, gripped them hard. "Send him in."

Ella's nod was quick, her smile limp yet comforting. She disappeared without a word.

Four days. He stared from one bedpost to another, then up to the ceiling that seemed to stifle him. *Four days, God, and I cannot even look for my son.*

The constable had done what he could. He'd asked questions, gone places, found a club where Ewan had gambled away his funds.

But nothing.

Still nothing.

Always nothing.

With a dreadful creak, the door came back open. The constable approached the bed with Ella at his heels, and he set his hat on the stand as if the procedure were becoming habitual.

"Well?"

"You can thank God for a man called Reeves."

"Reeves?"

"He's the only gent who remembered a thing about a little one." The constable crossed his arms and half grinned, as if the mystery appealed to his interest. "Fact is, he was there the night it happened. Sitting one table away, he says, and listening all the while."

"Listening to what?"

"The bargain."

Alarm jerked through Henry's stomach.

"Reeves said it was a game—piquet or something—and the winner gained the kid. Seems your brother lost."

"The man. Who was the man?"

"Now that is a question. Been asking myself all day, and if Reeves hadn't mentioned hearing the name Ashbrook, might have never known."

"Ashbrook?"

"Handsome lady, recently widowed. Visited her this afternoon and drank tea, if you can believe that." The constable uncrossed his arms. "Becker was the name."

Ella slapped a hand over her mouth as she sank into a chair with a muffled groan.

"Clement Solomon Becker—and from what Reeves overheard, he has plans to return your son." A pause. "For ransom."

∽

Hours, years, decades—and finally, they were alone. As soon as the constable closed the door behind him, Henry swung out of bed and groped for his boots.

She stayed in her chair. Not knowing what else to do, she gripped the wood of the chair's rough and grainy arms. "You are not well enough."

He didn't answer. He crossed the room and yanked on his tailcoat, then his greatcoat.

"We do not know where he is."

"If he is returning Peter, he will find Wyckhorn. When he does, we shall be there."

"Henry?"

"Yes?"

Courage almost abandoned her. "Does the name Becker mean anything to you?"

"Should it?"

"The m-man," she said. "The man at Darby's."

Now he turned, came around the bed, towered over her. "It can't be."

"It is."

"Doesn't make sense."

"I know."

"God, no." The prayer came out a whisper. He pulled her from the chair, then grabbed his hat. "Let's go."

CHAPTER 28

*J*t would have been the loveliest sight in the world, the familiar cliffside, the scent of brine and seaweed, the roll and crash of distant waves. If only Peter waited for them.

Strange, how Wyckhorn could feel so much like home when it had harbored such lies and hurt. What was here for her?

Nothing.

Nothing but memories left to taunt her. Nothing but tangible illusions of what might have been. Nothing but a sea of regret, its tides rising to drown her with every inch they drew nearer to the manor.

"He's back!" The welcome drifted over distance as the young stable boy raced from the stables.

Two other servants ran to them—one taking Henry's reins, the other helping Ella from her saddle.

"Groom them well," said Henry, as he swung down. "They have ridden hard."

"Yes, m'lord."

He started for the house, and Ella hurried behind him, falling into his shadow until it melted into the larger shadow of the manor. He took the steps with a limp, then swung open the door.

"My lord, you are back—"

"Get Dunn." Henry strode past the butler without shedding his coat or hat.

Hurried footsteps echoed between the high ceiling and the marble floors as the butler scurried to find the steward.

Silence.

Henry turned, glanced at her, wiped moisture from his face. "You may go and rest if you wish."

She shook her head.

His eyes stayed with her as if scrutinizing every inch of her face. What did he see? What did he want to see? Did it please him or bring more disgust? In the days they had traveled back, he had spoken so little and smiled not once.

She told herself it was worry, grief, illness—but not hatred. Could he have kissed her so lovingly if there had been hatred?

As if he knew her thoughts, he glanced at the door.

Seconds later, a haggard Dunn hurried through. "My lord, thank heavens you are returned." As if forgetting himself, Dunn grabbed Henry's shoulders and squeezed. "Are you well, my lord?"

"Yes." Noble lie. "Has there been a letter?"

"A letter?"

"A letter, a message—anything."

Dunn glanced at her for the first time, as if in hesitation to render more grief. Then his hands fell back to his sides. "No, my lord. There has been nothing."

"There will be." Ella urged the words past a knot. "There will be."

Henry turned away. Without sparing either of them another glance, he headed for the stairs.

God, help him.

Partway up, his sleeve brushed quickly across both of his cheeks.

The wooden blocks were scattered across the rug. Part of the tower still stood, as if the foundation had been too strong to crumble.

Henry bent. His fingers swallowed a block into his palm. *My Peter.* The last of his joy, the last of his sanity, the last of his peace. . .and now he was gone too. *Peter, my son. My sweet little son.*

Tears, more tears. Yet even still, they could not blind his eyes to the sight of the small bed, the wrinkled covers, the dented pillow.

God, give him back.

He dragged himself to the bedside where Peter used to whisper his prayers.

I'll give anything.

Buried his face into the bedclothes.

Anything.

Wept into the smell of his son.

God, please.

But even if He didn't, even if He didn't answer the prayers, even if He never brought Peter home to him...

God, I shall serve You. One last sob tore through him. *It is in Your hands.*

He was not coming.

Ella sat alone at the dinner table, her hands folded in the muslin lap of a fresh dress. Had she ever felt so clean?

The afternoon hours had been spent bathing, allowing a maid to comb her tresses, then retiring for a nap at Mrs. Lundie's persistent demands. A servant had been sent for her trunk, which he returned only hours ago.

Now, Mrs. Lundie carried a bowl of soup and lowered it before Ella. "Ye must eat something, dear. Try this."

"And Lord Sedgewick?"

"I shall hae a maid deliver something to his chamber."

"He has not eaten well in days."

"Och?"

"Nor has he slept."

"Poor man."

"And he is still unwell. Especially at night...the fever seems to return. He never says a word, but I know. I know he is unwell."

"There, there, lass." Mrs. Lundie gave her a pat. "Ye are getting yerself pure upset for nothing. I shall go up and see to him right noo—"

"That will be unnecessary, Mrs. Lundie."

Ella's skin erupted in bumps at his voice.

He brushed past Mrs. Lundie in tailcoat, pantaloons, and cravat—then took a seat at the other end of the table. Damp hair made waves about his face as if he too had recently bathed. "I shall be dining here tonight. Will you serve another bowl?"

"Ye ken I will, m'lord." And she bustled from the room with a tune.

If Ella had possessed any fortitude at all, she would have resisted the urge to stare at him.

The ghost only hours before had transformed into a living being—so like the old Lord Sedgewick that she could almost imagine nothing had changed.

If only it hadn't.

"You look well," he echoed her thoughts.

"As do you."

"You slept?"

"Yes."

"Good."

She slipped her silver spoon into the frothy soup. "Did you?"

"Pardon?"

"Sleep." She swallowed. "Did you sleep?"

He nodded, breathed in, looked away.

Mrs. Lundie returned with soup and a glass of cocoa, and the meal resumed without further conversation.

I do not understand. During those days they had been away, there had been one upheaval after another. She'd felt torn between his love and his hatred, never knowing which he truly felt, never secure in whether his glances would be warm or cold.

Then he had kissed her.

A mistake, a tragedy—but in the chaos, it had enveloped her with a sense of peace.

She had imagined his forgiveness. She had imagined many things. She had imagined, if even for a moment, that all the past was forgotten when he had whispered the words, *"Our Peter."*

But nothing was forgotten, and returning to Wyckhorn was only a necessary blow to send them both into reality.

"Excuse me." Ella clanked her spoon into the bowl, pushed out of her chair, and fled for the door.

"Ella?"

She froze halfway over the threshold. "Yes?"

A squeak of the chair, heavy footfalls, then he stood next to her. "Take this with you." He held out her half-eaten bowl. "I shall not have you lose your strength."

With shaking hands, she took the bowl and escaped into the hall. The soup sloshed with every panicked step.

As soon as Peter is found, I shall leave.

She locked herself into her bedchamber and gripped the bowl.

The sooner I leave Wyckhorn, the better.

The first day had been tolerable. There were a number of reasons Becker could have been delayed. How long had it taken him to learn the whereabouts of Sedgewick's home? And even if he had found it, could he write a letter?

The second day was more difficult. Still, if Becker had traveled by wagon, it was reasonable to assume that his journey would be prolonged. Wasn't it?

By the third day, Ella could think of nothing. Despair threaded strings across the house, tightening all the walls, suffocating the last of hopes.

More than once, she had seen Henry take his horse and gallop away. She wondered what he did out there and if he really thought such an aimless search would do him any good.

He always came back. She expected a wild look, a senseless fear that would make him strangely similar to Ewan.

But instead, Henry's face bore only quietness.

And peace?

At first, she thought the idea madness. But then she recognized the same peace in herself—the gentle Spirit that accompanied every prayer, the overwhelming calmness every time she opened the Bible she'd discovered in the library.

"Oh—Miss Pemberton."

Dunn stopped in the library doorway.

"I did not realize you were in here. Excuse me—"

"Please." Ella approached. "Do not go."

In the days since her return, his manner had closely matched Henry's. Courteous, considerate—but ever distant, as if they were strangers.

"Did you have something to attend to?"

"Yes," he said. "I was merely going to draw the draperies to let in a bit of light." He approached one wall first, pulled back the French window curtains, then crossed to the other side of the room.

"It is a mockery, is it not?"

"Miss?"

"That a day should dare be so beautiful when. . ." The sentence drifted.

Dunn cleared his throat. "Yes, Miss Pemberton. I quite agree."

"Has Henry been out today?"

"Early this morning."

"I see."

With the last of the curtains drawn, Dunn stood very still, his eyes landing everywhere in the room.

Except her.

She wanted to apologize again, to build back a broken bridge, to restore a friendship she hadn't realized she treasured.

But when he mumbled an excuse and left the room, she did nothing to stop him.

Instead, she changed into her half boots and took a walk outside. She strolled along garden paths that seemed less colorful, onto a seashore that lacked any vibrance. Even the wind tasted less delightful, more bitter.

Oh, Mother, Matilda. I only wish to be home.

What relief Abbingston Hall would bring to her now. Where she was loved unconditionally, where all her mistakes were forgiven readily, where she was comforted from all her pains.

Ella paused. Halfway up the slope from the beach, she turned back and glanced at the ocean.

Nothing.

Her eyes darted left, then right, then up above her where the path led toward Wyckhorn. Had she heard something? Or only sensed it?

But she didn't spot anything out of place. She ran back into the safety of the manor nevertheless.

Her imagination was doubtless at play.

Wasn't it?

Evening had grabbed the tail of time and locked it in a cage. The bracket clock's hands still moved just as steadily, but time could no longer move with them.

Henry leaned his head into the wing-backed chair. Dinner roiled his stomach in protest. What had he eaten? Venison? A partridge?

No, that was the dinner before. And the dinner before that.

He tried not to think how many dinners it had been, or what his son might have eaten, or if he'd eaten at all.

From across the room, Ella turned a page.

Should have stayed away from her. Should have sent her home. Should have chosen a different room of the house to endure the evening hours.

"What are you reading?" The words were out before he could stop them.

As if startled, she snapped the book shut. "Nothing." When he didn't look away, her shoulders wilted. "Just *The Tour of Dr. Syntax In Search of the Picturesque*, something I used to read to. . ." Why couldn't she speak his name?

Maybe Henry couldn't either.

He rose and approached, reached for the book. "May I?"

"Certainly."

He thumbed through the pages, the rhyming lines, the humorous illustrations. "It is good"—he handed it back—"that you read to him."

"I did very little that was good for him," she said. "You see, I knew nothing about children, only that I did not like them very much. Until I came here."

He should have been angry at her admission. Why wasn't he?

"And I—"

From behind, a door opened. Two servants dragged a dirty, hunched figure into the center of the room. The stable boy?

"What happened?"

"Sorry, m'lord." Blood dripped from the boy's nose. "I was out walkin' one o' the horses. . .the one with the sore hoof. I ne'er seen nothin' coming at me, m'lord. I swear I didn't."

"Set him on the couch."

"No." His thin shoulders shrugged away the servants' support. "I be fine, m'lord, but I won't be gettin' blood on e'erything."

"Anything broken?"

"Don't think so."

"Let me see that eye." Henry pulled him into the light of a wall sconce, inspecting the bruise that already swelled part of the eye. "Who did this?"

"I told you, m'lord. I don't know."

"You must have seen something."

"The first clout came from behind. . .and it was sort o' hazy after that. But I do know this." He dug something from the waistline of his trousers. "I was 'posed to give you this."

Henry ripped open the paper. Messy scrawl, almost unreadable. *Two thousand pounds. . .return of Peter Sedgewick. . .safe from harm. . .meet at the seashore tonight. . .midnight.* There was more. What did it say?

He stepped closer to the light, squinted. *Miss* something. . .*Miss . . .Pemberton?* His eyes hurried through the sentence until bile threatened his throat.

Ella had stepped close to him. He could tell by the unsteady, half-pant of her breathing. "Henry, what does it say?"

"Two thousand pounds at midnight. The seashore." The letter crumpled in his fist. "With one more stipulation."

"What is it?"

The core of his being shook. "You."

CHAPTER 29

I can get away." The lights in the room flashed, blinding her eyes, making her head swim. "I can get away. Do you hear me?"

He didn't answer.

Again.

Why wouldn't he talk to her?

She crossed the room to the mantel, ran her hand down the smooth length of it. "After Peter is safe, you can get help. There is nothing. . . nothing to fear."

The floorboards creaked with his steps. Pacing, always pacing. In the name of heaven, why wouldn't he speak?

Hurt carved into her chest, slicing, reshaping. *Dear God, how shall I bear this?* Sick everywhere, aching everywhere. So many lights in the room. Why were they so bright?

She rubbed her eyes. "It will be midnight in but a few hours. I had better change for riding." She made it no more than three steps before he seized her.

He held her at arm's length. Slowly drew her closer to him. "Go to your bedchamber and lock the door. Do not come back out."

"You ask the impossible."

"Ella—"

"No."

His face in hers, breath tingling her skin. "You cannot think I would surrender you to such a man. I will not."

"At the price of your son?"

"My son would not want this."

"But I do." She tore away from him. "And I will not bear having a child's life on my hands—nor can I expect that of his father."

"We would never get you back."

We?

"He would be gone with you before I could get help. . .before I could save you."

I know.

"If you tried to escape, he would kill you."

Then let me die.

"Ella." He grabbed her again, pressed her against him. "Ella, this is not the way. We shall save Peter. *I* shall save Peter."

"How?"

His lips firmed.

"How, my lord, do you propose to save your son's life?"

The words must have cut because he stepped away from her so abruptly that he nearly stumbled. He marched from the room and sent the door crashing shut behind him.

☏

There was no pain in gathering the money, in placing it in a woolen bag, in tying the string to secure it.

Henry sank behind his desk. From somewhere in the house, a clock chimed eleven o'clock. Oh, how he wanted to pray. Never wanted to pray so badly in his life.

Yet he couldn't.

He sat still in his chair, hands spread out in front of him, and couldn't form a single word.

Minutes sped by.

One.

Two.

Three.

Grabbing the bag, he went to find Ella. The drawing room was empty, so he limped up the stairs and rapped twice on her door.

No answer.

"Ella, let me in." He pushed the knob and slung open the door.

No figure on the bed or by the window or occupying the small chair. Only one thing caught his eye, a wrinkled dress tossed into the floor in a heap.

A green dress. The same one she'd been wearing earlier when she'd wanted to change into a riding habit, when she'd wanted to...

No. Henry hobbled back down the stairs, the money in his clutch. *No.*

∽

Night air pulled her hair from its pins as she lunged for the path. Her boots skidded over rock, sand, grass, until the slope evened into the beach.

I must do this. Over and over. Half coherent. A helter-skelter ghost racing the corridors of her mind. *God, I must do this.*

Her gaze swept from the shadowed rocks to the path growing more distant with each step. The ocean rumbled behind her as if taunting the lack of escape.

Where was Becker?

He should have been here. He should have been waiting. He should have had Peter with him, as he'd promised.

Or was the letter a lie?

No, no.

Couldn't be a lie, because that would mean her life was sacrificed for naught, her death sealed for—

"There."

A scream caught halfway up her throat, one second before a hand seized the nape of her neck.

"There," came the breath again. "My little biddy at last."

She didn't have time to answer, to move.

Hard metal struck her skull and drove her into the sand. Her vision blurred with pain, a ringing filled her ears. The world spun around.

"A little early, are you not, biddy?" He swung her over a shoulder. "Not that I don't gain pleasure from your presence."

Odors of cheap port and unwashed flesh fumed from his clothing as he deposited her at the base of the cliffside.

She landed on a rock, rolled, and sank into moist sand. Her vision cleared enough to see him looming over her. Fear dried her mouth.

"Lost a bit of spirit, eh?"

Her tongue slid over her lips.

"At our last encounter, you were a mite more. . .vigorous, it seems." He snatched her chin. "But we shall have plenty of time to discover your more exciting side, my maiden."

"Peter." Her jaw flexed under his touch. "Where is he?"

"Lying behind those rocks over there."

"Is he—"

"Aye, he is dead, little biddy. But let us not say a word until after his lordship appears with our request, hmm? I should not wish to be unrewarded."

Anguish gnashed at her, biting, ripping—until she clawed at his hand. "No." A scream, but his hand clamped over her mouth. *No, no, no.*

"There it is," he said. "A bit of life back into your feisty little soul. But come now, let us be rational. Do you really think I would do such harm to a little one—especially one of such great, shall we say, worth?" Amused eyes drew closer to her face. "Now, let us discuss other matters, for I do not wish to see this little meeting go awry, do you?"

She shook as he pressed her harder against a rock. The pressure of his hand stifled her breath, choked her.

"I had not counted on the lordy sending you down alone, but no matter. Just stay here out of my way, and I shall return to you with the money. You'll be happy to know I traded my cumbersome wagon for a steed, so our escape will be quite simple."

Peter. . .

As if sensing her thoughts, his hand loosened. "The little one shall come with me. An even trade. I foresee no gunplay, as I am certain his lordship would not pay so great a price, only to risk his son's death afterward."

"Y–you cannot think he will let you go unfollowed."

"Quite true, my maiden. But you see, I have already thought of this too. Why do you think I insisted on Miss Pemberton?" Voice thickened. Hands threaded through her hair. "Surely you are not so vain as to think I wanted you merely for pleasure?"

From behind his shoulder, something snagged her gaze.

A lantern.

Becker shifted on his haunches and followed her stare, then he uttered an oath. "Here at last, my biddy." With a gun pulled from his trousers, he weaved his way through several rocks, disappeared behind the largest, and pulled out a small figure.

Peter.

Walking, breathing, living.

Alive. She cupped her hands over her mouth, muffling broken sounds. *Dear God, he is alive.*

She watched as Becker hauled him out onto the beach. Stood a few feet away from Henry's rigid stance. Waited until the bag was thrown to Becker's feet.

Then Peter lunged forward. He tackled the legs of his father, became swallowed into arms that embraced him.

Ella's mind caved. She tried to look, to keep contact—but Henry was already carrying Peter away, and Becker was sprinting toward her.

"Fight me now, and I'll kill you." He snatched her arm with a panicked grip. "Now run."

God, please. Her legs pumped, digging into the sand. Twice, she slipped, but he yanked harder and dragged her on until finally they reached a horse.

He tossed her onto the saddle. "Hold this."

A heavy bag was shoved into her chest, then he heaved himself up. His arms enclosed her. Trapped her. Terrorized her.

My God, help me.

The horse charged into a gallop. No shots rang after them, not even the pound of horses or the shouts of men.

Not that she fathomed there would be. Not enough time. Only

seconds, minutes—yet already, they were so far away. How long would it take Henry to get Peter into the house, how long before he grabbed a gun, and how much distance would be put between them while he saddled his horse?

Agony doubled her over with cries that had no sound. *Dear God, no.*

Because Henry had been right.

There was no escape.

CHAPTER 30

*W*hoa." Racing hooves ground to a stop in the sand, as Becker yanked the reins to the left. "Now hold on my biddy. We might have a rough go of it."

She jerked as the animal lunged up a rocky path. Sweat trickled down her temples, formed along her palms.

Becker panted in her ear. A curse, a growl, then another shout to the horse.

Upward, upward, upward.

Closer to the road, farther from the beach. Escape would be simple, just as Becker had said, because as soon as they reached the road, they would be too far gone to—

A shrieking neigh pierced the quiet.

"No!" Becker screamed, followed by the scrambling of hooves on shifting stones.

Ella was flung first. Air rushed from her lungs, then she landed on hard, slanted ground. Pain kept her paralyzed. She couldn't breathe, only listen to the disconcerting shrieks of the horse and the high-pitched yowls from Becker.

Then silence.

At first she remained still, her bruised flesh comforted by the calm. *Beach.* The word flung her back to her feet. *God, the beach.* Skidding down pebbly ground. *Help me.* Leaping back to the sand. *Please*—

"Biddy!"

Panic tangled her feet, but she caught herself before a fall.

"A step more and I'll shoot."

She froze.

"Missed that fox." His voice came closer. "But think not I'll miss you." Within seconds, he was next to her, twisting her back around to face him. One hand struck the side of her face. Stung. "There." Was that blood on his forehead?

She couldn't tell. It was too dark.

"You have made me hit you, biddy, and I never wanted to do that."

"Let me go—"

"Come on, biddy. We haven't time to converse." His grip tugged her forward, but she wrestled against his arms until another blow sent her sprawling.

She tasted blood in her mouth, even as she tried to stand. "Please . . .let me go. . ."

"Never."

"You have no horse now. I shall only slow you down."

"I said no!" He seized her hair, hauled her up. "Now move!"

She staggered back toward the rocks, the cliffside, where he grabbed the money bag. She couldn't see the path, only ascended it blindly. Jagged edges cut into her palms.

"Almost there, biddy." He cursed, wheezed. "Almost to the road."

Her fingers numbed as she grasped the last rock, pulled herself onto level ground.

Becker climbed behind her and grasped her arm. With his free hand, he dragged a sleeve across his wet forehead. "All right, biddy." He jerked her one step into the road. "Now to—"

A horse's bray cut off the sentence.

Becker stilled.

Ella frantically searched the darkness. Had Becker's horse survived the tumble? Had he somehow climbed—

"One move and you are dead, Becker." The familiar timbre of the voice sliced through the night like a ghost. "Let her go."

⌒⌒

A thousand nerves twitched in Henry's finger as it slid across smooth metal.

Becker didn't react. He remained still with one hand wrapped around Ella's forearm, and the other clasping the bulging woolen bag.

"Let her go." Before he lost control. Before he pulled the trigger and murdered the wretched dog where he stood.

Becker's teeth flashed in the moonlight. "Now, this certainly is a predicament. Who are you?"

"I said let her go."

"I say, man. Can you not come into the light a bit? If I am to lose such a damsel, I should at least like to know who I am losing her to."

Henry's horse pranced but remained in the shadows. One wrong move and he'd blow him to—

"Besides, whatever his lordship has paid for her return will be scant reward compared to this." He raised the bag a notch and shook it, the coins clinking inside. "Name a price, my good man, for I have yet to be called unreasonable."

"All of it." Henry's heart thundered. "And the lady."

"Who the devil do you think you are, man?"

"Sedgewick—Lord Sedgewick."

"Impossible."

"Let her go."

"But you could not possibly have. . .have. . ." Becker flung her in front of him and looped an arm around her neck.

Henry's finger twitched again. Wild, cold rage surged through every vein inside him until his lungs pumped with fear. "I have servants at every escape route."

"Doubtful, man."

"You cannot get away."

"No?" Shuffling backward toward the cliffside. "Again, your words are doubtful, my lord. Myself, I think the chances are buoyantly high."

"Stop right now or—"

"Or what?" Becker's boots hesitated on the grassy ledge. "You have two options, man, and both would end in a rather painful finish for Miss Pemberton. You see, you can attempt a shot and let her act as my shield." He paused for effect. "Or you can remain on your horse and watch me sling her over this edge—though I must warn, it is a rather frightful fall."

Shivers crawled up his flesh. Helpless. . .helpless again. *God?*

"Be sensible, man, and ride away."

"No."

"Will you have her dead?"

The question roamed around the night without answer.

In the moonlight, Ella's eyes held fast to his. Glowing, moist, stricken. Her lips moved, but whether she murmured his name or not, he couldn't tell.

Then Becker spun, tossed her to the ground.

A bullet whizzed past Henry's ear. He fired back, lunged from his saddle, darted for the figure that collapsed halfway across the road. *God, help me.* Anger pulled his fingers into fists. Didn't want to kill again. Didn't want to end another life.

But when he bent over top of the body, it didn't move. When he grabbed the coat and turned him over, the face only lolled back to the side without sound.

Henry's rage depleted into realization.

He's dead.

∞

There was no sound for so long. Just the faint fluttering of leaves from across the road, the ebb and flow of ocean waves from behind, and the occasional pound of Miss Staverley stamping her foot, as if with impatience.

Then he started toward her. *Henry, Henry.* Without a word, his arms swallowed her up and carried her toward the horse. He lifted her onto the saddle with ease, settled behind her, then guided her hands to the horse's mane. "Just hold on here." Calm, with as much kindliness as if they were riding along Hyde Park instead of recoiling from a nightmare. "We shall be at Wyckhorn soon."

She never said anything. If silence had ever brought her comfort, it was now. There was peace in his control, trust in his arms, strength in the thump of his heart.

Henry, please. Without sound, her eyes welled. Tiny rivers eased down her cheeks, yet she didn't wipe them away lest he notice. *Please tell me it is over.*

As if to assure her, the strong tower of Wyckhorn Manor appeared before them. Every clomp of the horse matched the rhythm of her chest—first slow and weary, then quick and anxious as they neared the manor walls.

He swung her down into his arms.

I can walk. Why did she have no voice? *Henry, I can walk.*

"You are crying?"

She shook her head, but traitorous tears reappeared.

"Has he harmed you?"

Had he?

Slowly, he settled her onto her feet as he steadied her. "Did he?"

"No."

Henry's finger lifted to her lips, touched the cut, drew back with blood. "I am sorry."

"It is over."

"I wish I could have stopped it."

"But you did—"

"No." Strange, unfamiliar emotion deepened his voice. "No, Ella, I did not. I wish to heaven I could have spared you from this. I wish to heaven he would have never hurt you."

Did he care so much?

From behind, a door flung open and light spilled into the courtyard, followed by the eager scuff of approaching steps.

She heard Henry's breath come out weak, half sob almost, as she forced herself to turn.

In nightcap and gown, Dunn came hurrying toward them—with Peter's arms wrapped about his neck.

God, thank You.

The child leaped from the steward's arms to his father's, mumbling phrases none of them understood beyond the sobs.

"My son." Henry ruffled the scruffy blond hair. His lips pressed into wet cheeks. "You are all right, my son. Do not weep. You are all right. . ."

"I was scared."

"I know."

"I told him Mamma was dead."

"I know."

"He didn't believe me, Papa. . .he didn't. . ."

Dunn grasped Ella's shoulder from behind. "Miss Pemberton."

Ella nearly wilted beneath a touch so kind. "Dunn." She grasped his hands, squeezed. "Dunn, I. . ."

"You are overwrought, Miss Pemberton. You must let me help you inside, please."

She followed his lead until she reached the massive threshold. She glanced back only once.

Henry rocked his son back and forth. His gentle crooning melted over the air like a desert's raindrop. Never a man and boy so precious, so wonderful.

Her heart unraveled as she crossed the threshold.

If only they were hers.

CHAPTER 31

Ye better get some rest. I'll be pulling the bedclothes for ye, then."
According to Mrs. Lundie, Henry had returned inside only long
enough to place Peter in his nursery. She'd sat with the child until
sleep finally claimed him, then hurried to Ella's chamber.

Ella watched from her place at the upstairs window. Henry's long
strides carried him toward the stables. His hands moved as he said
something to a servant, and the stable boy brought out a second horse.

"Are ye listening to me noo?"

"Yes."

"What are ye looking at?"

"Nothing." Ella released the curtain, allowing the rose-shaded fabric to obstruct her view. The faraway sound of horses galloping away
reached her. "Where is he going?"

"Got to get the constable, they do. And his lordship cannae very
well leave the body, noo can he?" Gentle hands drew her toward the
bed. "Will ye come lie doon at last?"

She didn't want to sleep. Not when tonight was the end, the last
remnant of a world she would soon be lost to.

"There, there, child." Soothing hands guided her to the bed. "More
tears? Ye been crying since ye returned, ye hae."

"I want to see Peter."

"And so ye shall, in the morning—"

"No. I wish to see him now." Pleading welled with her tears.
"I must."

∞

Streaks of light backlit the sky before Henry returned to the stables.
He gave thanks to the servant who had accompanied him and handed

over Miss Staverley's reins. This once, someone else would need to brush and stable her.

Then he made steps toward the house. Hesitant steps—even though he wanted to sprint inside and bound through the door.

Sweat beaded along his hairline. For the umpteenth time, he removed his hat and wiped the moisture away. *God, for the first time. . .*

The sentence lingered, tugging at his lips, pulling them into something like a smile. When was the last time he'd smiled? When was the last time he'd approached his home without the gnawing at his stomach, the wretched dread, the hatred?

Was the curse over? Could the past be buried with Ewan, all the future restored with Peter, all the silence broken with Ella?

God, dare I hope to be. . .happy?

Fear made hope shrink back, but an underlying courage kept the thoughts ever in motion. Turning, rolling, forming, until he'd painted something lovely, a vision he'd do most anything to possess.

In the house, he discovered the breakfast room empty, the sidebar barren, the plates unused. Even the drawing room appeared lifeless and vacant, as if no one had disturbed the place since the evening before.

He pushed the haunting memories behind him. He'd done what he had to do—not what he wanted to do.

Tossing his hat to the side, he went for the stairs. They seemed to shiver as he strode up them—and had they ever been polished to such a shine before?

When he reached Peter's nursery, his happiness made unexpected moisture spring to his eyes. He blinked hard, fast, unwilling that tears should steal away the moment.

Then he crept inside.

What he saw must have been a mirage. His wishes—his heart's desire—playing with his sleep-deprived imagination.

But every step he took closer made them more real, until he bent beside the bed and touched his finger to the lace on her sleeve. The soft, quick breaths of his son mingled with the airy warmth of her own.

His gaze hesitated on her lips. Didn't want to linger there. Didn't want to see the small cut, where a man's fist had hurt her.

Henry had hurt her too. He mustn't forget that. Perhaps more, in deeper ways—and for his initial unwillingness to forgive, he would always be deserving of hers.

God, if only I were worthy to keep her. Before she could be disturbed, he turned and retreated across the nursery rug.

If only she wanted to be kept.

He stood at the base of the steps, almost as if he'd been waiting for her.

Nerves knotted and tied, she took each step with delicacy, held the banister, and looked everywhere but at him.

She never wanted to reach the bottom. She never wanted to be close enough to inhale his scent, his special scent, his dreaded scent.

"I've instructed Mrs. Lundie to keep breakfast waiting for you."

Only four more steps. "You needn't have bothered."

"Are you not hungry?"

"No." Three steps.

"Perhaps something warm to drink?"

"Thank you, no." Two more steps, one more step, then she stood before a man she couldn't bear to look at. "My lord, I . . ." Her courage bled and died. "Where is Peter?"

"Mrs. Lundie is helping him bathe."

"Oh." A pause. "How is your leg?"

"Improving greatly."

"Your fever?"

"Gone."

"Good." She edged backward, just enough that the air might return to her lungs. "My lord, I . . ."

"Yes?"

"I wish to speak with you."

His eyes made a slow drop to the letter in her grasp, half hidden behind the folds of her dress.

"I have written a letter." She outstretched the sealed paper. "I thought perhaps you would care to have it mailed."

He read her script, glanced up again. "Abbingston Hall."

"To my mother, my sister. They will want to know I am. . ."

"What, Miss Pemberton?" Something altered in his tone, deepened as his lips parted with her name. Hurt, angst, and a thread of longing. . .or was it hatred?

God protect her from the misery of that.

"They will want to know when to expect me." She tore her eyes from his and backed away. "I shall leave tomorrow morning."

Not even his argument that Peter was fragile after his ordeal and that her leaving now would certainly upset the boy anew succeeded in changing her mind. Henry had no right to express the damage it would do to his own heart. But Peter. . . Would she not stay a little longer, at least, for Peter's sake?

She could not be persuaded and in fact would brook no discussion of the matter. And could he blame her? What she had endured because of him was inexpressible.

She had retreated to her chambers for the length of the day. At both following meals, he had waited for her at the table, but she never appeared.

Peter asked where she'd gone.

He didn't know what to say, so he'd taken his son by the hand and occupied him out of doors. At first they strolled along the garden paths, talking quietly in the evening coolness. Then he'd helped Peter up the tree he'd missed so desperately, and Henry watched as the branches shook with the happy music of his son's laughter.

I am crumbling.

Every tie that held his heart together had been severed until the pieces broke apart inside of him. He tried to steady the trembling when he reached up and grasped Peter's hand. He attempted to hide the trace of anguish when he laughed with his son. He tried to banish the detestable moisture when he forced another smile.

But he was dying inside. Should have known this would happen. Should have known she'd never stay, that his unforgiveness would distance her, that the lies would take this too.

What was left for them?

Nothing. She was right in her choice. There was no other way, not after all that had happened, all the hurt between them both.

"Papa, see how high?" The light, cheery voice swept down from the treetop.

"I see, indeed."

"I missed my tree."

"Did you?"

"Yes, I did." A different branch creaked under his weight. "Papa, look at the window!"

Henry pivoted, raised his eyes toward the manor.

From a window at the west wing, a maidenly figure turned away, as if she'd been watching them from the distance.

"Was it Miss Woodhart, Papa?"

No. He was seared by the name he once believed in. *Miss Woodhart is forever gone from us.*

And Miss Pemberton had only a few hours left.

In the morning, she would carry herself downstairs with all the bravery she could feign. Without tears, she would kneel beside a child she loved, take his cheeks in her hands, whisper the goodbye she never wanted to make.

She wouldn't allow herself to imagine how easily she might have been his mother.

In the dark, Ella wandered toward her window. She touched the cool glass with numb fingers, tried to look beyond the blackness for the outline of an oak tree.

Too dark to see, though. All she had now was a vague memory.

Peter ascending the leafy boughs. Henry standing so far below, the way he spun back to look at her, the startling way she felt his eyes—even after she'd flung herself away.

God, I cannot live with only his memory. She pressed her forehead against the glass. *How shall I ever say goodbye?*

∽

Of all the rooms in the house, he didn't know what should have led him here. There was no sympathy in his mother's portrait. Her peculiar, distant eyes glared at him, as unreal in the painting as they had ever been in life.

Henry leaned against the wall. Quiet, this time of night. Everything still and motionless, with an uncanny sense of loss hovering about the air like dust motes.

For hours he waited, sometimes settling into an upholstered chair, other times roaming to the Grecian-style window, where he would trace his finger along smooth fabric.

But in the end, he was always drawn back to his mother. He was still the child who needed her, yearned for her, turned to her—even when he knew she wouldn't be there.

He touched the painter's brushstrokes. Hadn't he thrown her portrait from the wall?

Someone must have hung her back. Dunn, no doubt. In the name of goodness, why did no one destroy the thing? Must it hang here the rest of his life to taunt him?

Maybe it didn't matter. Maybe here or not, the image would follow his mind, infest his heart, suffocate him.

God, why can I not forgive her? He dragged his finger along the brushstrokes of her hair, lowering to the gentle slope of her cheek. *Will she inflict me with pain forever?*

His mother's face swam into a different memory. *My wife.* Shouldn't there be a portrait of Lucy too? Her betrayal had been as keen as his mother's. Perhaps worse, for she had wounded not only him—but their son.

And Ella. On the morrow, she would leave. He had no portrait of her, either. No single trinket to symbolize the devastation she was leaving behind. *God, how shall I ever forgive her for this?*

How would he forgive any of them?

Better hurry back to his hatred, his numbing hatred. Needed it, depended on it, too weak to battle without it.

Because with no hate, he was vulnerable. Defenseless. Unshielded.

Dear God, what do I do? The anguish pumped through blood that was cold. *Must there always be such misery?*

No answer.

Why? His lips shook as he whispered the word without sound. *In the name of mercy, why can't I be happy?*

Only he knew. Maybe he'd known all along but didn't have the strength. *I can't forgive them, God.* His breathing shallowed. *Please do not ask it of me.*

They didn't deserve it.

His mother didn't.

Lucy didn't.

Maybe Ella didn't either—he didn't know—but he couldn't pretend all the wrongs were not done, as if nothing had happened. He wished he'd never known any of them. He wished he'd never been the recipient of their smiles, their soft words, their few touches.

Yet even so, it wasn't true. God knew it wasn't true. He knew.

And he was weary of hating.

Please, please, help me.

Couldn't go on like this. Had to kill the hatred, had to destroy the bitterness until there was no more left inside.

He had no right to hate his mother, because if nothing else, she had given him life.

He had no right to hate Lucy because even in her treachery, she had given him Peter.

And he had no right to hate Ella. Could not ever hate her. Could no longer remember a reason for his lack of forgiveness.

She was guiltless. She was beautiful. She was courageous.

Whether she belonged to him, he loved her. Whether she was apart from him, he loved her. Loved her beyond himself. Loved her through his own failures, in spite of his past and weakness. Loved her more than the word itself.

It must end here. The realization came as slowly as the morning sun seeped through the draperies. He remained still until light bathed the room. *The hatred is dead.*

With eyes that stung with weariness, he grabbed his tailcoat from the back of the chair. He slipped through the sleeves, raked a hand through his hair, dragged in a ragged breath.

It was time to say goodbye.

Help me. Halfway through the door, Henry paused. He glanced behind him, beheld the portrait for one moment more. "Mother, I forgive you."

∞

Someone tapped the door.

With deft hands, she finished tucking her fichu. Then, with a smooth of her dress, she pulled open the bedchamber door. "Dunn."

The steward offered a wan smile. "How did you sleep, Miss Pemberton?"

Had she slept at all?

He cleared his throat, "The carriage is prepared. Are you certain you will have no breakfast?"

"Yes." She reached for her pelisse, hurried it on. "I am most anxious for an early start."

"It would mean a great deal to Master Peter if you could stay for breakfast—"

"No." The word left her sharper than she'd meant. Tears threatened. "No, I must leave now."

Dunn nodded, submissive, but he could never quite meet her eyes. "Very well, Miss Pemberton. If you will follow me."

The stairs again. Oh, why were there so many of them?

When they reached the bottom, no one waited for her. Relief

battled with distress for the length of time it took Dunn to reach the front door. He pulled the knob, held it open while she forced her legs to move.

"Where is Peter?" Raspy voice, even to her own ears. "I must tell him goodbye."

"He is not yet awake. Shall I fetch him for you?"

"Yes." This came from behind, rumbling and soft, followed by quiet footsteps. "Yes," Henry said again. "My son will want to say goodbye."

Ella never turned.

Dunn's footsteps melted away.

Emotion thrilled every cord until her body shook with a melody bittersweet. Oh, why didn't he say something? If she had strength, she would pass through the doorway. She would race outside, sprint down the stone steps.

Yet she remained, still as a marble statue, and the last of her fortitude drained away. "When I am returned to Abbingston Hall, my mother and sister shall know the truth. They will be infinitely contrite, for they have misjudged you so long," she said. "You must expect letters of apology."

"Do not defame your sister's name for my sake."

"You deserve good opinions, my lord."

His breathing was unsteady, hushed. "May I also expect letters from you, Miss Pemberton?"

"No, I fear you shall not."

"Why?"

"If my apology could not reach you before, I am convinced a letter would have even fewer hopes."

From behind, he took hold of her arms. Slowly, lightly, he turned her to face him. "Do not say such things, Ella."

"What would you have me say?"

He stared without answer. So many times, begging eyes swept to her lips. "Say you forgive me."

"My lord, I—"

"Please." Closer. "Please, Ella, do not leave without speaking the words."

"You have done no wrong."

"Haven't I?"

"Henry—"

"I have given you my love, yet tried so desperately to rip it back away. I have despised you for the same sin I am guilty of. If any forgiveness should be sought, then let it be from me." Miserable tears. "Please."

Against feeble warnings, her lips leaned upward to press against his cheek. She left a whisper in his ear, "Then it is yours." She tried to pull away, but his arms did not release her.

One heartbeat. Two. Three, until her senses began to drown in the citrus scent of him.

Looking away, he dropped his arms to his sides.

She fled through the door, as one who runs from an arena of lions. Her chest burned with the roars, heart wept from the ripping claws. *God, I must leave*—

"No, Ella." He seized her before she reached the carriage door. His arms crushed her in their strength, their power. "No, Ella, do not go."

"I do not want to. Never wanted to, but I. . ."

"Wyckhorn is yours. You must know that." His arms shook. "You must stay for Peter. . .can't you see, Ella, how he needs you?"

Her lips broke with a sound. "I know, but. . ."

"I need you."

Her world careened.

"Need you so much that I. . .I. . ." Half weeping.

She waited for him to go on, but he never did. Instead, for the second time, he let her go.

Her body nearly wilted.

His face turned away from her, as one of his hands hurried away the wet stains. "Heaven knows I love you."

"Henry. . ."

"Love you with all my unworthy heart."

She grabbed his hand and tugged him back toward her. Slipped her fingers to the lapels on his coat. "Henry, one of the truest things I have ever told you is this. I do not want to leave," she said again. "I never did."

He blinked, opened his mouth as if to speak, closed it, then finally said, "And with nothing held back, nothing buried except that which should be, may I ask if you shall marry me? Stay not merely for now, but for always?"

Their lips tangled before she had time to answer. With her first breath, she murmured the pledge, "I will."

EPILOGUE

Lonslock, Gloucestershire
May 1815

"*O*h Ella, you are the embodiment of loveliness and vibrancy." Tolling church bells sent ripples of excitement across the yard, half drowning Matilda's close whisper.

Ella took her sister's gloved hands. "Only because I am so happy."

"Yet not so much as him, I daresay." With the words, her sister's gaze flew to where the groom was being engulfed by the arms of his son. "Now go and say your goodbyes too, Lady Sedgewick."

Ella hurried a kiss onto her sister's cheek. "You had better take the best care of him."

"With mother in charge, you may depend on it."

Ella's laughter mingled with the last chime of the bell. Despite the rules of consanguinity and affinity, the vicar had been willing to perform the wedding ceremony. She was no longer just the woman who loved Lord Sedgewick.

She was his wife.

With one hand rescuing her trim from muddy ruin, she swept to the landau, which had been crowned with wreaths, tulips, and sweet-smelling lilacs.

Henry planted Peter back on his feet. "Have you no kisses for my bride, Son?"

With eyes strangely shy, Peter glanced up at her. "Are you not Miss Pemberton anymore?"

She bent next to him before she remembered the soggy ground. "No, Peter."

"You're not Miss Woodhart either."

"No, I am not."

Tiny brows came together, with an almost knowing smile. "What shall I call you?"

With mirth bubbling over into another laugh, Ella pulled him against her, pressed loving kisses against his cheek. "You may call me Mamma if you wish. What do you say to that, hmm?"

His arms tightened around her neck. When he finally pulled away, the sweetest moisture brimmed his gaze. "Can I come too?"

"Oh rubbish, dear." This came from Ella's mother, who snatched his hand in her lace glove. "One never takes a child on a wedding trip."

"Why not?"

"Just because," she said. "We shall find many more pleasures at home. You shall see. Now blow them both a kiss, my dear—and the two of you be off!"

They needed no more prodding. In one quick motion, Henry hoisted Ella from wet grass and whooshed her inside the landau.

A servant shut the door behind them. "All ready, Lord Sedgewick?"

"Yes, carry off."

The bright yellow wheels turned through mud, several hands waved in cheer, and one last *dong* sounded from the bell tower.

Henry reached for her hand. With a smile that traveled from one glowing cheek to the other, he peeled away the glove from her fingers. "I like it better this way," he said, as his lips caught her knuckles. "Do you not agree, Lady Sedgewick?"

She laughed, nuzzled her nose into his, then dropped an eager kiss upon his waiting lips.

As the landau carried them away, the strangest silence befell them. It was comforting, serene, a thrilling world exotic to them both.

For the first time, there was no curse.

And the silence was beautiful.

ACKNOWLEDGMENTS

I've been bubbling to spill my thanks for a long time. To the many, many people who have worked behind the scenes to make this book a reality, my gratitude is infinite. Much thanks to:

My mother, who believed in my dreams before I did, who endured an all-nighter editing spree, who attends every conference and reads every word I write. I love you more than you know.

My literary agent, Cynthia Ruchti, for being in my corner and always taking part in my excitement. You're the kindred-spirit agent I always prayed for.

Marcus Brotherton, for becoming my friend, being my fan, and encouraging my journey. Thank you for the connections you so graciously made happen for me. You're the best and I will ever hold a warm spot in my heart for you.

Steve Laube, for your advice, wisdom, and friendship. I wouldn't be where I am without the guidance you've given me over these last few years.

The incredible team at Barbour, for making my publishing dreams come true.

Granddaddy, for your unfailing support and love.

My church family, for your prayers.

All my awesome writer friends—Erica Vetsch, Lynnette Eason, Vincent Davis, Rita Gerlach, and more.

And above all, Jesus. The One who not only gives me words to write and stories to tell, but who also gives me life, hope, and peace. I love You endlessly. You are my rock.

Hannah Linder resides in the beautiful mountains of central West Virginia. Represented by Books & Such, she writes Regency romantic suspense novels. She is a double 2021 Selah Award winner, a 2022 Selah Award winner, and a member of American Christian Fiction Writers (ACFW). Also, Hannah is a Graphic Design Associates Degree graduate who specializes in professional book cover design. She designs for both traditional publishing houses and individual authors, including *New York Times, USA Today,* National, and International bestsellers. She is a local photographer and a self-portrait photographer, as well. When Hannah is not writing, she enjoys playing her instruments—piano, guitar, and ukulele—songwriting, painting still life, walking in the rain, and sitting on the front porch of her 1800s farmhouse. To follow her journey, visit hannahlinderbooks.com.

COMING SOON!

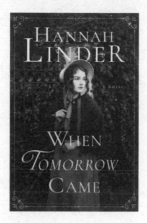

When Tomorrow Came
By Hannah Linder

They Waited Their Whole Lives for Their Papa to Return

Nan and Heath Duncan, siblings abandoned by their papa and abused
by their guardian, have no choice but to survive on the London streets.
When a kind gentleman rescues Nan from an accident, the siblings
are separated and raised in two vastly different social worlds. Just
when both are beginning to flourish, their long-awaited papa returns
and reunites them—bringing harsh demands with him. Soon dangers unfold, secret love develops, fights ensue, and murder upsets the
worlds Heath and Nan have built for themselves. Will they be able to
see through to the truth and end this whirlwind of a nightmare before
it costs one of their lives?

Paperback / 978-1-63609-440-3